A.D. 33

ALSO BY TED DEKKER

A.D. 33

A Novel

TED DEKKER

**CENTER
STREET**

New York Boston Nashville

Copyright © 2015 by Ted Dekker
Original map drawn by William Vanderbush

Cover design and illustration by Mike Heath
Cover copyright © 2016 by Hachette Book Group, Inc.

Ted Dekker is represented by Creative Trust Literary Group, www.creativetrust.com.

Center Street
Hachette Book Group
1290 Avenue of the Americas
New York, NY 10104
centerstreet.com
twitter.com/centerstreet

Originally published in hardcover and ebook by Center Street in October 2015.
First mass market edition: September 2016

Center Street is a division of Hachette Book Group, Inc.
The Center Street name and logo are trademarks of Hachette Book Group, Inc.

The publisher is not responsible for websites (or their content) that are not owned by the publisher.

The Hachette Speakers Bureau provides a wide range of authors for speaking events. To find out more, go to www.hachettespeakersbureau.com or call (866) 376-6591.

Library of Congress Cataloging-in-Publication Data
Dekker, Ted.
A.D. 33 : a novel / Ted Dekker. — First edition.
    pages cm. — (A.D. ; 2)
ISBN 978-1-59995-417-2 (hardcover : acid-free paper) — ISBN 978-1-4555-3624-5 (hardcover : large print : acid-free paper) — ISBN 978-1-4555-6408-8 (paperback : international) — ISBN 978-1-4789-5999-1 (audio cd) — ISBN 978-1-4789-0833-3 (Audio Playaway) — ISBN 978-1-4789-6000-3 (Audio Download) — ISBN 978-1-4555-3516-3 (Ebook)
I. Title. II. Title: A.D. Thirty-three.
PS3554.E43A643 2015
813'.54—dc23

                                    2015025676

ISBN 978-1-59995-411-0 (mass market), 978-1-4555-3516-3 (ebook)

Printed in the United States of America

RRD-C

10 9 8 7 6 5 4 3 2

MY JOURNEY INTO
A.D. 33

TRUE SPIRITUALITY cannot be taught, it can only be learned, they say, and it can only be learned through experience, which is actually story—all else is only hearsay. Surely this is why Jesus preferred to use stories.

For ten years, I dreamed of entering the life of Jesus through story, not as a Jew familiar with the customs of the day, but as an outsider, because we are all outsiders today. I wanted to hear his teaching and see his power. I wanted to know what he taught about how we should live; how we might rise above all the struggles that we all face in this life, not just in the next life after we die.

We all know what Jesus means for Christians on a doctrinal statement in terms of the next life, and we are eternally grateful. But we still live in this life. What was his Way for this life other than to accept his Way for the next life?

So I began by calling Jesus by the name he was called in his day, Yeshua, and I once again set out to discover his Way through the lens of a foreigner—a Bedouin woman who is cast out of her home deep in the Arabian desert by terrible tragedy. Her epic journey forces her to the land of Israel, where she encounters the radical life and teachings of Yeshua, which turn her world upside down.

As they did mine.

Although I grew up in the church and am very familiar with Christianity, what I discovered in Yeshua's life and teachings staggered me. It was at once beautiful to the part of me that wanted to be set free from my own chains, and unnerving to the part of me that didn't want to let go and follow the path to freedom in this life.

I grew up as the son of missionaries who left everything in the West to take the good news to a tribe of cannibals in Indonesia. My parents were heroes in all respects and taught me many wonderful things, not least among them all the virtues and values of the Christian life. What a beautiful example they showed me.

When I was six years old, they did what all missionaries did in that day and for which I offer them no blame: they sent me to a boarding school. There I found myself completely untethered and utterly alone. I wept that first night, terrified. I don't remember the other nights because I have somehow blocked those painful memories, but my friends tell me that I cried myself to sleep for many months.

I felt abandoned. And I was only six. I was lost, like that small bird in the children's book who wanders from creature to creature in the forest, asking each if she is his mother.

Are you my mother? Are you my father?

I see now that my entire life since has been one long

search for my identity and for significance in this life, though I was secure in the next life.

As I grew older, all the polished answers I memorized in Sunday school seemed to fail me on one level or another, sometimes quite spectacularly. I began to see cracks in what had once seemed so simple.

I was supposed to have special power to love others and turn the other cheek and refrain from gossip and not judge. I was supposed to be a shining example, known by the world for my extravagant love, grace, and power in all respects. And yet, while I heard the rhetoric of others, I didn't seem to have these powers myself.

During my teens, I was sure that it was uniquely my fault—I didn't have enough faith, I needed to try harder and do better. Others seemed to have it all together, but I was a failure.

Can you relate?

Then I began to notice that everyone seemed to be in the same boat, beginning with those I knew the best. When my relationships challenged all of my notions of love, when disease came close to home, when friends turned on me, when I struggled to pay my bills, when life sucked me dry, I began to wonder where all the power to live life more abundantly had gone. Then I began to question whether or not it had ever really been there in the first place. Perhaps that's why I couldn't measure up.

So I pressed in harder with the hope of discovering God's love. But I still couldn't measure up.

And when I couldn't measure up, I began to see with perfect clarity that those who claimed to live holy lives were just like me and only lied to themselves—a fact that was apparent to everyone but them. Did not viii • MY JOURNEY INTO *A.D. 33*

Yeshua teach that jealousy and gossip and anxiousness and fear are just another kind of depravity? Did he not say that even to be angry with someone or call them a fool is the same as murder? Not just kind-of-sort-of, but really.

So then, we are all equally guilty, every day.

How, then, does one find and know peace and power in this life when surrounded by such a great cloud of witnesses who only pretend to be clean by whitewashing their reputations while pointing fingers of judgment?

So many Christians today see a system that seems to have failed them. They have found the promises from their childhood to be suspect if not empty and so they are leaving in droves, causing leaders to scratch their heads.

What about you? You're saved in the next life as a matter of sound doctrine, but do you often feel powerless and lost in this life?

Think of your life in a boat on the stormy seas. The dark skies block out the sun, the winds tear at your face, the angry waves rise to sweep you off your treasured boat and send you into a dark, watery grave. And so you cringe in fear as you cling to that boat, which you believe will save you from suffering.

But Yeshua is at peace. And when you cry out in fear, he rises and looks out at that storm, totally unconcerned.

Why are you afraid? he asks.

Has he gone mad? Does he not see the reason to fear? How could he ask such a question?

Unless what he sees and what you see are not the same.

Yeshua shows us a Way of being saved in the midst

of all that we think threatens us on the dark seas of our lives here on earth.

When the storms of life rise and threaten to swamp you, can you quiet the waves? Can you leave that cherished boat behind and walk on the troubled waters, or do you cling to your boat like the rest of the world, certain that you will drown if you step on the deep, dark seas that surround you? Do you have the power to move mountains? Do you turn the other cheek, able to offer love and peace to those who strike you?

Are you anxious in your relationship or lack thereof? Are you concerned about your means of income, or your career, or your status? Do you fear for your children? Are you worried about what you will wear, or how others will view you in any respect? Do you secretly suspect that you can never quite measure up to what you think God or the world expects of you? That you are doomed to be a failure, always? Are you quick to point out the failures of others?

I was, though I didn't see it in myself. As it turns out, it's hard to see when your vision is blocked by planks of secret judgments and grievances against yourself and the world. It was in my writing of *A.D. 33* that I discovered just how blind I was and still often am.

But Yeshua came to restore sight to the blind and set the captives free. The sight he offered was into the Father's realm, which is brimming with light seen only through new vision. And in that light I began to glimpse the deep mystery of Yeshua's Way, not only for the next life, but for this life.

His Way of being in this world is full of joy and gratefulness. A place where all burdens are light and each step sure. Contentment and peace rule the heart. A new power flows unrestricted.

But Yeshua's Way is also opposite the way of the world, and as such, completely counterintuitive to any system of human logic. The body cannot see Yeshua's Way for this life—true vision requires new eyes. The mind cannot understand it—true knowing requires a whole new operating system. This is why, as Yeshua predicted, very few even find his Way. It is said that nearly 70 percent of all Americans have accepted Jesus as savior at some point, but how many of us have found his Way for this life?

Yeshua's Way is letting go of one world system to see and experience another—one that is closer than our own breath.

It is surrendering what we think we know *about* the Father so that we can truly *know* him, which is to experience him intimately, because this is living eternal life now. It is the great reversal of all that we think will give us significance and meaning in this life so that we can live with more peace and power than we have yet imagined.

In today's vernacular, Yeshua's Way is indeed the way of superheroes. In this sense, was he not the first superhero, and we now his apprentices, born of his blood, risen with him? Would we not rush to see and experience this truth about Yeshua, our Father, and ourselves?

In the Way of Yeshua we will bring peace to the storms of this life; we will walk on the troubled seas; we will not be bitten by the lies of snakes; we will move mountains that appear insurmountable; we will heal the sickness that has twisted our minds and bodies; we will be far more than conquerors through Yeshua, who is our true source of strength.

It is the Way of Yeshua for *this* life that I present in *A.D. 33*. Whenever we find ourselves blinded by our own grievances, judgments, and fears, we, like Maviah, sink into darkness. But when we trust Yeshua and his Way once again, we see the sun instead of the storm.

This is our revolution in Yeshua: to be free from the prisons that hold us captive. This is our healing: to see what few see. This is our resurrection: to rise from death with Yeshua as apprentices in the Way of the master.

So enter this story if you like and see if you can see what Maviah saw. It may change the way you understand and experience your Father, your master, yourself, and your world.

—*Ted Dekker*

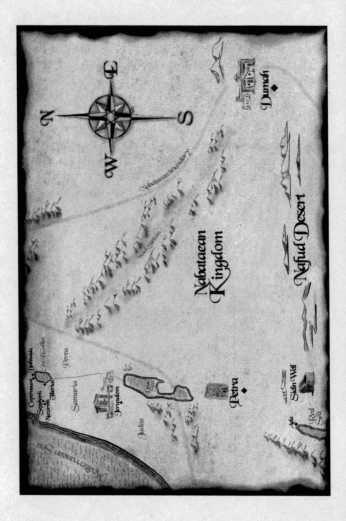

All teachings spoken by Yeshua in
A.D. 33
are taken directly from the
New Testament.
(See appendix)

DUMAH

"Love your enemies
and do what is wonderful to those who hate you.
Bless those who curse you
and pray over those who take you away by force."

Yeshua

PROLOGUE

IT IS SAID that there are four pillars of life in Arabia, without which all life in the desert would forever cease. The sands, for they are the earth and offer the water where it can be found. The camel, for it grants both milk and freedom. The tent, for it gives shelter from certain death. And the Bedouin, ruled by none, loyal to the death, passionate for life, masters of the harshest desert in which only the strongest can survive. In all the world, there are none more noble than the Bedu, for only the Bedu are truly free, living in the unforgiving tension of these pillars.

Yet these four are slaves to a fifth: the pillar of honor and shame.

It is said that there is no greater honor than being born with the blood of a man, no greater shame than being born with the blood of a woman. Indeed, born into shame, a woman may find honor only by bringing no shame to men.

Even so, the fullness of my shame was once far greater than being born a woman.

Through no will of my own, I was also an illegitimate child, the seed of a dishonorable union between my father, Rami, mighty sheikh of Dumah, and a woman of the lowest tribe in the desert, the Banu Abysm, scavengers who crushed and consumed the bones of dead animals to survive in the wastelands.

Through no will of my own, my mother perished in childbirth.

Through no will of my own, my father sent me to Egypt in secret so that his shame could not be known, for it is said that a shame unrevealed is two-thirds forgiven.

Through no will of my own, I was made a slave in that far land.

Through no will of my own, I was returned to my father's house when I gave birth to a son without a suitable husband. There, under his reluctant protection in the majestic oasis of Dumah, I once again found myself in exile.

Through no will of my own, my father was betrayed by my half brother, Maliku, and crushed by the warring Thamud tribe in the great battle of Dumah.

Through no will of my own, Kahil, the prince of the Thamud, threw my infant son from the high window of the palace Marid onto the stones below, where his head was crushed. And with it, my heart.

Filled with shame and dread, I obeyed my father's command that I go to Herod in Galilee and beg for audience with Rome, which had great ambition to conquer Arabia for its spice trade. I crossed the Nafud desert with Saba, the mighty warrior who could not be broken, and Judah, the Bedouin Jew whom I came to know as my lion. Our task seemed beyond reason and our trials unbearable, fraught with fear and betrayal at the hands of kings.

We did not find audience with Rome. Instead, at Judah's zealous insistence, we found audience with one far more powerful.

His name was Yeshua.

Some said that he was a prophet from their God. Some said that he was a mystic who spoke in riddles meant to infuriate the mind and quicken the heart, that he worked wonders to make his power evident. Some said he was a Gnostic, though they were wrong. Some said he was the Messiah who came to set his people free. Still others, that he was a fanatical Zealot, a heretic, a man who'd seen too many deaths and too much suffering to remain sane.

But I came to know him as the anointed Son of the Father from whom all life comes, a teacher of the Way into a realm unseen—a kingdom that flows with far more power than all the armies of all the kingdoms upon the earth joined as one.

One look into his eyes would surely bend the knee of the strongest warrior or exalt the heart of the lowest outcast. One whisper from his lips might hush the cries of a thousand men or dry the tears of a thousand women.

It was Yeshua who showed me how fear and judgment darkened my world; how shame deceived me, causing me to stumble in a stupor. It was Yeshua who told me that I was the daughter of his Father and that I too could find peace in the storms that rose to threaten me with their lies.

It was Yeshua who gave me the sight to see the sovereign realm when I was blind, and the mind to become as a child, in perfect peace through faith. It was Yeshua who gave me the power to prevail in the arena at Petra before King Aretas, an audience of many thousands who sought my demise, and his wife, Shaquilath, who had sent Judah, the man I loved, into captivity among the Thamud.

It was because of Yeshua that I was set free into Arabia with Saba at my side to gather any who might pay heed, and to liberate Judah and restore the livelihood of all those oppressed by the Thamud.

For two years I traveled from clan to clan with Saba at my side, offering the presence of Yeshua and a message of hope in the face of Kahil's sword.

At first they cried out against me because I was a woman, suited for bearing children, not for leading men.

But I returned their anger with a gentle, unyielding spirit. One by one, they began to spread word of my strength and compassion.

One by one, they joined me.

But I dared not approach the stronghold in Dumah until we were as many as the sands in the tallest dune.

Now, over two years later, that day had come. And now, following in the Way of Yeshua, I would save my lion from his dungeon.

For Yeshua came to set the captives free.

CHAPTER ONE

THEY STOOD deep in the bowels of the palace Marid, the two most powerful warlords in all of Arabia, and if not, certainly the most brutal.

Maliku son of Rami, called the betrayer, because he had deceived his father, Rami, ruler of the mighty Kalb tribe, and led their enemy into the gates.

Kahil son of Saman, benefactor of that betrayal, whose sword had led the Thamud tribe's butchery of Dumah, and of untold thousands throughout the desert.

A single torch cast amber light through the dungeon, revealing a third occupant who slumped in the corner of the expansive chamber. Rami, Maliku's father, once the powerful sheikh of Dumah, now a mere skeleton dressed only in sagging flesh.

Wielding bloodied swords, the Thamud army had forced all resistant sheikhs to their knees, and yet one now rose from the sands to bring them to their knees willingly.

She was not a sheikh, nor did she bear a sword.

She was a queen and she would threaten them with peace.

"There is only one way to defeat her," Maliku said, watching Kahil pace. "We cannot use force, unprovoked, or our honor will be stained for all of eternity."

"Honor." Kahil cut him with a cold stare. "This from a prince who betrayed his own people only two years ago?"

Indeed. But Maliku had long ago accepted this stain on his heart. He cast a gaze at his ruined father, whose head hung low, unmoving.

"Maviah must not be allowed to live," Kahil snapped. "This sister of yours—this dog who calls herself queen—she leads twenty thousand now, camped only six hours south. If we allow her to live, they will be fifty thousand within the year."

"That day will never come. We will crush her, but not until we have cause." He took a deep breath. "You *must* stay your hand and allow Maviah to take our bait."

"And if she does not?"

Maliku had underestimated Maviah once, and she'd humiliated him before the king of Petra and all of his subjects.

Never again.

"As much as I swore to you that I could deliver my father, I swear that Maviah will come upon us herself with all the fury of the gods." He turned to Kahil. "And then you will have your blood, and I, my revenge. We must appear to be at odds before your father, Saman. Only play your part until I deliver her to you, brother. It's all I beg of you."

Kahil studied him with a dark stare, then grunted

and yanked his dagger from his belt. He crossed to the slumped form of Maliku's father, jerked his head back, and slashed the old man's throat.

Blood silently spilled down Rami's bare chest.

Kahil shoved him to one side and strode toward the door.

"Never call me brother."

CHAPTER TWO

I PATIENTLY listened to our council of twelve, the only woman among sheikhs, as they argued as only Bedu men can—with great passion, as if each word was their last. They sipped tea and leaned against saddles and emphasized their words with dramatic gestures. I sat both with them and apart from them on a nearby camel hide, legs drawn to one side, leaning on one arm.

We were gathered under the spacious black tent of our eldest member, Fahak bin Haggag, in the Garden of Peace, the small, verdant oasis that sat a mere six hours south of Dumah, where my father had once ruled.

Those present in this tent were the most revered leaders from among the Bedu tribes who had survived the Thamud slaughter. For two years they had heeded my counsel and resisted Kahil bin Saman's tyranny. But they bowed to no king, and though they followed me as a queen, I would never rule them. This was neither their way nor my aim.

They had gathered to me because they heard the tale of my victory over the traitor Maliku, my brother—a victory granted to me by the power of Yeshua.

They had followed me because I offered them Yeshua's hope and power in the face of Kahil's sword. Though the Thamud had orphaned hundreds of children and seized our every resource, I made them a promise: as people of Yeshua's kingdom we would have nothing to fear. We would be restored.

But today the doubters raised their voices.

There were no lavish appointments in our camp. None among us could afford silk or drink from silver or sleep upon thick pillows. The sheikhs were all dressed in plain, well-worn robes, showing their status and tribes only by the colors in the agals wound around their headdresses. My own dress was the color of the sand, and I rarely pulled my blue shawl over my head save to protect my long dark hair from the wind and sun. My sandals were made of goat hide, bound by leather thongs around my ankles, and my wristbands from stained skins cut into thin strips and woven together with cords from the red reed.

Most everything else of value we had long ago traded for food and for she-camels, whose milk provided much of our sustenance.

The contrast between our meager Bedu means and the lavish courts of Herod and Aretas, where I had lived for many weeks, could not be overstated. Our camels, our tents, and the oasis with its spring and small spread of date palms and pomegranate—these are what allowed us Bedu, who could wring life from a rock, to survive in the middle of the forbidding sands that had defeated many an army from the north.

Fahak lifted his cup from the flat stone beside his saddle and took a noisy sip of the hot tea. His frame was thin and his hair clung to his head and chin as if it were pasted there by mud, waiting for a stiff breeze to blow it all away. Then he carefully set his cup back down, just managing to keep it from spilling, and cleared his throat.

"Do I not know the greatness of Maviah? Was I not the first to accept her among all sheikhs? Though Thamud, did I not decry the violent ways of my own tribe for her sake? Did I not single-handedly save her from the jaws of the mighty Nafud so that she might bring back the power of her new god, Yeshua, to join with our gods, Wadd and Isis and Shams and Dushares?"

Much of what he said distorted the facts, and no amount of explanation seemed to help Fahak understand the truth of what gave me strength. He would only listen to me with a blank stare, then dip his head in agreement and praise his god for bringing such a woman with her new god to help him overthrow the enemy.

"But Maviah does not carry a sword. To march upon Dumah is to march *with* the sword. And so, however grateful we are to Maviah, the time for men has now come."

He let his words sink in.

"The sword is not the issue, Fahak," the sheikh Niran said.

"Of course it is! Do you think Kahil would not slaughter eight thousand men who come to defy him without swords?"

"And do you think eight thousand armed men on

haggard beasts can stand against Saman's army of thirty thousand?"

"No man can defeat me!" Fahak cried. His cry faltered and ended with only a raspy breath, followed by several rattling hacks from his worn lungs.

"We must wait for more men to join our number," Niran argued. "Another month."

"We do not have the food to wait another month," another sheikh said. Habib. "In two weeks the camels will begin to starve and we will need to slaughter them for food, thus compromising our mobility."

"Then perhaps we march in two weeks, when we are at the end of our food but have more men," Niran said.

"More men will only require more food," Habib countered. "To go when we are weakest is not the Bedu way. Nor is it our way to confront the enemy without a sword."

A fourth sheikh, Jashim, the youngest of the leaders, spoke evenly. "We must go in peace. There is no other way to restore Rami's honor and liberate Judah, who is unjustly imprisoned."

"We must go with the sword and demand restitution for the Thamud plunder!" Fahak snapped. "We are free to couch camel and clan where the sands offer grace. This is the right of all Bedu for as long as man has set foot on the earth. And yet Saman's butcher son would slaughter us all. If not with the sword, then with starvation and poverty."

"A ruler without subjects is no ruler," Jashim said. "Our deaths are not in Saman's interests. Who would remain to attend to the many spice caravans that pay his taxes? Or deliver the food and wares the city requires?

Dumah is the jewel of the deep sands, but it cannot stand alone."

"No? Except for your desire to disarm us you speak with a sane mind." Fahak jabbed his forehead with a thin finger. "But Saman is mad. His son, Kahil, is worse. Are we to hope that the jinn who have eaten his brains will now spit those same brains back into his skull so that he might come to reason?"

The only member of our number who was not a sheikh, besides me, was Arim, servant of Fahak, who had helped save me from the deadly Nafud desert two years earlier. He had since sworn to protect me from any jackal who sniffed at my tent.

Seated behind the circle of elders, Arim raised his voice.

"Maviah wishes we march in three days' time to rescue my blood brother, Judah, and it is my wish—"

"Silence, Arim!" Fahak snapped up a trembling, bony finger in warning. "Do you now speak for the sheikhs with your wishes?"

"I only say—"

"It is time for sheikhs to speak and for boys to be silent!"

"Yes, Fahak. Forgive me. And yet you challenge her wishes to—"

"Not another word!"

Arim bowed his head. "Forgive me, mighty Fahak, most wise one. I speak out of turn."

"This is not news," the old man said, then coughed again.

Under other circumstances I would have offered a glance of courage to Arim, whom I loved like a younger brother, though I knew he sought affection of a different kind from me. He was perhaps eighteen, long since a man.

And I would have smiled at Fahak's antics, because, although he led the council, he did not seem to know the weakness of his aging bones.

Immediately the debate resumed, back and forth, around and around, bound by tradition and a pride that ran deeper than marrow. Should we go to Dumah in peace or with swords? Should we negotiate with Saman for restitution or seize it? Should we march in three days or in three weeks?

In my corner of the tent I held my tongue as they worked the fear out of their blood with words of bravado. Had I not known such anxiety many times? Did I not feel it even as I heard their doubts? Fahak was right: Saman's son, Kahil, might well slaughter us without thought.

Kahil, the one who'd thrown my infant son to his death upon the rocks.

Kahil, the one who'd once blinded me.

I closed my eyes and let my fear swell. I did not rest it. This would only fuel the offense. *Accept. Turn the cheek.*

Had not a storm once threatened to crush me on the Sea of Galilee? Had not I faced my own death in the arena at Petra? And yet I had followed the Way of Yeshua and emerged unharmed.

Still I felt fear, for now twenty thousand had put their trust in me. Kahil, who'd taken the life of my first son, would now surely threaten the life of my second, Talya. And of all the orphans gathered to safety here.

Judah's life was also at stake. Judah, my warrior and my lover, fading in the dungeons of Dumah.

Judah, my lion. My heart ached for him.

Talya, my little lamb. Forgive me. I would die for him.

Saba, my tower, stand by me. Yet he was not here to calm me.

Yeshua, my master, speak to me.

Peace. Be still...

I took a deep breath. Stillness came to my mind and I lingered there, drawing strength.

"... Maviah, our queen."

Arim had spoken. I opened my eyes and saw that he faced me, standing.

The council turned to me.

"Speak to us, Queen Maviah," Arim said. This time Fahak made no attempt to silence him. My time had come.

I gathered my dress and slowly pushed myself to my feet. I let my gaze rest on their faces, then bowed my head in reverence to Fahak.

"You are most wise, my sheikh. I am honored to be the queen of such powerful men who have seen the Light of Blood in my eyes and followed a path of bravery rarely known, even among the Bedu, subjects of no kingdom but the kingdom that reigns in the heart. It was you who saved me from the desert."

Fahak dipped his head. "Yes, it was I who saved you."

"Indeed. It was you who believed in me."

Another nod, but with some caution this time, because he'd often found himself cornered by my gentle words.

"The first to believe," he said.

"You, Fahak, were most wise for having believed in my name." My voice soothed like oil. "For I was the daughter of Rami, who was the greatest of all sheikhs among the Banu Kalb. And as the daughter of Kalb, I found the power of a new Father in the name of Yeshua, in whose name I believed. Is this not true?"

His response was slow. "It is."

I paced to my left, arms loose by my side, looking through the open flap at a gathering of children fifty paces distant, knocking about a ball of dried dung with sticks.

Unless you become like children . . .

"Tell me, Fahak," I said, turning back to him, "what does it mean to believe in the name of someone?"

He glanced at the others, because the answer was plain among all the people of the earth.

"To trust and so align with them," he said. "Am I so old that I cannot understand what is known by all?"

"Your age only makes you wise, mighty sheikh. To believe in one's name is not merely to acknowledge that they are who they say they are, or to know of their status. It is, as you say, to put your trust in the authority that comes with the name. And so to align yourself with them."

"So are alliances made and bonds forged," Fahak said.

"Indeed. And do you still put your faith in my name, Maviah, daughter of Yeshua?"

Again he hesitated, perhaps only now seeing where I was taking him.

"I do." He lifted a finger. "But only so long as what you say follows my own proven understanding."

"And yet I am here only because I surrendered my own understanding to Yeshua's Father, who is also my own."

"He is not my god."

"And because I trusted Yeshua's Father, though it was beyond any common sense, he gave me the sight and power to prevail in Petra. You see? Common sense is for the masses. Only the wisest depart from it."

His eyes narrowed slightly. But rather than ask him for his submission—for this would be too much to ask of an old Bedu warrior such as Fahak—I turned to the others and made my case.

"You are right when you say that Kahil has lost his mind and would not hesitate to slaughter every man who marched on Dumah, whether or not we go with swords. And you are also right when you say that we did not come to die. So then, we cannot march with eight thousand men in three days' time."

They watched me, surely having expected other words.

"She speaks the truth," Fahak said.

"Kahil would kill all of our men," I said. "But Saman will not allow his son, however mad, to kill twenty thousand Bedu."

"Thus he has not come against us," Jashim said.

"Then we might, instead, go to him. All of us."

Silence stretched long in the black tent.

Habib appeared confused. "You are suggesting that we take women and children as well?"

"We came together as one, did we not? In three days' time we might go twenty thousand strong to Dumah, unified and without a single sword, so that all may see our intentions for peace, not war. We must restore Rami to his people. We must free Judah. And we must negotiate for honorable compensation for our losses. Saman and Kahil may have hearts of stone, but the Thamud people, even their warriors, are not beasts. They too have wives and children."

"Among all Bedu it is forbidden to take the life of the desert's offspring," Jashim said, standing. "She speaks the truth."

"We cannot take women and children to war!" Fahak cried.

"It is not war!" Jashim returned.

Fahak looked dumbfounded—what I suggested was unheard of. But then his face began to settle.

"You suggest we leave the Garden and march to Dumah as one?" Fahak said. "All of us."

I dipped my head in respect. "Is this not wisdom, mighty sheikh? It was you who first put your trust in me."

For a long time the old man stared at me. Would he dare openly put his confidence elsewhere, after publicly declaring he trusted in me?

He turned to the others, then lifted one hand as if to silence them, though there was no need.

"In my eyes, made wise with age, I have seen a way. Like an eagle high in the sky, peering beyond the tallest dune, I behold that we might march on Dumah in three days' time. All as one. Without a sword."

Silence.

I don't remember who voiced the first objection, nor the impassioned exchanges that followed and would surely continue for hours.

I don't remember, because in hearing my own mind spoken so clearly by Fahak, I knew the decision was already made.

The fear I had felt earlier returned with unexpected

strength, like the scream of a demonic jinn in the middle of the night.

I was putting the lives of every man, woman, and child who'd followed me into the hands of the monster who'd killed my infant son.

Into Kahil's hands.

And yet I had another plan.

CHAPTER THREE

JUDAH BEN MALCHUS. It was his former name—he could remember that much, but darkness had swallowed the rest. Like a distant howl in the desert night, his old identity often haunted him, mocked him, then faded back into the void.

He was no longer son of Malchus of the Kokobanu tribe, those distant stargazers filled with wonder for the heavens and for the one who would, indeed *had*, come to save all of Israel.

He was now only son of bitterness, a man with no identity in which to place his hope or trust.

Judah lay unmoving in the pitch darkness next to a rough stone wall, only barely aware of the shackle around his ankle. The bars at the front of the dungeon were beyond his chain's reach—a security measure put into place after he killed two guards when they entered to tend the head wound he'd received in Petra.

The floor was muddy except for the strip where Judah now lay. They dumped the food through the gate, just within reach if he pulled his chain to its end and stretched out on his knees. A wooden bucket collected his waste and was emptied only once each week.

But his misery came from the darkness. Nothing could torment any Bedu accustomed to sun as much as two years of perfect darkness. No torches lit the chamber, nor the passage beyond, except when they came with food.

In the beginning, he was confused by the nourishment they served him and the care they took when disease took root in his body. Only after many months did he understand their intent.

Kahil meant to keep Judah's senses sharp and drive his mind into madness. Kahil inflicted no pain. No one discouraged Judah's obsessive strengthening or spoke words of confrontation. Darkness and solitude and utter silence were Kahil's tools of abuse. And these were unfamiliar enemies to Judah.

Realizing Kahil's purpose, he spoke to himself often and filled his mind with graceful memories of the past, reliving each over and over.

The liberation near Mudah, on the southern Nafud, where, at barely sixteen, he'd single-handedly tracked twenty camels stolen from his tribe, cut down two Tayy warriors on the outskirts of their camp, and skillfully avoided pursuit in delivering the camels back to his tribe. The elders learned then that Judah was not a common man among stargazers.

The day Rami bin Malik had taken Judah into his tent as his second in all matters of war. They had slaughtered ten goats and two camels that night, singing his praise until the rising of the sun.

Fighting by Saba's side in battle, knowing always that together they equaled twenty warriors. Were they not legend already?

Many such memories kept Judah occupied for weeks as he waited for deliverance, knowing that it would come in time. Saba was surely alive and free. Nothing could stop Saba.

The mighty sheikh, Rami, was also in captivity, but Judah had heard nothing of his fate. He served Rami still, but more, he served Maviah.

Maviah...

Nine of ten memories lingered on the woman he loved. Memories of her seated behind him after her camel had been swallowed by the storm in the Nafud. Her arms around his chest and her hot breath on his neck as he pointed out the stars that guided them by night.

Memories of her soft voice in his ear, asking him far too many bold questions for a woman. How he loved her for them all.

Memories of her lips upon his own, of her body pressed against his, seeking comfort and courage. Of her walking confidently into Herod's court, however unsure her heart. Of rescuing her from Brutus. Of her standing tall before King Aretas. Could anyone deny that she was a queen?

These and many other recollections were Judah's only companion for so long. These and his memories of Yeshua, the king who would liberate his people from Roman tyranny.

Yeshua, who had come with a sword to divide the people from their oppressors.

But in time, speaking became futile and the memories began to fade. Soon he could no longer recall what Maviah looked like without considerable effort.

Bitterness crept into his mind then, like a poison that at first fueled him, then began to eat away at his sanity.

Why had they not come? Or had they come, only to be defeated? But Saba would die before accepting defeat. So then, was Saba dead? The Thamud were still in control of Dumah. So then, had Maviah failed? And if so, was she still alive?

Eventually, the questions themselves drifted off into the darkness and he let them go, because he could not endure the pain they brought him.

It was then that Maliku started coming to his cell. There by the light of the torch, it had taken Judah a minute to recognize Maviah's half brother, the man who had shown his true colors of betrayal by leading the Thamud into Dumah to crush his own father, Rami.

Maliku returned to Judah's cell periodically after that, rarely speaking more than a few words, asking only if he might offer any comfort. In a show of mercy, he ordered the guards to place straw on the mud and empty the bucket of waste every day.

Judah was tempted to ask Maliku if Maviah was still alive, but he didn't think he had the strength to learn of her fate should she be dead.

Maliku continued to come, and Judah began to wonder if the man's Kalb blood had finally prompted regret for his betrayal. To live in such terrible guilt might be a fate worse than a dungeon.

Only yesterday a new thought crept into his mind. If Maliku suffered such dreadful guilt, what might have triggered it? Maviah's death. What else would cause such a turn in the man?

Maviah, the woman he cherished, was dead.

With that thought, Judah once again felt truly alive. For the first time in many months he could feel deeply. But the emotions crushed him, robbing him of breath so that he begged for his own death.

"JUDAH. You are needed."

The voice was still far away in his dreams. Maliku's voice.

Iron grated against iron and Judah slowly opened his eyes to see the amber light beyond the bars—torches held by three warriors dressed in black tunics and leather battle armor. Between them stood Maliku, watching him through the opened gate.

"If you would see Maviah, then you must come peacefully."

Judah blinked. Maviah? They had her body? Or she was alive...

"You must come in peace."

He pushed himself up, pulse surging. They were going to take him from the cell?

Maliku turned to the guards. "Free him."

They hesitated, then came in, and when Judah made no sign of resistance, they bound his hands behind his back, unshackled the heavy chain from his ankle, and hauled him to his feet.

Judah cleared his throat. "Your sister is alive?"

A moment of silence hung between them.

"Maviah has never been more alive," Maliku said. He nodded at the guard. "Bring him."

Surrounded by warriors, Judah walked down the corridor in silence, mind crawling back to life, filled with an urgent hope. Maviah was alive.

At the passage's end they were joined by two more guards, who led the procession up a flight of stone steps. Judah knew them well from his days as Rami's warrior, when the palace Marid had been ruled by the Kalb sheikh.

They passed into light. A ray of sunshine through a window both unnerved and mystified him. He'd forgotten what sunlight felt like. And yet, they would surely return him to the darkness below.

Then they were at the door leading into the chamber of audience, and then they passed into the large room where Rami bin Malik had once conducted his business with sheikhs from all corners of the desert.

But his power and wealth now belonged to Saman bin Shariqat, great warrior sheikh of the Thamud. The massive chamber's walls were covered by long silk drapes fashioned in the colors of the Thamud, yellow and red on black. Thick new carpets from Persia and India softened the fortress floor amid three elaborate pillars.

The tables were heavy with carved chests, overflowing with jewels and gold coins. Silver trays with matching tea sets from afar were on prominent display, likely gifts from merchants and rulers who'd passed through Dumah on their way to Petra or Egypt or Rome. Exquisitely stamped and appointed leather saddles, each separated by polished swords, daggers, and lances, lined the walls.

But silver and gold meant nothing to Judah now. He longed to see only one thing.

There was no sign of Maviah.

There was only Saman, dressed in the black fringed *thobe* of his tribe and seated on a large wooden chair banded in silver. On his head, a black agal bound a red-and-yellow headdress. Thick pillows with golden tassels rested on the floor, where those who came for audience would be seated. It appeared Saman had abandoned the customs of the Bedu for the ways of the kings.

Kahil bin Saman, the son who knew no mercy, stood at the window, hands held loosely behind his back, gazing out at the oasis of Dumah beneath the tall fortress. Judah wondered if this was the same window where he'd thrown Maviah's son to his death.

Like a coming storm, Judah's anger began to gather. And with it, nausea.

"Leave us," Maliku ordered.

The guards left them behind closed doors.

"Hold your tongue," Maliku said under his breath. "Trust me."

He pushed Judah forward, and with that shove Judah knew the man wore two faces in this room—both Kalb and Thamud.

Saman watched Judah with piercing eyes, chin planted on the palm of his hand. Kahil turned and walked toward him, studying his frame.

"I'd nearly forgotten we still had you in the dungeon," Kahil said. "You are what I do with dung collected on my boot. I can only hope that you will fully appreciate the sound and sight of twenty thousand dying women and children."

"Enough!" Saman stood, glaring at his son.

Kahil dipped his head in respect and backed up.

Saman stepped off the platform, eyes on Judah.

"To raid and overthrow is a sheikh's right in the sands. Did I not crush Rami and take all of his wealth? In the desert did I not subdue those who resisted my power? Am I not the rightful overseer of all the caravans that flow through my city now?" He spoke with sweeping gestures. "Answer me."

Judah offered the sheikh a nod, because this much was true.

"And yet even now they hover, twenty thousand beggars of all tribes, camped like stray dogs in the southern oasis. For a month now. On which winds did this illness infect the desert?"

"An illness that must be eradicated," Kahil said absently.

Maviah. It had to be! No one else could have gathered so many.

"She calls herself the queen of the desert," Saman scoffed.

Judah's heart pounded.

"She is no more than a fly to be swatted," Kahil said.

Saman's brow arched. He retreated to his chair, sat heavily, and sighed. "You see what I have," he said to Judah. "A son who cannot lay down his sword long enough to enjoy his spoil, and a traitor who would give me council."

Judah looked at Maliku. What standing did the man have among the Thamud now? A traitor was a traitor, even in the eyes of those he'd benefited.

"Maliku claims that she will come unarmed."

"This is the expectation of our informant," Maliku confirmed.

"Only fools would come unarmed." Kahil sneered. "But let them come—it will save us a march."

"Cutting down twenty thousand unarmed Bedu, twelve thousand of whom are women and children, might be"—Maliku searched for the right word—"misunderstood." He turned to Saman. "Would you have their blood on your hands, my sheikh?"

"We're already drenched in blood!" Kahil said. "What is a few more?"

"Peace will change the story that is told about the Thamud," Maliku said. "It will change the tale for generations to come. Peace offered by Saman bin Shariqat of the Thamud. Not by Maviah, who is Kalb."

But peace was not in Kahil's blood.

"Do you think they will simply vanish into the sands because we offer them peace?" Kahil demanded.

"They need some compensation for their loss. Many of their sons and daughters have been slain. But this might be a small price to pay for a legacy among the Bedu."

Kahil's face darkened. "They won't stop until they've retaken Dumah!"

"I only offer my opinion to the great Saman." Maliku bowed before the sheikh.

Something had tested and changed Maliku, Judah thought. Here stood a wiser man, tired of bloodshed. Could he be trusted?

Saman spread his hands. "To slaughter or not to slaughter. What do you, mighty warrior of Rami, have to say to this? Maliku insists that you are the prize Maviah would seek."

Judah stared at the sheikh. To think they'd brought him into audience for his advice was absurd. Something else was afoot.

"Well? Have they cut your tongue out as well?"

Judah cleared his throat. "Though Maviah is a warrior, she has no thirst for blood."

"And what of you?" Saman asked.

"I only say what I—"

"Do *you* have any thirst for blood?"

Did he? An old, seething rage churned in his bowels. But he dared not betray it.

"If there's any thirst left in me, it's for the blood of those who oppress my people in Palestine."

Kahil grinned, brow raised. "And the woman who calls herself queen? You have no thirst for this whore?"

The rage in Judah's gut rose, heating his face. But he would not lash out, not until the day when he could drain the blood from both Kahil and his father. That day would come.

He spoke in a soft tone. "Am I to be ashamed of my love? To sit by the fire once again with a song in my heart and Maviah by my side...I would trade all the swords in the world for one night of peace with her."

"You are a fool."

"Do not underestimate him," Saman said. "Bedu like Judah know only how to seek revenge."

The sheikh sagged in his seat of power, eyeing Judah with suspicion as he absently twirled strands of his beard.

"There cannot be two rulers in this desert." He paused, lost in thought. "We will march tomorrow."

CHAPTER FOUR

TWO THOUSAND black tents covered the rolling slopes of sand beyond my tent. I watched tendrils of smoke rise to the sky as women tended fires fueled by camel dung. Beneath a layer of coals and sand they would bake unleavened breads to be spiced, buttered, and rolled with dates. Few men were in sight; they were behind a partition in those same tents, doing what Bedu men did when not hunting or raiding: exchanging embellished news of their past exploits and fearlessly proclaiming the imminent defeat of the Thamud.

I had to find Saba now. Saba, my tower of strength, who was with my son Talya, now eight. I'd adopted Talya after coming upon him abandoned among the Banu Abysm tribe, the same tribe of my mother, who was now dead.

If Saba wasn't by my side, he could be found in the hills alone or with Talya, who had become like a son to him. Politics and conflict offered him no intrigue.

I descended a sandy slope and approached the small, spring-fed pool that brought life to the reeds and green palms and bushes. The camels were bunched around the drinking trough just south of the spring, or strewn across the sands, searching for stubborn tufts of grass, or sleeping in the sun.

During the last month, we had slaughtered more than a hundred of the male camels, each drawn by lot. The owner was awarded the most prized meats—liver and head—and the rest was divided among that family's clan.

My own she-camel, whom I'd named Zahwah, as white as the brightest sand, would be near my tent, for she loved me and never strayed far. If she was selected for slaughter I would weep, then gratefully give her life to save the children.

The moment the little ones saw me, they ran to me, leaping with arms swinging high. "Maviah, Maviah, Maviah!" There was Sayd and Salim and Mona and others—I knew them well, most younger than my Talya and so perhaps even more trusting of those who cared for them.

"Leave her!" Jalilah cried. The old woman's stained dress was ragged, made of finely woven camel hair worn thin by years of use. Her feet were bare, soles thickened by a life on the sands. With one hand, she steadied a heavy skin of water on her back; with the other she waved at the children, scolding. "Maviah isn't a goat to be played with!"

"Let them come, Jalilah." I smiled and her scowl softened, but I had countered her authority and immediately sought to repair her pride. "Only a moment before you chase them away," I said, lowering myself to one knee to receive the children.

Mona reached me first and flung herself into my arms. I kissed her dirty cheek, wondering how many days since she'd washed herself.

"How beautiful you are, Mona!" I said, kissing her filthy hair. "You are like the morning sun."

Then the other children reached me, clambering for as much love and affection.

"Salim is killing his goat tomorrow," little Mona said, eyes bright. "We're having a great feast because Salim is slaughtering the goat!"

"Oh?" I grinned at Salim, who wore his age with pride, for he was the eldest here, perhaps seven—already a warrior in the making. "Salim has a goat to slaughter?"

The young boy shrugged, knowing he'd spoken more than he could deliver. "It's my uncle's last goat. He says we will eat it soon. And I will kill it with my knife."

"Well, won't that be the day! I will feast with you, Salim. We all will."

"Now leave her!" Jalilah scolded, shooing them with her free arm. "You're children and know nothing! Leave, leave!"

I gave Salim a nod.

They scampered away, knowing not to test Jalilah. I felt the full weight of so many lives upon my shoulders.

I found Saba alone with Talya beyond the spring amid five staggered boulders, arms crossed, shaded by a date palm stripped of its fruit.

Saba had long ago traded his battle dress for a loose tunic and pants, which looked whiter than they were next to his black skin. His bald head towered over the frame of a small boy with dark curls, dressed nearly identically to his teacher.

My heart leaped at the sight of Talya. The new name I had chosen for him meant both "child" and "lamb" in Aramaic, the language of Yeshua, because he was small, even for an eight-year-old. And precious.

I pulled up short on the slope, realizing they hadn't yet seen me.

"And what do we call it?" Saba asked in his soft, rumbling tone.

"The kingdom," Talya said.

How sweet was Talya's young voice. I slipped between two boulders and watched, unseen, treasuring these gifts of mine to love.

"Which kingdom?" Saba settled back against one of the boulders, arms still folded.

Talya answered without pause, having learned Saba's teachings well. "The kingdom of heaven. There are two—the realm of heaven and the realm of earth. But only the realm of heaven is eternal, with no beginning or end."

"And where is this eternal realm called heaven?"

"Everywhere," Talya answered, using his little arms to demonstrate. "Inside, outside, high and low and wide and deep."

"Even among the Thamud?"

"Yes, but they cannot see it. They are blind."

"Why are they blind?"

"Because they see only with the little eyes in their skulls. They are blind like Hamil."

"Hamil is blinded only by old age and too much sun. Perhaps he sees the kingdom of heaven better than any of us. But blind, yes. Excellent!"

Saba clapped once, straightened, and tossed Talya a date from his pocket.

"And how sweet is this gift of earth, for which we are eternally grateful."

Talya stuffed the date in his mouth, then clapped as well. "How sweet it is!"

Saba chuckled. "But not nearly as wonderful as Talya, who has opened the eyes of his heart so he may see more than the realm of earth."

A lump gathered in my throat.

Saba had become a new man in the two years since we'd left Petra to gather the oppressed in Arabia. While I tended my place as mother to all, Saba often retreated to the sands to quiet his mind in prayer and contemplation. In this way he exchanged his own understanding of the world for a deep intimacy with the Father. This was his process of repentance, the way of attaining *metanoia*, which is a changed mind—a mind transformed and made greater.

He was obsessed with the path to truly *know* the Father and his realm. This, Saba believed, is what Yeshua meant when he spoke of entering the eternal realm of heaven.

He often called this path the forgotten Way of Yeshua, because that Way into the realm, so opposite the ways of the world, was difficult to keep in mind, even for those who had once seen.

Saba paced, hands on his hips, gazing at the horizon, wearing a track in the sand.

"As I have often said, to follow in the Way is to find salvation from the storms that rise to crush us. So this demands a question. How?"

"How?"

"Yes, how does one now walk in the eternal kingdom of heaven, which sets us free from anxiety?"

"By believing in Yeshua," my son said.

"Yes. But what does this mean? Tell me."

Talya absently mirrored Saba's pacing, though with far shorter strides. The sight of them together in this way melted my heart.

"To believe in is to trust," Talya said most seriously. "To have faith."

"To have faith *in*," Saba said, accentuating *in* with a raised finger.

"Yes, to believe *in*," Talya returned, finger also raised.

Saba flattened his hand, palm down, and swept it to one side. "Not merely to believe *about*. Even the demons believe that Yeshua is the Son of the Father, for surely they have ears." He spat to one side.

"To believe only about Yeshua is nothing," Talya said, spitting.

"A small first step in the right direction, perhaps," Saba said.

"But this is not the Way."

"To believe *in* Yeshua gives one the power to find peace in the storms of this life. This is the work of the Father, to believe *in* the one he has sent. This is eternal life, to *know* the Father. This is what Yeshua taught. Now tell me, how does one know if or when they are believing *in* Yeshua as opposed to just *about* Yeshua?"

"We know we are believing in him when we are in peace, without worry or grievance."

"Yes, peace. If you have a grievance against any threat, such as a storm or an illness or a brother or even an enemy, it is only because we are putting our faith in the power of the storm, rather than in Yeshua and the realm of the Father."

"But putting our faith in Yeshua makes us the greatest of all warriors, able to move mountains and calm the storm," Talya said.

"Indeed."

Saba stopped his pacing and tossed another date to Talya, who deftly caught it and threw it into his mouth.

"And how sweet it is."

"How sweet it is."

I almost walked out then, so strong was my longing to sweep Talya from his feet and embrace him. But Saba spoke.

"So then—and now we are almost finished—if this *kingdom* is our only obsession, like a treasure in a field or a pearl of great price, and if faith is the *path* into such a place of great beauty and power, what is the means to this path? How will you find such a narrow path called faith?"

He was explaining it all in terms a child could understand, and I was filled yet again with wonder, though I already knew the answer to Saba's question.

"By seeing with new eyes."

"Perception! Perception is the means to true belief. Because the eye is your lamp. If your eye is clear you will see light. If not clear—if it is blocked with a plank of offense and judgment—you will remain blind. You will be trapped in the darkness of grievance, offense, and judgment."

I heard the voice of Yeshua in my heart. *Do you still believe in me, Maviah? Are you saved from darkness?*

Yes, I thought, because right now I trusted in Yeshua and felt no anxiety.

"Listen to me, Talya." Saba lowered himself to one knee. "All grievances are as destructive to you as murder, and they arise only from fear. Fear will render you blind. Yes?"

"I want to see."

Saba nodded once, satisfied. "And so you will. Do you understand what I have told you?"

"Yes, Saba."

"Of course you do."

He stood and spread his arms. "Of course you do!" he said with more volume, gazing at the sky. "You understand because you are a child, and unless you become like a child you cannot follow the Way of Yeshua!"

Saba then lifted his face to the sky and closed his eyes. "You too will calm the storms that rise against you in this life!"

He was speaking as a sage, I thought, and my heart pounded like a drum.

"As a child you, Talya, will lead them. With faith you will move the mountain. They will know you for your love and for the peace that passes all understanding. You too will walk upon the troubled waters of this life and help the blind to see. The captives will be set free and all of heaven will invade earth as no army can, for you will bring light, not darkness, and you will show them the Way of Yeshua!"

A heron chirped in the bushes behind me. The air felt thick. My heart had gone quiet.

My son finally spoke in a soft voice, full of wonder.

"If I will move the mountain later, can I move a stone now, Saba?" A beat passed. "Can *you* move a stone?"

Saba lowered his arms, hesitating. "Not yet," Saba said. "But I am less of a child than you. To begin, think of moving the stones that block true sight into the realm of Yeshua."

"And how can I remove the stones that blind me?"

Now Saba was even slower to respond. This was the question that had often bothered Saba. If clear vision was required to see the path of faith into the kingdom, by what means could one's sight be restored? We would one day return to Yeshua to uncover the mystery of this question.

"You can only see this path by taking your eyes off of all other paths," Saba said.

Talya thought about this for a moment. "How?" he asked.

"When the time comes, you will know how," Saba answered, but I didn't think the response particularly helpful.

I could not contain myself a moment longer. I stepped out from between the rocks and hurried toward them.

Saba turned his eyes toward me, then lowered his arms. Seeing Saba's gaze, Talya twisted back, saw me, and raced for me, face lit like the stars.

I stooped down, flung my arms around him, and swept him into the air, twirling.

"What a big boy you are!" I said, kissing his neck and his cheek. "I love you more than life itself."

"Saba is teaching me, Mother! I will move the mountain. The Thamud cannot stand against me."

I set him down and I pushed my fingers through his tossed curls, wiped the dust from his cheeks. "Of course you will move the mountain, my dear. With a single word!"

His eyes were the color of almonds beneath long lashes. Not a mark scarred his tender, smooth skin. He'd come from my mother's tribe—scavengers who were the lowest in standing among all of the Bedu. Compared to the first five years of his life in the sands, our paltry existence was, for him, like living in a grand palace.

How little it took to give an orphan a new life. Surely, this was Yeshua's Way.

Saba watched us with approval. "You must only follow everything Saba teaches you, and you will be the mightiest stallion in all the desert."

"A stallion who can fly," Talya said.

I laughed, setting him down. "A stallion who can fly through the heavens."

Talya skipped away, arms stretched like wings, then scrambled up the nearest boulder.

Saba dipped his head. "My queen."

I returned his greeting with my own. "My strength." I walked up to him, smiling. "You are taking your student far, I see."

"He has far fewer lies to unlearn than any grown man."

"Perhaps too far for a little lamb. 'A child will lead them'?"

He searched my eyes. "The meek will inherit the earth. Only as children can we follow or lead."

Strange, to hear such words from the strongest and most skilled warrior in the desert. His entrance into any tent always commanded attention, for it was well known that he could take on twenty of the best in any camp and leave them all bloody on the sand if he chose.

I looked toward Dumah, six hours distant.

"The council has reached a decision," Saba said.

"Yes."

"And yet I see concern in your eyes."

I glanced up at Talya, who balanced along the rock.

"We will march in three days' time," I said, "with all the people and no weapons, to camp at Dumah's gates. If Saman refuses our request, I will offer myself in Judah's place. He will set Judah free and take me in his stead."

So... there it was.

When no response came, I turned back. Saba stepped forward and took my arm, nearly frantic.

"No, my queen! I cannot allow this!"

I was taken aback by the force in his voice. Saba the peaceful sage had fled.

"Saman will put you to death!"

"He will not," I said, breaking Saba's grip on my arm.

Surely Saba knew this. Saman held Judah hostage because of my love for him, but his life hung in a precarious balance because Judah's death would not inflame the rage of the desert.

Killing me, the one revered among so many Bedu, on the other hand, would make me a martyr whose legend would outlast Saman's, a fact that could not escape the Thamud leader.

Once I was in chains, word would spread through the desert and many thousands would come to join our peaceful revolution. In the end, Saman would reconsider, surely.

And if not...

I gently placed my hand on his chest. "Listen to me, Saba. You must not fear for me. You must only think of restoring Judah to his full strength. You must think of the orphans and the lost tribes who have entrusted themselves to us. You must keep Talya in perfect safety, no matter what happens. I will need you to lead, and only you. Tell me you will not waver from this duty."

He spoke slowly, at a loss. "I will not waver."

I stared down the slope at the sprawling sea of black tents dotting the white sands.

"I have seen death," he said.

I looked at him.

"My death?"

"Many deaths, like locusts upon the sand. Who is among them, I cannot say."

My mind spun with visions of battle and bloodshed, for this was the Thamud way. I pushed the images away.

"Are you saying that going to Dumah is a mistake?"

"No."

My irritation flared.

"What's your intent in telling me this? If we die in peace, we die for generations to come."

"Yes."

That was all. Just yes.

"Then what is your point?"

He faced me, and I saw his eyes misty with emotion. Fear, that ancient familiar enemy I'd held so long at bay, approached me.

"If I am to be slain, or you," he said, "then know that I would gladly give my life for yours. I have found my life because of you and would trade it for yours without a thought."

I studied his eyes for a long moment, seeing there an honor he had never given me before. More than honor. Losing Saba would be as painful as losing Judah.

The thought surprised me. I couldn't deny how close we were—after so much time with him by my side, I depended on him for more than guidance.

But I loved Judah.

I removed my hand from his chest.

"Forgive me, Saba. Forgive me."

CHAPTER FIVE

PREPARATIONS WERE UNDERWAY for one last feast at my request, for I had decided that we would march with bellies full, confident of many more feasts to come. All of the children would be bathed, even if the same basin of water was used to wash many, spilling not a drop on the sand. I wanted them clean and smiling, for celebration was always a delight to them.

The morning after the council's decision was announced, Habib was placed in charge of securing all weapons, each delivered to a large cache prepared on the south side of our camp. After verbose discussion the men had come to peace with the notion of forsaking their "right arm," as they called their swords and daggers. Had anything like it ever been seen in the desert? Never!

One by one, drawing courage from those who'd gone before them, they solemnly approached the great pit, kissed each of their blades, and carefully laid them in the sand as they might a treasure.

I had left this ceremony and was with Saba in Fahak's tent, discussing the best strategy for marching with so many young and elderly, and so few camels for them to ride, when Talya burst in, running.

"Mother!"

I glanced up. He was pointing to the north.

"Camels! Many!"

Saba leaped to his feet and I joined him, gripping his elbow. Together we raced to the top of the dune near my own tent where Talya had seen. My camel, Zahwah, was couched in the shade.

They stretched across the flat sands to the north, hundreds abreast, moving at an easy pace. It could only be army, for caravans traveled in a single column.

"Thamud," Saba said.

I whirled to Zahwah and grabbed her lead. "Talya, to Saba! Summon the council members."

I quickly gathered my dress and flung my leg over my camel, already clucking my tongue. "Up, up, Zahwah." I tugged as she protested and rose to her feet.

"Maviah—"

"Tell only the elders—we must not spread panic! Bring them to me at the northern flat."

TWENTY OF US arranged ourselves abreast on the sand, I in the middle, seated upon my white camel with my dark dress flowing in the breeze. My long, dark hair was loose as I faced a wind that portended this coming storm of Thamud. They approached at a steady trot, hundreds wide and three or four deep. Banners of the red-and-yellow crest flapped high above those who rode at the center.

My heart was in my throat as their faces came into

clear view—Saman bin Shariqat and his son, Kahil. And there with them, my half brother, Maliku.

Had they come with a thirst for blood? Saba had seen many dead upon the sand.

"No one will speak but Maviah," Saba said to my left. "Not a word."

"This is business for men," Fahak said.

"Not for men who hold no swords. Hold your tongue and let your queen gain us favor or you will deal with me."

It was enough to bind the elder's pride, but Fahak didn't know how to remain silent for long any more than a lion knew how to leave its head buried in the sand.

Saba turned on his mount. "Remember Yeshua's words, my queen. This is only another storm on a forgotten wind. See with new eyes."

Those words flooded my mind. *Why are you afraid, Daughter? See with my eyes. Calm the storm. Walk upon these waters.*

Father... Open the eyes of my heart to see as you see.

I could see only the storm:

Saman, now slowing his camel to a walk, looming close.

The plodding hooves of a thousand camels bearing warriors dressed for war. Swords and daggers glinted in the sun at their sides.

Kahil, the one who'd killed my son and then blinded me, his dark eyes staring into my soul like a hawk eyeing its prey.

Maliku, my half brother, whose betrayal had led to the slaughter of so many.

Father...

Kahil lifted his right hand, and the sea of Thamud pulled up to a thudding halt.

My heart raced.

I fixed my eyes on Kahil, returning his glare with pointed disinterest. The knowledge that I had nothing to fear from him filled my mind. He was ruled by bitterness, I by acceptance. He, then, was the slave of this harsh taskmaster called earth, not I. For I was in the world but not of it.

And yet I still felt fear, because in that moment I did not *know* it as Saba spoke of knowing. Did he know? Was he at peace?

Saman stared at me, curious. A camel to my right roared, followed by a haunting calm. To a man, the Thamud stared at our small group clad in little more than rags.

"So..." Saman gave me a short nod. "This is the woman they would call queen of the sands."

I sat still.

"And there is Fahak by her side," he said, glancing at the elder to my right. "Thamud by blood and yet slave to a woman born in shame to a whore."

Fahak spat to one side but held his tongue.

"My son says we should enter your Garden of Peace and assist the women with their bleeding." His insult could not be mistaken, for it was believed throughout the world that all women were born lesser because they could not control their blood, which was the source of all life.

"You have only eight thousand men," he continued. "All mangy dogs."

"You underestimate pure Bedu blood," I said.

He hesitated, for it was well known that even a common Bedu warrior could fell a hundred men. And perhaps he remembered that I had once cut him and brought down his horse with nothing more than a dagger.

"And still vastly outnumbered," he said.

"Would a Bedu sheikh of such high standing as you slaughter so many?" I asked in a low voice. "Already your son has taken mothers and fathers from thousands of children. Or does he suggest you drink the blood of children as well?"

A wicked smile crept over Saman's face. "She can speak with clever words."

"She speaks only on my behalf," Fahak said, unable to restrain himself.

Saba cut their exchange short. "We have no desire for blood."

"No," Saman said. "Because in this desire you all would meet the gods by the setting of the sun. Even so, I hear your queen can also wield a sword." He drilled me with a stare of curiosity. "Perhaps you would pit yourself against my son and settle all of this absurdity without subjecting your slaves to an early death."

"I desire no blood," I said. "Only the freedom of my father and Judah, and honorable repayment for the blood Kahil has spilled in the sands, unprovoked."

Kahil spat to one side. "She should be sliced, like her father."

A pool of emotion rose from deep within me at this news of Rami's death. I had longed to honor my father, however much he'd wounded me. I still desired him to see the daughter he'd thrown away seated in high standing among his own people.

The sound of pounding hooves on the flat behind me

cut my thoughts short. All but Saba turned to see the brown camel racing toward us, whipped into a full gallop by its frenzied rider.

It was Arim, the young warrior who served me with an unabashed heart. Arim, with drawn sword waving in the air, headdress flowing in the wind.

"Back, you fool!" Fahak shouted, arms waving.

Jashim joined in. "Get back!"

Fahak's camel startled and stomped sideways to make room as Arim rushed in, reining his mount to an abrupt halt alongside me.

"You will not touch my queen!" he cried, sword extended at Saman. "You will not insult Maviah, for I am her slave and I will slaughter a thousand Thamud if they approach! Her god, Yeshua, will use my arm to cut any jackal who even threatens his chosen one!"

The intrusion was so sudden and bold that none could quickly respond. The sheikhs were surely outraged—none more than Fahak, because Arim found his courage in Fahak's own tent as part of the same clan.

The Thamud were surely amused, because all Bedu men respected such daring.

Saba only ignored the boy.

But Arim's fearlessness in the face of such an overwhelming enemy immediately reminded me that I was loved by a Father who saw no storm in this circumstance.

"Thank you for joining us, Arim," I said.

He stared at me, then at the Thamud. Then at the elders.

"We have no problem here. You may throw your sword on the sand."

He turned to me again, eyes wide, breathing hard.

"I heard there was to be trouble—"

"And yet there is none. Do as I say."

Sitting tall and with a stern face, he took one last look at Saman, then tossed his sword into the sand.

Saman chuckled. "Some Thamud blood at last. Give me a hundred like this one and I will rule the world."

"We do not lack heart, mighty sheikh," I said. "We have more courage than all who stand before us with swords at their sides. Ours we leave behind."

This gave him a moment's pause. His eyes shifted to the horizon behind me and he sighed.

"I too grow tired of war." Eyes back on me. "So then..." He shoved his chin in Maliku's direction. "Make peace with her."

Maliku prodded his camel forward three strides, then stopped, eyes on me. Clearly, he'd come to play this role.

He bowed his head and when he looked up at me again, I could see only fear in his eyes. I'd rendered him powerless once before, in Petra. He had no appetite to engage me again.

"It is true that you come in peace without any desire to retake Dumah?" he said in a soft voice.

"Where is Judah?" I asked.

"Judah is alive and well. But you must speak to me now. Speak from your heart so all can know the truth. You have no desire for Dumah?"

"When did they kill our father?"

He hesitated. "Surely you know that there can be only one ruler. Think of his death as proof that the sheikh too desires peace."

In the Bedu way, it made sense.

"We have no desire for Dumah," I said, calming my anger. "The desert is rich enough for all true Bedu."

"Then demonstrate your sincerity by leaving this place, never to return, and you will be protected by Saman so long as no one raises a sword against him."

"We require compensation!" Fahak croaked.

Saba grunted a warning.

I let Fahak's statement stand.

"This is impossible," Maliku said. "But peace, you can have. This very day. I beg you, accept this offer from them for the sake of your children."

Them? He spoke as one who did not want to be associated with the Thamud.

Seeing my reluctance, my brother motioned to the rear.

The warriors parted and a single camel plodded through their ranks. A body dressed in a muddy tunic was tied facedown on the camel's hindquarters. His head was bound by swaths of cloth.

My father's body?

"You cannot expect repayment," Maliku said, "but Saman will offer you life."

The warrior dismounted, untethered the body, and let it fall heavily to the ground.

Only then, as the tunic pulled free of his arm, did I recognize him. My heart seized in my chest.

"Judah!" Saba was already on the sand, rushing forward.

"Back!"

I don't know who barked the order, for my eyes were on Judah's body, which lay unmoving on the ground. I could not speak. I could not move. I could scarcely form a thought.

Saba pulled up at the command, breathing hard.

"Keep your distance," Maliku said. "He is senseless but otherwise unharmed."

"Judah?"

The voice was my own. I felt myself slipping from Zahwah's back. Landing on the sand. Hurrying forward.

The warrior who'd brought him stepped into my path, and without a thought I grabbed his arm, shoved my knee behind his left leg, and slammed him to the ground with enough force to knock the wind from his lungs. And already I was at Judah's side.

Saba seized my elbow and pulled me back. "Not now, my queen."

I was trembling. But Saba's voice, which had guided and comforted me through the desert, brought me to reality.

"Leave her," Maliku snapped, motioning the stunned warrior back to his camel. "Or would you die today?"

The man scowled, then drew his camel away.

Kahil folded his hands. "So you see, Maviah...My word is also true. Judah is alive and well, and he is yours if you agree to Saman's terms. For the sake of all those you lead, take your lover and go back into the sands. I beg you."

"You would send us away without food?" Fahak cried, unimpressed by Judah's deliverance. "You have taken all we have! We cannot enter the sands without food and camels!"

Maliku faced Saman, who considered the request and offered a curt nod.

"I will return with—"

"A *thousand* camels!" Fahak said.

"Don't be absurd." Kahil sneered. "Food for scavengers is all you require."

"A thousand camels or we butcher the lot of you where you stand!"

They said more, but my mind was on Judah, because I knew already that I was to be reunited with the man I loved.

"A hundred camels and two hundred goats," Saman said, cutting the discourse short. "No more."

"And wheat!" Arim said.

"Silence," Fahak snapped.

But Arim went on. "And tea. And spices. And ten coins for each family so that we might trade for food on the long journey far away from you."

Saman grunted, then conceded with a sigh. "Food and five hundred coins—no more. And let my mercy be known."

Fahak spat once more, earning the respect due him, sheikh to sheikh.

Maliku spoke again, watching me closely.

"Maviah. Take what is offered and live in peace. As your brother, I offer my word. It's all I have left."

I turned my head and stared at Kahil. His eyes were dark, and deep lines of bitterness and treachery were etched upon his face. I knew I would see him again, and the next time he would not be held back by a father weary of bloodshed.

"I would see Judah's eyes," I said, facing Saman.

Saman nodded at Maliku. My brother stooped, stripped off the cloth bound about Judah's head, and pulled free a scarf that muzzled him. Lowering himself to one knee, he gently slapped Judah's face.

But Judah's eyes remained closed. So Maliku

quickly retrieved a skin and splashed water on his face.

Slowly, like a rising sun, Judah's eyelids opened. And then, lying there on his side with his cheek pressed against the sand, my lion's bright eyes gazed up at me.

I turned to Saman. "We agree to your terms. Return in two days' time with all you have offered. Now take your army from our Garden of Peace."

CHAPTER SIX

THE THAMUD hadn't broken Judah's spirit, but they had chased it into the shadows.

So I took him with me to the desert, where he could regain his strength free of prying eyes. I left the camp and Talya in Saba's hands and went to the red cliff called the tower, two hours west.

Using one of the waterskins, I gently washed Judah's stained body and bathed a wound on his head, then trimmed his beard, allowing him the silence he required. I held his head in my lap and let him weep while I hummed and stroked his hair. I knew that his spirit would return, but not as it was.

Only when I made a fire late in the afternoon and served Judah some hot tea did the sparkle begin to return to his eyes, but then only for brief periods.

He made a feeble attempt to help me prepare food, but I hushed him and served him as he'd served me during our journey across the desert two years earlier.

We ate goat meat cooked on the fire, and flatbread that I baked with coals in the sand—these served with dates and butter, for it was all we had. Then I drew milk from Zahwah and we drank it warm, still frothy.

I told him about Talya, my son. I told him how Yeshua had saved me from the storm and healed me of my blindness in Petra. I told him about Stephen, who'd jumped out of the boat to go to Yeshua, and about Sarah, who'd been healed of an issue of blood. I told him of all the wonders, and the more I told him, the more he wanted to know.

He was Jewish to the bone, and I could see that his longing for his Messiah and for Israel tugged at his heart.

As it did mine. We would find Yeshua together, I said. We would rush to him and fall at his feet. He, not I, had brought salvation to the desert. He, not any queen or sheikh, was master.

As dusk gave way to night I left Judah by the fire and went to retrieve Zahwah, who'd wandered off in search of desert grass. By the time I found my she-camel and returned, it was dark. The fire smoldered, unattended.

I dropped Zahwah's lead rope. "Judah?"

Zahwah folded herself to the ground near the hot coals as I scanned the sands.

"Judah!"

We were at the base of the red cliffs. Surely he hadn't found it in himself to climb them. To the south, two dunes rose high, black against the sky.

I spun around, wicked images of Kahil suddenly large in my mind. We had two blades, for there are many prowling beasts so close to an oasis. Both weapons still leaned against the rock where I'd left them.

"Judah!" I cried.

And then I saw him, outlined against the night sky on the dune behind our camp. Relief cascaded over me as I snatched up a sword and hurried up the slope.

But when I reached him, his hands were up and his head tilted back, and I knew that Judah had found his stars.

He was of the Kokobanu tribe—the stargazers who'd first been led to Yeshua when he was a child. The nights of our desert crossing flooded my mind. How many hours had he spent teaching me the constellations? How many songs had he sung about the lights in the sky?

Indeed, these were the very stars that had led me into Judah's arms, for I was the brightest star in his sky.

"Look, Maviah," he said, smiling wide. "Look at them all!"

I stepped up beside him and let the sword slip from my fingers. "Yes. Look."

"I haven't seen them for two years."

My heart broke for him—keeping Judah from the sun and stars was like keeping any other man from food and water both.

"They are the lights of truth, which cannot lie," he said. "It was these that drew us to Yeshua."

"And me to you," I said.

His arms were wide and high and he shook them at the sky, as if soaking in a powerful force. "Look at them, Maviah! Just look at them!" He laughed and turned slowly around, beaming like the moon. "Look at them!"

I was smiling, delighted by his enthusiasm, and then laughing with him.

He swept behind me and grabbed my arm, lifting my hand in his to point skyward.

"There, remember? The hare. And there, the snake. When two point to a sign, forecast with hope; when three, forecast with confidence," he said, reciting the rule of the stars' foretelling. "Do you remember?"

"I remember."

I could smell the scent of the spice he'd chewed to cleanse his mouth, borne on his hot breath against my neck.

He placed an arm around my waist from behind and turned me to the northern sky. "There, the brightest. Do you remember?"

"The north star," I said.

He said more, but my mind was consumed with his passion, returning to him like water rushing into a parched wadi after a sudden storm.

I turned in his arms as he spoke, and I placed my hand behind his head and gently drew it down, as if he was one of those very stars, now for me to worship.

FOR TWO DAYS Judah and I remained, caught up in the heavens, dancing among the stars rather than under them.

With each passing hour, more of Judah's strength returned. Not once did he talk about his time in the dungeons, and I did not press him. Only occasionally did the darkness rise in his face or words. But then it quickly vanished.

"You will see, Maviah," he would say, hurrying for more wood from our small pile. "All that is wrong in the world will be made right."

And I would laugh, for no reason other than to be full of joy by his side.

"You will see, Maviah," he said, pouring tea at noon. "We will one day own a thousand camels and give two thousand away."

And I would smile, for there was no heart greater than Judah's.

"You will see, Maviah," he said softly, poking at the fire. "I will kill Kahil and return to bring Rome to ruin."

To this I had no reply.

On the morning of the second full day, Saba and Talya came for us, riding a camel.

"Mother!"

I spun to the sound of Talya's voice just as his head came into sight on the high dune. Saba swayed with the camel's plodding gait and steadied Talya as he stretched for the sky.

I was filled with joy but not yet ready for my time with Judah to be broken. Once back in the camp, the demands on me would be high and we would have little time to ourselves.

Talya jumped into my arms and I kissed his cheeks. "You're growing like a reed."

My son stared at Judah. "You are the mighty warrior."

Judah glanced at Saba and grinned. "Is that what they say?"

"That's what Saba says."

"And Maviah has told me that you too are a lion," Judah said. "But you must not believe everything Saba tells you. He's the far greater defender in these sands. Has he told you about the time we were set upon by the Tayy in the Nafud canyon lands?"

Saba dropped to the ground, eyes bright. "That is the past, my old friend. We wash these memories from our minds." He clasped Judah's arms. "The desert treats you well."

"And you, Saba. Tell me that Maviah taught you to sing while I was visiting the enemy."

"I sing all day," Saba said. He tapped his head. "Here, where the angels join me."

Judah smiled. "It's a good start, Saba. Soon you will be singing with me around the fire while all the young maidens watch. But now..." He hurried toward the fire. "We must drink tea and exchange the news."

Saba dipped his head toward me. "My queen. Maliku has come as promised. He awaits your audience."

"Let Maliku wait," Judah said, turning back.

"He is most insistent. He claims—"

"And I insist he wait," Judah snapped. The bitterness in his voice could not be mistaken. "Did I not wait for him these two years?"

Saba gave him a nod. "Then tea."

We took the steaming cups, saluted Judah, and sipped in the customary fashion while Talya climbed atop Zahwah.

"Now tell me, my old friend," Judah said, looking up at Saba. "What is their weakness?"

"Whose?"

"Kahil and his butchers, who else?"

Saba glanced at me. "The same weakness of all men."

"Which is?"

"Pride."

It wasn't what Judah was looking for, but he accepted the answer with a raised cup.

"Then we will stuff this pride down their throats." He drank. "Before they know what has hit them."

The air suddenly felt heavy. But could I blame Judah? No.

"We cannot raise our swords against the Thamud," Saba said.

"No? Then what? Lances? Daggers?"

"We offer them only peace."

Judah stared at him, then at me, taken aback.

"Peace comes when Kahil is dead. I will offer them my sword alone if I have to."

Talya spoke innocently from his perch upon Zahwah.

"Yeshua teaches that whoever lives by the sword, dies by the sword."

Judah looked at him, speechless, for what could he say to such a young boy?

He faced me and spoke in a low voice. "If Kahil took your own child to his dungeon, would you not raise your sword to behead such a vile creature?"

My heart was stung. His bitterness smothered me.

"My mother's heart says yes," I said. "Yeshua says no."

"Yeshua? And what can you know of his full teaching? You have seen him only twice. Even now your mother's heart would rage. You would ravage the Thamud and rescue your son!"

A chill washed over me.

Talya slid off Zahwah's back and hurried up the slope. I let him go. The sun was high and I had no desire for him to hear these words. He would not go far.

"Am I not the child of God?" Judah said. "As are all the children of Israel. This is why Yeshua came, to save us from oppression."

I held my tongue.

But Saba was perhaps more practiced in the Way than I.

"To set the captives free, yes," he said. "But not by the sword."

"Did he not say himself, 'I've come to divide by the sword'?" Judah said, setting his cup down, eyes on Saba.

"And yet that sword will be wielded by those who oppose him, not by those who follow him. Does he or those who follow him use the sword? Yeshua has surely come to divide so that those who follow him will be known for their love, not the sword."

"No! You will see that he and all of his disciples will use the sword." Judah spat into the sand. "I cannot accept this twisting of his words!"

Saba hesitated, then spoke in a soft tone.

"I cannot condemn the use of the sword, only point out what Yeshua makes plain. To live by the sword is to be subject to it, and so die by it. So you see, the sword is also madness. It is by the sword that so many have fallen, seeking an eye for an eye as is the way of the desert. Who, then, will break the cycle?"

Judah stood, enraged now. "The enemy slaughters and crucifies and you would twist the words of the Messiah who has come to set us free, both in Judea and in Arabia."

"Do you think by using the sword we will end the slaughter, so that in a thousand years there will be less death? Yeshua's Way is to love the enemy, even those who persecute you."

"Evil must be loved only with force! How can you speak so flippantly about the suffering forced upon all of God's children?"

Saba hesitated, for he wasn't normally a man of many words. He glanced at me, perhaps looking for my support. But even I was divided by Judah's suffering.

"Forgive me, Judah, I mean no disrespect," Saba said. "I only speak of Yeshua's Way, which is so easily forgotten when the harsh storms of this realm blow across our minds. But there is also another realm at hand. Yeshua teaches that those who would walk in this kingdom of great power must turn their cheek and not resist the evil man who comes against them."

Judah stared at him, aghast. Saba continued, words flowing like honey, defying all that was known in the world.

"To resist force with force makes one a king in the realm of earth. To offer forgiveness instead makes one a prince in the realm unseen by human eyes. To forgive is to release offense. To yield. In this way the sting is not felt."

"Sting? And what of Kahil's butchery, and the Romans? You would see God's children as sand to be crushed under their feet?"

"And yet a thousand have been crucified in Israel. Yeshua has seen this with his own eyes. Still, he refuses to speak out against the Roman butchers. Instead, he teaches a way of far greater power. Can the Romans heal the heart? Can they calm the storm? Can they make the blind see? And so the whole world is made blind by planks of offense and judgment, kept in place with harsh words and bloody swords. But Yeshua came to bring sight to even we who are blind, and to set free those imprisoned by their offense."

Judah slowly sank to his seat, calmer now. But his jaw was set.

"In your way of speaking, Rome will inherit the earth, even as Kahil has inherited the desert."

"The meek will inherit the earth," Saba said, quoting Yeshua. "Kahil and Rome are slaves of this master called earth. You can only serve one master. Never two. You will serve only the system of the world, or the realm of peace and love."

Judah stared at Saba for a long time, and for a moment I wondered if he was softening, because Saba's words reminded me of Yeshua's Way, as they so often did. In Yeshua's Way of peace, I had become queen at Petra.

Judah turned to me, face downcast, eyes pleading for understanding.

"Maviah...Surely you would defend Talya and the orphans with all of your might. Surely you will rise up and crush Kahil's brutality with all of your means. Surely you don't expect my people in Galilee to submit to crucifixion without resisting!"

How many times had I pondered this question and accepted the path of nonresistance, even as I had in Petra? But the pain in Judah's eyes pulled my mind into a fog.

Or was I seeing clearly now?

"I beg you, Maviah," he said. "Do not cast me aside."

My heart broke for him.

"Never," I said. "I will never leave you."

"Swear it to me."

"I swear it."

For how could I forsake what I loved?

A single tone drifted through the sky above us. A pure and gentle note, piercing the still air with perfect clarity.

I glanced up at the red cliff that rose thirty yards to its crest. There, on the precipice, stood Talya, stripped of his tunic, wearing only his loincloth. His arms were spread down by his thin thighs, and he faced the horizon with eyes closed.

My little lamb was singing. Long, beautiful tones that were at once haunting and full of wonder.

He'd found his way up the dunes and climbed to the top from behind, and for a moment I worried that he might slip and fall. But his song stilled my heart and then filled me with a strange sense of amazement.

A lump gathered in my throat and the air became difficult to breathe. Saba slowly rose to his feet, staring up at his little apprentice. I thought to join him, but I dared not move, fearing I might break the song.

The wind had stilled. The camels did not move.

Still he sang, in pure and unbroken notes that swept away all of my fear.

As though requiring no breath, Talya's high notes cut through the desert air. Tears misted my sight. A tremble came to my fingers. Talya was in another world, I thought. My young son was seeing into another realm.

Talya, my dear Talya! How beautiful you are!

Only then did his last note fade. The desert went quiet.

Talya opened his eyes and stared ahead as though mesmerized by the horizon. His mouth parted and broke into a smile. Then he looked down at me.

"A garden, Mother!" he said. "There is a garden called Eden."

Eden... A paradise of delight.

This was the eternal realm called heaven on earth?

Talya snatched up his tunic, spun around, and disappeared from the edge to climb back down and join us.

"He sees," Saba whispered, still staring up at the cliff. He shifted his astonished gaze to me.

There was no such amazement in Judah's eyes. They remained in the darkness of the dungeons that had held him captive so long.

But this would change. Yeshua had come to set the captives free from their blindness.

I would take him to Yeshua.

I would take him the very next day.

CHAPTER SEVEN

JUDAH STARED at the man who stood at the entrance to Maviah's tent having made his plea before Fahak, Saba, and their queen.

Maliku, the betrayer of them all.

The one who might even betray the Thamud.

As promised, Maliku had brought the camels and the food as well as Saman's coin. Compensation for the people's suffering had been promised and delivered. Fully emboldened and triumphant, Maviah's men had retrieved the swords they'd placed in a cache. The surrender of weapons made little sense to Judah.

Distant cries of victory and excitement filled the valley. The women were busily preparing for celebration.

But Maviah was wary. She was their mother as much as their queen, Judah thought.

The sheikh Fahak sat on a white camel hide in her tent while she stood over him. The unprecedented sight attested to the honor she'd earned among the Bedu. Had he not always known she would be queen?

How beautiful she was! How majestic the movement of her hands and her mouth and her every step. Her blue shawl fell to her waist over a white dress. Leather bracelets accented with red twine were fastened about her wrists and forearms. A necklace with a single round pendant carved from green marble rested upon her breastbone.

How stunning were her brown eyes, like windows into another world. How commanding was the curve of her soft lips beneath high cheekbones. Though in a simple Bedu tent, she stood as a bronzed sculpture in the courts of Petra. How utterly intoxicating, this queen of the desert!

His queen.

To her right, an oil lamp and a bowl filled with ghada fruit sat upon a chest. Her sword and dagger rested against the chest. Propped against the wall were two sticks with a ball of twine for a wheel—a child's toy pushed about the ground.

Maliku lowered himself to one knee before Maviah, marking his abject humility.

"I beg you, sister. Hear the sincerity of my heart. Though I have sinned against you and our father and all of the desert, forgive me now. I cannot live among the Thamud another day. My guilt eats away at my flesh and I cannot sleep. Saman has cast me out! He sees my eyes downcast in your presence and no longer trusts me. I beg you—"

"Because you are as trustworthy as an adder!" Fahak snapped.

"Even an adder poses no threat if its fangs have been pulled," Maliku said. "I beg you—"

"Until he grows new fangs to poison once more," the old man said, pointing a bony finger at Maliku.

Maliku took the second knee and kept his pleading eyes to Maviah. "Was it not I who persuaded Saman to accept your terms? Do you think they could not have come here with a far larger army and crushed you? And yet I saved you."

"We are Bedu!" Flecks of spittle collected on Fahak's wiry beard. "No one may crush us!"

Maliku twisted to the sheikh, adamant. "And yet Kahil knows no mercy, as you have seen."

"It is Kahil who would send you among us to beguile us with twisted words in our tents while gathering an army in Dumah!"

"Even in Dumah, I sought peace. I beg you, for this wayward warrior has seen his sin and throws himself on his sister's mercy in light of our father's death."

She watched him without betraying emotion, speaking not a word.

Maliku's voice trembled. "I saw it in Petra, when you rendered me powerless before all. I knew even then I had made a terrible mistake and must repent."

"You kept Judah in the dungeon for two years!" Fahak snapped. Though honoring Maviah, he would not relinquish his role as the one to be addressed.

"This was Kahil!" Maliku cried. "It was I who persuaded him to keep Judah strong with meat. It was I who showed Judah mercy, even in his suffering. It was I who delivered the price you required for peace!"

Maviah looked at Judah and searched his eyes. "He treated you well?"

He glanced at Saba, who offered no direction. Then at Maliku, on his knees, humiliated.

"He visited me often in these last few months."

"To ply your mind!" Fahak said.

"There was only guilt in his eyes. When they brought me before Saman, he alone was my advocate. It is true."

To this, Fahak said nothing.

Maviah folded her arms, eyes upon the oil lamp's wavering flame. How often had she been required to make such judgments? She, like King Solomon of old, was wise beyond years.

"Tell me, mighty sheikh," she said to Fahak. "What is thicker than water?"

His brow arched. "Blood."

"And why is this?"

"By blood, life comes to the desert among the Bedu, where water only sustains it."

"And how are bonds forged?"

"By blood," he said.

She dipped her head. "So you have taught me. And by the Light of Blood I once forgave Maliku and so was honored by Aretas. By the Light of Blood I became queen and led our children here, to peace. Is this not so?"

He hesitated only a moment.

"It is as you say."

"And is it not said among all sheikhs that mercy is equal to the sword in power?"

Her path was clear, and Fahak's tone as much as his words conceded the truth. "This too is true."

"Maliku is a sinner, born of Kalb blood and forgiven in the light of my blood. Fahak is honorable, the most powerful for showing mercy in the face of accusations against my brother, all of which are true. Is this so?"

Knowing he had been bested, Fahak returned the question with a twisted grin. "You are far too clever," he finally said.

"Only with you at my side, my sheikh." She bowed.

"Only."

"Then it is agreed?"

Fahak regarded Maliku with disdain. "Your life is owed to your sister, now twice. Pray that it is never in my hands. The Bedu gods do not turn their cheek like Maviah's god called Yeshua." He spat to one side. "It is agreed, with caution."

"With caution." Maviah regarded Maliku for a long moment. Her brother's head tilted down, barely perceptible. And with that slight movement, it was done. But with caution.

She lifted her eyes to Judah. "Protect us all from him, Judah. Your tormentor is in your hands now. I only ask that you show him mercy."

JUDAH SPENT the day inspecting the camp with Maviah and Talya, having sequestered Maliku with Saba, because Judah was now Maviah's protector. Her way with each man, woman, and child she engaged amazed him. She loved them all, no matter how dirty, or thin, or ill, or healthy, without any notice of their status, though she paid respect to all elders as was custom.

But her heart was stolen by the children, many of whom were orphaned. To each she would offer an embrace and a wide smile, ruffling their hair and wiping away any tears.

How they loved her. And how they loved Talya, who

walked among them without realizing how precious he was in the sight of all. In the Bedu way, Talya was son of a queen and so, a prince.

Judah knew many of the people from his years as a warrior in Rami's service, and yet they regarded him with even higher praise now, knowing he'd emerged unscathed from Saman's dungeons. He embraced them, one by one, and exchanged the news, quickly reacquainting himself with his own reputation.

But no matter how deep they ventured into the camp, he could not free himself from the images of Saman and Kahil, only a short distance north in Dumah. There, the serpent coiled with forked tongue, testing the air for the right time to strike at their heel.

They slaughtered twenty camels and twenty goats for the gathering that night, and Judah saluted the roar of twenty thousand Bedu when Maviah raised her hand for all to see.

And even more, Judah's mind was drawn north, to the lair.

The moon was full and high when Judah excused himself from Fahak's tent to check on Maliku. He found the betrayer at Maviah's tent with Saba. Talya was already asleep behind a curtain.

"Sit with Maviah and the elders, Saba. They are missing you." He looked at Maliku, who was poking at the coals of their fire with a stick.

Saba grunted. "There's no need."

"I would speak to my captor alone," Judah said. This was to be understood.

Saba gathered his white robe and stood, eyeing them both. "Watch Talya closely."

Judah watched him leave, then sat across the smoldering fire, glancing at Maviah's brother. For a few minutes, neither spoke.

"You know the Thamud too well," Judah said.

Maliku stared at him.

"To honor Maviah, I won't blame you for what you've done. I only seek to know my captors as well as you do."

"Then your heart will be blackened as surely as mine was," Maliku said in a low voice.

"My heart was blackened long ago."

"And for this I beg your forgiveness."

Maliku stood and retrieved a waterskin and poured water into a pot for heating.

"Tell me their weaknesses," Judah said. "Do their warriors not sleep? Are they impervious to poison? Does Kahil remain in the palace night and day?"

At this, Maliku stopped pouring. The night was quiet. All the children and most of the women had retired. There remained only whispers around a thousand campfires.

Judah continued. "You and I both know that there can be no peace for Maviah so long as the serpent lives. They send her away in peace, but we both know they fear her and will hunt her to the end.

"Help me crush the head of that serpent, Maliku, and you will once again be known as victor among the Kalb. Hear me: I seek a way for only one. If I go alone and fail they cannot retaliate against the whole tribe—only me."

The coals popped. Talya slept.

"There is a way," Maliku said. "But it would have to be done quickly."

Judah glanced over his shoulder. "How?"

The water began to boil, forgotten. Maliku might have been a statue. He laid it out quickly, barely above a whisper.

"Every full moon, Kahil and Saman take to the desert north of Dumah at the high point—"

"I know it." Judah's pulse thrummed. "It's where I first took charge of Maviah the night you betrayed her father."

Maliku blinked. His betrayal had now come full circle.

"They go this very night to offer sacrifice to the moon god, Al-Quam, who gives them power over the darkness. And then the next day they sacrifice to Dushares, the Nabataean god of the sun, victor over the day. On the third day they celebrate and return."

"The moon is full tonight."

"And they go as Bedu, taking only their high guard from—"

"How many?"

"Perhaps twenty. But you must know that they are the best warriors—"

"The best mean nothing to me." Judah was already pushing himself to his feet.

The teapot rocked on the coals. It occurred to him that Maliku might be setting him up, but to what end? If the Thamud wanted him dead, they would have killed him already.

"You have to plan carefully. Kahil is no ordinary warrior."

"What is there to plan?" Judah spat. "They won't suspect anything so soon. They know Maviah has no heart for war and think me crushed, but they don't know Judah's heart. The moon is full to lead me. It is my God, not theirs, who offers power over this night!"

"Judah..."

But he was already moving into Maviah's tent, certain of his path. Nothing had been clearer to him in two years. He snatched up the long sword that leaned against the chest, and her sheathed dagger, then stepped back out into the night, mind fixed as surely as the cold blades in his fists.

Maliku stood.

"Tell Maviah I take her camel and sword. You know only that I wished to be alone. For your own sake, confess nothing else, do you understand?"

The man did not object.

"I'll be back with the sun."

Maliku stared at him. "You have no armor."

"I'll take it from the first man I kill. Watch over Talya."

And then he was running for the camels.

CHAPTER EIGHT

A BITTER wind swept in from the deep desert, and yet Judah accepted the cold as a gift. All of his senses were on edge as he pushed Zahwah to her limit over the sands, guided by the moon and a thousand bright stars.

Riding now with blade in hand and retribution in mind was as much life to him as water was to the sands. This was the Bedu way.

This was the way of God, who demanded blood on the altar in payment for every sin. Saba was wrong to suggest God would lay down the sword and turn his cheek.

Judge not lest you be judged, Yeshua had taught—and now Kahil would learn the truth of those words.

The glory of Judah's people would be restored by this single blow. The head of the serpent—Saman the eyes, Kahil the fangs—would be crushed by the very warrior Kahil had shackled in darkness. All would then know.

Maviah, the mother and queen. Judah, the sword and her right arm.

Eden would be restored in the desert. Then they would return to Israel and join with the chosen one to find liberation from those who oppressed and crucified God's children.

Maliku would hold his tongue for fear of falling out of Maviah's grace. And if Maviah objected to the deaths of Saman and Kahil, the tribal sheikhs would rejoice. All would soon be forgiven and more, celebrated.

These were the thoughts that nourished him as he crossed the sands.

And his desperate need for justice fired his bones as he cut through the wind.

He came to the base of the high point before the first light had grayed the eastern sky, and there he couched Zahwah. The dark towers of rock stood tall four hundred paces ahead, silhouetted against the starry sky.

Studying the terrain for any sign of movement, he stripped off his white tunic, leaving only his dark pants, which he quickly bound to his calves so they would not catch. Taking up the sword and dagger, one in each hand, he faced the wind, chest rising and falling with each breath.

It only took him minutes to reach the first sign of Bedu—their camels, couched in a shallow depression east of the rock formation. Beyond the beasts, black tents bore red-and-yellow Thamud banners that rose lazily on a breeze. Seven tents. The fires were out and unattended. The camp was asleep.

Crouched low behind the crest of a dune, he scanned the encampment, searching for the largest tent, which would be occupied by Saman and Kahil. There, beyond the seven, were three more tents against the rocks. Wider and taller with five posts.

Unease crept along his spine. They would have posted guards at the least, but he saw none. For a long time, Judah kept his eyes on the terrain, seeking any sign of defenses. But there were only the couched camels and, beyond, the tents.

The faintest hint of gray edged into the eastern horizon. Dawn would come within the half hour.

He decided to skirt the wadi and come upon Saman's tent from the rock formation behind. Speed was now his closest ally.

Shoving the dagger into his belt, Judah quickly picked his way around the dune. The night was cold, but his chest and arms were slick with sweat by the time he reached the boulders jutting from the sand.

Still no sign of any guards.

The tent might be occupied only by priests or other sheikhs from Saman's court, less concerned with security than those they served. He rounded the nearest boulder and pulled up sharply.

There, only five paces away, stood a single guard leaning on the rock with his back to Judah. Before the man could turn—in movement born of a thousand raids—Judah slipped forward, breath drawn.

Sword in one hand, dagger in the other, Judah reached the Thamud in three long strides. He dropped the sword and, before the blade struck the ground, grabbed the warrior's hair while bringing his dagger across the man's throat, intent on severing vocal cords first.

Judah's sword landed with a thud.

Voiceless, the man flailed as Judah dragged him back and down onto the ground, as if bringing a camel to its knees. There, with eyes wide, the man quickly bled out on the sand.

Judah retrieved the sword he had dropped. Already, his eyes were on the other rocks. Where there was one guard, there would be more.

He leaped over the slain body and skirted the boulder, edging closer to the tents, expecting another warrior, perhaps two.

Instead, there were four. All with swords drawn. All facing him across a ten-foot clearing of sand. All confident and poised.

They'd expected him?

But they did not know Judah.

It did not matter if Kahil bared his fangs with weapons drawn—Judah could not be defeated in single combat. But if Kahil made an escape, all would be lost.

Judah surged forward, then spun, crouching low, swinging his sword waist high. The two closest guards leaped back, stunned by his swift strike. But he'd anticipated the evasion; the reach and speed of his sword was sufficient.

The tip of his blade sliced cleanly into their guts.

Using his momentum, Judah veered to his right, spinning to one knee, bringing his sword up for the head of the third guard.

He felt the jarring force of blade striking bone, but he didn't wait to see the man fall. He was already turning back toward the fourth guard.

And yet three more appeared, dropping down from the rocks above. All had found their voices. Their alarm cut through the night air.

In the space of a single breath, Judah calculated what must now happen. Kahil would flee from the sound of warning. Engaging these warriors would only delay him. He had to reach the tent quickly and cut off Kahil's escape.

Judah spun back the way he'd come, leaped over the first slain guard, and sprinted into open desert, intent on rounding the rock formations at full speed to reach Kahil's tent from the side. But where the desert had been vacant only a minute earlier, a long arc of warriors mounted on stallions now blocked his path.

He pulled up, stunned by the sight. Seventy, at least.

And then he knew the truth. They'd expected him. Here, at the high place.

Maliku had betrayed him.

Why? They could have killed him instead of returning him to Maviah.

The blow from behind struck his shoulder blades, cutting deep into his flesh. Dropping his dagger, Judah spun, sword fully extended in both hands.

The blade separated the nearest warrior's head from his shoulders. But already four more were upon him.

He took off an arm and drove his sword into another's thigh before a heavy blow slammed into his head.

The night swallowed him.

LIGHT.

Judah's eyes fluttered, then opened. He was lying on his back, facing a blue sky. Memories flooded his mind. He'd been freed days ago. Maviah comforted him in the desert and he'd remembered his destiny.

Maliku had come. The events of the previous night, like mocking jinn, whispered through Judah. He'd abandoned Maviah and chased after those jinn, lured by his own rage.

"He wakes."

The voice that spoke those two words pulled Judah back into an abyss of the deepest darkness.

Kahil, his tormentor.

Judah attempted to push himself up but found that his arms were bound to his waist at the elbows. A warrior grabbed his hair and jerked him up to a seated position.

He was in their camp, a few paces from a fire that warmed a teapot. Several dozen loitering warriors looked his way as if he were only a stray dog found upon the sand.

Before him stood Kahil, one brow raised, lips twisted. He was dressed in black without a headdress, so his long dark hair, unbound, gave him the appearance of a raven.

The rage Judah courted was swept away by Kahil's confidence, because in that moment, Judah knew that his enemy was not afraid. Judah was only the wounded jackal at his feet.

Fear rushed in to take the place of Judah's anger. And then more fear with the realization that he was succumbing to them now after retaining his dignity for so long in their dungeon.

He slowly turned his head toward the sound of feet upon the sand.

Saman approached holding a half-eaten leg of lamb. He bit into the meat, wiped his chin with his forearm, then motioned at Judah with his meal.

"Five men. That's what this absurdity of yours has cost me." Saman made no attempt to hide his disgust. "Do you think me a fool?"

Judah's thoughts plowed through a fog. He'd failed Maviah's trust. So then, what was he now?

"He's a Jew," Kahil said. "A Jew who is Kalb makes only for a mad fool. Did I not tell you?"

"Silence!" Saman cast Kahil a harsh stare. He reacquired Judah's eyes. "Answer me! Why do you think me so stupid?"

But Judah couldn't form thoughts.

Kahil struck his face with an open palm, then grabbed his hair and jerked his head back so that Judah was forced to see his disgust face-to-face.

"Showing only mercy, my father set you free into the arms of the whore you would take to your bed. This is how you repay his kindness?"

"Release him," Saman snapped. "You are no better than he!"

Kahil gave Judah's head a shove and turned away. "We should have killed him with Rami."

Saman took another bite of his meat and spoke around the food.

"My son and Maliku conspired to test you. Without my knowledge, I might add. Had I known, I wouldn't have expected you to fall prey to their plot so easily. And yet here you are."

Their play was now obvious to him: Maliku had thrown himself on Maviah's mercy to gain access, and to suggest to Judah that Saman could be taken here, at the high place.

Why?

"I only want peace," Saman was saying, waving the lamb about. "But it seems the slaves of the desert cannot accept defeat when it is handed to them. Stubborn as oxen, the lot of you!"

Judah had to understand reason for their actions. He tried to speak, but his voice failed him.

"Tell me that you've learned the foolishness of your ways," Saman said. "Or if I release you, will you return to me again like a rabid dog?"

"He will not return." The voice came from behind Judah.

Maliku approached them, still dusty from a night of travel.

"Never mistake shrewdness for kindness, my friend," he said to Judah, then spat to one side. "You deserve death. But the sheikh offers mercy yet again. Accept your defeat in the same way all Jews have accepted theirs in your motherland. It is the fate of your people."

Saman took one last bite from the mostly eaten leg, tossed the rest on the ground, and pulled on his beard to clean his greasy hand.

"Return to your whore and all those who follow her with a clear message. Saman cannot be defeated. Though you violated his terms, he will allow the queen to take her outcasts away in peace."

"*With* assurance," Kahil said.

"Bring them," Saman ordered, motioning toward the tent to his left.

A warrior emerged, leading several bound and gagged children into the sunlight. Judah's heart faltered.

"Maliku has delivered these to us so we could demonstrate both our strength and our mercy," Saman was saying. "If you have not peacefully vacated the springs in three days' time, they will die."

Seven children. Judah recognized only the boy at the end, who stared at him.

Talya.

Maliku had taken Maviah's son.

CHAPTER NINE

———————

WHAT CAN BE said of the worry a mother feels for her lost child? As in the storm on the Sea of Galilee, the dunes that surrounded us rose up to crush me. Yeshua's words, spoken before those frightening waves, haunted my memory.

Why are you afraid, Daughter?

"My son is missing..."

Do you still have so little faith?

"This is Talya!"

What do you see, Maviah? The darkness in these waves, or the light of peace in your own heart?

I tried to see light, but my vision was clouded by a terrible anxiety. Maliku had sent word through my maidservant, Nudia, that he and Judah had taken Talya into the desert to teach him the way of a man.

How could Judah leave with my son in the dead of night, knowing that I would worry?

"Find them!" I'd commanded Saba.

But it was dark and there was wind on the sand—
Saba needed more light to track their camels. He assured me that Talya was in good hands with Judah. I
spent the night trying to believe him, praying for their
hasty return.

When morning came there was still no sign of them.
Worse, the wind had swept away their tracks. And ru-
mors came that several other children had gone missing.

I prayed that Judah would appear with my smiling
lamb atop the camel at any moment.

But he did not appear. And as the hours passed, my
fear deepened.

I was pacing alone when Saba broke into my tent
with news.

"Judah has come. He rides a black horse."

A horse?

The ululating cries of first a dozen and then a hundred drifted into the tent from beyond. News of Judah's
return had spread.

"Hurry."

I was already moving, sprinting past Saba into the
open, where I pulled up.

Hundreds were pouring from their black tents in response to the commotion, peering at a single rider on a
dark horse, who stood tall in the saddle as he raced toward us, sword held high over his head.

"He calls for war!" Saba said. He ran for a camel and
flung himself on the roaring beast's bare back. "Hurry!"

I sprinted for another, leaped into the saddle from
behind, and tugged the languid she-camel to her feet.
We galloped, Saba just ahead of me, trying to catch the
surge of Bedu flooding into the valley at the camp's center, which was kept clear for gatherings.

Thousands had been swept up into the commotion. Above the din, Judah's faint cry was too distant for me to hear clearly.

My camel thundered past dozens of children racing through the sand, squealing with delight, oblivious to the crisis at hand. Only as the gap closed could I make out Judah's cry.

"I have sinned before you all!" he cried, weeping with his words. "For this I would pay with my very life. In my hatred of Kahil and Saman I went alone to crush them. But I was betrayed by Maliku, who came among us like as a wolf."

I feared the worst.

"I, Judah, who would die for Maviah, have sinned, and my sin cannot be undone. It can only be paid for in my own blood."

Just ahead of me, Saba crested the rise above the camp's center and sharply pulled up his camel. I came to a jarring halt beside him and gazed at the chaos. Other voices were crying out, urging silence so that Judah could be heard.

Bedu men of all ages had already filled the shallow valley. Women and children joined them, fixated on Judah. Why had he subverted me to whip up such passion?

"Talya, our queen's very son, has foretold our victory! Hear me, my Bedu brothers! Hear the voice of your own gods and my own. Hear Judah, protector of the outcasts and all who would honor the fallen Rami, whom I served with sword and blood!"

My eyes searched for any sign of Talya. There was none.

"Hear me when I tell you that I was with our prince in the desert." Anguish laced Judah's voice. "There

Talya, son of Maviah, spoke of a garden called Eden, which is well known to my people, the Jews, who, like all of you, are oppressed by tyrants. In this garden there was also a woman who had dominion in peace."

He paused for breath, turning his rearing stallion back harshly. Eden...He was speaking of Talya's song. My heart stuttered.

"But into this same garden called Eden, there came a serpent to deceive the mind and to steal the heart and to kill the body. The head of this serpent is Saman and his son is Kahil! They would crush our queen in Eden and enslave all Bedu!"

Judah had told me this ancient story about the garden Eden and only now did I connect it with Talya's song. I wanted to call out then, demanding to know where my son was, but his words had immobilized my tongue.

Stillness was upon us all.

"But it was foretold that the seed of the woman would rise and crush the head of that very serpent. Can there be any doubt that this woman is Maviah, our queen? And her seed, the beloved son, Talya? Would you not, every one of you, rise with your queen and lay down your very life to save the innocent children from the fangs of the serpent?"

Judah hurled his words out. The horse pranced back and forth. A chorus of agreement rose, for the Bedu passion for children could not be questioned. All of life depended on the preservation of innocent blood.

"Saman cannot crush the spirit of the Bedu! He cannot steal our children and rape our women! He cannot rob us of our land and poison our hearts with cowardice!"

As one the people raised their fists in support of Judah's bravery, which they took as their own.

Judah thrust his sword high in the air, reining in the rearing stallion.

"I went to crush the head of the serpent alone, and I will go again. And again. And again. And again!"

They stilled, eager to hear of the news he was to share, for only the bravest warrior would dare undertake such a raid alone. But I knew the worst was to come, and I felt ill.

"I will go again because the serpent has come like a thief in the night. Maliku has delivered seven of our children to Kahil, who will kill them in three days' time if we do not run like dogs into the sands."

Not a voice save Judah's could be heard now. It was morning, but in my heart night was already falling. I could stop the darkness sweeping into my heart no more than I could hush the words that next came from Judah's mouth.

"Saman has taken Talya, our prince, son of Maviah, who is our queen."

I felt faint. Judah cried out, but I heard the words that followed as if in a dream, muted by a terrible rage that swallowed my mind and my eyes and my ears. My heart was beating like a hammer in my chest, pumping outrage.

"He has taken him because I went to crush the head of the serpent, and for this I will die."

He was seeking their understanding for his offense, but I no longer cared for understanding. I could only see my precious lamb thrown into the same hole where Judah had lived for two years.

For a moment, I hated Judah. But I could not hate

the one who had gone to save me. I hated instead the one who had deceived him and taken my son. In my heart I saw my Talya, and I was already screaming and swinging my blade to sever the head of the serpent coiled about him.

Judah's voice rang out.

"At my queen's word, I will go this very day to the high place where Saman and Kahil sacrifice to their unholy gods. I will slay the beasts who have stolen our children! If I must, I will go alone, and I will shed my blood in the service of Maviah, my queen!"

His sword flashed in the sunlight and he thrust the blade toward me. For the first time, Judah had acknowledged my presence from his mount on the far slope.

At least ten thousand had found their way to the camp's clearing by now, and to a man, woman, and child, they turned to stare at me, seated upon my camel next to Saba, overlooking them all. But all I saw was Judah, standing as one with all Jews under Roman tyranny.

Judah, who would die for the boy he had unwittingly betrayed.

Judah, whose hatred I now embraced, even as it blackened my sight.

I had heard Yeshua's teaching on enemies. I had seen the storm calmed as he opened my eyes. I had embraced his teaching in the arena at Petra without regard for my own fate. Not once since then had I lifted a blade against any man for any reason.

And yet now Talya, not I, was in a storm, and it rose to crush his head even as my first son had been crushed.

Talya, my innocent lamb. Talya, my only son.

My horizon was dark. I could not see how any light or peace would come without a sword.

Slowly, I turned to Saba, because I knew my mind was already lost. He had always guided me.

But Saba did not guide me now. He stared at Judah across the wadi, jaw fixed, muscles taut, knuckles white on the camel's lead rope. Talya was as much his son as mine. The father in him offered no words of wisdom. His refusal to return my stare emboldened me to do what only I could do.

I looked down at Fahak, then Habib and Jashim and the other elders—all awaited my word. Judah lowered his sword and sat still, eyes on me.

Tears seeped from my eyes and trailed down my cheeks. I could not contain the fury raging through my bones, for I had been betrayed and yet would now betray. But I could not contend with these abstractions. I was a mother, and my son was to be slaughtered like the lamb that he was.

My voice and my intent were clear.

"Today we will save our sons and our daughters," I said in a voice that trembled but left no room for doubt.

I let all restraint in my voice go and lifted my fist for all to see.

"Today we will crush the serpent's head with the sword!" I cried.

My heart sought to tear itself free from my chest and I drew in air, breathless. Still they waited, wanting more.

"Today we will kill Kahil, or we will die!"

My last word echoed over their heads, chased by silence.

Then ten thousand voices erupted as one, joining in a roar that shook the Garden of Peace.

And Saba did not protest.

CHAPTER TEN

THE MOON was waning in the latest night hours and still we waited, because light wasn't our friend. We had embraced darkness.

Our army had quickly armed for speed and agility. Stirred by outrage, those women skilled with weapons had insisted on joining us until the sheikhs finally relented. They added one thousand to our number. A terrible need for justice had consumed us all, and I said nothing to discourage it.

We struck north—six thousand toward Dumah and three thousand to the high point outside of the walled fortress.

There would be no victory in a clash between armies, for the Thamud were four to our one. But in the desert, shrewdness was equal to might. Our shrewdness lay in the lethal speed of our counterattack in the face of our enemy's assumptions.

The assumption that I would not take up the sword.

The assumption that we were worn thin by hunger.

The assumption that we wouldn't take such a risk for seven children.

Our plan was simple: in the blackest of night three thousand of our strongest—all men save me—would hit the high point first, where the Thamud would be least fortified even if they did anticipate us.

The other six thousand would cut off the high point from Dumah, separating Saman and Kahil from aid.

We did not wear leathers nor carry heavy lances or axes. We wore only black tunics and belts that girded up our dress, and we carried only blades and bows, which were lethal in our hands and silent in the night. The six-hour journey took us ten, as so many of us were on foot.

The Bedu did not speak. They did not eat. They only rode on a dark surge of bitterness and rage.

And was I not the same?

No...Had I not come to the desert as queen to save the children? Is this not what Yeshua himself had sent me to do? Had not Talya sung of Eden? Was the snake's head not to be crushed under my foot, as Judah said?

Of us all, only Saba seemed unresolved. His thoughts were surely torn by the teachings of Yeshua. I too felt their distant call, but here in the desert Yeshua's words seemed to have abandoned me. I had forgotten what had once been so clear, and even knowing that I had forgotten, I couldn't seem to retrieve it.

Our course was set.

Now Saba, Judah, and I sat abreast upon our camels, awaiting the scout who would return in the night with news. Arim sat on Saba's far side, eager to be seen as one of my protectors.

A cold wind was in our face, carrying our scent to the

depression behind us where the three thousand waited, still mounted and ready. Once couched, a camel protested too loudly when prodded to rise. The roar of so many being mounted at once would travel too far in the still night air.

Jashim and Habib led the six thousand who now waited east of the high point. A scout had already informed us that they made no contact with the Thamud. All was as we had expected.

There was nothing to say now. Typically boisterous Bedu chatter always surrendered to perfect silence on the cusp of any raid or battle. Nothing could be allowed to distract intention or focus.

Though Judah had explained himself to me as we drove north, I could not bring myself to engage him then. There was too much darkness in me. I could only listen.

But now I felt compelled by compassion to speak. He had suffered more than I and suffered still, suffocated by betrayal.

"Judah..." I said in a soft voice.

He hesitated, then responded quietly. "Yes?"

"Whatever happens now, know that I hold you in the highest esteem."

He said nothing, so I faced him.

"I hold no blame in my heart. What you did...I know of no braver man who lives. I am proud to be by your side."

When he finally turned, I saw that his eyes were misted.

"I would die for you, my queen."

"I know. But tonight there will be no dying. Surely God did not bring you this far in vain."

"He comes," Saba said.

The scout trotted his camel across the shifting sands.

"A hundred warriors on guard," he said, pulling his mount around. "Their fires are out."

Judah's jaw flexed. "Then it is time. Tell the others. Remember, quietly until we are upon the camp, then like thunder as we have discussed. You've informed our brothers to the east?"

"Yes."

Judah nodded, then studied me.

"Maviah... We will be on camel. Your skills are on the ground. I beg you—"

"I go, Judah. He's my son."

He took a deep breath and let it out slowly, staring ahead into the night. Then Judah stood tall in his saddle, twisted back, and held up his fist. Without another word, he prodded his camel forward with Arim close behind.

"Saba?"

"Yes, my queen."

"Stay beside me."

"Like your shadow," he said.

"Do not worry, my queen," Arim said, twisting in his saddle. "No harm will come to you. Judah is my brother! I will fight for his love."

Judah took the point, twenty paces ahead. We gauged our advance by his. He slowed at the crest of each rise, scanned the dunes, then pushed forward. Like a swarm of black locusts, our tightly formed army crept over the sands, encroaching on the unwitting Thamud.

We made not a sound other than the soft plodding of camel's feet in the sand and their occasional snort.

They too sensed the urgency of their masters and knew to serve us. For half of the hour we proceeded in this way, drawing nearer to the towering pillars of rock.

Saba grunted. I turned and saw that he was scanning the horizon. He looked at me, eyes white in his dark face.

"I don't like it. Stay with me."

Judah had crested the last dune and now shoved his fist into the air. Leaning forward and whipping his mount, he plunged over the peak.

Like a wave the Bedu warriors swept past Saba and me, rushed up the hill, and vanished over the top.

"Easy, Maviah," Saba warned. "Let them deliver the first blows!"

Judah was right. I wasn't accustomed to combat from the back of any mount. I hesitated and the rest surged past us, but then I could hold back no longer.

Talya was on the far side of this dune.

We reached the crest and I was already over when Saba's sharp warning stopped me.

"Wait!"

I pulled my roaring camel to a standstill and stared down the slope. "What is it?"

Two rows of black Thamud tents hugged the towering boulders at the high point a hundred paces distant. Our warriors now streamed toward the encampment in a show of overwhelming force with swords in hand.

Then I saw what Saba saw. Truly it was what we did not see.

The camp appeared to be vacated other than a handful of warriors who were already mounting to flee.

Judah had already reached the tents and was now on foot, racing into the largest. From the corner of my eye,

I saw the retreating Thamud warriors dragged to the ground by a throng of Bedu in full battle cry.

But my eyes were on Judah and that tent.

"Hold..." Saba warned again, reaching for my lead rope.

I could not breathe, for Talya was either in one of these tents or had already been dispatched to Dumah. If the latter, then all hope was surely lost. I begged Judah to emerge holding my son.

"They come," Saba grunted.

They? Who? My eyes followed his to the north.

At first, I thought I was seeing a black cloud rolling in from the night. But this black cloud was led by tall lances flying red-and-yellow flags. It was formed of both horses and camels, and it was sweeping in like a sandstorm.

The Thamud army. Thousands. Many thousands.

"They knew," Saba said.

Judah burst from the tent, confused, spinning. By now a cry had erupted from my people, for they too had seen the Thamud rushing toward them.

"Maviah..."

I twisted to see more Thamud rushing up the slope behind us. I knew then that the sand would soon be red with our blood. Fear swept through my bones.

"Follow me!" Saba ordered. "Now!"

He took his camel down the slope, looking back to see that I was with him.

"With me, Maviah!" he demanded. "Only with me!" I had never heard such authority in his voice.

We plunged down the hill into the thick of our warriors as the Thamud swarm swallowed them in brutal conflict.

Judah had to know that he'd been led into a slaughter. I watched as he threw himself onto his camel and rushed toward us. Using only his knees and heels to maintain his seat on the beast's back, he swung his sword with both arms and decapitated a Thamud camel with a single blow.

The beast's severed head dropped free and the camel stumbled, catapulting its rider toward Judah, who cut the man's body in half with the back stroke of the same swing.

"Judah!"

He spun, already bloodied from head to foot, and I caught sight of his eyes, fired with life as he saw me. But only for a moment, because he sensed the enemy at his back and jerked to his right to avoid a thrusting lance.

That warrior he took with his dagger. The thrown sidearm slammed into the man's temple and sent him back over the rump of his mount.

Without clear thought, I dropped to the earth, sword in hand, screaming. I stepped up under a Thamud camel and took the leg off a warrior bearing down on me.

My mind was on Judah. I had to reach Judah. We had to find Talya!

"Maviah!" Saba's gruff cry came from behind and I heard his blade thudding into flesh.

"Judah!"

I ran, surrounded by beasts and blades and blood. Two more fell under my sword as I sliced through them. But I had lost sight of him.

"Judah!"

And then a hand grabbed the nape of my tunic and

plucked me from the ground. I twisted, intent on bringing my blade to bear, but Saba caught my wrist.

"Not now."

He swung me onto his mount's rump, fended off a spear, and cut through the sea of carnage.

"Judah—"

"Judah is a warrior!" he roared. "He is no good without a queen. Stay close and low!"

I clung to his strong body with both arms, pressing my head between his shoulder blades.

I dared not look now, for the bloodshed was too much for me. My mind was lost on Talya, and yet the price being paid for him was more than I could bear. Saba took me from that battle. How, I can hardly imagine.

Only when Saba pulled the beast up on a rise did I turn to see the battleground. Hundreds lay slain. Many more were crying out in pain, and those who could were scattering over the dunes into the night. Of the three thousand, at least half would not see the sun rise.

"My queen!"

I turned to see Arim rushing up to us on his camel.

"We have been slain!" He pulled up hard. "The Thamud have—"

"Have you seen Judah?" I demanded.

"Judah . . . Yes."

"Where?"

"They have taken him." Arim's eyes skittered to Saba, then back. "I tried to save him, surely I did, but the Thamud are like mad jinn this night. I swept in—"

"Who took him? Where?" I was beside myself with fear.

He pointed haphazardly. "Into the night."

"Where?" Saba demanded. "You point to the sky!"

"There, to the north," Arim said.

Saba studied the night, then Arim. "Can you still serve your queen?"

"But of course. Would I not die for—"

"Then take her to the oasis. If you must, strike deep into the sands—"

"No," I said, dismounting from Saba's beast. "I have need of your camel, Arim. Find another for yourself and go to the oasis alone." He dismounted. "Tell Fahak to take the Bedu deep into the desert. To the Shangal valley. Do you understand?"

"Yes, my queen."

Saba started to protest but I cut him short.

"You are to remain hidden at the Garden of Peace to send any who return from the battle. Yes?"

I gave Arim my weapons and took his beast.

"Yes. I will do as you say. Then I will return—"

"After one day, you will go to the Shangal and wait for me."

"Where will you go?"

I faced Dumah, less than an hour away.

"I go to my son."

CHAPTER ELEVEN

⸻

DUMAH. The ornament of the desert. All caravans from the east and south laden with frankincense and spices and treasured silks and wares of great value traveled through the city on their way to Petra, Palestine, and Rome—caravans of a thousand camels each, heavily taxed for passage.

The sprawling oasis fed a fertile landscape rich with date palms and fruit-bearing trees. Here the nomadic Bedu had settled in lavish homes, violating tradition. True Bedu did not establish roots in a city, for a city could be made one's prison if conquered.

High atop the city stood the palace Marid, jewel of Dumah, where I had once lived in service to my father. And beneath the palace lurked the dungeons that had held Judah in darkness for two years.

The very dungeons in which Talya was now imprisoned.

Morning light cast a red hue over the white and

gray homes as Saba and I approached. My frantic heart had given way to a plodding rhythm that matched my camel's steps.

I was drained of life. Devoid of hope. Cast into the sea and drowning. I had forgotten the Way of Yeshua, and now life had forgotten me. Not because I had lifted the sword against my enemy, but because I could not remember how to have faith in the midst of the storm.

I intended to throw myself at Saman's feet, seeking his mercy. He, rather than Yeshua, would become my savior, would he not? I was slave to Saman even as Judah was slave to the Law of Moses. So then, we were all slaves to the systems of the world, rather than free in Yeshua's realm of heaven on earth.

The city was just rising as we drew near. Dogs barked, smoke drifted from chimneys, camels were still couched on the sands.

"They know we come," Saba said.

"Then they know."

He withdrew the sword from his scabbard and dropped it on the sand. Then two daggers from his waist. Blades could not serve us now.

"We come as guests," Saba said.

"Slaves," I said. And it was true.

"We are blind, Maviah. We have lost our way."

I let his statement stand for a moment. My failure was too great for me to bear. Indeed, seated there upon the camel, a small part of me hated the Way of Yeshua as I had understood it.

Perhaps I had misunderstood him.

"Then we must find it again, Saba," I finally said.

Two guards loitered by the front gate as we approached, neither taking much notice of our haggard forms. We had both replaced the white dress we typically wore for black tunics and pants. Our sandals were dusty from travel, and dirt had dried with the sweat on our faces. Saba wore no headdress to cover his bald head. I'd pulled a dark blue shawl over my hair.

They saw only two common Bedu.

But I was surely wrong. They had been watching us, knowing full well that Maviah, queen of the outcasts, and Saba, her tower of strength, came to beg for mercy.

When they pulled the gate wide without challenging us, I was certain.

Within the walls of Dumah, warriors stood on either side of a hard-packed path. Hundreds of them, spaced out by a sword's length, stretching deep into the city, leaving no question as to where we must go.

They were tall, dressed in black from head to foot, wearing well-worn leather armor, and headdresses tightly bound with red-and-yellow agals. All bore lances planted in the ground and polished daggers in their red sashes.

I had entered Herod's courts in shame, a hypocrite on a stage, playing my part as queen. I had marched into Petra's arena with my head tall and there became a real queen. For two years I had gathered the orphans and the outcasts, promising great power through peace in the Way of Yeshua.

Now I entered Dumah as a slave once again.

Saba and I guided our camels down the narrow way, staring at the palace Marid high upon the hill. No orders were given; no word was spoken. The only noises were the gentle padding of our mounts and the distant sounds of a city stirring to life: a dog, a spoon in a pot, a child crying, the pounding of wheat into flour. The city was well ordered and swept clean, but few emerged from their homes to watch our procession.

At the end of the main street, the way to the palace was blocked. Here a lone warrior on horseback stepped out before us and led us toward the center of the oasis. Toward the gardens, where my father had planted many flowering trees and pruned the palms for beauty.

Why? Talya was in the palace, surely. My pulse surged and my breathing became shallow. I wished only to reach Talya and offer myself for him.

Today the garden was a dazzling array of white and red and yellow—fruits that would make any Bedu salivate and blossoms that would attract the wonder of any traveler from afar.

This was Saman's own Garden of Eden, I thought. Watered with the blood of the fallen.

We broke through a stand of palms leading down to the main spring, and both Saba and I stopped and stared at the scene before us.

A hundred warriors stood in formation around the pool, facing a platform that had been erected on the near side of the oasis. Upon this platform stood Kahil in regal attire, watching us.

Thick branches from a large tree reached over the platform, and from the thickest branch extended a frayed rope. At the end of the rope hung a limp body.

For a long moment that refused to release me, I could not breathe. I could not mistake Judah's swollen face.

I could not move. My eyes would not leave the vision of death. Saman had executed Judah in the most demeaning fashion. Even as my heart had beat with Judah's, so they ceased together.

And Talya?

I quickly scanned the scene and found no sign of him.

"Be strong, Maviah," Saba said. But I could hear the revulsion in his soft voice.

The warrior who'd been leading us turned back, saw that we'd both stopped, and spoke for the first time.

"Come."

Judah... My dear Judah! What have I done?

I followed Saba, numb. I had done this. I had allowed Judah to embrace his rage. I had joined it! How many times had Saba repeated Yeshua's teaching that those who lived by the sword would die by the sword? How many times had he said that all would reap from others what they sowed into them?

Talya...

All I had now was my son.

We stopped ten paces from the platform and I kept my eyes on Kahil now. To look at Judah again would be to lose any strength I still had.

He returned my gaze, wearing a twisted grin. Then he turned to two warriors and motioned to the body. They crossed to the rope, lowered Judah, and freed his neck from the noose. As if he were only a sack of grain, they hauled him to the back edge and dumped his body to the ground, out of view.

Then they fixed the rope in place so that the noose hung from the limb, empty.

"They say that to hang a queen is to invite demons into your bed," Kahil said, pacing along the platform's edge, hands behind his back. "But my priests tell me that hanging you now will chase them away." Kahil faced me, resolute. "You are the queen who betrayed us. What would you advise?"

I swallowed the pain in my throat and spoke, but hardly more than a whisper came out.

"Are you a queen?" he cried. "Speak like one!"

I took a deep breath and gathered strength.

"Where is my son?" I bit off.

"Ah...Yes, of course. The child. You will have your child if you wish."

My heart leaped.

"But first...tell me, was this insanity your own notion, or Judah's?"

"You took my son!" I screamed, unable to restrain myself.

"Because Judah sought to kill my father's son!"

He was speaking of himself.

Kahil stroked his beard. "Maliku played you perfectly, did he not? He knew that Judah would raise the battle cry if he took the children. And that the Bedu would lose their minds. History will show our actions fully justified. Not once did we attack first. You, not I, have brought all of this upon your people."

His reasoning was twisted but acceptable in the Bedu way.

"You attacked a king," Kahil said. "I have no choice but to hang you from your neck until you are dead."

In a flash I saw the utter insanity of the ancient way, which sought an eye for an eye. There was always one more retaliation to be had, one more grievance to be righted, one more life to be defended.

Only Yeshua's Way of forgiveness could stop the endless cycle of punishment and retribution. Without it, the way of the desert would trade in violence for thousands of years to come.

This is what Yeshua had taught.

And then I thought of Talya and Judah, and I forgot that teaching.

"Then take my life if you must," I said. "Only give my son to Saba and let them live free. I beg you."

Kahil lifted his hand, fingers heavily ringed in silver and gold. "But you are no longer as valuable to me dead, dear Maviah, queen of the outcasts. You still have so much work to do."

Warning whispered through my mind.

"Today, I have satisfied my need for blood by taking the life of your lover. But I still have an empty noose. Bring him!"

Two warriors led a hooded child out from behind the ranks, and I immediately recognized Talya's small form. A chill washed over the crown of my head and spread down my back.

"No!" I cried. Without thinking, I dropped from my camel and tore toward him, even as Saba started to dismount.

"Stay!" Kahil said, shoving his finger at Saba.

Three warriors stepped out and blocked my path, grabbing my arms and hauling me back.

"He is a child!" Saba roared.

"If you dismount, then neither this child nor his mother will have a warrior at their side!"

"I'll kill you!" My voice was frayed and I saw only the darkest night. "Don't touch my son!"

The warriors pushed me and I landed on my back. Flailing, unable to catch my wind, I scrambled for purchase and regained my feet, gasping. Talya stood near the noose with his hands tied behind his back, black hood over his head, breathing steadily.

But he wasn't panicking that I could see, and this gave me a sliver of hope.

"Do not disgrace yourself in my garden, Maviah," Kahil said, clearly satisfied. "Be a queen before this king."

I called out to my son. "Talya?"

"He is gagged. Unharmed, I assure you. And so you know, I have no intention of hanging him today. Nor the other thirty-nine that we have taken."

Thirty-nine?

"I could have taken more while your band of despots was seeking to kill us, but I thought forty was the proper number. One for each tribe that has followed you. Forty, including your son who, I might add, is a very brave little boy."

He reached over and pulled the bag from Talya's head. My son's mouth was bound by a brown swath of linen. But his tender eyes were bright, nearly green in the light. He was staring directly at me, unblinking.

There was no fear in him.

There was only Eden in him, I thought. And that thought deepened my anguish, for his innocence would be crushed in Kahil's thick hands.

"Do you see what mercy I show?" Kahil said. "For the third time in the same week we extend a branch of peace to you."

"What do you want?" I demanded, struggling to show my son bravery.

"You will return to your forty tribes, and you will persuade each of them to swear their allegiance to Saman in the Light of Blood. Every sheikh, every warrior, every Bedu who would rise against me must kneel."

What he demanded was impossible. I had gathered

twenty thousand, some from each tribe, but to gather them all... Bedu blood was too thick and their pride too ancient for such subservience. Asking any Bedu sheikh to bow to Saman would be no different than asking them to fall on their own swords. Most would prefer death!

"For this, I will give you sixty days. Two full months. And then, if you fail, I will raise my sword once again and water my garden with the blood of your sons and daughters."

I was watching Talya's eyes as Kahil spoke, trying to offer him assurance and courage. But it was I who needed it, not my son. He looked at me, making no sound nor offering any resistance.

I glared at Kahil, awash in outrage. "You are a viper," I snarled.

"And your son, the viper's prey," he said. "Return him to the cell."

They pulled the bag back over Talya's head.

"Talya! Do not be afraid, my son!"

I felt deathly ill. They dragged him away, and still he made not a sound.

"Wait!"

But they did not wait. Panic battered my mind. What might I say to offer my precious boy love and courage?

"Make sure that you eat all of your food!"

They were the only words I could form in such a state of anguish.

Saba offered more.

"Do not forget the Way, Talya. See his realm! Only his realm."

Kahil nodded at me. "Sixty days, Queen. Not a single one more."

CHAPTER TWELVE

UPON LEAVING Dumah, I wept rivers of tears known only by a mother who has lost her son and a woman who has lost the man she loves. Was my Father in heaven weeping for me? If he was, I could no longer enter his love.

Saba tried to comfort me with soothing words, uttering not a single suggestion that I should change my outlook or be stronger. Only once did he speak of Yeshua's teachings.

"When we are blind," he said that night as we were seated by the fire, "there is no sight of the light. And so we are in darkness. But this doesn't mean that the realm of Yeshua's eternal light has ceased to exist. Only that we cannot see it. We have been blinded by our own grievance."

I knew his words were true.

"Why, Saba?" I asked, staring into the flames

through my tears. "Why do we go blind, having once seen? True sight now seems like an illusion."

"Perhaps we have lived too long attached to this world." He gathered me into his gaze from across the fire and spoke softly. "But Talya is uncorrupted, Maviah. He has seen and sees still. Our little lamb has surely found Yeshua and laughs with him even now."

They were the kindest words he could have spoken to me.

"Yeshua will restore the joy of our salvation," he said. "He knows no sorrow. We must go to him now."

Yes... But I was a queen called to her people and a mother desperate for her son.

"Perhaps, but first we will go to Petra."

"Petra?"

"I've shown myself worthy to King Aretas and his wife. Shaquilath is a mother as well as a queen, like me. She might speak to Saman on behalf of the children."

He thought a moment, then nodded. "Then Petra."

That night I slept with my head on Saba's chest, calmed by the rising and falling of his strong breast. I fell into a deep sleep, crying for Judah.

More than a thousand of our warriors had perished in the raid, and the Shangal valley was still filled with the terrifying sounds of wailing when Saba and I joined the survivors there the next day.

I wept with them all, embracing as many as I could.

I gathered the council and told them of Kahil's demand that the forty tribes bow to him. They tore at their beards and cried bitter words of rage. But I calmed them and begged them not to take up the sword. Instead, they should retreat into the desert and rebuild their lives until I returned from Petra with the power of Yeshua, for Kahil was temporarily appeased.

After two hours of argument, no more was heard. They agreed with me.

But I asked for more. I insisted they not breathe a word of Kahil's demands to a single soul, for this would only enrage hearts and flood the sands with the blood of our people.

After yet more impassioned deliberation, they swore their compliance, Fahak last.

"I would beg you reconsider this ill-advised journey," Fahak said through a frown. "When have any Nabataeans come to the aid of the outcast?"

But there was no other way. Arim insisted that he be allowed to accompany Saba and me, for he was blood brother to Judah. And so it was decided.

Later, with an anguished heart and darkened soul, I stood upon a dune above the valley and tried to offer courage to thousands who looked to me for guidance. But my words carried no courage, only remorse.

"I will go to Petra in the name of Yeshua and secure an alliance," I said for all to hear. And then louder as my mind cleared: "Yeshua, the lover of all children. Yeshua, who heals the sick and calms the storm. Yeshua, who empowered me to prevail in Petra once before."

They stared at me in silence, for they had put their faith in me, not in a distant god or a foreign prophet.

"Kahil has offered me two moons to submit. I swear to you, I will return before the second moon with all the powers of heaven and earth to save us all."

Someone took up the cry, *Maviah*, and then more until thousands thundered my name. *Maviah, Maviah, Maviah.*

I, who had already failed, was their last hope.

And King Aretas was now mine.

I felt ill in heart and mind.

TALYA SAT in the corner of the large cell, shivering in fear, watching the other children. Most of them huddled in small groups on the stone floor. Two large lamps burned, one on each wall, sending black smoke toward the dirty ceiling. There were three tables in the room, each with two benches. And there was straw on the ground, but not enough.

For three days, the room had been filled with the sound of terrible weeping. No one knew why they had been taken and placed in the darkness underground. All of them cried for their mothers, even the orphans who didn't have mothers. They'd cried until the Thamud Kahil had come and cut Salim's chest with a blade because their wailing could be heard all through Dumah, he said. If they didn't stop, he would cut their throats.

Since then they'd cried softly, into their arms or the straw.

Talya was strong at first, because he was sure that Saba would come for him. So would his mother, who was queen and commanded the sands. Nothing could stop them. Both were of the realm that flowed with light. Both would bring a hundred thousand warriors to save him.

He clung to that vision. The others were afraid, but he knew they would be saved at any moment.

Then the serpent, Kahil, had taken him to the pool and pulled the bag off his head.

His mother and Saba had come for him! But of course they had!

Even when his mother was crying, telling him to be strong, he was sure he would be saved. Even when they led him from the platform.

It wasn't until the long walk back to the palace that doubt and fear came to him. Not until he was led back into the dungeon that his tears began. And once they started he couldn't stop them for a long time.

Two days had passed. Now he wasn't crying. Now he was only shivering. Shivering and trying to remember his vision of Eden and the forgotten Way into the sovereign realm.

But fear darkened his mind.

CHAPTER THIRTEEN

THE LAST TIME I traveled to the west, Judah had led us through the formidable Nafud sands by night. The wasteland had nearly taken our lives on more than one occasion. This time we traveled along the Wadi Sirhan, the same route well traveled by caravans laden with treasures. Saba led me by day and his footing was as sure as his camel's.

But I could not shake the darkness that hovered over me nor the despondency that seeped from deep within me. I could not release the fear I felt for Talya, nor forgive Kahil for taking him. And so I suffered.

I mourned Judah nearly as much as I feared for my son. What cruel fate had delivered him to me for three days only to take him away forever? The sands would never again hear his song; the stars would never treasure his gaze. His laughter had been forever silenced.

Arim spoke incessantly, eager to pull me out of my misery.

"Do not fear, Maviah! Kahil is nothing, you will see! I myself will lead the army of Aretas and dispatch the Thamud as easily as I dispatch a worn cloak."

In many ways he reminded me of a thinner, younger Judah.

"Just like a cloak?" I said. "That easily?"

"Just throw it off, you see?" Arim stood upon his camel, balancing easily, and stripped off his tunic. He threw it on the saddle and sat back down, using it as a cushion.

"The sun is no enemy to me," he said. "Nothing can hurt Arim. And with this same power that delivered you in Petra, I will slay the beast in Dumah!"

Even Saba could not resist a grin.

"And just so, you can throw off the dark cloud that follows you, Maviah."

Saba looked ahead, rolling with his mount's gait.

But I could not find the power to make it just so.

On the fifth night, when Arim had gone looking for his camel, which had wandered from the camp, I sat close to Saba as he tended to a dying fire.

For the first time since leaving the tribes, I spoke of Dumah and of Judah and of Talya. Tears seeped from my eyes as I quietly poured out my heart to him.

And Saba listened.

Where had I gone wrong? How I mourned Judah. Had not Yeshua sent me back into the desert to set the captives free? How many mothers were now without sons? Was not the blood of all those slain on my hands?

"No, Maviah. You only did what any mother would do."

"And look what suffering it has brought us all."

"More suffering than the desert knew before?" he asked.

No.

He poked at the fire with a long stick. "For as long as I can remember, there has been suffering on this earth. And for as long as I can remember, that suffering has been judged and opposed by force, which has only brought more suffering. Using the sword must have its place, but now we see that to live by it is to die by it, just as to live by wealth is to pay the price of that wealth. Both are cycles without end."

Yes.

"So tonight, I offer you no judgment. Perhaps if you stopped judging yourself, you might find love for yourself, rather than condemnation."

My heart stilled, and in that moment I think I loved Saba more than I had ever loved any grown man or woman. Not as a lover, but as a human being.

We came into Petra, the towering rock city without rival in all of the world, on the ninth day. Arim had never been to any city so grand, and he gawked as we passed a great marketplace bordered by majestic columns of red limestone.

A thousand traders sold and bought wares and linens and spices and frankincense and myrrh. Coins and jewels were passed and agreements made with spit upon the hand.

As we moved deeper into the city, headed for the court of Aretas, Saba attracted attention. None could mistake him for less than a warrior of great stature. But seeing Saba, some pointed also to me, whispering.

"They see us and know how mighty we are," Arim said.

We reached Aretas's court without incident. And this time, my name alone was enough to gain us entrance.

KING ARETAS, surely the most powerful man in all of Arabia, could not hide his respect for me. Had I not bested his greatest challenge in the arena and filled his coffers with gold two years earlier?

Because of Yeshua, I had won over Aretas.

Because of Aretas, I had become queen of the outcasts.

His elegant queen, Shaquilath, swept into the lavish dining hall where we had been presented, her face lit like the moon. We were not dressed for the opulence of that court with so much silver and gold and silk on display, but this, I believe, was a part of our appeal. She cast a disapproving glance at my pedestrian dress but quickly played to her higher self and embraced me as a queen.

"So..." Shaquilath spoke with one brow cocked, wearing a guarded smile. "The great Maviah returns to Petra."

I bowed. "My queen."

She wore a long purple dress that clung to her body, dark hair braided with golden thread. Silver rings set with emeralds sparkled on her manicured hands, and she wore a heavily jeweled gold necklace, the value of which might have fed our entire tribe for a week.

Shaquilath looked at Saba. "The dark warrior still by your side. Phasa would be jealous. If she hadn't found a husband, she might seduce you still."

"Saba isn't easily seduced," I said. "As Phasa already knows."

"I see." Her smile seemed to suggest she suspected how deeply I cared for him.

"Maviah!" I turned to see Phasa rushing in, gown flowing behind her, ever a stunning vision. "I knew you would return!"

Her pleasure in seeing me lifted my spirits.

"Phasa..." We embraced like two sisters reunited. "It is good to see you again."

"But look at you!" she said, standing back. "I've heard so much of your exploits in the desert." Her eyes went to Saba, brightened for a moment, then ran over his body, settling on his face. "Saba."

He dipped his head.

She glanced between us. "So the stallion is now yours," she said.

"He serves me—"

"Of course he does." She gave me a knowing smile, then redirected, touching my scarf as if to test its quality. "You've journeyed far, we must eat! Do you care to bathe before? My servants could dress you."

"Thank you, but I have urgent matters and I prefer the dress of my people."

"Then a hot bath at least. The desert enters with you. Did they tell you I have found a husband? One who could give even Saba a match."

"Please, Phasa," Shaquilath said. "There will be time."

"There's a new bath salt you must try, Maviah. From Rome. It leaves the skin—"

"Phasa!"

"What?" Phasa snapped. "I haven't seen my dear friend in two years. If not for her, Herod would have murdered me!"

"Yes, and we are grateful. But now she comes with urgent business. Please, give us a moment."

Phasa turned to me. "This is your wish?"

I took her hand. "I must speak with the queen. Then I will come. I promise."

"Very well. But you must bathe before we eat. I insist."

"Of course."

She left, humming.

"Phasa has a free spirit, wouldn't you say?" Shaquilath said with a smile.

"As always."

"Petra wouldn't be the same without her. Now, where were we? Ah, yes, urgent business."

Her eyes went to Arim, who stood stunned in the presence of such wealth and power. Draped in little more than rags, he was too much for her.

"Please have your slave wait outside—this is not a stable."

"I can never leave my queen's side!" Arim said. "There is no greater queen in all of the deep sands, and I am her greatest warrior. No man may lay a hand on her in my presence and live."

"Oh?"

"Forgive me, my queen," I said, "but I kindly request that Arim, the Thamud warrior who once saved my life in the Nafud, remain as my right hand."

Standing to Shaquilath's side, Aretas was clearly intrigued.

"You see what spirit these Thamud have," he said, grinning. "It is no wonder Maviah finds so much trouble at Dumah." He swept his hand toward a table heavy with food. "Maviah's companions are welcome in my court."

And so we reclined at a table spread with grapes and

melons and steaming venison, with tall vessels of red wine. Attended by three servants dressed in golden tunics, we guests of honor appeared to be the poorest in the room. Which we were.

Aretas set his goblet down, ready to hear me. "Tell me, Queen of Outcasts: what is all this trouble in Dumah that I hear about? Tell me what I do not already know."

I quickly told him everything about my followers from among the forty tribes, my council of twelve, our camp in the Garden of Peace, Saman's release of Judah, the ill-fated battle that ended in our defeat, and the captivity of our children.

When I came to the last, my resolve to remain strong failed me and I had to turn away, overcome with emotion.

"I see," Shaquilath said after a long pause. "You are mother to your outcasts as well. And now your own son has been taken by the monster who rules Dumah."

I tried to swallow my sorrow. "The same one who took the life of my first son two years ago."

She nodded, sympathetic. But her words revealed her heart.

"Don't you know, Maviah, that the desert is full of monsters? Ruling them means becoming one yourself."

"You are too harsh," Aretas chided, plucking a grape from the silver platter. "What she has accomplished in two years is more than any army could have." He lifted the grape to me. "I salute you, Maviah." Then he tossed it into his mouth.

"I only speak the truth," Shaquilath said. "You came into our arena blind and sure to be killed. And by whatever means, I do not know, you left the victor, seeing.

But now you also see that you should have killed Maliku that day. By offering him mercy, you only freed a beast."

I turned to the one I could trust more than myself.

"Saba...Speak for me."

He looked between us, then addressed Shaquilath with a gentle yet sure voice.

"What Maviah means to say, my queen, is that in taking an eye for an eye, there are no eyes left to see. The whole world is blind. What she saw in your arena was the *only* path to truth and freedom and the greatest power as spoken of by Yeshua in Galilee. Only with his sight can faith, which calms any storm, be found."

"And you, dark sage," Shaquilath said. "Can *you* see what none of us can see?"

"Sometimes. And sometimes I am blind. Yeshua's Way of sight and faith is easily forgotten."

"Can you see it now?"

He hesitated.

"What Saba means," I said, "is that I have gone blind once again. The way once so plain to me has gone dark. I come to you for mercy in my time of deepest need."

Shaquilath sat back, thinking on this.

"And what manner of mercy do you seek?" Aretas asked.

"That in the kindness of your heart, you persuade Saman to return our sons to us. We want no more bloodshed, only peace."

For a long while no one spoke. How could a mother such as Shaquilath deny mercy to children?

"I don't think you grasp the simple truth, my dear," the queen finally responded. "Are we not all children? You mention Yeshua, who speaks for the children of Israel. His children are captive to Rome as surely as your own are captive to Saman. Are we to rescue these children of Israel from their oppressors as well?"

"They are a kingdom, not orphans," I said. "I beg you. One word from you and Saman would return Talya to me."

"Would he? He was within his rights to take your children. Judah attacked him."

"Judah was only raising his sword against those who took him captive!"

"So you see... an eye for an eye. And now Saman has taken one of yours. So then take one of his. But we cannot take his eye for you."

Aretas regarded me, sympathetic but one with his wife. "Our agreement with you wasn't to offer you an army, only our blessing for you to raise your own," he said. "Each ruler is responsible for her own children. At the right time I will exact a punishment from Herod for his offense against Phasa. That is my responsibility. Your son is not. He's your own."

An eye for an eye. There was no end to judgment for offense. Saba was right. The whole world was already diseased by blindness and now I as well.

"I am not asking you to take an eye for me," I said. "Only to ask Saman for mercy on my behalf. Is this too much for a mother to do?"

"He will see it as weakness," Aretas said. "Much gold comes to me from Dumah's trade. The only reason Saman pays our tax is because he knows that to refuse will bring my wrath upon him. He's a dangerous man with a powerful army. Any sign of weakness and he might lose his head."

The balance of fear. This was the power wielded by

the threat of an eye for an eye. It had offered a necessary balance for a thousand years.

And yet Yeshua spoke of a new way.

"If I may speak for my queen," Arim said.

He had eaten all of the food in his reach, surely overtaxing his belly. He was out of his league but too bold to know it. And so he continued without permission.

"If you are so afraid of this viper called Saman and his vile son called Kahil, then you might be wise to crush their heads. Maviah will rule Dumah in peace. You will not fear her as you do Saman and there is no greater ruler in all of the sands than my queen."

Aretas grinned. But I couldn't fault Arim's point.

Shaquilath, on the other hand, could.

"We do not break our agreements or betray our allies. Without them, power is stripped from even the greatest king." She turned to me, tapping her nails on the table. "But perhaps we could be persuaded that you are a greater ally than Saman."

Renewed hope flowed into my mind. "Anything," I said. "I am at your mercy."

She smiled, daring. "I know how much you like challenges. Saba claims that Yeshua's way of seeing is the path of greatest power. Saman has given you two months. Stay with me and show me this way of seeing. Convince me that Yeshua's way is the only way to true power. If you succeed, we will have audience with Saman on your behalf."

Dread snuffed out my light.

How could I show her what I had lost? And more, show her what I had failed to show the sheikhs in the desert? Again I turned to the one I could trust.

"Saba?"

His gentle gaze held me.

"For this we must first go to Yeshua."

Yes, of course. What had escaped me only moments before suddenly seemed plain. I would find my sight with Yeshua once more, and this time I would learn to show the way to others. Was this not what it meant to follow him?

I faced Shaquilath, having taken Saba's confidence.

Seeing my agreement, the queen made her final offer.

"Then go to your sage, this Yeshua. Find your power once again. Return and show me how you defeated Maliku in our arena."

She studied me. The king offered no objection.

"Bring us Yeshua's power," Shaquilath said. "If you can, we will save your children."

BETHANY

"He who holds his life dear is destroying it;
And he who makes his life of no account in this world
Will keep it to the life of the ages."

Yeshua

CHAPTER FOURTEEN

FILLED WITH urgency and a renewed hope, we remained in Petra only one night, long enough to bathe and resupply for the journey. And to dine on rich foods with Phasa, who begged us to stay a few more days.

Although neither Saba nor I took the lavish clothing she offered, she insisted we at least take some costly spices and perfumes as well as some silver to aid us if we ran into trouble.

Arim was less modest. He made a plea for a new headdress and a white tunic brightened with a wide cotton belt the color of pine. He also persuaded Phasa's servants to give him new leather sandals and a pair of sheepskin boots embellished with golden stones, the latter of which he delightfully stowed away in his saddlebag for special occasions.

I had not anticipated how much Arim would lighten my heart, for he, like Judah, carried the stars in his eyes and the sun in his heart.

Leaving Petra the next morning, I was desperate to find Yeshua. I would throw myself at his feet and beg for his salvation in the desert. I would beg him to heal my heart as he'd healed my sight once before. I would weep in submission and drink of the living water that only he could offer.

And then I would return to Petra, filled with power, and save my son and all of the Bedu who were enslaved.

We rode long days and far into each night, speaking often, eager to reach the northern shores of Galilee where we'd last encountered Yeshua. In conversing with Saba now, I felt as though I was speaking to Talya's father as much as to my protector.

Even more, I became aware of how deep was my friendship with him. For two years he had been my pillar, never yielding, always honoring me over all else, ever my faithful adviser in all matters. Truly, I knew Saba far better than I had known any man.

Arim, who had never failed to show interest in me as a woman, now seemed to abdicate this role in Saba's company. Surely he saw in Saba something far more than he could offer me.

The journey to Capernaum was to be six days, but our journey was cut short near the north shore of the Dead Sea in Perea. There, on the caravan route, we met a Nabataean Jew named Elhizer returning from Jerusalem with his two sons. When Saba inquired of a teacher named Yeshua from Nazareth, the man became still.

"Yeshua, you say?"

"Yes. You've heard of him?"

"The worker of wonders?"

My pulse surged. "You know of him?"

"It is said that he has raised the dead," the man said, clearly unnerved. "That he is dangerous."

"Only death finds him dangerous," Saba said. "Where is he?"

Elhizer eyed him suspiciously. "They say he stays with the one he has resurrected. In the village where the outcasts and lepers tread."

"Where is this village?" Saba demanded.

"Near Jerusalem."

"Where?"

The man looked between us, as if unsure he should divulge this information.

"Give us a name, man!" Arim interjected, making his presence known. "Are all in Palestine so unhelpful to a queen?"

I glanced at him. "Please, Arim."

"Forgive me, my queen. I speak too quickly."

The man looked at me who'd been called queen.

"Bethany," he said. "The place of unripe figs and misery. Less than an hour east of Jerusalem, near the mountain of olives."

BETHANY. On the fourth day of our journey we cut due west across the Jordan River and came upon the small village when the sun was still high.

We drew our camels to a halt on a small rise, overlooking perhaps fifty ramshackle hovels made of mud and straw and nestled at the base of the mountain of olives—a large hill covered in olive groves. Beyond it must lie Jerusalem, sacred city to all Jews, crowned by their great temple.

I had heard many tales of the majestic city, heavily fortified by Antipas's father, Herod, who built the lavish palaces and a grand arena for games and gladiators. An hour's walk from Bethany, Elhizer had said.

I returned my gaze to what I presumed to be Bethany. From our vantage the town indeed appeared to live up to its namesake. It might have been Nazareth. A few children played on the jagged path through the village. So poor, so insignificant, and yet had not Yeshua always preferred the company of outcasts? Hadn't he been raised by his mother, Miriam, in a village like this? So then he would be at home among the poorest of the poor. Among the diseased and destitute. Among women and the shamed.

Among those his religion punished for being unclean.

Still...If Yeshua was there, among the humble homes, surely crowds would be gathered as they had in Capernaum and Bethsaida. We had journeyed for thirteen days away from my son for an audience with the master. I could not bear the thought of one more.

"What if Elhizer was wrong?"

"There can be no doubt but that he deceived us," Arim said, spitting to the side. "Not even the poorest Bedu could abide in such a place."

This was true. Even the poorest Bedu lived on windblown sands, however humble their tent. Only in villages and cities could such poverty appear so entrenched. Arim had likely never seen this kind of living.

"Elhizer wasn't wrong," Saba said quietly.

"How can you know this?" Arim asked. "A god cannot live in such squalor."

"You do not know this god." Saba stared ahead, resolved. "I can feel him."

The afternoon became perfectly quiet. A light breeze

cooled my neck. The skin on my arms prickled, as if by an unseen power. Saba was right, I thought.

"His realm is not of this world," I said, and I nudged my camel, who snorted once and plodded on.

We rode three abreast into Bethany. When we'd arrived in Nazareth two years earlier, the children had run out to beg, but here we were barely noticed. Perhaps because, unlike Nazareth, Bethany was so close to a large city and accustomed to travelers.

But where might we find him? Arim was the one to ask.

"You there," he said to a boy dressed in rags, hurrying past. "Is the prophet god called Yeshua near?"

The boy stopped, hesitated a moment, then pointed to a house at the edge of the village, back the way we had come. "You have gone too far," he said. "Lazarus, there."

Arim drew his camel about. "Lazarus, you say?"

But the boy was already running off.

"Arim?"

"Yes, my queen."

"Do not call him god aloud in this land. They would stone him."

"Forgive me, Maviah. I will call him prophet only, though you call him a god."

Arim could not yet understand. And could I?

"It is mystery," I said. "The mind cannot fully understand."

The house of Lazarus sat by itself, a modest yet relatively clean hovel attached by a courtyard to another home behind it. Two goats chewed on stubborn tufts of grass along the wall. A large shade tree rose from a garden beyond the house, spreading its branches over the courtyard.

Soft voices reached us from within.

Without waiting for me, Saba dropped from his camel and strode for the gate. But before he could reach it, the door was flung wide and a man dressed in a simple tunic and sandals stepped out, head down, intent on his passage.

He took two steps and pulled up sharply, seeing us and our five camels. His eyes went from Saba to me. I recognized him immediately.

"Stephen?"

"What is this?" he cried, rushing up to Saba as I slid from my saddle. "Saba, my old friend!" Stephen clasped his arms and kissed his cheeks. "What joy has visited me this day!" Then he kissed Saba again.

"It is good to see you, my friend." Saba dipped his head, grinning.

"Maviah!" Stephen stepped around Saba, pressed his hands together, and offered me a bow. "The queen of the desert has returned as bright as the morning star." He spread his arms wide. "Welcome, my dear friends, to the land of splendor!"

I hurried up to him and clasped his arms, overcome by gratitude, because Stephen was like a brother to me. He was also the certain way to an audience with Yeshua.

"Thank you, Stephen! Thank you." Tears sprang to my eyes unbidden.

He stared at me, quieted by my outburst, then glanced at Arim, who had dismounted and stood holding the camels' lead ropes.

Stephen looked into my eyes. "You've come with a heavy heart, dear Maviah."

Was it so obvious? But to Stephen, it would be.

"I must find Yeshua," I said. "My son..." There was too much to say.

"You have a son? With Judah?"

"No. I've taken an orphan as my own."

"Then you must not fear. The kingdom of the sons is upon us. There is much to speak about! Everything is changing, my friends. Everything!" He motioned me toward the house. "Come, all of you. You must meet the others. Leave the camels. No one will steal here in Bethany."

He grabbed Saba's arm and was halfway to the house before turning back to Arim. "Forgive me. And what is your name?"

"I am Arim, protector of my queen, Maviah of Dumah."

"And I am Stephen ben Gamil, slave of Yeshua, who is king of the world. Come!"

Even as I approached the gate I became certain that when I stepped into the courtyard, I would find Yeshua. If his presence was like a warm breeze laced with spice, it was in the air already.

But there was no breeze in the courtyard. Nor any scent but that of baking bread. And there was no sign of the master.

Instead, I saw two women seated on a mat, quietly weaving, and two men at an old table, eating dates. One of the men was thin, with a graying beard and no more than rags on his bones. The other man was younger and well groomed. He wore a dark beard and a threadbare brown cloak.

Both paused their quiet conversation and turned to us. The eyes of the younger man were amber like honey, and I found myself bound to them for a moment before remembering myself and looking away.

"May I present Saba, mightiest warrior in all of Arabia; Maviah, queen of Dumah; and her protector, Arim," Stephen said, stepping to one side. "They are dear friends to us all, disciples of the master."

The two women had stopped their weaving and looked up. Both wore head coverings, as was the Jewish way for all women, and plain dresses. Sisters, I thought—their faces mirrored each other.

There was mystery in all of their eyes, I thought. Something wonderful and inviting. They, like Stephen, were close to Yeshua.

None spoke, but their hearts pulled me in. After so long on the dry sands, Saba and I had finally returned to those rare companions who understood what the Bedu could not.

Stephen introduced each in turn.

"This is Lazarus," he said, indicating the younger man, and our dear friend Simon the leper, though as you can see, his skin is now like a child's."

The old man flashed a sheepish, nearly toothless smile. I was immediately taken by him.

"This is Martha and her sister Mary. They are both sisters to Lazarus."

The woman called Martha was the first to stand and hurry toward us. Then Mary, though she held back, watching me tenderly.

"Welcome to our home," Martha said, offering me a kiss. Then they all approached with customary greetings, Mary the last. There was a quality about Lazarus that I could not fathom. Perhaps the secret lay in his eyes.

"They call you the leper?" Arim asked, staring at the old man who'd hobbled over. "I see no disease."

Simon had worn his grin since Stephen's introduction. "I am called the leper because I was always called Simon the leper. I do not wish my brothers to see me differently."

"You were a leper, then? How is this disease gone?"

"Yeshua," the old man said. "The healer."

"This is not the half of it, Arim," Stephen said. "Come, you must be hungry. Martha, give them water. Sit, sit...We have much to discuss. Yeshua comes for a feast at Simon's house tonight!"

"Tonight?" I said.

"Tonight! But first, sit. Maviah, tell us your troubles."

At Stephen's coaxing, I told them my story with help from Saba, who came alive among them. He told his story as well. And Arim, his, though this took only a few minutes.

There were chairs for only six. Martha busied herself in preparing dough for flatbread, interjecting questions freely, offering gasps when surprised and clucks of the tongue when sympathetic. Mary sat on the mat, weaving quietly, hardly speaking a word.

They were silent for a moment when we finished.

"Do not worry, Maviah," Stephen said. "Yeshua will know. You will see. He comes this very night and you will know what you must do. And you, Saba, who have become wise beyond most. And you, Arim—Yeshua vanquishes death for all."

Mary pushed herself to her feet and approached the table. She took my hand. "Will you walk with me?"

I glanced at Stephen.

"Go," he said. "We men will talk among ourselves. Go with Mary."

"And me?" Martha asked. "Am I man to remain?"

"No, Martha. You will prepare, will you not?" He smiled at me. "At times I think Yeshua comes to Bethany mainly to eat Martha's bread. This is her gift to us all."

Martha arched her brow, but she was pleased by Stephen's praise. "He comes for mine, and the rest of the world comes for his bread." Her eyes fell on Lazarus. "For life itself."

"Come," Mary said.

She led me by my hand through a gate into a field with scattered olive trees. Ahead, a path cut back and forth up the large hill that they called the Mount of Olives.

We walked together hand in hand, like two sisters, Mary at peace. I couldn't begin to guess her intentions. How wonderfully unique were these poor in Bethany.

Just beyond the homes, we crested a knoll and came to a grove. Mary smoothed her dress and sat on a patch of grass beneath a sprawling olive tree, patting the ground.

"Sit with me, Maviah."

I lowered myself to the grass beside her.

"Your name is similar to my own," she said, smiling. "If you lived in Israel, we could be sisters."

I was drawn by her soft tone. "I would like that."

"I cannot imagine what it's like to live where you do. And to be queen to so many outcasts. You are not married?"

"I was to be married to Judah."

"But of course. I'm so sorry. Then you might now marry Saba."

"Saba?"

She was smiling. "I see his eyes. Not even the strongest man can hide admiration."

"Saba is a beautiful man, but my protector. And my sage." Yet hearing her put it so plainly, I knew that he was becoming more to me.

"Then better," she said. "A man who nurtures you with mind and body. You must snatch him up!"

I blushed.

"What of you? So beautiful and still young yet I see no husband. And Martha."

Her smile softened. "It's not easy for those who have been shamed and unclean. We are cast aside and can never marry."

Why, I didn't know—perhaps she too had been a leper, I thought. Or an offender of the Law in some unforgivable way. She didn't elaborate and I respected her silence.

"But Yeshua sees no stain," she said, gazing past me. "I saw it immediately, when he first came to Bethany long ago. He breaks all tradition by teaching women at his table. My sister was at first angry that I should sit at his feet with the men while she prepared food. Do you know what Yeshua said to her?"

"Tell me."

She lifted a finger as if scolding. "'You are worried and upset about many things, Martha. But only *one* thing is needed. Mary has chosen what is better and it will not be taken away from her.' Imagine that!"

"I can," I said. "I have eaten with him as well." Memory of our meal in Capernaum returned to me in vivid color. "So what do you think he meant by one thing?"

"Only knowing the Father matters," she said, as if this truth was plain. "But to Yeshua this knowledge is not like common knowledge. It is to know intimately, as a woman knows a man. I think this truth is more easily seen by women than men."

"How so?"

She shrugged. "Men rule over women with judgment." She frowned and continued in a stern voice. "*Walk this way. Don't be seen! Be silent! Shame on you!* And they make God in the same stern image. They respect written codes and abounding knowledge. Women live more from the heart, don't you think?"

"I would say yes. If allowed."

"So it's the same in Arabia?"

"In many ways, yes."

She nodded. "Yeshua offers no judgment and speaks of the Father in the same way. The very code that men lord over women, Yeshua upends. If Yeshua speaks out against any, it's only against the brood of vipers who judge others."

I recalled his teaching against the Pharisees.

"For someone so shamed as me," Mary said, "this is good news." She plucked a blade of grass. "I worry for him."

"For Yeshua?"

"Those in power hate him. His power terrifies them. They would stone him for blasphemy."

"Saba says that Yeshua cannot be killed."

"Perhaps he is right—he has said, 'Everyone who lives and believes in me will never die.'"

"Yeshua says this?"

"Yes."

So then Saba was correct. I could hardly fathom it.

"Still, I worry for him," she said. "He seems to acknowledge the threat against him more. It drives him underground, to small villages. Too many follow him during the day for the authorities to strike, but he must be very careful at night. He avoids Jerusalem."

This surprised me. "Yeshua is afraid?"

"No. He's more resolute than ever. But still...I worry. I worry even as his mother in Nazareth worries." She turned her eyes to me. "Even as you fear for your son."

I was suddenly taken back to Nazareth, where I had wept on the shoulder of Yeshua's mother, Miriam, after losing my first son. And then my mind went to an image of Talya, so precious, so innocent, singing high on the rock about Eden.

Then an image of him muzzled and bound on the platform under Kahil's ruthless glare. A lump gathered in my throat.

"I am so sorry for your loss, Maviah. My heart weeps with yours." Mary took my hand in hers. "Miriam comes from Nazareth soon. I have known no greater woman. She comforted you once. She will again."

But my sorrow would not wait for the mother of Yeshua. I was gripped by a sudden urge to rush back to Dumah to rescue my son.

"I brought you here to tell you a story. Would you like to hear it?"

When I didn't immediately respond, she pressed.

"It will lift your heart."

"Yes, of course. Forgive me..."

Mary drew a deep breath.

"Not so long ago, my brother, Lazarus, whom Yeshua loves dearly, fell ill. Desperately ill. Filled with fear, we sent word to him, knowing that if Yeshua knew, he would surely come. But Lazarus died before word reached him."

I wasn't sure I'd heard correctly.

"Your brother?"

"Yes. Lazarus died of terrible illness. When Yeshua heard, he told Thomas and the others that Lazarus had only fallen asleep and that he would awaken him. But his disciples didn't want to undertake such a long journey only to awaken a man. Yeshua then told them plainly that Lazarus was dead and they must go to wake him. In Yeshua's mind, sleep and death are the same. This is a mystery to me."

I blinked. "So which was it? Was he asleep or was he dead?"

"He was dead, I can attest to that. Dead and buried for four days by the time Yeshua arrived."

"Buried where?"

"In a cave among the other tombs." She pointed to the south. "I will show you, if you like. He was there—we buried him ourselves."

She took a breath.

"Martha rushed here, to this very grove, to meet him. She was overcome. He was waiting for her. Hearing her anguish, Yeshua comforted Martha and told her Lazarus would rise again."

"She believed him?"

"I don't know. But she hurried back and found me. So I ran to him here and fell at his feet. By then others had heard and followed me." Her voice was soft and distant. "I was weeping, as were others, still in mourning. And in my anguish, I was beside myself. I accused him. I said, 'If you'd been here, my brother wouldn't have died.'"

How deep was their relationship that she could speak such words to one so esteemed? I was mesmerized by her story.

"What did he do?" I asked.

Mary looked at me and I saw tears in her eyes.

"He wept. He wept as I wept. As you weep for your son. My heart broke. I'd questioned the loyalty of the only man who has truly loved me, you understand."

"Yes. I think I do."

Mary toyed with the stalk of grass in her hand.

"He was weeping for me, Maviah. The others thought he was weeping for Lazarus, because he loved Lazarus so deeply—they are like brothers. But Yeshua already knew that my brother was dead. He knew in Galilee. It wasn't until he saw me weeping that he wept."

She swallowed deep emotion. Her admiration for Yeshua was palpable.

"He doesn't weep for his own loss," she managed to say, "but in compassion for us. For *me*. Seeing my anguish, he wept."

The one who had cautioned his own disciples for their lack of faith and then calmed the storm with a word had wept with Mary.

With a woman.

"And after that?"

"We took him to the tomb."

"And he raised your brother?" I knew already, but part of me still couldn't quite accept it.

She sniffed and gathered herself.

"Yeshua told us to take away the stone. Martha objected, fearing the stench. Only then did Yeshua point out her lack of belief. So they took the stone away. And yes, we could smell the death."

She stopped.

"Then?"

When Mary faced me this time, her face was bright. My heart beat heavily.

"He thanked the Father so that all could hear. For our benefit, so that we would know his authority."

"And?" I was eager for more.

"I will never forget it," Mary said, scrambling to her feet.

She faced the tree and set her jaw. "He spoke to my brother there in the grave." She was pointing at the tree as if it were the tomb. "He called out to him, commanding in a voice that might scatter goats." She spread her arms now, legs planted firmly beneath her, and leaned into her cry. "'Lazarus, come out!'" Mary glanced at me. "Just like that: 'Lazarus! Come out!'"

"He just came out?"

"I saw his arm first, bound with the very linen that I had wrapped around his flesh. My heart was leaping in my breast. Then he came out, still in linen."

Mary lowered her arms and turned to me. She lifted her finger, making her point certain.

"This, Maviah, is the power of Yeshua! My brother, Lazarus, was dead, but Yeshua raised him from that death."

I didn't know what to say. My fingers were trembling. I pushed myself to my feet, mind still caught up in my imaginations of such a scene. But there could be no doubt—Lazarus was buried four days and yet I had just met him. And in seeing him I had known that he contained a mysterious life.

"You see?" Mary said. "It was a message to us all. Yeshua came to Bethany to awaken my brother, who had perished. So you must not be worried for your son. Not even death can defeat us!"

I stood in awe. In awe of Yeshua, who could do such a thing. In awe of Mary, who was like Yeshua's sister, a small woman more powerful than a thousand men. And in awe of my own failure, for I'd forgotten his power, once so plain to me in Petra.

"How foolish I was to doubt him after the life he gave me," Mary said. "Today will be the first time he returns to us since those days. I am the lowest in all of Judea, scorned by all but the lowest man." Her soft voice trembled with emotion. "And yet Yeshua wept for me."

Her shame had been as deep as my own, as a slave.

"This is what he does, Maviah. He makes us all queens, like you. And yet I have nothing to offer him."

"Your life," I said.

"Yes. He has it already. But still..."

I thought of Shaquilath's gift to me before leaving Petra.

"I brought something you might offer him."

"A gift?"

"A vessel of nard given to me by the queen of Petra. I offer it as a token of appreciation for inviting us into your home."

Her eyes lit up. "Nard... Fitting for a burial."

"Even more so for new life."

"Yes." She beamed at the idea of offering this precious perfume to Yeshua. "You are most kind, sister."

"It is the very least I can do."

She gazed past me, lost in thought. "Nard..." she whispered. "It is perfect."

My mind was still on the resurrection of Lazarus. I could not imagine the man I'd just met, now with such bright and peaceful eyes, being in the grave for four days.

"Does your brother remember being dead?"

She blinked and looked back at me. "Lazarus? He's changed. He was always close to Yeshua, but now they seem to share something words cannot express. At times I think he cannot truly understand what happened to him."

"What does he say?"

She hesitated.

"He has no fear of death now. None. Truly, I believe he longs to be absent of body once again. He saw much but can explain little. But more, Lazarus knows only love for others now. It seems he has become a child once again."

Talya came to my mind, but now my fear for his safety had subsided. Yeshua would surely save my son, even as he'd saved Mary and her brother. Even as he'd saved me.

"Maybe Lazarus saw Eden," I said.

"Eden?"

"The garden. My son once said he saw it. In a vision."

"Eden. The garden of perfection. Perhaps this is the kingdom of heaven on earth."

"Where death cannot touch us," I said.

"And shame is no more."

Mary smiled and stepped up to me.

"Well then, Maviah...We will believe that your son is in Eden, and we will have no fear. Death will not come to him. Yeshua will save him, you will see."

She took my hand in hers.

"Now we must return to help Martha prepare before she scolds me. Yeshua comes to dinner tonight!"

CHAPTER FIFTEEN

⟞⟝

TALYA DIDN'T know how long he and the others had been in the dungeon. Twice each day they were brought food—heaps of flatbread, dates and other fruits—and water. Never enough, so he took only a little. Once each day, Kahil, the one his mother had called a viper, came to check on them. A perfect hush came over all of the children when the gate at the end of the passage opened.

Talya was sure that Kahil came only to look at him, which he did with dark eyes before leaving without saying a word.

Salim's wound had festered, then finally started to heal, but hatred had come into his eyes, and he did his part to make as many of the children as miserable as himself. As the oldest he demanded their food and shoved them away if they asked for some of his straw.

Many of them had developed running noses and coughs. Many of them were growing skinny. Many of them came to Talya to ask what they should do, even though he was the youngest, for he was the queen's son. But he didn't know what to say except that Saba would come. That the queen would rescue them.

After a while they stopped asking. And soon he forgot to tell himself that story as well. He was only a small boy full of fear.

When night came, the guards put out the lamps and left the children in darkness. Soft crying would fill the large stone cell, and Talya would curl up in the corner to keep warm, covering his ears with his hands.

It was then that he tried to remember the Way. Then that he tried to find Eden as he dreamed of walking in the dark desert, alone. But although he could still remember some of Saba's teaching, the light never came.

And then it did.

He was asleep in the cell, but in his dreams he was there again in the desert, standing and looking at the stars, lost in the darkness and full of fear. Suddenly, a star streaked from the black sky, like a falling star, only larger.

He blinked, thinking it would vanish. Instead it grew bigger. Like a ball of fire streaking straight toward him.

Barely able to breathe, he watched it hit the sand a hundred paces away. A blinding flash lit the entire desert, and faster than possible the light spread.

The moment the light hit him, he felt its power blow through his hair. Through his chest, through his heart. And with it, a song. Only one note, the same note he'd heard and sung in the desert before. The light itself was like a song!

Suddenly it was day. Not a day with a sun, but day by the light of that star. As if by magic.

But there was more. Much more.

He gasped, sucking in the air, which seemed to be the light itself. And with that breath his arms began to tremble. Peace and joy as he'd never known them filled him from the inside out.

But there was more. Much more.

Immediately grass began to grow from the parched sand, and vines became full of grapes, and small trees grew into large ones heavy with green leaves. A clear blue pool sprang out of the ground, and many birds flew through the sky. On the rolling hills he saw camels and lions and lambs and foxes and many wonderful creatures that he didn't know.

All of it happened quickly, in the space of only ten or fifteen breaths.

And with each of those breaths, Talya inhaled the light, knowing that it was the light of the world. This was the Father's sovereign realm, surely.

This was Yeshua, creating the world. Eden.

This was what he had seen in the distance from the high ledge. But now...now he was *in* it. He spun around with arms spread wide, singing that song in a pure voice that joined with the light.

Only then did he see the large black serpent with green and yellow and red stripes sliding into the meadow, not ten paces from him. He stopped and stared, captivated by its beauty.

The serpent slipped slowly through the grass, flicking its tongue, eyeing him with golden eyes. It hissed in one long sound that grew, overwhelming the pure song that had filled the air.

Talya felt his pulse quicken. The hissing was at once beautiful and cutting, drawing him and repulsing him at the same time.

The serpent suddenly coiled. Then opened its jaw wide. Talya watched, stunned, as a round fruit rolled out of the serpent's mouth and onto the grass. The fruit was half-white and half-black—not just white like the sand, but white like the sun. And not just black like the shale, but black like a hole that had no bottom.

The hissing grew louder.

As Talya watched, a woman who looked like his mother stepped out from behind a tree, eyeing that fruit.

The snake hissed at her, and she watched it for a while, as if listening. She didn't seem afraid, only curious.

Then the woman walked up to the fruit, picked it up, and stared at it in her hand. She surveyed the garden for a moment as if undecided about what to do.

Looking at the snake one more time, she gave a slight nod, then lifted the fruit to her mouth and took a bite.

Immediately, the light winked off and the garden disappeared, leaving only the woman on desert sand at night. The song and the hissing stopped.

Talya stood with his mouth open, filled with fear.

The woman crouched and spun around with the fruit still in her hand, trying to see, terrified. The serpent darted out from the darkness, fangs flashing, and bit her heel. She screamed and dropped the fruit, grasping at her leg.

She staggered to the edge of the meadow and then collapsed.

Talya spun to see the serpent still there, coiled, watching him with beady eyes. Surely the viper would bite him as well.

"Who are you?"

The gentle voice spoke from deep within Talya and also from the sky, like a soft wind drifting through him. He blinked in the darkness, straining to see.

"What is your name, my son?"

He swallowed and spoke in a thin, ragged voice.

"Talya."

"And what does *Talya* mean?"

"A...a lamb."

"And what does *lamb* mean?"

An image of his mother stroking his hair filled his mind. Was the voice his mother speaking? No, it was more. Far more...

"It means innocent child," he whispered.

The darkness was silent for a moment, and then the voice came again.

"I have given you power over the deceiver, who brings the knowledge of good and evil to blind you. I have given you authority to trample on serpents and overcome all the power of the enemy. Nothing will harm you."

Talya trembled.

The serpent was still there, tasting the air with its tongue, eyeing him.

"Crush the serpent," the voice said.

"The serpent?" Talya said, still shaking.

"Yes. Crush the serpent, then you will see."

Still full of fear, but desperate for the light to return, Talya slowly walked up to the serpent, amazed that it did not slither away. He lifted his foot and stomped on its head with all of his might.

Thunder boomed overhead. Immediately the darkness rolled back like a scroll, revealing the garden exactly as it had been before.

Once again the light flooded Talya's body, and the song his mind.

"Ha!" Talya cried, jumping, smiling wide. "I did it!"

Somewhere far away, a door squealed and then shut, like the door in the dungeon, pulling him from the dream.

He jerked up, gasping. Torches were lit and many of the children were already sitting up, leaning against the walls or sitting cross-legged, faces flat or strained with dread.

Truth came to Talya then—he was to bring light into this dark world. This is what Saba had meant when he'd said a child would lead them! This was his place here, to help them see what they couldn't see.

Eden was here, beyond the darkness, he was sure of it!

He jumped to his feet filled with courage and spoke without thinking.

"We will be saved!" he cried.

They turned to him with dumb stares.

He stepped forward and lifted one hand. "It's dark in here, but I have seen the light. It's here if we only look. It's always been here, everywhere, we are only blind to it!"

"Be quiet, you spoiled little dog," Salim spat from his corner. A couple of the others who were eager to impress the older boy snickered.

But this meant nothing to Talya. He took another step, eager to be heard.

"I had a vision, and in this dream I saw the serpent blind the world with a fruit of darkness. The fruit of the knowledge of good and evil. But that serpent is powerless against us! If we be like Yeshua. If we only open our eyes to see the light!"

"Quiet before I knock your teeth out!"

"No, Salim! This is the light you seek!" He glanced around. None of them seemed to care. How could it be?

"No one will listen? All of you would rather remain in this darkness, weeping for your mothers? Please...I beg you—"

"I will listen," a soft voice said.

Talya turned to his left and saw that Mona had risen to her feet. Her eyes were wide with wonder.

"Tell me about the light."

He stepped toward her. "I will. I'll tell you everything."

A chuckle echoed through the room, and Talya twisted to the bars that caged them in. There, in the dim light beyond the cell, stood Kahil, grinning. The sound he'd heard in his dream...The door...

"So...the little prince has found his courage once again."

Talya blinked. "This is the serpent," he said, stretching out his arm. "But he has no power over us."

The room was deathly quiet. Kahil's smile flattened. The courage in Talya's blood began to leak away and he lowered his arm, caught in the man's glare.

Kahil nodded at him once, as if accepting the challenge. Then he stepped to one side and spoke to two guards behind.

"Bring him."

CHAPTER SIXTEEN

———⟪⟫———

WORD THAT Yeshua was coming to Bethany had fil-
tered through the village—the air was filled with great
expectancy. But nowhere more so than in Martha's
house, where Mary and I joined her in preparing food,
while Saba spoke in quiet tones with Stephen, Lazarus,
Simon, and Arim.

They spoke of the kingdom; they spoke of the wonders of Yeshua. Of the time he'd healed a deeply frac-
tured man with many demons, who went by the name
Legion. Yeshua had cast these demons into a herd of
swine, and the man immediately found a sane mind.

I listened, and my mind was on Yeshua. If he could
save such a broken mind, Yeshua could surely protect
Talya.

They spoke of death and of resurrection. Lazarus
declared that Saba, who had no religion, could accept
the mysteries more easily than those steeped in religious
tradition. What he'd experienced while being dead and

then coming back to life defied all common reason. In this, he knew what Yeshua meant by his repeated use of children as an example for all who want to enter his kingdom.

"He speaks of being born yet again," Lazarus said in a gentle voice. "Of the Father revealing himself to infants and hiding himself from minds of reason. 'The kingdom of God belongs to such as these,' he says of the babes when they are brought to him." He glanced at me, a mother. "And 'anyone who will not receive the kingdom of God like a little child will never enter it.'"

"You experienced this rebirth, upon waking?" Saba asked. "As an infant?"

"I can only say that nothing looks the same to me now," Lazarus said. "There are no words for it. All that I saw before has grown strangely dim." His eyes twinkled. "I feel as though I am just now alive. As though reborn into the light."

"You see, Saba?" Stephen said, smiling. "Reborn, like infants. Are you then an infant?"

Saba only stared. He knew of this teaching but was now knowing it again with Stephen and Lazarus. My tower was indeed like a small child among them, I thought. And I loved him for it.

They spoke of many other wonders and healings and casting out of devils. There was surely no end to the power Yeshua had shown all through the villages and towns.

But his teachings had become too hard for many to follow, and so many had abandoned him. "They wanted to see the wonders, but they could not follow this narrow way, which defies all common sense," Stephen said.

The old man Simon lifted his finger to make a rare point. "But this too has changed. Hearing of Lazarus, many are returning. All of Bethany saw him dead and buried. All knew that he was in the tomb for four days. And now all see him alive." He chuckled, baring what few teeth he still had. "Word has spread like a fire through the field. Every street in Jerusalem whispers of this news."

After the sun set, under Martha's continuous direction, we took baskets filled with warm loaves of flatbread along with dates and honey and wine to Simon's home. Two other women arrived with portions of a small lamb they'd slaughtered, and together we laid out a humble feast.

"Put the fruit back on the small table," Martha said to Mary. "This table is too cluttered." To me: "Maviah, dear, did you sweep the floor?" I had done so twice. She even lorded over the men so familiar to her. "Must you leave your cloak on the chair, Lazarus? You would make this house a barn?"

None of us minded. This was her way of honoring Yeshua.

Simon's house was larger than he could have possibly purchased or inherited. It had been offered to him by a wealthy man in Jerusalem named Zacharias, whose sister had been healed of leprosy a year earlier.

The dinner was to be a small gathering in Yeshua's honor. The lamps were lit; the long table set just so, fit for a humble king; ten of us were gathered. There was room only for ten around the table, and these seats were reserved for Yeshua and the disciples who had traveled. The rest of us would recline on couches set along the walls.

All was prepared.

The time grew late, but still they had not come.

"Are you certain he said tonight, Simon?" Martha asked.

"Tonight," the old man said, grinning. "You will see."

"Not tomorrow but tonight—you are sure this is what Bartholomew said?"

"I am old, but not deaf. Tonight."

"You are absolutely positive, Simon?" Stephen said, standing in the corner.

"They will be here!" Simon croaked. "Do you think my mind is gone?"

Arim was at the window, peering out. "Perhaps he has fallen into the hands of the enemy." He turned back. "I would help Stephen search the path for him."

"Don't say such things," Mary said, hurrying toward the door. "You must not even think—"

A knock on the door stopped her. She gasped. And with that gasp we all went perfectly still.

"He's here!" Martha whispered. Then she was moving, rearranging food that was already perfectly set, smoothing her dress.

I was standing beside a bench in one corner as Simon hurried to the door, pulled it open, and stepped back.

The first in was Peter, whom I recognized immediately, though he'd lost some weight. Then Levi, at whose home I had first met Yeshua. Then John and James and one named Judas—all whom I'd seen in Bethsaida. Did they remember me?

They poured in, seven of them, the famed disciples chosen by Yeshua to be his inner circle. These remained with him night and day. Only five were not present.

But Yeshua did not enter. He was not among them. My palms were clammy and my heart raced.

Grinning wide, Simon stepped outside. I heard words too soft to be understood. The door remained empty, and beyond it only darkness.

But then that darkness was gone, replaced by the frame of a cloaked man who wore a mantle over his head. He took two steps into the house and stopped.

Yeshua.

Only my knowledge of him made his entrance so grand. To those who didn't know him, his arrival might have been nothing more than the arrival of a shepherd after a long day in the fields. But I did know him. And I could not move.

I could hardly breathe.

I did not see his eyes at first, because the blue-and-white mantle hid all but his gentle, bearded smile from my vantage. His cloak was dusty and his sandals worn thin. In his right hand, a walking staff.

He scanned the room slowly, taking in each face as Simon pushed the door closed behind him. When his light-brown eyes met mine, they lingered for just a moment.

But that moment felt like an eternity to me. He was seeing into me. Through me. Holding me in a gaze of deep understanding. For two years I had served him in ways that only Saba and I could know, and yet he seemed to know every breath I'd taken in that desert already.

Eyes still on my own, he dipped his head ever so slightly. A simple acknowledgment by any standard. Yet in my mind, he might as well have washed my feet—this was the power of acceptance and honor that extended from him. I wanted to weep with gratitude.

Yeshua reached up and pulled his mantle from his hair. The old man Simon stood behind him, beaming with pride. Lazarus stepped forward and clasped his arms.

"You came."

"Have I not always come to you, my brother?"

"Always," Lazarus said.

"I see that Martha has been busy." Yeshua stepped past Lazarus and warmly greeted both Martha and Mary, exchanging soft words I could not make out. Besides his disciples and his own mother, these were Yeshua's closest family.

"Saba..." Yeshua clasped his arms and looked into his eyes. "I see that you have been learning."

He knew? Saba was caught without words.

"You do so well, my friend. So very well." His eyes shifted to Arim. "And who is your Bedouin friend?"

"Arim," the boy replied. With that Arim fell to his knees and gripped Yeshua's hand, head bowed. "I am Maviah's humble protector, who worships her prophet and protects him also from any who would raise the sword. My life is now yours, mighty sheikh."

Yeshua's brow arched. "Then serve me by serving those who show you the Way," he said gently.

Arim rose and stepped back, then bowed again. "With the very last drop of my blood."

Yeshua turned and approached me.

"Maviah...The daughter from the desert comes with a heavy heart."

My fingers where trembling. It was all he said. And

if he had said more, I might not have heard it, so overcome was I.

He went on to greet the others, but my mind was already ruined. I could not understand the waves of emotion washing through me. I had been deeply affected by his presence the first time we had met, two years earlier, but not so overwhelmed as now.

Perhaps because he would save Talya.

They were moving about the room—taking their places at the table, gathering up food, washing their hands in a basin as was customary—but I lingered there in the corner, lost and found at once, wondering when I should tell him about Talya.

I took some bread and settled next to Mary on a couch, but I had no appetite.

His disciples filled me with awe. I wondered what it was like to be the right arm of such a powerful master, to see all they had seen. And yet they were quiet in his company, yielding to his authority.

The last time I'd seen Peter, he seemed far more uncertain than he now appeared. It struck me that after so much time at Yeshua's feet, Peter must now be like a god among men.

Levi too seemed to carry an air of authority about him. As did the others—James and John and Philip. They were comfortable near their master. And yet perhaps they, like Mary, sensed the danger that followed him.

Judas, whom I'd only seen from a distance before, made the case plain in a hushed tone.

"We should not have been traveling so late this close to Jerusalem," he said to Peter under his breath. "There are too many threats now."

"We travel when he says we travel, Judas. Do you doubt after so long?"

"Of course not. But it is our place to attend to these matters. Support is coming our way, finally. All the more reason to be careful until we win many more."

He was a Zealot, I thought. Like Judah.

"You worry too much, Judas," Peter said. "He will show his power when he's ready, not at our beckoning."

Judas turned away, clearly unconvinced.

But none of this seemed to concern Yeshua, who was eating and listening to Lazarus's soft voice in his ear. I watched as he tore pieces of bread from a loaf, dipped them in honey, and carefully placed them in his mouth. Then he took a sip of wine from his stone cup.

I watched his strong, gentle hands. They had healed so many with a touch and yet appeared worn and callused, like those of any who lived off the land.

I watched his mouth, from which came words of such power and authority, and yet it was only lips and tongue and teeth, like any human mouth.

I watched his brown eyes, windows into another world full of mystery and love and unfathomable peace. With a single glance, he could surely halt any army. Yet they were just eyes, like any other human's.

There was nothing in his appearance alone that moved me.

It was his presence.

Twice he caught me staring and I felt compelled to glance away, though I saw only acceptance and honor in his gaze.

Like the last time I'd eaten with Yeshua, the conversation was muted, perhaps in respect, perhaps only waiting for Yeshua himself to direct what might be said.

This was the way a court might gather around a king of highest honor, though Yeshua's power came from neither wealth nor armies.

Here sat a humble master in a humble home. One who healed the heart and raised the dead. Aretas of Petra would surely tremble at Yeshua's feet.

Slowly, even the hushed conversation fell off, leaving the room to the sounds of eating and drinking. Even Lazarus fell silent. Yeshua's eyes were now cast down, gazing at his cup of wine, which he slowly turned with his fingers.

I should speak now, I thought. I had lost my sight, and my son was held in chains. I had to save myself to save Talya.

But I couldn't speak. It would be irreverent. I would be speaking out of turn. And yet I must.

"Master..."

His eyes lifted to me, inviting.

"My son, Talya. The Thamud have taken him. I..." Tears blurred my vision. "I'm powerless to save him. I don't know what to do."

A gentle smile. Then words, like a healing balm.

"Maviah...What a precious daughter you are."

He held my eyes for a moment, then looked at the others.

"Suppose one of you has a hundred sheep and loses one of them. Does he not leave the ninety-nine in the open country and go after the lost sheep until he finds it? And when he finds it, he joyfully puts it on his shoulders and goes home. Then he calls his neighbors and friends together..." His eyes shifted to me. "He calls them together and says, 'Rejoice with me; I have found my lost sheep.'"

Talya. Meaning little lamb. He was speaking of my son...

With a sob, Mary suddenly rushed forward and fell on her knees before him, weeping, hands wrapped around the pint of nard I had given her.

"Master, I am that lost sheep!" she cried. "I give you my life...all that I am and all that I have. I, the lowest sinner, was made whole by you."

She opened the bottle of precious perfume and I knew that she meant to anoint him with some of it. But she didn't.

She anointed him with all of it.

Weeping, she poured some on her hand and anointed his head, then poured the rest over his dusty feet and let the bottle fall to the ground.

She began to wipe the nard from his feet using only her hair. "Forgive me...Forgive me..."

Emotion welled in Yeshua's eyes as he watched her.

In that moment, I became Mary. She, the woman who had been crushed by unforgivable shame in the life she'd left behind; I, the slave who had been thrown away by my father, the powerful sheikh.

And Yeshua, our savior from all of the shame this life might heap upon us.

He'd spoken of my Talya, surely, but he'd also spoken of me and of Mary and of all those in the room. We were all there, weeping with her, offering him what was reserved for a king.

Judas broke the moment when he slowly stood to his feet.

"Why wasn't this perfume sold and the money given to the poor?" he asked. "It's worth a year's wages!"

Peter reached out to him. "Judas...Not now."

"Do we not tend to the poor? How dare you rob the poor with such waste!"

Still Mary wept, wiping Yeshua's feet with her hair.

Judas looked at Yeshua. "Master..."

"Leave her alone," Yeshua said quietly, lifting misted eyes. "She's done a beautiful thing. It was intended that she should save this perfume for the day of my burial. You will always have the poor among you, Judas. But you will not always have me."

Judas hesitated, then slowly sat.

Yeshua leaned down and placed a kiss on Mary's head. "I rejoice with you, Mary. What you have done will be remembered by all the world, wherever the good news is received."

She grabbed his hands and kissed them. "Rabbi." But she had no other words.

She whispered something, and he nodded. Then she gathered herself, picked up the empty bottle, and hurried back to her seat near me, eyes bright like a proud child's.

Yeshua looked around the table. The certainty of his authority, like the extravagant scent of the nard, filled the room.

"Have you not heard me say many times that you cannot serve two masters?" he said. "You will hate the one and love the other, or you will be devoted to one and despise the other. You cannot serve both God and mammon. So then, which master do you serve? But I tell you the truth...No one who has left home or wife or brother or parents or children for the sake of the kingdom of God will fail to receive many times as much in this age and in the age to come. Eternal life."

He was talking about more than money. He was

speaking about all that enslaved one to this world's system, be it sword or wealth or religion. There are two kingdoms, Saba so often reminded me: the realm of the world and the realm of the Father. Serve only one, the Father, to master the world.

But surely Yeshua did not mean for me to abandon my own son.

"Tell me, Saba," Yeshua said, turning to him. "What is the Way of which I speak?"

Saba, the strongest man in the room by twice, was among giants, I thought. He glanced around and cleared his throat.

"There are two realms, heaven and earth, both among us, both within us. To find the priceless treasure, which is the eternal realm of the Father even now, one must trust in you and so come to know the Father intimately. The means to see this path is new eyes that see the realm of peace instead of the storm. This is to be reborn, as an infant, with new eyes. Only then can one be saved from the storms in this age."

All stared at him. Stephen looked as though he might burst with agreement. "And the age to come," he said.

"Yes," Saba said, glancing at Stephen. "And in the age to come."

Yeshua smiled, offering neither agreement nor disagreement.

"And what of love?" he asked.

"Love without judgment is the expression of the realm of heaven on earth."

No one voiced an argument.

"I only ask this," Saba pressed. "If one must have new sight to see the realm of peace in the storm, what is the way to gain this new sight so that our eyes might be opened?" He hesitated a moment. "Is surrender the means to sight, then?"

For a long time, Yeshua regarded him without speaking. Slowly his smile faded. He looked through the window into the night.

"If any would come after me, they must deny themselves, take up their cross daily and follow me." He paused. "Anyone who does not take up his cross and follow me cannot be my disciple."

I wasn't sure I had heard right. But I heard more.

Yeshua's eyes rested on Saba again. "Whoever wants to save their life will lose it, but whoever loses their life for my sake will save it. What good is it to gain the whole world yet forfeit your soul? If anyone comes to me and does not hate their father and mother, their wife and children, their brothers and sisters—even their own life—they cannot be my disciple."

He paused, looking from one to the other.

"Again I say, you cannot serve two masters; you will hate one and love the other."

To hate as he said it meant to hold of no account...As if to say it was impossible to have faith in both this world and the realm of the Father at the same time. But how was one to do this of everything pertaining to life in this world? Even their own sons and daughters? He was speaking of a new kind of surrender that staggered my mind.

Yeshua stood and faced us all, fingertips on the table, then he turned and walked to the door. He put his hand on the frame and tested its strength as a carpenter might.

"Suppose one of you wants to build a tower. What will he do, John?"

"He will first sit down and estimate the cost to see if he has enough money to complete it," John said, as if familiar with the teaching.

Yeshua released the door frame and faced us. "Or suppose a ruler is about to go to war against another ruler. Will he not first sit down and consider whether he is able with ten thousand men to oppose the one coming against him with twenty thousand? If the ruler is not able, he will send a delegation while the other is still a long way off and will ask for terms of peace."

He was speaking of the Thamud? No... Of me.

"In the same way, any of you who does not give up everything he has cannot be my disciple. So then, first count the cost."

Why Yeshua's call to unconditional surrender drew me, I don't know. Perhaps only because I was so desperate to know his power.

I looked away. *Have mercy on me. Save me from the trouble that has swallowed me! Save your son, Talya. Save my son, I beg you.*

"Maviah..."

I jerked my head back to face him.

"Know this, Daughter," he said. "I have overcome death. He who believes in me will never die. Do you understand this?"

"Yes, master." My voice was weak.

"Do you, Maviah?"

Tears were flowing from my eyes, unbidden.

"Yes."

He walked over to me. Then, gazing down into my eyes, he gently rested his hand on my head.

"Then do not worry about your son. Even as I will not die, so neither will he. You wish to know what to do...Only remain in me. Come to me when I call. Stay in Bethany with your sisters. Then you will know what to do."

"Yes..." Gratitude washed over me. "Yes, I will."

Deep introspection filled his eyes. He walked up to the window on my right and gazed out. We watched, silent in anticipation.

"In two days, after the Sabbath, we will go into Jerusalem," he said quietly. Then turned to face us.

"It is very soon now."

CHAPTER SEVENTEEN

IT IS SAID that the Bedu can *feel* a storm in the air before the rains come to nourish the desert with life-giving water. There is a power in the air that finally bursts forth with jagged bolts of lightning from the gods.

This was what I felt in Bethany. My skin prickled with the power in the air. Talya would be saved...I knew this like I knew I still breathed. How, I didn't know, but Yeshua could not fail.

He stayed with Simon as the guest of honor, and I did not see him on the Sabbath or the morning that followed. When Yeshua wasn't with them, he was gone to the Mount of Olives, where he went to be alone for many hours.

Remain with your sisters, he'd said. And so I did. Sure of my son's deliverance, I allowed myself to embrace the presence of Yeshua that hummed in our bones like a silent thunder.

Many had come from Jerusalem to see him, and

many others were traveling through Bethany on their way to Jerusalem for the feast of Passover, one of the holiest of celebrations for the Jewish people. On that day they would slaughter a lamb and atone for their sins with its blood.

Bethany swelled to three times its size. Visitors came with gifts of wheat and barley and fruits, and Martha busied herself baking at all hours, for there were many to feed. Mary and I helped as much as Martha allowed. I had never baked so much bread in one day.

Our talk was of Yeshua. Always Yeshua. Mary didn't speak of her time of shame, for it was now in the past—a season that no longer held any significance to her other than the fact that it was past. Though Dumah and the plight of my people hung always in the back of my mind, I spoke of it rarely.

Thoughts of shame and death were far away from us. If only Judah could have seen what I was seeing! How my heart broke for him. His prison had first enslaved him and then finally crushed him. But he was now with the Father, I thought. Perhaps he was watching over me like the stars, and if so, he was surely smiling, singing a song of gratitude.

But Saba...I can't rightly describe the shift in Saba after that first night. He was gone, always, hovering near Yeshua when possible, or talking to Stephen, or retreating to the hills by himself. I was glad for him.

And yet he also seemed distant from me in spirit. I didn't realize how much I had come to expect his affectionate company until then.

When we gathered to eat, he was at my side, offering me food, but his eyes were not attentive. And he would quickly excuse himself to be gone.

At first I dismissed this retreat into himself as completely understandable. But on the second night I saw with more clarity. We were alone in the courtyard, having shared bread, and he was eager to leave.

"You go to find him now? It's late, Saba."

"I would be alone."

"Yes, of course. But you've been gone all day. We've hardly exchanged a word. You might stay with me for a little while."

Normally he would immediately agree to such an invitation. Now he turned his face away from me. "Yes, my queen." This out of obedience rather than desire.

I felt wounded. Worse, I was surprised that I would be.

"What is it, Saba? You seem distant."

"I am here, my queen."

"Are you? Where is your mind? With Yeshua, of course, but will you not love me as well?"

"Yes... Yes, always."

But his heart wasn't in his words.

"And yet?" I rose from my mat and crossed to his, then sat down next to him, placing my hand on his arm. "Saba, speak to me..."

"I find that I have become a slave to my affections for you," he said softly. "How then can I follow his teaching?"

Then I understood. Yeshua's teaching: *If anyone comes to me and does not hate their father and mother, their wife...*

I removed my hand. "I'm not your wife. And if I was, what does it mean to hate?"

"To let go," he said. "To make of no account... He speaks of the chains of affection for this world."

"Then you would make me of no account?" I had been so enraptured with Yeshua's promise to save Talya that I'd given little thought to this difficult teaching. And thinking of it now, I was sure that Saba must be wrong.

I was also hearing his confession that he found himself enslaved by affection for me.

The former nagged at my mind; the latter did not bother me.

"You are my closest companion, Saba, not my husband."

He glanced at me. "Yes..." But there was some pain in his eyes, and I regretted being so blunt. My words didn't properly express my own affection for him.

He was struggling with his emotions for me, thinking they distracted him from seeing Yeshua's kingdom clearly. And had not my own desperate need to save Talya made me blind too?

Yes, but there had to be another way of seeing such bonds.

"Stephen says you cannot truly love someone unless you also hate them," Saba said. "Only when you release all expectation of them can you love them without condition, as the Father loves all."

These teachings cut at my heart. You could not serve both the system of the world and the Father, Yeshua said. But wife and son? This was impossible. The teaching was opposite the way of the world—and my way as well.

"You would hate me so you can love me," I said, aggravated.

He hesitated, then rose.

"I don't know..." He remained still for a moment, then turned. "I must leave."

I watched my tower slip out the back gate. He was shaken by his affections for me. Saba, so strong, would have no great challenge in forsaking himself or his desires for anything the world could offer him—this I had seen many times.

But when it came to me...I was a different matter.

Saba was in love with me. Secretly I cherished this realization, now made so plain.

And if anyone could sever his affection for a woman to walk in the realm of Yeshua, it would be Saba. This was also plain.

I silently pondered all of this as I lay on my sleeping mat in Mary's room that night. We would know what Yeshua meant soon enough. Tomorrow we would be with him.

THE SUN was already in the western sky the next day when Arim burst into the courtyard.

"We go to Jerusalem!" he cried.

Mary, who was sweeping some spilled flour, spun. The broom dropped to the floor. "Now?"

"Yes." Arim had made no secret of his hope to see the great city. "Jerusalem!" He hurried for his saddlebag, which contained his prized boots.

Saba strode in. "We go to Jerusalem."

"I've told them." Arim pulled out his boots and set about dressing himself for the occasion.

Saba dipped his head. "We must hurry, my queen."

My queen...whom you would hate so you can love.

Mary and Martha were already scurrying about, grabbing their shawls, throwing bread into a basket.

"It's late!" Martha said.

Mary's face was pale with anticipation. "It will only take an hour on foot."

"We have nowhere to spend the night!"

"We will return for the night."

"We can't travel in the dark!"

Mary spun to her sister. "Stop worrying, Martha! He calls for us. It is Yeshua."

We didn't need the camels, Saba said, urging us out of the house. All would walk. The disciples were already leaving from the west side of Bethany.

"We must go, my queen."

"There's no need to call me queen here, Saba. Only Maviah."

He caught my eye but said nothing.

"We can catch them on the mount," Mary said. "It's shorter this way. We can meet them going up. Hurry!"

We followed her out the back gate and up the same small path along which Mary had led me when I'd first come.

"Hurry!"

We hurried. Over the knoll, through the olive trees, while Mary explained why this path was shorter than the one through the village. We would surely come upon them just over the next rise.

My heart pounded as much from my anticipation as from our climb. He was my savior, you see. I and my son and Saba and all of the outcast Bedu in Arabia hung in the balance: death at the hand of Kahil, and life at the hand of Yeshua.

All thoughts of my exchange with Saba the night before were gone.

Arim overtook Mary, urging us on in his new boots. "This way! It will be even faster."

"No! Stay on the path!"

He corrected his course, eyeing Mary. "Yes of course. Then I will carry your bag."

"She can carry her own bag," Martha objected.

He reached out for it anyway, and Mary gave it willingly. I saw the look that passed between them. They were fond of each other? I hadn't noticed until then.

In less than five minutes we crested the second rise and pulled up, taking in the scene below us with a single glance.

He was there in the wadi, on the path that eventually climbed the Mount of Olives, walking just ahead of his inner circle. Directly behind them: Simon, walking with a cane, Lazarus, very much alive, and Stephen, who was waving at us to join them.

A group of perhaps sixty or more—men, women, and children—followed fifty paces behind the disciples, buzzing with excitement while respectfully keeping their distance.

But my eyes were for Yeshua.

Yeshua, who walked with his staff, wearing the same clothes he'd worn to Simon's house, hooded beneath a blue-and-white mantle. Yeshua, keeping to himself as he walked toward Jerusalem.

Yeshua, who slowly turned his head, looked up the hill at us, held his shrouded gaze for a few paces, then faced forward once again. I couldn't see his expression.

Mary and Martha were already plunging down the slope. "Hurry!"

I felt Saba's guiding hand on my elbow. "We must hurry, my queen."

A gentle breeze cooled my neck.

"I told you, Saba. Don't call me queen." And then I ran.

We joined Stephen just behind the disciples, now ten in all, who gave their master space after his time with the crowds. They spoke in hushed tones, aware of the danger that going into Jerusalem presented.

Peter turned back, slowing for us to catch him. I had spoken to him only in greeting before, but now his eyes were on me. Gentle brown eyes tinted with green, filled with confidence.

He smiled. "You are Maviah…"

"Yes."

He matched our stride. "The master says that you are a queen from Arabia. From among the Bedu, deep in the desert."

Yeshua had spoken of me to them? My pulse quickened.

"Yes. We are outcasts who have been crushed by the Thamud in Dumah."

"And Judah? Where is he?"

Saba answered for me when I hesitated. "Judah has been taken by the sword."

Peter glanced at Saba and shook his head, tsking. "I am sorry. He was a good Jew with a wild heart." To me: "And you, are you now Saba's wife?"

"He is my right arm," I said quietly. "But no."

Peter nodded, looking ahead. "Yeshua speaks highly of you both, though you aren't Jews. Perhaps you will follow his Way and make good Jews in the desert."

To this I had no response. Peter obviously understood Yeshua only within the Jewish context. I didn't know enough of their religion to be a convert, much less to make more good Jews.

"He is more than a prophet, you understand," Peter said softly. "I would gladly give my life for him. He brings a new kingdom in peace and love. The world will then know their king. You understand this?"

"Yes."

"Then you too will be a part of that kingdom." He paused. "He would speak to you and Saba soon."

I blinked. "He would?"

"Yes."

"When?"

"Stay close. Now I must rejoin the others."

I watched Yeshua, who continued to walk alone, and I tried to imagine what he was thinking. The air was full of excitement, and yet I wondered what burdens Yeshua held close to himself, there on the path ahead of us.

His words about his own journey, spoken to me on my previous visit to Galilee, whispered through my mind.

To the Hebrews it will one day be written of me: "During the days of Yeshua's life on earth... Son though he was, he learned obedience from what he suffered."

Had he already suffered all he needed to suffer to learn this obedience? Surely. Or was he still to learn more?

Around me, all were speaking as we ascended the Mount of Olives, and I as well, but all the while my eyes were on Yeshua, walking ahead, always ahead, leading the way.

We had come to a small vineyard that drew his attention. He stopped on the side of the path, studying the tangled vines and leaves. He looked back at us. The disciples too had stopped, giving him space.

Then he dipped his head, making his intentions known to his disciples, who knew his way.

Peter turned and beckoned us.

I hesitated, but Mary nudged me from behind. "Now," she whispered.

"He calls us," Saba said, striding forward already.

Arim followed on our heels, not to be left out, though Peter hadn't specified him. We hurried through his inner circle, which parted for us.

Yeshua looked at each of us and yet I felt as though he was looking only at me. So close to him, the air was heavy and my heart was pounding wildly.

"Arim, always the eager one," Yeshua said with a smile.

Arim stared at him, grinning sheepishly.

"Walk with me." Yeshua resumed his stride up the path. Behind us by ten paces, the disciples followed, and beyond them, the crowd.

"Do you know vines, Saba?"

"*I* have known them," Arim said. *Arim, always the eager one.*

Saba cleared his throat. "Yes, master."

"But do you *know* the vine?"

To know. Not to know about.

"Listen to the truth as I will tell it to the others," Yeshua said, facing me. I looked into his eyes. Eyes that beckoned me like an ancient memory, daring me to listen. "Will you know?"

"Yes." My mind swam in the intoxication of his gaze.

Yeshua looked at the path ahead.

"Then know that I am the true vine." He paused. "My Father is the gardener. He cuts off every branch in me that bears no fruit, while every branch that does bear fruit he prunes so it will be even more fruitful."

This was familiar imagery to me. My master in Egypt

had tended a small vineyard beyond the house. Careful tending of the branches by pruning away the rubbish produced far more fruit.

So he would prune away the waste in me...

"No branch can bear fruit by itself; it *must* remain in the vine." He turned to me. "Do you understand this, Daughter?"

Did I? I thought so.

"Yes, master."

"If you remain in me and I in you, you will bear much fruit. Apart from me you can do nothing, but if you remain in me..." He paused. "Ask whatever you wish, and it will be done."

The promise of such power to ask anything—I could feel it in the air. If such power came by remaining *in* Yeshua, which was true faith, how then did one remain in him? This had been the essence of Saba's question.

Is surrender the means to sight?

Surrender. But surrender of what? My own son?

"You have many questions, Daughter," Yeshua said in a gentle voice. "And you, Saba."

We had come to a large olive tree, and Yeshua stepped off the path into its shade.

"Arim, will you do something for me?" he asked, turning with a smile.

"Anything. Only speak it, and it will be done."

"Bring Philip and Andrew to me. Wait with them until I call."

Arim twisted toward the disciples, who were waiting. He began to go, then spun back and bowed. "It is done. I will bring Philip and Andrew immediately."

"When I call."

"Only when you call." And then he was off.

Yeshua walked up to the tree, placed his hand on the gnarled trunk, and looked up at the branches. He was carrying a burden that I could not fathom, I thought. But when he turned to us, his gaze was even.

"They study the scriptures diligently because they think that in them, they have eternal life," he said. "Tell me once again, Saba... What is eternal life?"

"To intimately know the Father."

"And where is his kingdom?"

"Neither here nor there, but within and among us even now, as you have said."

"And would you walk in this kingdom, Saba?"

"It is the only thing that matters now."

I could feel Yeshua's presence, like something that could be breathed.

"Many will come in my name... They will deceive many. Beware of false prophets who come to you in sheep's clothing but inwardly are ravenous wolves—you will know them by their fruit. Good trees bear good fruit, but bad trees bear bad fruit. And what is this good fruit?"

"To love neighbor as self. All is summed up in this: love the Father with everything, and love neighbor as self."

"Even so, know that many will say to me, 'Lord, Lord... did we not do many mighty works in your name?' And I will tell them plainly, 'I never knew you.' Do you have ears to hear this, Saba?"

Saba stared as if he were a young boy. He spoke with a slight tremble on his lips. "Many religious ones will represent you without intimately knowing you or the Father—they will only call you Lord and claim your name, doing mighty works. But they have no good fruit, the truest of which is love without judgment, because the Father judges no one."

Yeshua nodded once. "Neither do I accuse you before the Father. I did not come to judge the world but to save it. I do not judge, but the very words I have spoken will judge those who do not accept them."

"Neither you nor the Father judge," Saba said. "The Law is the accuser. The Law and your teachings judge those who are of this world. But you and those who follow you are not of this world. We only live in it."

Yeshua smiled. "You hear my words well. In it. And in this world, you will have trouble. But take heart, I have overcome the world."

He shifted his gaze to me.

"Do you understand, Daughter?"

"I think so..."

"Can you forgive? Can you surrender? Can you live without judgment? Can you love even your enemy?"

His teaching from Galilee flooded my mind.

"I...I think so."

The breeze lifted a strand of hair edging from beneath his mantle.

"Do you remember what will be written of me?"

That through his suffering he learned obedience...

"Yes, master," I breathed.

"But they will write more: 'Once made perfect, he became the source of eternal salvation for all who obey him.' So then...can you, like me, also obey?"

I felt a tear slip down my cheek. "Yes."

He stepped up to me, then lifted his hand and wiped away my tear with his thumb.

"We won't be together much longer, Daughter, but I will not leave you as orphans; I will come to you. The world will not see me, but you will see me. Because I live, you also will live."

He was speaking of the orphans—all of us and the children, I thought. And Talya. My heart soared.

Yeshua removed his hand and looked between us. "The Father will send you a helper to be with you forever. The Spirit of truth. The world cannot accept him because they neither see him nor know him. But you know him. He lives with you and will be in you."

My mind swam. His words were like a fragrance—I could not fully understand the scent nor explain why it affected me so; I could only *know* it.

There under the olive tree with Yeshua, I knew his love and power and truth far beyond what my mind could comprehend. I knew it in my heart, where love is revealed in a way never grasped by the mind alone.

I wanted to fall to my knees and kiss his feet, as Mary had. I wanted to scream of my son's deliverance for all to hear. I wanted to throw my life away and live in Yeshua's presence always.

But I stood still, like the tree behind him. Breathing in his fragrance.

"Thank you..." I managed. "Thank you, master..."

"Soon, Maviah... Very soon."

"Yes, master."

He slowly turned his head and stared at the knoll fifty paces up the path. Beyond this was a small village called Bethphage, Stephen had said. And beyond Bethphage, a garden Yeshua often prayed in, called Gethsemane. Then the Kidron Valley, which led up to the celebrated city.

A heaviness seemed to settle over him.

He stepped past us, strode back onto the path, and called to his disciples. "Philip. Andrew."

The two Arim had been sent to retrieve hurried to join him.

"Master?"

"Go into the village ahead. As you enter it, you will find a young donkey tied there on which no one has ever sat. Untie it and bring it to me. If anyone asks you why you're untying it, say this: the Lord needs it."

Philip and Andrew looked at each other.

"Hurry," Yeshua said.

"Yes, master."

They bowed and ran up the path. Yeshua watched them crest the knoll and vanish from sight.

"So then," he said under his breath. "It begins."

CHAPTER EIGHTEEN

———————

KAHIL DRAGGED Talya from the larger dungeon, pushed him down the passageway, through another door, and threw him into a small, square cell with a dirt floor.

"If I could kill you, I would," he said through the bars. "Like I killed Judah, who lived in this same cell for two years. We will see how long you last before the serpents come to sink their fangs into your tiny mind."

And then he'd gone.

For a long time, Talya had stood alone, not sure what to do. The cell was cold and wet, the small patches of straw soggy. The only light came from a slow-burning torch down the passageway.

There in the cell, all of the hope he'd found in his dream seemed far away. Unable to remain strong, he'd walked to a tiny dry patch in the corner, squatted to his heels, lowered his head, and wept.

But none of his crying made the cell warmer. Or dried the ground. Or brought any comfort. Hours later he was still alone with no one to hear him. So finally he wiped his tears, sniffed his last, and curled up into a ball, praying for sleep so that he could dream again. If he could dream, he would find the light, and in that light he would find peace.

But for all of his trying and praying, he couldn't sleep.

A guard came with some food and water and Talya ate it, but then it was silent again. He was left with only his thoughts, and soon even they seemed pointless to him.

He closed his eyes and slowly sank into a kind of nothingness that left him empty. And it was then, much later, when he was awake with a quiet mind, that the voice spoke to him again.

"Take courage, my little one," it said very gently.

Immediately the darkness was gone. Replaced by light.

Talya gasped, startled. He was in the garden again! It didn't arrive on a star this time—it was just there. Once again he was standing in the meadow.

This time he cried out with relief and joy, spinning around with arms spread wide. And this time there was no serpent. But of course, because the serpent was dead!

Instead, there was a lamb as white as the brightest cloud, eating the grass next to vines heavy with grapes. The lamb was him, of course it was. But it wasn't him. No, it was *like* him. Or he was like it.

Either way, that lamb was somehow everything that was innocent and pure, the opposite of the deceiving serpent who tricked the woman into eating the fruit of the knowledge of good and evil. At least that was how Talya saw it.

He jumped for joy, arms up in the air, crying out for the whole garden to hear, "The lamb, the lamb, the lamb!" He wanted to run to the lamb and hug it. He wanted to dance with it and sing with it even though sheep neither sang nor danced.

And then, suddenly, the garden was gone, and he was alone in the cell again.

He sat up, eyes wide. "No!" His voice bounced off the stone walls.

Talya quickly lay back down and clenched his eyes shut, begging the vision to return. But it didn't.

Not in the hours before they came and snuffed out the torch. Not that night when he slept. Not when he woke in the morning, weeping.

Not when he grew quiet and slumped on his side, realizing that he might never see Eden again. But it didn't matter, he thought. *I know it's there and if Kahil kills me, I will be there. So then, I am well.*

I am well.

Not until then did he see the garden once more. Again with the lamb by the vines. Again filled with light. Again filling him with peace and joy.

"Do you want to remain?"

At first Talya thought the lamb had spoken, but it was only five paces away, eating the grass. No, of course it wasn't the lamb. Sheep didn't speak.

"Y-yes..." he answered.

"Eat my fruit and live."

My fruit?

"The fruit of the vine," the voice said. "Love. Forgiveness. Peace. Surrender. Joy. Eat it."

He stared at the only fruit nearby—the grapes on the vine. Then he walked over, plucked a grape, smelled it, and bit into it.

Warmth flooded his body.

Talya began to laugh.

CHAPTER NINETEEN

SO THEN... It begins.

What would begin? The sentiment among Yeshua's followers had infected me, and I was swept up with this one thought: Yeshua will triumph here in Jerusalem by overcoming the world, as he had said.

He would conquer the world of Roman rule with peace, then usher in his kingdom of peace. Though Judah and all rulers would have used the sword to establish a new kingdom, Yeshua would do so with his power, which was of the heart and of Spirit.

He was indeed their Messiah, as Judah had said.

And by following Yeshua, I would save the children in the desert from their oppression.

The moment we began our descent toward Jerusalem, everything changed. It began with the donkey Philip and Andrew had been sent to fetch. No one seemed to understand its significance immediately, but there was something about Yeshua's reaction to the donkey that arrested everyone's attention.

He stopped on the path, staff in hand, watching his disciples coming up the path. Philip had the donkey by its lead rope and led him dutifully to Yeshua's side. But more than a donkey had come with them.

Many from the village had followed Philip and Andrew. Clearly, they'd heard the news—Yeshua, the one who worked wonders and had raised Lazarus from the dead, was coming into Jerusalem.

It was the number of people, both behind us and before us, that surprised me the most. Hundreds by now. They would not have come unless deeply moved by hope and anticipation.

Yeshua put one hand on the donkey's neck and slowly stroked its mane. Not a soul made a sound. All watched in silent anticipation.

Yeshua gazed back at his disciples. Still no one moved.

I turned to Stephen, who stood by my side. "What's he doing?" I whispered.

"Yeshua walks, always."

"And if he rides, what—"

"Shhh, shhh... Watch."

So I watched, not understanding what I saw.

Yeshua nodded once, tossed his staff to Philip, and mounted the donkey, which, though never ridden, accepted him without protest.

I watched as the disciples began to run. They were joined immediately by those behind us, who now ran past. Like a swell from a storm, they rushed to Yeshua, who now rode the donkey slowly down the path between large olive trees.

Their cheer began quietly, and then was joined by many caught up in the moment.

"He's going to make an entrance!" Stephen cried, spinning to me. "Don't you see?"

There was triumphant celebration in the air, and I was caught up in wonder. But why such celebration over an entrance?

"I don't—"

"Listen to them, Maviah!"

Then I heard what they were crying. "Blessed is the King who comes in the name of the Lord!" Other cries, but this one, *Blessed is the King*, impacted me the most.

He was going into Jerusalem as a king? Surely the authorities would object!

"*Fear not, daughter Zion*," Stephen whispered. "*See, your king is coming, seated on a donkey's colt...*" He spun to me, eyes flashing. "This is written of the Anointed One, in the book of Zechariah. You see, it is him! He orchestrates this with intention!"

My mind spun.

"Herod has come to Jerusalem for the Passover, but now comes the true king!"

Herod was in Jerusalem? I didn't know what to think of it...

Then Stephen was running and Saba as well, turning back to urge me on. "Stay close, my queen."

Arim, though having no clue, surely, had thrown himself into the frenzy, mimicking their cries with arms raised. He cried out to me over the din. "Come, my queen! Come!"

We rounded a bend and came to a long stretch of open ground with only a few olive trees, and I saw that many more people were coming out to meet us. How many had heard?

Yeshua hadn't been in Jerusalem for some time, but his reputation, once so widespread along the shores of Galilee, had overtaken the great city. The raising of Lazarus was perhaps the greatest of his wonders, and all had heard.

In a land crushed under Roman rule, only Yeshua offered any hope of salvation. He was approaching Jerusalem on donkey, as foretold in their scriptures, and he was accepting their cries of *King!*

I saw now that some of them had brought palm branches and were lined along the path, waving the fronds, crying out, "Blessed is the King. Blessed is the King."

Yeshua gazed ahead without reacting to their praise in any way that I could see as I ran to catch up. Some were spreading their cloaks on the ground before the donkey as it approached—also a sign of the highest honor.

Many children ran alongside him. A boy of Talya's age leaped up and down beside the donkey, waving a small frond. His mother hurried, weeping, reaching out a hand to Yeshua.

Still, Yeshua rode in silence.

A new king was riding toward Jerusalem. I could not fathom what the Roman occupiers would say to this. Or the religious authorities, who had already denounced Yeshua, and he them. It all seemed terribly dangerous to me.

I was so enthralled by the scene that I didn't at first notice that the city had come into view as we topped a small knoll.

Yeshua rode like a conquering ruler, eyes fixed ahead, always ahead. His mantle had hidden his face from my sight, but now I could see him—his face and the tears that wet his cheeks.

My heart stuttered. He was weeping! I turned to follow his gaze.

The sight took my breath away. From our high vantage we could see all of Jerusalem, like a sprawling castle carved in limestone. Their renowned temple, built into the eastern wall, stood in splendor.

I spun back to see his silent tears flowing. These were not tears of joy, but sorrow, I thought.

Alarmed, I stepped into the path, wanting to comfort him, though it wasn't my place. I wasn't his mother. I wasn't even one of his inner circle, and I almost pulled back. But then I heard—he was speaking below the din, as if to the city itself.

"If you had known in this day, even you, the things which make for peace." He paused, swallowing. "But now they have been hidden from your eyes. The days will come when your enemies will throw up a barricade..." I lost some of his words in all the celebration. "...they will not leave one stone...because you did not know the time of your visitation."

He was speaking of the city's destruction.

Stephen was on his other side, and he too had heard. We exchanged a glance and I saw the confusion in his eyes.

Then the moment was over and Yeshua spoke no more. Quickly, his weeping subsided.

But the cries of the crowd did not. Not until we had passed through the Kidron Valley. Not until we had approached the gates.

When Yeshua dismounted, walked past six guards at the gate, and entered the city, the crowds began to disperse, as if knowing the consequence for such a display within the city itself. But they did not vacate us. They spread out and continued to follow, eyeing Yeshua's every move without wanting to be seen as part of an insurgence.

I understood then just how dangerous was that processional calling him king. Yeshua had orchestrated it himself in calling for the donkey. So then he was *inviting* confrontation with the Romans?

An elderly man with a shriveled hand called out for healing as Yeshua passed. Many beggars shook their cups and cried out, "Son of David, son of David, have mercy…" A young boy in rags ran toward him, but one of the disciples guided him away.

Yeshua walked on, looking neither to the left nor the right, followed closely by all of his inner circle, which Stephen and Arim had joined.

The Roman soldiers eyed us curiously but made no move against us. Word of the processional clearly hadn't reached them yet, I thought.

"What's happening?" I asked Mary. "Where is he taking us?"

"To the temple," Mary whispered, glancing around. She didn't appear to be at home in these streets. Not any longer. "You must be careful, Maviah." Her eyes were wide. "They are everywhere."

"Who is?"

"The ones who despise Yeshua and those who follow him."

I then imagined all who were dressed in tassels to be eyeing me.

"If we are with Yeshua, we are safe," Saba said. "Stay close, Maviah. Remember his words."

I remembered. Ahead of us walked the one who had calmed the storm and raised the dead. He would not die. We would not die. But Mary still wasn't at ease.

"Only be careful," Mary said. "You are a foreign woman. Stay close."

I had been in Dumah. I had entered several cities in Egypt. I had seen Sepphoris and Petra. But none of them could compare to Jerusalem.

The city had swelled with pilgrims from many corners of the world, come to celebrate their Passover, a tradition that recalled the deliverance of the Jews from Egypt, led by Moses.

Merchants were everywhere, selling wares from afar. Silks and linens and spices. Clay pots and grain and fruits... there was no end to the variety of items bought and sold on the streets of Jerusalem.

But more than these, I was struck by the massive walls and the towering buildings that rose on all sides. And even more, the temple ahead of us.

We walked up its steps amid many who'd followed, all converging here to see what Yeshua might do. The sun was already halfway down the western horizon.

Something was going to happen... Surely the news of his triumphant processional had already reached the authorities. Yet by going to the temple, Yeshua averted any Roman interference, for the temple was under the authority of the religious leaders.

We followed him into the outer court reserved for Gentiles, and there with at least a hundred others, I watched as Yeshua walked to the center of that vast courtyard, past all the merchants. He stood with his back to us, facing the inner court, alone now.

Yeshua commanded the waves; he walked on water; he raised the dead. Surely he could bring the temple to its knees with a single word, without lifting a single finger. And if he did lift a finger, it would not be in anger, but to demonstrate his authority.

For a long time he only stood still with his hands down by his sides. All had seen him. All watched. Even the buyers and sellers had paused and watched his incursion into their space. Everyone seemed to know that something would happen.

Then Yeshua turned to us, studied those who'd gathered for a few moments, and walked past us, back out of the temple the way we'd come.

He'd done nothing.

"What's he doing?" Martha asked.

"Follow him," Saba said.

So we followed him. Back down the steps, back to the gate through which we'd entered, back out of the city onto the path that led over the Mount of Olives to Bethany. A smaller crowd now followed the disciples who, like the rest, appeared at a loss. There were no more songs of praise—only confusion. And yet a charged sense of anticipation remained.

I turned to Mary and Martha at my side. "We go back to Bethany?"

Both were too distracted to respond.

"Mary..."

"This is his way," she said. "With Yeshua you cannot predict what happens one moment to the next, but he knows what he does."

I looked up at Saba, who was staring at Yeshua walking ahead of his inner circle in an even stride.

"Saba..."

But Saba was too fixed upon Yeshua to pay me mind.

Louder: "Saba. I don't understand..."

He blinked and looked at me. Then quickly pulled me to the side of the road out of the hearing of our companions.

"He's a tactician," Saba said. "Don't you see?"

"See what?"

Saba glanced about, not wanting to be heard. "He comes as a king and then goes at will. But his eye is on the temple. So then... What argument can the Romans have against him? His challenge is with the religion of the Jews."

"He intends to overthrow the religious leaders, not the Romans?" I asked, looking at Yeshua.

"I don't know. But everything he does now is orchestrated. In coming today, his statement is unmistakable. He, not they, controls his movements."

Yeshua had stopped on a small rise ahead of us and was facing a grove of olive trees. The disciples were talking among themselves, some urgently. Half the initial crowd had departed or remained in Jerusalem to conduct other business.

"There, you see?" Mary pointed to carefully kept grounds. "It's called the Gethsemane garden. He prays there often. Maybe he will go there now."

A garden. My mind recalled Talya's song of the garden in the desert.

The disciples and others closer to Yeshua had also stopped.

One of his inner circle hurried up to him and spoke,

then retreated. For a moment, Yeshua stared at the garden. Then he turned to the disciples and the others and began to speak.

Saba touched my arm. "Come…"

I couldn't hear what Yeshua said at first, because I was rushing forward and he was too far away. But then he raised his voice.

"…if it dies, it produces many seeds." Then, louder: "He who loves his life loses it, and he who hates his life in this world will keep it to life eternal."

Again that word *hate*, now in regard to one's own life. A requirement of those who wished to experience the Father's eternal realm. His voice carried to me, laden with distress.

He paused, then spread his arms and lifted his chin.

"My soul is troubled… What shall I say? Father, save me from this hour?"

I pulled up, struck by the distress in his tone. My heart began to break with his. I had never seen him so despondent.

"No!" he cried. "It was for this very reason I came to this hour!"

He took a deep breath, arms still spread, and faced the sky. Now his voice carried for the whole valley to hear, a gut-wrenching cry that took my breath away.

"Father… Glorify your name!"

His voice echoed through the valley and faded. We stood still, taken aback.

A long peal of thunder rolled across the sky, though there were only a few dark clouds far to the west. But how could that be? I blinked, trying to make sense of thunder so close.

But then I wasn't thinking of the thunder at all, because suddenly that very thunder was in my mind. Yet it wasn't thunder as much as a voice. A deep, rushing voice that shook through me.

"I have glorified my name and will glorify it again."

I gasped and jerked my head to see that Saba was trembling and staring at Yeshua.

Murmurs and cries broke out as others ducked and jumped off the road, grasping at their ears. They too had heard, the thunder at least.

Thunder. Then something that had sounded like a voice, and yet not a voice, as if from my own bones. I stood aghast.

The world seemed to still around me. I had heard the voice of God?

I have glorified my name and will glorify it again...

By "my name," I knew this meant the Father's identity, for a name was one's blood in the desert. But how had God glorified his identity, and how would he do it again?

I was trembling from having heard this thunder in my very soul.

When I looked back up the hill, Yeshua was gone. Only the disciples and those gathered remained. Mary, who'd fallen to her knees, was pushing herself to her feet. Arim was running back toward us, eyes wide.

Yeshua had gone to be alone.

So then... it begins. His words, spoken under his breath hours earlier, now became mine, and my spirit soared. Nothing had happened in the temple, but I knew in a way I could not yet understand—everything had just happened.

There could be no doubt. Yeshua would rise to power for all to see.

CHAPTER TWENTY

I WILL GLORIFY my name again...

I cannot begin to describe how elevated I felt in the wake of those words over the next three days. Not just I, but all who had heard. Saba, Stephen, Arim, Mary, Martha, Lazarus...the disciples, though I didn't see them after returning to Bethany that night.

No one knew quite what it meant, but there was no end to speculation.

A great mystery had swarmed us, and we lived in the hope of its imminent revelation. The staggering power of Yeshua, who had spoken to the storm and walked on the sea of trouble, was sure to invade the realm of this world even as that voice had.

Every passing day was one more in which harm might be done to the children in the desert, and yet I knew I would receive the power for their salvation here.

Then I would rush to Shaquilath and show her.

Then the serpent in Dumah would be crushed.

Then our children would be swept up in the arms of their mothers, and I would kiss the cheeks of my precious lamb. Together we would find Eden, led by Talya. As Saba had said, *a child will lead them.*

I did not see Yeshua during the next two days, but I didn't need to. His word that my son would not die, even as he would not die, was certain.

I did not see Yeshua, but I heard. And everything I heard pointed to the manifestation of the Father's glory. Yeshua did not merely speak of the Way; he showed us that Way in everything he did.

I heard . . . that when he emerged from his solitude the next day there was undeniable authority in his eyes. He walked as one who could not fail.

I heard . . . that he showed his power by cursing a fig tree so that it would bear no more fruit. The tree then withered, showing that he did not want those who followed him to place such value in the fruit of this world. It could not compare to the fruit of his vine—the glory and power of the Father's realm.

He turned to Peter by that wilted fig tree and made the extent of that power clear: *If anyone says to this mountain, go throw yourself in the sea, and does not doubt . . . it will be done. Whatever you ask . . . believe that you have received it and it will be done.*

Again, such power for those who believed.

To believe was the key! And I knew in my bones that one could not believe in Yeshua and also hold *any* grievance for *any* reason in the face of *any* storm, because to do so only exchanged one's faith in the Father for faith in the storm. This rendered one powerless to find peace.

The withering of that fig tree showed both his power and the obstacle to that power. My faith was like a torrent. I had no doubt that I could do this and become like Yeshua, able to heal and love and move any mountain.

I heard...that he went back to Jerusalem and straight to the temple courts. But this time his intentions were utterly clear. Because this time he overturned the tables of the money changers, drove out the merchants with a cracking whip, and stood in the way of all who would bring goods into the temple.

Again he made his meaning clear. *My house will be called a house of prayer for all nations. But you have made it a den of robbers.*

Was it not the way of all earthly religions and false prophets to seek their own gain on the backs of their followers?

I heard...that when asked about taxes, Yeshua said, *Pay to Caesar what is Caesar's*, for Caesar's image was on the coin. And *pay to God what is God's*. And I thought, I am made in the image of the Father, so then I will pay and sow myself to the Father and let the Thamud and the world have what is theirs. They, like me, would reap what they sowed.

I heard...that the people were amazed by his teaching and authority, and the religious leaders were terrified by it. That a great gulf was dividing Jerusalem. And yet those who hung on Yeshua's words were too many for the religious leaders, who now tested him whenever he showed himself.

I heard many other accounts, and they all pointed to the same thing: a great storm was coming. We all knew it. We didn't know what it might look like, but one thing was certain: from the thunder of that storm, the glory of the Father's realm would be made known.

I could feel it in the air.

But all of that shifted on the afternoon of the third day.

I was with Saba, alone in Martha's courtyard. She and Mary had gone to the orchard for fruit when Yeshua's inner circle returned to Bethany that night. During the days his disciples went with him to Jerusalem or kept watch as he retreated to be alone on the Mount of Olives.

Miriam, the mother of Yeshua, would arrive the next morning for Passover, and the women had been like birds building their nest, anticipating her arrival. Mary in particular was deeply taken with Yeshua's mother, because Miriam had shown her great compassion, just as she had comforted me in Nazareth two years earlier.

Saba, who dutifully remained near me despite my assurance that I would be safe with Mary, had returned from the hills with an armful of firewood. He'd kept to himself through those days, lost in contemplation of that thunder in his own heart. And perhaps still lost in thoughts of what it meant to hate one's wife to love her.

The gate was suddenly thrown wide and I turned to the clatter. Arim stood on the threshold, beaming like a sheikh who has taken a new bride.

"I see it!"

Stephen stepped in from behind him and strode into the courtyard, eyes bright. "He sees it!"

Their excitement was infectious.

"What is it you see?"

"This power to move the mountain," Arim said, marching in with a finger in the air. "I too can have it, and I will."

There, full of wonder, my young Bedu brother still wore his new boots to impress Mary.

I smiled. "Oh? Then tell me."

Arim glanced at Saba, who stood from the woodpile and walked toward us.

"Tell them, Arim," Stephen urged.

"I am blind!" Arim cried.

I waited for more, but he was fixed by this statement alone.

"This is how you see? By being blind."

"No, my queen. But one must first *see* that they are blind! You see?"

"You see?" Stephen said. "Tell them more. All of it."

Arim paced now, sticking a second finger in the air as if to count what he'd learned from his teacher.

"My inheritance of eternal life is this glory we heard on our return from Jerusalem: the eternal realm of Yeshua, in which his power becomes our own. The power to do as Yeshua does. To be great mystics who can heal and calm the storm and walk on water."

Arim paused, then went on, shoving a third finger into the air.

"In order to inherit this eternal life for *this* life and become a water walker who needs no sword nor even a single harsh word, I must see the world as it truly is, with clear vision. But a veil over my eyes hides the world of light and power. Thus, true vision beyond this veil is my greatest need."

He was right, I thought. It was as Yeshua repeatedly taught. But Arim didn't stop there.

"It is as Saba says..." His eyes glinted with daring and he snapped up his fourth finger. "To abide in Yeshua, one must surrender!"

Arim made a fist.

"Then, and only then, will I command the storm!"

Hearing it again, that easily forgotten Way seemed so simple.

"Surrender what?" Saba asked, eyes now on Stephen.

"Everything," Arim cried, sweeping his arms wide. "The whole world!"

"Everything," Stephen said, grinning. "Yeshua has said always, give up this life to find true life; hate your life to find the eternal realm; take up the cross even every day; hate even wife and son and mother. Call no man on earth father."

"No man!" Arim said, thrusting out his thin fingers. "For your true Father is in heaven, which is within and at hand even now."

Stephen stood like a proud teacher. "There are two worlds—the kingdom of the Father and the world of mammon. You can have faith only in one. You can serve only one."

"Hate the world of mammon and the law of the world to see and love the other," Arim cried, jumping onto the bench beside Martha's table, spreading his arms wide, eyes bright. "All the world has placed its belief and hope in the laws of the world and Moses and mammon and wife and children, rather than putting their faith in Yeshua and his kingdom of staggering power!" He was speaking as much with his hands as his mouth. "But you can serve only one master. Surrender the other. Put it to death, as he says."

"Deny yourself for his name's sake," Stephen said. "Surrender your name, which is your identity, for his instead, and so find his life! True life! Rivers of living water! Then move the mountain."

"Then heal the leper!" Arim cried. "Knowing the body is not master and is to be held of no account!"

They were trading words back and forth, teacher and student. I knew that these were Yeshua's sayings, but I wasn't so sure about their interpretation.

"And what does it mean, to deny yourself?" I asked. "Surely, I am still a mother."

"Are you? Yes, in the world of mammon, but even Yeshua says all are his mother. If a son has many mothers, then a mother has many sons not born of her womb."

"And so I am to hate my son?" I felt irritation swell in my breast.

"With man it is impossible," Arim said, reciting what Stephen had taught him. "In the Father, all things are possible. Only in this way will we be like him and have this great power. You must hate—"

"Stop it, Arim!" I was surprised by my outburst. "Are you a mother to suggest I should hate my son?"

He stepped back on the bench, pale. Then stepped down to the ground. "No, my queen. I did not mean . . ."

He glanced at Stephen, who'd lost his smile in the face of my eruption.

"Isn't that the way of the Gnostics?" I pressed. "Don't they teach that this life is evil?"

It was Saba who rescued us.

"No, not like the Gnostics, Maviah. You misunderstand. In the same way the world doesn't understand true love, it doesn't understand Yeshua's teaching on surrender. He doesn't teach that this world is evil. He teaches us to love all, mostly the outcasts. To hate only means to hold of no account, as Arim says. To have no attachment to mammon and food and your own body and son and father and wife and all the world. This is what he teaches. That you should sever your faith in the things that command you in this life, and instead place your faith only in the Father's realm. Then all these things will be added to you, because you hold them of no account."

"Of course," Arim said. "This is what it means. Even if they try to kill Yeshua, what does this mean? Nothing! He speaks of his death, but this means nothing."

I stared at him, stunned. "His death?" The thought horrified me. "Where did you hear this?"

He blinked, perhaps fearing another outburst from me. "It was said by one of the inner circle in passing."

"No . . . No, that can't be—"

"No, Arim," Stephen interrupted, casting him a corrective look. "This death he speaks of is only a figure of speech! Yeshua will not die. He has overcome death!"

"There will be no death," Arim said. "It is only a figure of speech. The death he mentions is only a death to all that enslaves."

"You will see," Stephen insisted. "By overcoming this world of illness and death, he is no longer subject to it. He's no longer mastered by his body. And he will prove it by escaping death, otherwise all he has taught is thrown into question."

But a fear had taken root in my heart. I thought of the sadness in his eyes, the lines on his face, his bold maneuvering in Jerusalem . . .

"What did they say, specifically?" I asked Arim. "About his death."

He glanced at Stephen but received no support.

"That he would be handed over to the authorities and killed." Arim hesitated. "But as Stephen says, this is only symbolic. He is saying that even if he were, it would mean nothing, because he holds no account of his flesh. But no man can touch Yeshua."

"No man," Stephen said. "It is only symbolic. Have no fear. In the end, he will triumph for all to see, no matter how it looks to the eyes. This I swear to you, Maviah!"

"Yes," I said. "Yes, you are right."

But a hundred thoughts crowded my mind, and a chill washed over my body. What if they were wrong?

More was being said—something about mastery of life—I wasn't listening.

Yeshua could not die! All that I knew and hoped for would be destroyed. I knew he wouldn't die, of course he wouldn't. But what if?

Panic lapped at my mind, and I turned away so they couldn't see my face, sure that it would betray my fear.

In the fog of my heart, a new thought sparked to life. What if I had been drawn to Jerusalem for more than Talya, my lamb? Was not Yeshua the good shepherd? What if I had come to serve him as well, so that he could serve my lamb?

Like a lamp struck in a dark room, I suddenly knew.

Herod!

Stephen said that Herod had come to Jerusalem from his palace in Tiberias for the Passover. The king would hear me. If he knew I was here, he would even seek me out, for I had outwitted him once. And Herod had the power to protect anyone in his kingdom.

He a king, I a queen...

Yeshua's words came to me: *You will know what to do.* Was this not what I knew to do? My heart pounded.

I turned and saw that Saba was staring at me while Arim went on, pacing.

"Saba..." I said.

The gate creaked behind me and Saba looked to it. And by the look in his eyes, I knew. By the sudden stillness, I knew.

Yeshua had come.

I spun around. Yeshua stood at the courtyard's entrance, watching us beneath his mantle.

His face sagged from lack of sleep, and his hands hung by his sides, tired. His eyes were full of the same glory I had felt when the Father spoke, but I imagined him filled with sorrow.

His sandals scraped on the stones as he walked into the courtyard. Several of his inner circle waited for him beyond the gate.

Saba sank to one knee, head bowed. Then Arim to both knees, and seeing them, Stephen. It was the Bedu way of giving honor to a conquering sheikh.

Yeshua's gaze settled on me, perhaps because of my stricken look. He drew near and I was about to fall to my knees when he reached out his hand, palm up. I hesitated, then placed mine in his. The mere touch of his warm skin sent a familiar power through my bones, as if he was filling me with his same glory.

My hand began to tremble, there in his. I could not breathe. I wondered then if he'd actually sought me out.

"This too will pass," he said gently. "Do you understand, Daughter?"

He was speaking of my sorrow in a voice that as much became anguish as washed it away. I nodded.

"Soon. Very soon."

Then he released my hand, looked at Stephen, and smiled. "I was hoping for some of Martha's hot bread."

Stephen stood and looked about, at a loss. But there was no bread yet, I knew.

"Tell her I'll be at Simon's house later."

"Of course, master."

Then Yeshua turned and walked from the courtyard, leaving us four rooted to the ground.

"He is a god," Arim breathed, staring at the gate.

And I had been brought to Bethany for him as much as he for me, I thought. I would help the one who had once helped me.

I would go to Herod.

CHAPTER TWENTY-ONE

FOR FIVE DAYS Talya found peace and joy with the lamb in that garden called Eden. For five days he found that even when he wasn't dreaming of it, he was aware of it, just beyond what his eyes could see. For five days, he knew that nothing could harm him.

Nothing, no matter how horrible it might seem. He knew because he *knew* that the garden was somehow more real than the cell they kept him in. That he was in the cell but not of it.

He was a part of the song in the garden. He was in the light. Everything else was real, but less real, and as long as he could see the garden, he was saved from the serpent called Kahil.

At least that was how Talya saw it in his mind.

But on the fifth day that changed.

On the fifth day he was dreaming of Eden, lost in the wonder of that realm, when suddenly, for no reason that he knew, the black serpent with beautiful colors came out of the brush, slowly slithering through the grass.

Talya jumped back, expecting it to vomit up another black-and-white fruit. If it did, he would only have to crush the snake again, as he had before.

But this time the serpent ignored him. This time it turned and streaked toward the lamb. Before Talya could move, it spread its jaws wide, sank its long fangs deep into the lamb's flesh, unlatched itself, then sped away, hissing loudly.

Immediately the lamb's song, so pure and beautiful, became a scream.

Talya dropped to his knees and grabbed his ears, terrified.

Horrified, he watched as the lamb bleated, faltered, then stumbled to the ground, where it closed its eyes and lay still. Dead.

The world sputtered once, then winked out, leaving him in utter darkness. But this wasn't like the other kinds of darkness he'd experienced, because now that darkness was still screaming.

And when he jerked up from the floor fully awake, it was his own scream that filled the cell.

He knew then.

He knew that he too was going to die.

CHAPTER TWENTY-TWO

I COULD hardly sleep that night. Once the idea had taken root, not even Saba could rid me of it. We would go to Herod of our own accord, and there I would tell him everything. He, being the king from Galilee, would hear me. Yeshua must not be harmed.

Saba worried for my safety. There was no need to save Yeshua, who could not be hurt. I would be the one in danger, he insisted.

"Then we go for me, Saba," I said. "This will be my act of faith, throwing myself into danger for his sake. I've stood before kings—this is what a queen does! I must go."

Seeing my resolve, he offered no more argument.

I commanded Arim to remain in Bethany, despite all of his begging to come for my protection. But I insisted. In the event anything happened to us, he must take word to the tribes. All of the desert would depend upon him. This seemed to satisfy him.

I bathed with soap and drew my hair back with Mary's help. Both she and Martha were eager to assist me, for my seeing Herod, whom they feared, filled them with wonder.

They washed my long white tunic and red shawl, which certainly appeared queenly to them, particularly matched with my blue mantle and the silk sash about my waist. I chose to wear this and the silver necklaces that Shaquilath had insisted I take, though I hadn't yet worn them.

"You are a vision for any king!" Mary whispered as I mounted my camel.

"You're being too kind."

"Nonsense! Herod will be watching you like a hawk. Just be sure that you pay no mind to his eyes. He's not to be trusted, that one. There was never a more poisonous viper."

Mary did not know the more poisonous snakes, Saman and Kahil. She knew no other ruler, for that matter.

But this one, Herod, I had once both seduced and foiled. It was then, seated high upon my camel, that my standing returned to me. Was I not the queen who had bested two kings?

I turned to Stephen. "Take good care of Arim. He's lost without you."

Arim would have none of it. "Have no fear, my queen. It is I who will see to Stephen!"

With my role as queen of Arabia in mind, Saba and I once again struck out over the Mount of Olives for Jerusalem while the sun was still on the eastern horizon.

Mounted, our journey took far less than an hour, and we arrived at the gates of Jerusalem before the city had fully risen. Merchants were just beginning to set out their wares. Pilgrims from the far corners, dressed in all manner of headdresses and tunics signifying their status and position, loitered in doorways as they watched us clop down the deserted streets.

Saba had learned the location of Herod's palace, which was on the western side of Jerusalem. No one could possibly miss such a lavish structure, so elegantly built by Herod's father, also called Herod. The high walls were made of massive white marble blocks. Three towers rose on the north side, overlooking all of Jerusalem.

But we did not easily find entrance. Nor had we expected to, for the hour was early and we were not expected.

We approached the barred gate, which was under the watch of four guards—two Roman and two of Herod's, distinguished by their black armor. The sun was only just growing hot.

Saba stopped his camel beside a tall palm thirty paces from the entrance. "Wait here." He dropped to the ground, then bowed to me, showing himself to the guards as my servant. I watched my tower striding toward them, wearing his sword.

Saba, the most powerful warrior in all of Arabia, so tall and muscled, yet gentle as a dove.

Memories of the violence in Dumah flooded my mind. Saba had saved me then, even as the Thamud overpowered Judah. But I was the one who'd subjected Saba to choose such violence.

Saba, who would sever a hundred heads and then die to save me.

Saba, who loved me, despite his intention to hate me.

I had pushed him too far, I thought.

He talked to the guard and presented his sword in good faith. *The queen of Arabia, known as Maviah, has come for an audience with Herod*, he would be saying. And what would Herod say?

What was I to say?

You will know what to do, Yeshua had said. This is what I knew to do.

I turned to the east and looked beyond the city. Yeshua was there, somewhere. There was no account of him since he'd left Martha's courtyard last night. Had he spent the night in the hills, then returned to Bethany? Or was he on the Mount of Olives still? Or perhaps somewhere in Jerusalem, even now?

Stephen had said Yeshua would surely share in the ritual Passover meal with his disciples later, as night fell. Today was the first day of unleavened bread, which held great significance for the Jews. They would slaughter a lamb and paint the doorposts with its blood, as had been done in Egypt to avoid the angel of death. This marked the start of their seven-day Passover festival.

Thin lines of dark clouds were forming on the distant horizon. A storm might build, I thought. Or the clouds might pass—they often promised rain to a dry and thirsty land, only to dash hope.

I'd stood before Herod and Aretas and Saman and Kahil, and always, I had stood tall. But here I suddenly felt alone.

Saba returned.

"What did they say?"

"That we must wait," Saba said. "He sleeps."

I grunted. Herod loved his wine.

We waited. Three hours at the least. Not until the sun

was halfway up the eastern sky did a guard approach us with a servant close behind.

"Leave your camels, they will be taken care of. Come with me."

Saba nodded at me. So then...Our time had come.

But I was wrong.

We followed the guard up sweeping steps into the courtyard and I was immediately taken aback. Herod's father, who'd built the palace, had spared even less expense than his son had in Sepphoris, or Aretas in Petra.

The vast courtyard was made of stone floors that surrounded a garden, complete with grass and trees and two round pools. White doves fluttered about the branches; geese floated lazily on the water. Bronze fountains spewed precious water, which ran through canals to the pools.

On either side, covered walkways with hundreds of white pillars were richly furnished with cushioned seats and tables. Many of the lampstands and ornaments were made of silver and gold.

Many guests of great wealth, likely in Jerusalem for the Passover, lingered on benches and chairs, eating fruits and sipping wine from silver chalices. Only a few looked our way.

Far across the courtyard, steps rose to the inner chambers, but we were led to a wing to our right. It mirrored a second wing on the far side. There was enough space to house many chambers for hundreds of guests, I thought.

"Wait here," the guard said, motioning to a cushioned seat.

And so again we waited. A young servant boy tended

to us, offering us grapes and figs with water and wine. We waited in silence. There was little to say now.

Those distant storm clouds were making a slow approach, like an army marching toward Jerusalem. But when I mentioned them to Saba, he suggested they would be blown south by the wind.

The sun was already well past noon when we were finally approached by one of Herod's chamber guards.

"The king will see you now."

Saba caught my eye as he stood. "Only remember who you are first, my queen."

And who was I first? Queen of the outcasts in Arabia, or daughter of the Father?

The moment I stepped into Herod's court, I became queen first. Familiarity came back to me in a single breath. The lavish settings drenched in gold and silver, the slaves waiting to serve at a moment's notice, the guards at the door, the stately thrones of power on a raised platform.

The seats were occupied by two men, one in white, whom I'd never seen, the other in red, whom I knew too well.

Herod.

His eyes were on me as I crossed the polished marble floor and stepped around a black table at its center. Saba stayed one step behind me. A thin smile cut Herod's face beneath piercing eyes as he toyed with his graying beard. I couldn't tell if he was pleased or sneering.

The stately man, clearly Roman by his robe, stood as if to leave.

"Stay a moment, my friend," Herod said, eyes still on me. "I would like to introduce you to Arabia's queen of outcasts."

The man regarded me without emotion. His clean-shaven face remained flat. He struck me as one who either didn't appreciate his position in Herod's courts or found himself enslaved by it.

"And so she returns with her slave once again," Herod said, standing.

I offered him a slight bow. "My king."

He returned the courtesy. "My queen." Then to the Roman, sweeping his heavily ringed hand toward me in grand gesture. "Maviah from Dumah, queen of the disenfranchised Bedouin. By all accounts she's become something of legend."

The Roman ruler offered only a slight nod, unimpressed.

"This is Pontius Pilate," Herod said. "Roman prefect, who governs at the mercy of Tiberius, my dear friend."

I knew Herod to be favored by the Roman emperor, Tiberius. He was using our introduction as an opportunity to emphasize this point. For my benefit or Pilate's? Were Herod and the prefect at odds?

I dipped my head. "It is my honor, Governor."

"Honor?" Herod quipped. "And what do the Bedu know of honor?"

"Only that betrayal has no part in it," I said, reminding him that it was he who had betrayed me.

He smiled and glanced at the Roman. "Never underestimate the Bedu, prefect. Nor a woman with such spirit."

Pilate grunted. "Arabia is the curse of Rome. How many legions have we lost in those impossible sands?"

"Too many, I'm sure," Herod said. "And yet Maviah

rides through them like a ghost and gathers the tribes like a prophet."

Pilate's brow arched. "Then perhaps Rome would enjoy meeting such a queen."

"Perhaps. But only with a king's blessing."

"Oh? I didn't know that Herod had such far-reaching authority."

Herod looked at the Roman prefect and chose his words carefully. "It seems that we have often been confused about who has authority where," he said.

Pilate gave him a conciliatory bow. "Indeed. Now, I must return. As you can imagine, these festivals tax any man's endurance."

"Of course." Herod dipped his head. "Prefect."

Pilate glided down the steps in his long cloak and walked toward a table heavy with scrolls.

Without waiting for the Roman to exit, Herod continued his business with me. "So tell me, Queen, what have you come to steal from me this time?"

"If you mean the gold paid to Aretas, that was payment for your wife, Phasa, as you know. And I was only a messenger."

"Of course." He plucked a grape from a silver tray held by a servant beside him, and sat down again heavily. "And whose messenger are you this time?"

I hesitated, only because I wasn't sure where to begin.

"Yeshua's," I said. But there were many Yeshuas in Palestine, so I clarified. "Yeshua the Rabbi."

Pilate was by now near the door, but when he heard me speak Yeshua's name, the sound of his sandals on the marble floor stopped.

He turned back. "Yeshua the Rabbi, you say?"

"You know of him?"

Pilate approached, clearly intrigued.

"This is the one celebrated by the crowds as king?"

"Yes." The air suddenly felt heavy.

Saba spoke for the first time, stepping to my side. "He's a peaceful man who heals the sick."

"And yet accepts the people's praise," Pilate said, eyeing Saba. "But it seems his trouble is more with his own religion than Rome. He's a clever man."

"He's far more than clever."

"Perhaps. All I know is that he has deflected Roman concerns." He glanced at Herod. "Do you know this man?"

"The whole world knows of him." Herod was eyeing me with deep curiosity. "Impossible to pin down. They say he has great power from beyond this world. I've always wanted to question him."

"My wife, Claudia, dreamed of this prophet last night," the governor said. "A serpent disturbed her sleep. It's curious."

A dream?

"What did she see?" I asked.

"She wouldn't say. I'm sure it's nothing. A woman's dreams." He paused, and I thought he might say more, but he let it go. "But duty calls," he said, excusing himself again.

This time Herod waited until he was gone before speaking.

"You cannot imagine the trouble this governor has caused me. It's difficult enough to keep the religious fanatics happy without having to trade conflicts with a governor who thinks only of his own self-interests."

"And yet the whole world is infected with this—"

"Do you know what this fool did to me?" the king interrupted Saba, jabbing his thick finger at the door. "Only last Passover, he killed seven Galileans and mingled their blood with the sacrifices. You can imagine the outrage in Galilee. I can't tell you why Tiberius has allowed such a fool, who knows nothing of the Jewish ways, to be seated here as governor. The Romans are daft."

He stared at me, red-faced, as if expecting me to solve his problem. Then he sighed and sat back.

"But I'm tired, Queen. I never asked for all of this nonsense. Why can't a king enjoy his wealth and power without playing nursemaid to the world?" I followed his gaze out the window, far to my right. Clouds were still dark on the horizon.

"So now I must pay respect where none is deserved, if only to keep the peace," Herod said, facing me. "Now, back to this business at hand."

One of his administrators approached with a scroll, but Herod waved him off.

To me: "You say you come on Yeshua's behalf."

"Yes."

"To what end?"

"I request your favor and your trust. One day Dumah will be mine. And then I will use diplomacy to beg the mercy of Aretas on your behalf. Only then will he listen to me."

Herod stood. "Aretas? What has he to do with Yeshua?"

"When Aretas marches, as is still his intent, his army will crush yours. But I might speak for you."

Herod's face was ruddy again, but he didn't argue. Two years ago I had warned him of Aretas's unquenchable anger, though the king of Petra would bide his time. Even if Herod thought he could defeat Aretas, he wasn't the kind of ruler interested in battle. Wine and women were his vices.

Herod scoffed and turned away, incredulous.

"This is all nonsense! How will you take Dumah if you don't believe in the use of force? And even if you succeed, how can you be sure Aretas will yield to your diplomacy on my behalf? And *again*, what has the troublemaker Yeshua to do with any of it?"

I looked at Saba, who had not moved, and I kept my eyes on him as I answered, drawing his strength.

"I will do all of this with a power that comes through Yeshua. And so I ask you to protect him."

Herod faced me, caught flat-footed by what surely sounded even more absurd than my offer to beg Aretas for mercy.

A smile slowly formed on Herod's face.

"So you too have been taken in by all this talk of his magic."

"Magic? He casts no spells and uses no incantations. He speaks only for God, from whom his power comes."

"Give me one soldier," Herod said, lifting his finger. "Only one to put up against this so-called prophet of yours, and he would be dead with a single blow."

"No." Saba's voice rumbled with unmistakable authority as he stepped forward. "Forgive me." He dipped his head in respect. "But you are wrong. And I speak as a warrior who could crush twenty men of your choosing pitted against me in this very chamber."

We were both taken aback by his boldness, but Saba wasn't finished.

"What good is your sword against the one who raises

the dead? Which eye can you pluck out that Yeshua cannot heal? What storm can you conjure that he cannot
still with a single word?"

His nostrils flared and his stare was sword enough
against Herod, who stood rooted to the floor.

"This is the man you have heard of, but even what
you've heard means nothing. I, Saba, greatest warrior
among all Bedu, have come face-to-face with Yeshua,
and in his presence, my knees are weak."

His words seemed to push the air from the room.

"Then maybe *I* should fear him," Herod said.

"What is there to fear of love?" I said. "Only the religious leaders who dread the loss of their own power fear
Yeshua. Would you take their word over ours, who have
nothing to gain or lose in your country?"

He looked between me and Saba, then settled.

"Well then, what is your word?"

I clasped my hands behind my back and stared out
to those distant storm clouds couched on the horizon,
like a massive army in wait. Strange that they didn't appear to have moved.

"I once saw him calm a storm on the Sea of Galilee.
It was as if his words, spoken from the boat, carried a
power to which all of nature was forced to bow. Only
three words—*peace, be still*—and the clouds rolled back
like a scroll before my very eyes."

I faced Herod, who listened intently, however skepti-
cal.

"But I first met him with Phasa in Capernaum, on
the northern shore, where I watched him heal the hearts
of all who came seeking peace," I said.

"Phasa?" he said, surprised to hear this of his former
wife.

"Yes. She made a way for us to go while you were on your way to Rome." We both knew that he'd gone instead to his lover, Herodias, and conspired to have Phasa killed so that he could take Herodias as his wife. But I wasn't there to accuse.

"Go on."

I went on, telling Herod all that I'd seen of Yeshua's love and power, including the regaining of my full sight. Saba joined me, fueling my recollections with his own. We spoke quickly and with each account, our courage grew. So did Herod's interest. Finally we came to the sound of the Father's voice in thunder.

"Thunder?" Herod said. "There was no storm on that day."

"I cannot say it was thunder, only that it sounded like thunder to those gathered."

"You must understand." Saba stepped closer. "All that we have said is true. Did not your own prophet, Elijah, hear out of thunder? And did the kings listen to him? So then, you must realize that what happens here in Jerusalem will forever change all of history. You must not stand in the way of that history. It will only destroy you."

Herod stared at him, at a loss. But he had heard. More, he hadn't scoffed.

"I see." He shifted his eyes past me, still lost. "What can a man say?"

"Nothing," I said.

Herod sighed, climbed the steps to his seat, and lowered himself into the chair. Elbows on the golden throne, he slowly tapped his fingers together.

"Now I really must talk to him."

And join him, I thought. Perhaps this was what Yeshua had intended.

"You must realize that if he is taken by his enemies— if this rebellion of his looks to fail—even those closest to him will surely abandon him. This land has seen no end to prophets who have been killed, and their followers soon after."

I blinked. How could he say such a thing after all we had told him?

"Never," Saba said. "Not after what they have seen."

"What they've seen will have value only if they also see him take authority where influence matters. On earth, not merely in heaven."

We had to be careful, I thought. Though Saba and I both knew the extent of Yeshua's authority on earth as well, it wasn't our place to put fear into Herod.

"I can see that Yeshua's power isn't lost on you."

"No. No, I suppose not." He sighed. "So then, tell me, what can I do for you?"

"Only follow your heart. Allow him to do what he is destined to do without interference. Let his Way be heard in all of Jerusalem without any fear of harm."

"And in exchange for this, you will be my advocate for peace when you come into power—if such a day ever comes?"

His doubt was obvious.

"Did you ever think that I, daughter of Rami, who first came to you in Sepphoris, would one day steal your wife back to Aretas, relieve you of so much gold, and prevail in the arena at Petra to be made queen?"

Herod's face softened.

"No," I said. "And yet here I stand. Throw away your doubt. If I'm right, you have everything to gain. If I'm wrong, you lose nothing."

He finally nodded.

"Stay as my guests," he said to us. "I will give you an answer when the sun rises."

The thought of remaining the night unnerved me somewhat, but this was now my duty as queen.

We had won Herod's ear, and maybe more. I had trusted Yeshua before and he had given me sight when I'd fully surrendered to that trust.

I must do so now as well.

It was afternoon. Yeshua would celebrate their Passover in a few hours. Lambs were prepared for the slaughter.

I offered Herod a shallow bow.

"Then may the sun rise to offer me your grace, my king."

CHAPTER TWENTY-THREE

PASSOVER.

On the Jewish calendar, every new day began at sunset, and in this case that new day was the beginning of Passover celebration. Saba and I ate alone late in the lavish chambers Herod ushered us into, remembering Judah, the mighty Jewish lion.

Judah, whom I still loved.

As I thought of him, sorrow filled my heart. And yet, here in Jerusalem, a new day was dawning and with it, new hope. After five days in Palestine, my hope in Yeshua's power to deliver Talya only continued to grow.

We had stepped out of the boat and were walking on water, as Stephen would put it. It was one thing to contemplate wonders in heaven; it was another to walk the earth, full of heaven's wonder. This took faith.

There was a large bed in the chamber, this to our

right, covered in red and white silk sheets. Three oil lamps, all silver, lit the lavishly appointed room. Kings and princes had slept here, Herod said.

"It is because of Judah that we are here," Saba pointed out, watching me across the low, Roman-styled table beside the couch. "Maybe this too was by God's design."

I could hardly reconcile Judah's death and Talya's imprisonment with anything good.

"No, we are here because I forgot my way."

"Perhaps that too." Saba stood from the couch and walked to the window, hands on his hips. The night was already late and darkness hid the clouds that had been encroaching on the city. "Or perhaps we've never truly found the way," he said. "Yeshua calms the storm with a spoken word. We struggle to rise above even the simplest fear."

Yeshua's words, spoken so long ago, returned to me: *What you will see now is only the half*, he'd said. *There is far more to be revealed in time. Only then will you be able to follow where I will go.*

"Only the half," I said. "But we are finding the other half, don't you think?"

He stared into the darkness with his back to me. "Yes."

It struck me that Saba was like a little boy. Like Talya. There in the dim light he was a black stallion, so majestic and powerful in this world's eyes, but inside he only wanted to trust.

I pushed myself up and approached him from behind. I could still smell the scented soap he'd used earlier. He had shaved, as was his way, and his skin glistened in the light of the flame.

"I often think the stormy sky is like our minds," he said. "Darkened by clouds."

"And yet the light always comes in the morning." I put my hand in the crook of his elbow and stepped up beside him. My head reached his shoulders if I stood on my toes. But tonight I preferred to rest it on his arm, not for my sake but his.

"We follow a mighty Way, Saba," I said. "His path is enough to make the head spin."

"It shatters all common sense."

"It defies the most destructive storm."

Saba put his hand on mine, there in his elbow.

"Soon, my queen. I can feel a great illumination rising in the darkness. It is the end of all suffering. In the same way that he has overcome the anguish of this world, so will we, as we surrender."

Talya's song of Eden was the promise of Yeshua—to live in glory even now while the world slogged through pain and death.

"I think it must be beautiful, Saba."

He hesitated. "Surrender?"

"Yes," I said. "I think in surrendering as Yeshua has surrendered through his own suffering, we will find only peace."

"More than we can imagine."

"Snakes cannot hurt us. Death will be far away."

"Love alone will rule our hearts," he said.

A beat.

"Saba?"

"Yes?"

"I know you are meant to hate me ... But do you love me?"

Several breaths passed before he answered, barely

above a whisper. "More than you can imagine, Maviah."

His words flowed through me like honey.

I smiled in the dim light, staring out at the dark sky.

"Then let's swim in this love that he brings us." I pushed back and twirled away. "Let's open our eyes to see the light and vanquish all darkness because he's come to bring sight to the blind!"

He was grinning when I faced him again.

"Dance with me, Saba!"

"Dance? I don't know how to dance, my queen."

"Nonsense! Dance, Saba, dance!"

He began to clap slowly, his way of dancing. But it was enough for me. So I twirled to the table, plucked a grape, threw it into my mouth, and turned back to him.

"Then drink with me, Saba," I said picking up my goblet. "Let us drink in remembrance of the light that has come to us in our darkest hour. We, who were blind, are beginning to see!"

"This," he said, marching forward with one finger in the air, "I can do."

From that moment, accepting such a powerful alignment between us, all darkness was vanquished from our minds.

We ate more food than we could possibly need— dates and cheeses and pomegranates and oranges, spitting out the seeds into a silver bowl. And we laughed. Not only a chuckle but true laughter and at the silliest things, like the juice running down Saba's chin and my spilling of wine as I filled his goblet.

I learned something that night: Saba truly was a child at heart. His many hours in silence before the

Father had transformed him. It was no wonder Talya adored him so. They were both children.

I finally collapsed on the bed, exhausted yet brimming with life.

"We must sleep, Saba. A new day, full of the sun, dawns tomorrow."

He was on the couch, smiling. "Do you want to know what I think, Maviah?"

His calling me Maviah rather than Queen pleased me.

"Tell me."

"I think Yeshua will send us back to the desert soon. Perhaps tomorrow."

I sat up. "You think so?"

"He said he would join us there, in spirit. You've done what he's asked of you here, now he will send us back to Petra with power. This is what I think."

"I hope you're right."

"If not tomorrow, then soon. Very soon." He climbed to his feet, grabbed a pillow, and tossed it onto a large sheepskin across the room. "So you're right...We must rest."

I watched as he blew out two of the lamps, then crossed to the third, which he picked up.

"Sleep well, my queen," he said, gazing over the flame.

"Good night, my tower."

He blew the lamp out and went to the sheepskin, which he preferred to the couch.

"Saba?"

"Yes?"

"Do you think Talya is in suffering?"

He answered me in a tone that left no doubt. "Talya

is full of Eden, Maviah. He is like Yeshua—they do not suffer as we do. As Yeshua himself says, do not worry about Talya. Only become like a child."

It was the kindest thing he had said to me.

"Are you sure?"

"Without question."

"Thank you."

"Now sleep."

Within minutes, I could hear his breathing deepen, and I knew that he had fallen asleep.

I pulled the silk sheets over me and settled into the deepest peace I had known in weeks.

I DREAMED. I dreamed of many things, but then I dreamed I was in the desert and thundering storm clouds promised torrential rains. A hundred thousand Bedu were dancing as rain pelted the dry earth. And Talya was there, watched by all, smiling like the sun. Green sprouts began to spring from the sand. Life had come!

Suddenly I was on a boat in the thundering storm once again. The sky above me was pounding. And Yeshua was there on the bow, fist raised to the dark skies above.

"I saw Satan fall like lightning from heaven!" he cried, lowering his fiery eyes to me. These were the very words he'd spoken to those he'd sent out in his name a year ago, Stephen had said. "I have given you authority to trample on snakes and scorpions and to overcome all the power of the enemy. Nothing will harm you!"

Serpents! I was filled with courage. Who could touch me? Who had overcome me? Not that viper Kahil.

Who could know true authority? Not Herod.

"But rejoice that your names are written in heaven!" Yeshua cried.

My identity is the Father's daughter in his realm even now, I thought, even as his disciples' names were written in heaven long ago. And there we could not be harmed.

The sky pounded.

"Yes?"

Saba...

I was jerked from my sleep by the sound of his soft voice and I sat up to see him at the door. A servant stood beyond the threshold, holding a lamp. He'd been pounding on the door and woken Saba.

The sky was still dark outside.

"What is it?" I asked.

Saba turned. "Get dressed, my queen. Herod calls for us."

"Herod? At this hour? It's—"

"He calls." Saba gathered his sandals. "Hurry."

I flew out of bed and grabbed my shawl and sash, at a loss as to why the king would call us to his chamber before the sun had risen.

We followed the servant down a hall, then turned to a massive door. My own sandals were still in my hands, and I thought to put them on, but then the door was opened and the servant was ushering us into Herod's chamber.

I stepped up behind Saba and blinked in the lamp-light. Herod was standing by a table, dressed only in a nightshirt and a waist robe. His hair was tangled and he held a goblet in hand.

He turned to us looking put out. "This is why I hate Jerusalem," he said. "They know no respect."

I didn't know what to say.

"Well then...You have your answer. Courtesy of the Pharisees. You see who they think they are to demand an audience with me in the middle of the night. It never ends."

This wasn't what I'd expected. "They came to you? Who?"

Herod set down his cup.

"One named Nicodemus. He insisted on my waking and begs for my intervention on the behalf of this prophet."

Nicodemus! Stephen's uncle, and friend of Yeshua.

"Which prophet?" I asked. But I already knew. "Intervene how?"

"Your Yeshua, have you forgotten? The Pharisee claims he will be betrayed to the religious authorities before the sun rises."

My heart was in my throat. Arim's words on death crashed through my mind but then were gone, because I refused to believe them. Stephen was right...In the end, Yeshua would show his power. And my visit to Herod was part of that.

"Didn't I warn you about these religious fanatics?" Herod was saying.

I couldn't think straight. "Will you?"

"Intervene? Even if I could, why should I? You say he cannot be stopped—so then let us see. If he is who you say, he will show himself as such and I will bow to him myself. There is your answer."

His words sucked the air from the room.

"Where?" Saba demanded.

"Where will I bow?"

"Where is he to be betrayed?" The force in his voice stilled even Herod.

"In a garden," the king said. "One he frequents."

A chill swept through the room.

Saba grabbed my arm. "We must go."

I was already turning, my mind on one thought alone: Gethsemane.

"Return to me with proof, Queen," Herod said. "Convince me!"

But I, like Saba, cared about only one thing now.

We had to get to the garden just outside of Jerusalem. Yeshua must be warned. This, I saw now, was why my heart had been nudged to visit Herod.

Reaching the expansive courtyard, Saba began to run, then turned back and grabbed my hand.

"Hurry!"

"Hold on..." I leaped to a couch and quickly pulled on my sandals as he faced the eastern horizon. The Mount of Olives. Now with full view of the sky, I saw that the ominous storm clouds rose like a wall beyond that peak. The sight filled me with dread.

I sprinted after him, through the courtyard, down the sweeping steps of the palace, to the gate.

"Our camels—"

"There's no time to secure them," he snapped. "Stay close."

The streets of Jerusalem were deserted, and we ran through them as if for our very lives. The temple was a lifeless white monument against the dark sky.

We returned by the same route we had taken only yesterday. Past a hundred homes and shops. Past the guards at the city gate who watched us curiously as we ran. Up the path that led through the Kidron Valley to the Mount of Olives.

We did not speak—doing so would have only wasted

our breath, which kept cadence with the slapping of our feet. Saba loped two steps ahead; I was at a full run, trying to keep up.

There was no sign of violence or threat, and this calmed me somewhat, but I could not shake the weight of those massive clouds towering on the horizon. I had once faced a storm in Galilee. But Yeshua spoke calm to the storm. Now a new storm was gathering against him.

I didn't know if we would find Yeshua in the garden so late. Nor whether he'd already been betrayed. Nor who might have conspired against him. Nor why Nicodemus had been prompted to wake Herod.

I only knew that I had to run, because I had information that few could possibly have guessed.

But more, I ran to be by Yeshua's side. To remain in him. To be with him always, for my sake, but perhaps now for his sake as well.

A hundred questions spun through my mind, and still I ran.

ONLY WHEN we reached the section of road where we'd heard the voice of the Father in the thunder did Saba veer from the path and slow to a walk.

"He's there?" I whispered, staring at the garden ahead of us.

Saba surged ahead, offering no response.

Slowly, my breathing settled. Large olive trees rose about us and Saba led me through them, picking his way easily, eyes ahead...always ahead.

"Saba."

He lifted his hand and absently shook his finger to silence me, leaning into the darkness. Then he pulled up short, listening.

I heard nothing but the sound of crickets. But Saba had ears to hear a ghost in the night.

He shifted his gaze to where the trees edged a shallow basin. Then, in the stillest moment, I heard what he heard, however faint.

A gentle, deeply anguished sob.

The sound drained me of life. I knew immediately, without thought, who the sob belonged to.

It seemed the whole world was weeping in that single sound, for it came from one who could not possibly utter such a terrible cry.

Saba stood frozen. And then it came again, very soft, but filled with agony.

Alarmed, Saba cut straight for the cry beyond the trees, forgetting that I existed. But I too had to reach the man crying in the garden.

And then I saw him, between two trees. I knew his cloak. I knew his blue-and-white mantle, now drawn off his head. I knew the sound of his voice.

Yeshua lay at the base of large tree, facedown with both arms extended over his head. His body was trembling.

And now I heard the guttural words he uttered.

"Abba…Abba…"

Neither Saba nor I could move. How could this be? How could the Son of the Father who knew no death be so undone? Hadn't his Father promised to glorify his name even here, in this very garden?

"Abba…Father…" He drew a deep breath, then another, begging through a trembling groan. "All things are possible for you. Remove this cup from me…"

Confusion swallowed me. I could not breathe. My eyes flowed with an ancient sorrow they could not contain.

"I beg you...remove this cup from me..."

What cup, I did not know. The reason for his pain was unfathomable. But in that moment, I became only a mother like his own, Miriam, who had offered me compassion.

I wanted to rush out to him. To comfort him. To wipe his tears and hold him close and tell him that he did not need to be afraid.

I wanted to, but his dread immobilized me. I had never imagined him in such a place.

"Abba...Abba..." Each desperate cry crushed me. "Remove this cup..."

Then it struck me: Yeshua knew that he would be betrayed.

He *knew*.

I tore my eyes from his lament and saw that Saba's face streamed with tears.

Yeshua wept with heaving sobs now, body hitching with each cry, fingers dug into the earth as he lay, forehead pressed into the dirt.

I could rush out and tell him. *There will be no cup! Please, Yeshua, please. Do not be afraid. Only have faith.*

But I could not move.

Yeshua began to settle. And when he did, hope flooded my heart. Now it was over. Now he would gather his faith and rise. *It's over, my son. It's over and now you will be safe. Now let me hold you and wipe away all of your tears.*

But it wasn't over. His sobbing overtook his body again with even greater torment, until I believed he bore the suffering of all the world upon his shoulders.

Now Saba sank slowly to his knees, arms spread by his thighs, tearful eyes fixed upon Yeshua as silent sobs began to shake his body. Saba, whom I had never seen broken, breaking from the inside out.

Now I was mother to him as well. And to Talya and to all who suffered in this world.

I was mother, and so I put my hand on Saba's shoulder, but I had no further courage to offer, for I was lost in my own anguish.

And yet, something unseen was happening, I thought. Here, in this garden, something greater than my understanding. I knew it like a gentle whisper of solace from beyond time.

He learned obedience through what he suffered...

Right now Yeshua was like me. He too suffered without advantage, and this truth drew me to him as I had never been. There, the one who calmed the storm wept in its presence, even as I wept for Talya.

Yeshua drew his hands under his chest and pushed himself to his knees, and I thought, now...now it's over.

Then he spread his arms with fists clenched, lifted his face to the sky, and settled back on his heels, arms now spread by his side. By the light of the stars in the west, I could see the long trails of dark tears on his face.

"Not what I will, but what you will, Father."

Not his will...In this moment, the will of his mind and the Father's will were not one.

Then I understood. He was surrendering his will. He was overcoming the ancient call of man's will to be God.

Yeshua's expression began to settle. For a long time, he remained still on his knees, facing the heavens, eyes closed. His breathing became steady and deep, his body relaxed to some unseen balm that seemed to wash over him from head to foot. He did not smile, but his face was at perfect peace.

His body was overtaken by a brief tremble. I believed it to be one of power and love, not fear.

For a long time I stood numb, unable to move. I could feel the presence of his newfound peace, as if an angel had come to offer him comfort and I had been touched by the wind of its wings.

Then Yeshua lowered his head and let out a long breath, and finally pushed himself to his feet. He stared into the darkness for a moment, then walked toward another small grove close by.

Saba sank back on his heels and hung his head. I settled down beside him, watching the night into which Yeshua had vanished. My hands were shaking and a terrible knot had seized my throat.

"Saba?" I whispered.

His eyes were closed and he breathed deeply, trying to calm himself.

I put my hand on his back. "Saba—"

"He knows that they come for him," he said. "He knows and he allows it."

I nodded. "And this cup he speaks of?"

Saba looked at the grove where Yeshua had gone. "I don't know. But he overcame his fear. You saw it?"

"Yes."

"He overcame and will show his power now. No man can touch him."

Again, I nodded. Then I asked the question I hardly dared to ask.

"Why was he so filled with fear, Saba?"

He gave no reply. He had none.

Yeshua's distant voice carried to us, speaking calmly.

"The spirit is willing, but the flesh is weak." Then more regarding sleep, and what sounded like Peter in reply, but I couldn't make out the words.

Saba suddenly turned his head to the west, and I too heard the sound of running feet approaching.

"It is enough," I heard Yeshua say, speaking with more authority now. "The hour has come. The Son of Man is betrayed into..."

And then I heard no more, because both Saba and I were jumping to our feet as the runners passed us, just north of where we crouched.

I started to run toward the grove where Yeshua waited, but Saba grabbed my arm.

"No!" He hurried past me. "They must not see a woman here."

"I can't stay—"

"Wait!" he snapped. Then he gave a curt nod and ducked into the darkness, leaving me alone.

I understood. There was no telling what the indignant religious would do to a woman caught with men so late. I drew behind the closest tree, trying to calm my breath so that I could listen. But there were many voices now, some soft, some angry—Peter, the one I thought might be Judas, others from those who'd descended on the grove. But I couldn't make sense of them except to know that Nicodemus had been right.

They'd come to arrest him. They had, but they could not succeed in this, surely. Yeshua had overcome his anguish. I'd seen him with my own eyes find that great peace.

A cry cut through the night and I jumped. Then a scuffle with loud shouts. Then more calm words, these from Yeshua, though I still couldn't make them out.

And then they scattered. Feet were running in different directions. Confusion overtook the garden and I withdrew further behind the tree.

Wild imaginations flashed through my mind of soldiers trying to bind up Yeshua and failing. Or succeeding and hauling him away in chains, however impossible it seemed to me.

I had flashes of Saba crushing all of Yeshua's enemies. He could do it easily.

Then the sounds faded and I was alone with the pounding of my own heart.

Twigs cracked to my right and I spun. Saba rushed in from the darkness, eyes wide. Alone.

"What happened?"

"They've taken him." A breath. "He's arrested."

I blinked. "He's arrested? To what end?" And then harshly, before he could answer. "Why didn't you stop them?"

"He went willingly!" Saba snapped. "Peter drew a sword and stuck one of them, and Yeshua rebuked him."

"Peter, who slept while Yeshua wept? How could they allow this?"

I clenched my hands to still their trembling. I knew it wasn't Saba or Peter or the others who'd allowed any of this. Yeshua himself had allowed it.

Yeshua, who had intentionally poked his finger into the religious leaders' eye by riding into Jerusalem as their Messiah. Yeshua, who had poked a finger into their other eye by cleansing the temple. Yeshua, who had come here at night, so close to the city, knowing they would come for him. Yeshua, who had handed himself over to them.

This was the cup he'd begged his Father to remove. And now he was giving himself over to it.

A moment of deep anger welled up within me. I didn't understand that wrath; I only felt it as one who has been betrayed even as Yeshua had been betrayed. Betrayed by life...

Betrayed by Yeshua.

But I immediately cast the anger aside. *A way will be made even now. Yeshua will not die, even as your Talya will not die. He promised it.*

"We must speak to Herod again," Saba said, turning already. The warrior in him was emerging.

"Who took him?" I demanded.

"The religious leaders. Judas brought them."

"Judas?" Yeshua had been betrayed by one of his inner circle? How could any of them turn their backs now? The heat of rage burned my face.

"Then we must run again," I said, rushing past him. "We have to turn Herod!"

CHAPTER TWENTY-FOUR

———※———

IT WAS STILL dark when we reached Herod's palace, winded.

Still dark when we demanded entrance. Still dark when a stiff-lipped steward ushered us into his court.

That darkness was as much in my heart as in the sky. A terrible confusion had blinded me. I could see no reason to explain what Yeshua had done.

Yes, he had spoken much about danger and even death, but his were symbolic teachings, not predictions of his own troubles. He was bread and comfort to orphans and outcasts; he was calm in the face of storms and death; he was life to the dead. He would surely show his power again.

But his agony in the garden disturbed me deeply. In seeing his fear, I found my own, fully alive. So I took it upon myself to intercede. I could not allow his demise, for his sake as much as for Talya's. And my own.

I stormed into Herod's court with my jaw firm. And

when I saw that he was dressed in a purple robe and adorned with silver chains and many rings, seated upon his ornate chair of power, displaying all of his majesty, my dark mood only deepened.

I stopped with Saba by my side. Scanned the room now lit by ten torches. A dozen of his guard were stationed to our right and our left, all watching us with keen eyes. So then, the moment he heard of our return, he'd called warriors.

Why?

"What's the meaning of this?" I snapped, striding forward. "Am I now your enemy?"

Two guards bearing spears stepped toward us, one from each side.

"Maviah, Maviah..." Herod said. "Always the impetuous one. Enemy, no. How can a mere Bedu woman from the wastelands be considered an enemy? But you come to me with anger in your eyes. What is a king to do?"

"He's been taken," I bit off.

"So I heard. Pity."

His guards were close now, spears half-lowered. They feared nothing from an unarmed woman. My mind, dark already, lost itself.

I flew at the nearest guard in two long steps, even as his eyes opened wide with surprise. Deflecting his spear with my right arm, I stepped under him, grabbed that same spear arm, and threw him to his back using my shoulder for leverage.

The other guard rushed at me with a grunt, but Saba was already there. His palm struck the man in the chin, knocking him up and back, clean off his feet. The guard landed on the step at Herod's feet, unconscious.

"Stop!" Saba spun and held his palm out to several

other warriors who were already running for us. "She will restrain herself."

The man I'd thrown was clambering to his feet, but I paid him no mind. My eyes were set on Herod, who appeared both stunned and impressed. My mind began to settle.

"Forgive me, I had no right," I said. "But you aren't seeing clearly. The fate of the world is at stake and you sit, a king as blind as I once was. I beg you pay me heed."

Stillness filled the court. The torches' flames licked the air like thirsty tongues. A thin smile slowly edged onto Herod's face.

"I've paid you more heed than any woman from the desert. And I've already given you my answer. The fate of this prophet is in his own hands. If he is who you say he is, no one can stand in his way."

"Are you so powerless in the face of these religious leaders who've taken him?" I demanded.

"But you miss the point, Queen. The question is, is *he* powerless?"

I balked. Yes. I knew this. But I had seen Yeshua's struggle, and fear had worked its long teeth into my mind.

"Your conduct doesn't speak of one who believes her own words," he said. "If he has such power, why are you so afraid?"

I had no answer for him.

"Let me be clear again. Since Yeshua is from Galilee, he may well end up in my court. If so, and if he proves himself, I will give him his just reward. Either way, I am not one to condemn him."

It was all I could ask.

"When?" I demanded.

"When he is brought to me. *If* he is brought to me. And for the record, I hope he is. I would like to see what all the fuss is about. These wonders of his have certainly terrified the Sanhedrin and the rest. I can't imagine they fear him for blasphemy alone."

"Where do they have him?"

"The house of Caiaphas, the high priest. But I can't have you storming their courtyard, now can I?" He eyed Saba. "You've proven that much."

"You have my word." I turned to leave.

"Your word will no longer do." He motioned to his chief. "Put them under guard. If this Yeshua is brought to me, I will call for them." Then to me, with smug satisfaction: "Or will you object to this as well?"

"We will not," Saba said, answering for me.

Herod's right brow cocked. "Your slave speaks for you?"

I glanced at Saba, who stood tall, an unbreakable tower. But there were cracks even in his foundation, I thought.

"He's not my slave," I said, watching him. Then to Herod: "If they don't bring Yeshua to you?"

"Then you will be free to go. You and I have unfinished business with King Aretas."

I DON'T KNOW how long Saba and I paced in the small holding chamber under heavy guard, waiting—begging—to be called. It felt like a lifetime but could not have been more than an hour.

Saba kept to himself, sitting on a wooden bench or standing by a small window. Our mood was heavy, like those black billows hidden from sight by darkness, but still present. Neither of us was able to speak.

And yet my mind spoke always, pummeling me with questions and doubts and fears.

Where was Yeshua now? What was he saying to the leaders, whom he'd always foiled with the cleverest words? Was he even now speaking calm to the storms in their hearts? What had happened to his inner circle?

This was Yeshua's Way, I kept telling myself. To put himself in the middle of the storm and there rise above it, unscathed, shining with light and power. Even as I had trusted the Father in Petra's arena, so he would stand in the den of wolves only to emerge the victor. Not by sword, but by love and word alone.

Slowly, his assurance returned to me.

Slowly, my fear ebbed.

"They cannot hurt him, Saba," I said, staring at the gray dawn light. "They can't even threaten him."

"No." His voice sounded distant.

I swallowed and turned to him, arms crossed. "I allowed fear to blind me."

Saba was slow to respond. "I as well."

"There's nothing as blinding as fear."

"Nothing."

I approached him, arms still folded, seeking comfort in his expression. Then I leaned my head against his chest and closed my eyes.

"I'm still afraid, Saba…"

I felt his hand settle on the back of my neck. "He will take our fear away and give us rest."

They came for us only a moment later, while I was still close to Saba. I spun to the sound of the opening latch. Four guards stood outside the door, eyeing us with distrust. When they saw no threat in us, the closest nodded.

"He is here."

My heart jumped. I hurried out of the chamber, mind on Yeshua alone. I had to see him. I had to know that he was safe. To look into his eyes and find comfort in the bottomless gaze that had always swallowed me with love.

Ignoring the guards, I rushed past them and strode down the passageway with Saba close on my heels. One of them grunted a warning. Herod's distant voice had reached me from his grand chamber ahead.

"... Yeshua of Nazareth. So close to where my own palace rises by the sea. And yet not once have I seen you." Many crowded the side entrance at the end of the hall, blocking my sight of the chamber. "Why have you avoided me all these years?"

His question echoed to silence. I might have heard a pebble drop.

"You have no answer for me?"

I pushed through a tangle of humanity and pulled up next to several armed guards. The lay of court came to me in a single glance.

Perhaps a hundred had congregated before Herod— soldiers and aristocrats and servants, lining the walls and crowding into the center where twenty or more religious leaders stood in an arc, several deep. These were dressed in formal apparel with square hats and long, richly woven robes, black and white with golden tassels.

There was no sign of his disciples.

There on the rise stood Herod, staring at Yeshua, who wore a torn white tunic. Rope bound his hands. His hair was tangled and his lower lip was bleeding.

If Herod acknowledged our sudden appearance, I didn't notice. My eyes were fixed on Yeshua.

He stood with his head bowed, eyes closed, his breathing unlabored and steady. The room felt like a distant abstraction to me in that moment. Someone began to speak—one of the religious, deeply agitated—but my mind was consumed with the image before my eyes.

With Yeshua.

He looked utterly innocent and frail, yet he stood at ease, as if oblivious to the number and strength of his enemies. He was only biding his time. Herod would see. At any moment he would understand the power of the man standing before him. The man who would not bow to any kingdom on earth.

I glanced up to see Herod looking my way. Our eyes met briefly before he faced Yeshua, who hadn't moved.

"Why do you refuse to speak to me?"

Silence.

The man I took to be the elder of their Sanhedrin extended an accusing finger. "He is silent before you because he fears you. Before us and before all men he claims to be the Son of God. He says he will tear down the temple and rebuild it in three days. That he—"

"Silence!" Herod snapped. "You bring him to my court for me, not you, to judge. You've had your say. He will speak."

The leader lowered his arm, face red.

Yeshua would speak. He would speak because he always spoke. How I longed for the sound of his voice to bring peace.

Herod paced with hands on his hips, a lion before cubs. "They say you have power to bring sight to the blind, and to cast out devils. Is this true?"

Silence.

"Hmmm? That you can control the sea like Moses and raise the dead. Yes?"

Yeshua stood like a statue with his head hung. I could hear the sound of Saba's breathing to my right, and my own, silently begging Yeshua to open his mouth. Only one word... A single word and they would know...

But he said nothing.

"Do you know who I am?" Herod demanded. "I have the power to save you. You've shown all of Galilee this power, so then show me, your king."

Still Yeshua refused to speak or move.

A chill washed down my back. *Show him!* I wanted to cry. *Show them all what you've shown me... Speak to Herod, who is a king far below you!*

"Are you deaf?" Herod demanded, eyes glaring in the face of such defiance. "Speak to me!"

Yeshua's silence extended, crushing hope.

Someone grunted. A soft chuckle. Heat flooded my face.

Three more times, Herod questioned Yeshua, each time with increasing frustration, demanding he speak something, or show some power, or at the very least offer respect.

Three more times, Yeshua did not even acknowledge him.

Herod threw his arms wide, now livid. "Are you mad, man?" His voice echoed through the chamber. "I am the king! Speak to me!"

And yet Yeshua stood in silence, a lamb before that lion.

"He claims to be king of the Jews," the chief of the Sanhedrin sneered. "This is—"

"Silence!" Herod thundered. "Are you deaf as well? If an outcast without a sword claims to be king, then so be it! Insanity is not a crime in Galilee. If it were, our prisons would be full."

He paced, face red, watching Yeshua again.

"You refuse to show me your power. You refuse to speak to me. So then you must be mad. Tell me at least that much. Are you?"

Confusion and fear smothered me; I could no longer bear such humiliation.

"Yeshua..." My voice was weak and strained, but I knew he could hear me. "Please..."

Yeshua remained still, head down.

Herod glared, jaw set. "You are a king?" He snapped, turning for his throne. "Then of fools." He snatched a long purple robe draped over the back and flung it at the closest guard. "Show me how a king of fools looks."

Laughter broke out. The guard tossed his spear to another and approached, wearing a grin. He draped the robe over Yeshua's shoulders, then stepped back.

"Behold," Herod cried out, arms spread wide. "Yeshua, king of the Jews, who brings sight to the blind!"

The room erupted with delighted mocking.

Still Yeshua did not move.

Tears filled my eyes and slipped down cheeks.

"Here then is the mad king who threatens all of Israel!" Herod thundered.

"Yeshua..."

I felt Saba's hand close around my elbow.

"Yeshua!"

Only then did Yeshua lift his head. Slowly. Not toward Herod, but toward me. His eyes—now open—met mine. The same brown eyes that had always reached into my soul and filled me with deep assurance.

My heart stilled with that look. He wasn't smiling, but I saw a calm in him, defying even this storm.

But then I saw that there was more than calm and I blinked.

His eyes were misted, betraying a terrible sorrow that he could not hide. A tear slipped down his cheek and my fingers began to tremble.

Herod was saying something, but I couldn't hear his words. The guard who'd dressed Yeshua spit on his face, then slapped the back of his head to the uproarious approval of all those gathered.

Still Yeshua held me in his gaze, now filled with tears that leaked down both cheeks.

Without thinking, I started to move toward him—to rush out and defend him—but Saba's firm grasp pulled me back. And then away, through the throng fixated on the spectacle.

"Wait!" I cried out.

But he would not.

I tried to pull away, terrified to leave Yeshua in such a state, but Saba would not loosen his grip. By my elbow, he hurried me into the outer court.

Laughter erupted behind us. They weren't done. I started to turn back, but Saba took my face in his hands, focusing my attention on his eyes.

"Hear me, Maviah."

More laughter...

"Listen to my words."

"Saba—"

"Listen to me!"

He was being strong, but his eyes too were misted. I nodded, pushing down my panic.

"He is Yeshua. He will find a way."

The words cut through my fear.

"Do not allow darkness to blind you. Find your faith. Promise me."

I hesitated, then nodded.

He stared at me for a moment, then took a calming breath and lowered his hands to my shoulders.

"You have to go to Bethany. The others—"

"Bethany? No! I can't leave him."

He touched his finger to my lips. "I will stay. Stephen and Lazarus, his mother, they're all there. Tell them. Bring them."

"Why?"

"They must be told. There's no more you can do here without putting yourself in danger."

"Danger? He's in danger! I can't just—"

"He is Yeshua!" Saba thundered, releasing me. Then again, with eyes blazing, thrusting his trembling finger toward the inner court, "Yeshua! Have you forgotten his Way?"

I swallowed. Then settled. Saba lowered his hand.

"Bring them," he said. "They must be here when he is released."

My mind filled with images of Stephen plunging into the Sea of Galilee at the sound of Yeshua's voice. Of Yeshua's mother holding me as I wept in Nazareth. Of Mary anointing Yeshua's feet with nard.

I nodded.

"Find the camels. Take both."

Another nod.

He took my hands into his own and held them for a moment, then squeezed them. "Run."

I ran.

CHAPTER TWENTY-FIVE

THE SUN had risen but the sky was encased in billowing gray clouds as I rushed through Jerusalem on my, leading the other by its rope. I don't remember passing through the streets, nor the faces of those yelling at me when I galloped by, nor the nature of the guard's warning as I crashed through the gates. I don't remember the path leading up the mountain, urging the camel to run faster.

There was only one Way to find salvation from the troubles of this world, and he had gone silent. Once again, I was lost.

Mounted and at a full run, I must have made the journey to Bethany in less than half an hour, but it seemed endless.

Stephen would know what to do.

His mother, Miriam, would offer comfort.

Yeshua would save us all. He had to. Talya depended upon him as much as I did. The world depended upon him.

If any in Bethany had heard of Yeshua's arrest, his followers would be rushing to Jerusalem already. But I met no one on the path over the Mount of Olives.

And when I reached the village and drove the camels toward Martha's house, I saw only smoke there, drifting up lazily from the courtyard, as on any other morning.

I dismounted before the camels came to a halt and I ran for the courtyard. Gentle laughter reached my ears. I crashed into the gate and flung it wide.

There: Mary, eyebrow raised at Arim. And Martha, holding a bowl with one hand on her hip, ready to scold. Stephen was bent over the fire, blowing at the coals. Lazarus reclined against the wall, one knee hooked in his elbow.

And Miriam, the mother of Yeshua, turning from the table with a smile on her face. The laughter had been hers.

One glance at my disheveled hair and distressed face and they all stopped.

"Maviah?" Mary stood. "What is it?"

Miriam's smile began to fade.

"Tell us," Martha snapped. "What is it?"

I held Miriam's gaze, afraid to speak her son's name, because in that moment she became me, receiving news about my little lamb.

"Yeshua," I said.

Only that. Only his name, and yet she knew the rest already. For a moment her eyes looked dead to the world, as if she'd always known this day would come.

"He's been arrested," I said. "Only arrested."

"By whom?" Stephen demanded, on his feet now. Lazarus stood behind him, watching me without expression.

"The religious leaders." My words tumbled out. "I was there, in Herod's court, when they brought him. It was your Sanhedrin. And Saba sent me. He's there with him..."

"Take a breath, Daughter," Miriam said quietly.

And with those words all of the emotion I'd battled crossing the Mount of Olives overwhelmed me. I lowered my face into my hands as gentle sobs shook my shoulders.

I felt a hand on the back of my neck, then an arm, pulling me close.

"Hush, my dear Maviah." It was Miriam, whom I should be comforting. "Do not fear. My son knows what he's doing."

I wrapped my arms around her and held her even as she held me.

"I'm so sorry. Forgive me." I sniffed, determined to be strong. Yeshua was mocked, but he wasn't hurt. "I saw him. He's fine."

"Yes. That's right."

"I've never seen anyone so strong," I said, pulling back.

Tears had filled her eyes. "No one," she said.

Then she took a breath and nodded. "So we must go to him."

She gathered her dress, turned from me, and spoke to Martha as she crossed the courtyard.

"Bread, Martha. And a clean tunic, if you have one."

"I do," Stephen said, heading for his bag.

Lazarus stopped him. "Mine. It will fit him." He stepped into the house.

"Ointment," Miriam said to no one in particular. "And bandages."

She was being his mother. Only that.

Arim approached me, full of courage. "Do not worry, my queen. Yeshua cannot be harmed. He will need none of these things."

"Some clean cloth, Mary," Miriam said. "And water. Hurry."

They moved quickly under the direction of Miriam. The urgency was palpable, as was a haunting dread, but they'd all grown accustomed to threats and danger, and none offered their thoughts beyond what had already been said.

We four women mounted the camels and were led away from Bethany by Stephen, Lazarus, and Arim, who hurried before us. When we were halfway up the Mount of Olives, Stephen spoke.

"Whatever happens, you can be sure that with Yeshua, all is well," he said. "You have no reason to fear for your son, Miriam. None."

She nodded once. Seated behind her, Mary had wrapped her arms around Miriam and pressed her head against her back, perhaps both drawing and offering courage.

We pushed the camels, who might have objected after the hard ride from Jerusalem. But they were quiet. The towering clouds over our heads drew only passing comments from Arim who, being from the deep desert, regarded them as a great promise of rain.

"You must remember," Stephen said, "we see the storm, but Yeshua sees only peace in the place of this storm. To him, all that threatens in this world is like a ghoul without power."

Miriam was silent. As were the rest of us.

We urged the camels onward, trotting where the road leveled, leaning into the steeper sections.

"You will see," Stephen pressed. "There's nothing to fear. Tell them, Lazarus."

"There's nothing to fear," Lazarus returned after a moment.

"You see, Miriam?" Stephen clapped his hands once to make certain the point wasn't lost. "Not even death!"

Miriam said nothing.

Neither did I. I had looked into Yeshua's eyes and watched tears trailing down his cheeks. I knew that his inner circle had fled. I had seen Yeshua's fear in the garden and heard his cry of anguish, as if all the world's troubles were heaped upon him. How could I face any storm without fear if he, the master of storms, couldn't?

All of this I kept to myself. I couldn't speak my concern in front of his mother. Nor the others. Nor hear them voiced aloud myself.

All I knew was that Saba had to be right. Yeshua had to make a way because Yeshua *was* that Way.

So I clung to this promise and I rode in silence, casting occasional glances at Miriam, who kept her thoughts to herself and her eyes on the road ahead.

We did not stop until we crested the knoll from which we could see across the Kidron Valley. There Miriam slowed and then brought her camel to a halt. As one we looked at the great city ahead of us. Jerusalem, crowning glory of the Jewish world. Jerusalem, with her towering white walls and majestic temple.

There was no sign of trouble. No sign of any uprising or impending doom. No sign that the city was even awake.

"It was here that Yeshua wept for Jerusalem," Stephen said, voice subdued. "He did not weep for himself, because this world holds no power over him. Isn't this what Yeshua has shown us?"

He didn't wait for our response.

"And if he claims he will tear down the temple and rebuild it in three days, though symbolic, who will do it if he cannot?" He turned back to us, eyes bright. "No one but Yeshua! You see? His work isn't finished!"

He was right, I thought. And Stephen wasn't finished either.

"Hasn't he shown us his power before?"

"Many times," Martha said.

"Many times. You, Mary, with our own eyes, saw your brother walk from his tomb."

A grin crept onto her face. "I did."

"And you, Lazarus! You were that dead man and yet here you stand, breathing!"

There was a far-off look in Lazarus's eyes as he smiled there beside Stephen. "Yeshua has overcome death," he said.

"As have we!" Stephen thrust both of his index fingers into the air now, marching with great courage. "Do we not have that same power even now? Will we not do what he has done and even more? Will we not ask what we will in his name and see it done? Will the mountains not tremble before us and the storms run in hiding before our voice?"

"Yes," I said. All that I had forgotten crept back into my mind.

"Will we not calm the storm and heal the sick and raise the dead and handle those vipers who would sink their fangs into our flesh?"

"Yes," Martha said, staring at Jerusalem.

Stephen spun to her sister. "Yes, Mary?"

Her grin now split her face. "Yes!"

"Yes, yes, and yes!" Arim cried, both fingers lifted like his teacher's. "Before all the gods and unlike any other, Yeshua would make us gods on this earth!"

Stephen lowered his hands and looked at him. Blinked.

Seeing the question on his teacher's face, Arim quickly corrected himself. "No, we will not be gods. Only have the power of this god."

"Close enough." Stephen faced us. "You must not bring your fear into Jerusalem. It only mocks all that he has shown us! See peace instead of this storm; see light instead of darkness; see his power in the face of death, because Yeshua will not be harmed. In this way we will follow him. If the leaders mock him, they will also mock us, but we, like him, have overcome even death!"

His excitement had winded him.

"None of his teaching will have any power if he is taken from us now."

Yes, I thought. So then, I should let all my fear fall away and put my faith in Yeshua instead.

"Let us enter Jerusalem as Yeshua did, with cries in our hearts for the coming king!" Stephen said. "We don't have the crowds, but all the angels rejoice even now. Yes, Miriam?"

Miriam hadn't removed her eyes from the city. Neither had she smiled. But she was his mother.

She hesitated, then offered a single nod. "Yes," she said softly. "We must hurry."

CHAPTER TWENTY-SIX

WE ENTERED Jerusalem with spirits buoyed by Stephen's faith. Still there was no sign of trouble that we could see; none that we could hear on the east side of the city.

We'd dismounted and led the camels by their lead ropes, hurrying for Herod's palace and Saba on the west side. We would find Yeshua there as well—unless he'd been freed, a prospect that Stephen put great faith in.

The others knew the city far better than I, but I led them, walking quickly. Merchants and pilgrims now crowded the streets and I wove through them, eyes on that palace rising against the gray sky.

None of us spoke as we neared, not even Stephen. We were all consumed by the same hope. Yeshua would fulfill his promise to us and we would see it with our eyes.

I broke into a run when we emerged onto the street that led to Herod's palace, just ahead.

"Maviah..."

But I ignored Stephen and ran faster. And then they followed, sharing my urgency, their feet rushing behind me. The only thing that mattered to me now was reaching Herod's court.

At the gate, one of his guards recognized me—a younger warrior with brown hair and kind eyes. The moment he saw me, he hurried forward and stopped in my path.

"Herod awaits you, Queen of Arabia."

I slowed to a quick walk, relieved. So…I was expected. Something had happened.

I stopped before him to catch my breath. "And Saba?"

"Your slave?"

"Yes. He's with Herod?"

"I don't know." His eyes darted to the others, who'd caught up to me.

"They're with me. What do you mean you don't know? You haven't seen my slave?"

His eyes were still on the others. "With you? I…Then I will have to send word to—"

"No!" I quickly calmed my voice. "Forgive me. Yes, I understand, but they must come with me now."

He hesitated.

"Herod will demand to see them," I pressed, searching for the right words. "The king has Yeshua in his court, and I've brought Yeshua's mother, also from Galilee." I pointed to her. "It is critical that he question her immediately."

The guard blinked. Then glanced between Miriam and me.

"Yeshua, the prophet?"

"Yes. You've seen him?"

"They took him."

My heart skipped a beat.

"Who took him? Where?"

"To the prefect, Pilate. But..."

He stalled, as if unsure he was authorized to say more.

"But what?" I demanded.

"I was told that he is to be crucified."

Crucified? I hadn't heard him correctly.

"Crucified?"

"Yes."

"No, you don't understand. I mean Yeshua, who was with Saba. The one from Nazareth who raises the dead."

"Yes. Yeshua, the prophet."

I felt the blood drain from my face.

"No. No, Herod would never condemn him. I'm speaking of Yeshua! *Yeshua!*"

He backed up a step, alarmed. "It was Pilate who condemned him."

My mind was unable to comprehend this news. The very thought of crucifixion was unbearable. To punish him or scourge him or put him out of the temple, I might have understood. But to crucify?

Behind me, Mary began to weep. I glanced back and saw that Miriam's lips trembled as she silently wept. Beside her, Stephen had gone pale as clay.

I faced the guard and strode forward. "No! There's a mistake. You have the wrong man."

"Forgive me, but this is what—"

"No!" I shouted, face hot, grabbing his breastplate. "No, no, this can't be."

Mary's cry rose to a wail.

"No!" I was moving before my mind could stop me. I slapped the guard's face. "No, this cannot be!"

"Maviah." Stephen, behind me, voice strained.

Images of a Roman crucifixion pierced my mind. Revulsion rose through me, seizing my lungs until I couldn't breathe. To kill Yeshua, who had never lifted a sword, was unforgivable.

But to *crucify* him...

My hands were trembling. In the periphery of my vision I saw two other guards hurrying forward. Miriam was behind me, and I might have turned to weep with her. Stephen was there; I might have turned to him for guidance. Saba was somewhere; I might have rushed to find him.

But my mind refused to accept what I'd heard.

"Where?" I growled. "Where is he?"

The guard motioned to the city behind him. "There, beyond the city wall. Golgotha."

I was already running, sprinting down the side street without so much as a glance behind me.

I had to find him, you see.

I had to know that the guard was wrong.

I had to prove to myself and to the world that Yeshua could not be killed. Not him. Not the one who'd calmed the storm. I had to make them understand that to crucify Yeshua would be to end the world.

Rage pushed me as I tore up another street, angling for the northern wall. I didn't care where my feet landed, nor who I pushed out of the way to reach the gate.

Where was Saba? My mind spun with dizzying fear.

I called out his name, but my voice was swallowed by a thickening crowd that suddenly seemed to be hurrying in the same direction as I—to the north. Their voices swelled with excitement.

Something was driving them. Something was drawing them. Some spectacle.

"Saba!" I screamed. But he was nowhere and I was lost in a sea of humanity, swept forward now with a hundred others. The sound of weeping reached me. Not one or two, but many women, wailing. A whip cracked.

Now blind with panic, I tore around the corner, shoved my way through a wall of onlookers, broke into the open, and recoiled.

The first thing I saw was his flesh, exposed through his shredded tunic. I saw his skin, but strips of it were gone, and his body was a bloody mess. Even his feet, which staggered under the weight of the massive crossbeam he bore on his shoulders.

All of this I saw at a glance, unable to attach meaning to the scene before me. I gasped and felt myself beginning to retch, and I impulsively snatched my hand to my mouth.

In that single moment, all I had come to know of Yeshua and his realm was undone.

Mocked. Crushed. Gone.

I knew it was Yeshua—this was his body, his hair, his strong hands. But it wasn't the Yeshua I had known. They'd reduced him to a slave, the kind bought for the sadistic pleasures of vile men who fed on their own bloodlusts.

And he had yielded to them.

He stumbled to one knee, groaned softly, then struggled back to his feet with a bystander's help. Someone jostled me and I stumbled forward on numb feet, carried along by the surging crowd.

Four grisly Roman soldiers, the kind recruited for loathsome cruelty, beat the pressing onlookers back, barking orders. A woman rushed in with a cup of water, her weeping eyes on Yeshua, but one of the guards struck the side of her head with the butt of his whip. "Away, you whore!"

She cried out and stumbled back.

This wasn't the Yeshua I had known on the Sea of Galilee. This was the one who trembled in the garden, begging for this suffering to be taken from him. The one who stood before Herod without uttering a single word to defend himself. The one who surrendered his flesh to be torn under their whips and chains. The one who seemed to have no power. The one who was only a man, subject to the kingdom of anguish and death.

Yeshua was like Talya now, at the mercy of tyranny.

The realization of his frail mortality swelled through my mind, and with it, a new thought consumed me.

I had to save him!

Every bone in my body cried out with this compulsion. I, who had been saved by him in Petra's arena, could not stand by while they tried to rob him of his power in this arena.

"Yeshua!" I ran out into the street and threw myself to my knees in front of him. "Yeshua," I breathed, battered by dread. "Tell me what to do."

I didn't know what I expected or what I possibly could do, but it didn't matter. It didn't because I saw his face, marked by trails of blood from a ring of thorny vines they'd shoved onto his head.

A voice was yelling at me, "Get back! Get back!"

But I was fixated on Yeshua's eyes, so hollowed by

pain. Terror sliced through me. The anguish in those eyes was bottomless.

From the corner of my vision, I saw the guard draw his whip back. "Away, you bloody—" But then Saba was there, snatching his arm as if it were a twig. Throwing the smaller man back. He reached me in two strides, grabbed the back of my tunic, plucked me from the ground, and pulled me through the mob to the corner of a building.

Saba enfolded me in his arms and held me close, blocking my sight of the horror.

I leaned into him, weeping bitterly as the procession moved on. Saba hushed me gently, though his muscles vibrated with tension.

I could not contain my thoughts and, there in my shattered mind, Yeshua's demise became his fault.

He could have stopped it, I thought. Even as he could have saved Talya. He still could stop this! There were only four guards close to Yeshua—they were no match for Saba, who could snatch Yeshua and rush him far away from all of this.

Overcome by this impulse, I pushed away from him and shoved my finger at the procession. "Save him!" I cried. "Save him! Kill them all!"

Tears flooded his eyes.

"Don't just stand there!" I trembled from head to foot, screaming at him now. "Save him! I am your queen, you are my slave!" I slapped his cheek and thrust my hand out again. "Save him!"

His face contorted in anguish, and his hand remained latched onto my tunic so I couldn't twist away or run.

I was breathing hard, but now Saba's own pain

reached me, and I felt my anger melting. I began to sob and lowered my forehead onto his chest.

"Forgive me," I whispered. It was all I could press past my aching throat.

I was only dimly aware that the march of death had passed through the gates leading up to Golgotha. Stephen would have reached Yeshua, surely.

But I could not bear to look at Stephen now.

I imagined Yeshua's mother, with a broken heart, reaching for her son. But my own shame would not allow me to console her.

Mary and Martha and the others—all were likely near him, weeping.

I was only near death. And near Saba, who held me like a tender flower, silently wetting my hair with his own tears.

The Romans were going to crucify Yeshua.

For a long time we remained as we were, broken and powerless. For a long time I stood immobilized, not daring to turn my head, much less follow the procession to watch. Unlike those from Palestine, I was unaccustomed to crucifixions.

How could I watch such brutal torture?

And if it were Talya?

My body trembled. If it were Talya, I would watch. For his sake.

"My queen." Saba had lifted his tearstained face and was staring after them.

Something shifted in me then. I took a deep breath and set aside all of my selfish thinking and became who I was—a queen for the outcasts and a mother to the broken.

Miriam would care for her son in death.

I would care for Saba. He was all I had left. He and Talya.

Wiping his wet cheek with my thumb, I took his hand without any regard for the traditions of this land, which prohibited contact between a man and a woman in public.

"Come, Saba."

We walked in the procession's wake, silent. The path was stained with blood. Ahead of us, women wailed and men cried out, some ripping their tunics. Others laughed, and still others mocked him.

But Saba and I walked beyond the walls in stunned silence, two foreigners who no longer belonged in this land of death. Our own awaited us, far away. Dark thoughts came to me then like black ravens in the night, and I batted them away, determined to be strong.

We followed the people up the hill called Golgotha, where two other crosses already bore criminals for all to see. But I did not lead Saba to the crowd gathered around the execution atop that knoll.

Perhaps I was too weak—too unfamiliar with the inhumane death penalty. Perhaps my own shame had imprisoned me once again. Perhaps I could not bring myself to watch as they nailed all of my hope to that tree.

"Come." I guided him to an outcropping of rock fifty paces beyond the crowd and there sat down next to Saba, who hung his head between his knees. I wanted to comfort him further, but it was all I could do to numb my own pain.

For a long time, we said nothing. But we saw. And we heard. And we wept. It was the third hour by Jewish time—nine in the morning by Roman time.

We saw large hammers rising and falling, heard their heavy strike on nails that penetrated flesh and wood, heard Yeshua's guttural cries of pain.

We saw the crossbar being lifted into place under a sign affixed to the vertical beam—*THIS IS THE KING OF THE JEWS*. Heard the ropes scrape over the wood as they hauled up his body. Saw them drive a spike through his feet.

We saw Yeshua with his arms spread wide, stripped of his tunic, hanging from the beams, still wearing thorns for a crown. Heard his weeping.

We saw his mother on her knees comforted by John, one of only three from the inner circle that I could see. We saw the others—Stephen, who lay prone on the ground, sobbing loudly. Lazarus, with John and Miriam, dumbstruck. Mary and Martha with other women, wailing. Arim, who had fled upon first sight of Yeshua carrying his cross, had returned to Saba and me and sat in silence behind us, speechless.

We saw the other two crucified with Yeshua; heard one mock and one cry for mercy.

We saw the soldiers cast lots for his clothing. We heard the jeering of those same Roman thugs calling for Yeshua to come off the cross if he was the king of the Jews. Several religious leaders called out: "Let him save himself if he is the Christ!"

We heard Yeshua's words in response, straining for the heavens, "Father... Forgive them, for they know not what they do..."

The silence following his cry was deafening. Terrible offense rose up within me.

How could he say such a thing to such vile creatures as these Romans? They knew exactly what they were doing! They had crucified hundreds, thousands, and each time they knew the full effect of their torture, and they took pleasure in it.

How could Yeshua pardon them in the very act of their brutality against him? How could he release the religious leaders from their guilt so easily?

"He turns his cheek," Saba said with wonder.

Yes. Like the Father who did not judge. The Father who had abandoned Yeshua in the bowels of this horrifying nightmare. But I dared not confess my thoughts to Saba while he suffered.

It was all I could do to not throw myself at Yeshua's tormentors even as they stood at the foot of the cross.

The hours passed. Neither of us seemed able to move. I knew that Yeshua saw us, because his slumping head was often turned in our direction, and when it was, I could not hold back my tears.

Others who had followed him during the past few years now sat on the ground in small groups, weeping softly or dumbstruck.

A hundred times I thought I should approach him and give him my tears. Or rush up and end the torture somehow.

A hundred times I found myself unable to move.

At noon, the dark clouds that had been encroaching upon Jerusalem for the past day finally swept over the city like a black woolen blanket, blotting out the sun. Even the sky now seemed to mock Yeshua as he overlooked Jerusalem, not as a king, but as a dead man.

Those clouds smothered Golgotha with silence, and I thought, *Now it will end*. But it didn't. The soldiers waited, some seated, two standing.

I swallowed. "Saba."

He looked at me.

"What is the Way of Yeshua? Tell me again."

Saba looked at the bloody crosses against the dark sky, and I thought he wouldn't answer because that Way seemed to have failed even Yeshua now. But he did, in a trembling voice.

"There are two realms, heaven and earth, both among us, both within us," he said, as if reciting. "To enter the eternal realm of the Father even now, one must be reborn with faith, as an infant who knows the Father. The means to see this path into the realm is new eyes that see the realm of peace instead of the storm."

His throat tightened as he swallowed. He continued, resolved.

"The means to acquiring this sight is surrender. To deny oneself and follow him."

His words hollowed out my heart.

"Love without judgment is the expression of the realm of heaven on earth. This and the power to chase away the storms."

A tear snaked down his dark cheek.

"He surrenders his life," he said.

Then Saba fell silent.

"And where is his power now?" I said under my breath.

The horizon roiled with black clouds.

"I don't know. But he will send his Spirit to comfort us."

"I don't want his Spirit," I said. "I want him."

"His Spirit is him."

"No, Saba!" I said, gesturing to Yeshua's bloodied body sagging on the beams. "*That* is him."

And then I lowered my head and gave in to my grief.

Saba placed one hand on my back. I wanted to say more, to air all my doubts, but I couldn't bring myself to shatter Saba's reverence. Nor question Yeshua's character.

Now I understood why his inner circle had fled. Why one of them had betrayed him. Why Peter was now absent.

Their master had failed. He who claimed to be one with the Father had proven himself to be just a man. He, like all, was only human, subject to the world and to death.

Lightning stuttered through the black layers of cloud on the distant horizon. A cry tore through the air.

"My God!"

I jerked my eyes toward Yeshua and saw that he'd managed to lift his head and prop it against the vertical post. He was staring up at the heavens.

"My God! Why have you forsaken me?"

For a moment he struggled to keep his head lifted, then he let it drop and his body sagged.

I heard someone cry out, saying that Yeshua was quoting a scripture that seemed to hold meaning for them. But it meant nothing to me. Terror flooded me, thinking he had died.

I pushed myself up and hurried forward, stumbling on the broken ground, eyes fixed upon him. Tears spilled from my eyes and I began to run. Past Stephen who was kneeling with head bowed, now silent and rocking in his defeat.

Past two groups of women seated on the ground. Past a Roman soldier absently watching the crucifixion.

I could see Yeshua's face close now and I knew. Behind those closed eyes he was swimming in turmoil.

Nails like fangs bit through his hands and feet, bleeding him. The serpent that was Rome and the world had struck its fatal blow with the help of religious leaders.

Yeshua... Yeshua...my dear forsaken son...I'm so sorry. I'm so very sorry...

Then I was there, at the foot of the cross. I fell to my knees and gripped the bloody post with both hands and began to sob, head hung low. I was alone there, kneeling in his blood, ruined with sorrow as all of my anguish spilled from me.

I thought I should say something to Yeshua, but I couldn't lift my head. And I had no words. My whole body shook with hitching sobs.

Dear Yeshua, my son... Do not feel forsaken... Forgive me... Forgive me...

They were the only thoughts that washed through me now as I wept—for how long I don't know. For me, time was no more.

I sobbed because he was a son. I sobbed because he was in pain. I sobbed because the Son of Man was forsaken by his Father.

I sobbed because I was his mother.

None of the soldiers ordered me to leave. They had grown deathly silent. And still I wept uncontrollably, as if my heart had been torn from my breast.

Then, when my sobs began to quiet, he spoke from the cross, words filled with resolution and unreserved relief.

"It is finished."

I opened my eyes, struck. The ground at my knees was soaked in blood. Death had taken him?

Without thinking, I lifted my head. There, the post in my stained hands. There, his feet punctured by a thick spike that pinned them to a wedge of wood. There, his ravaged body and his head, hanging and tilted to one side above me.

His eyes were still closed. Beyond him, the black sky.

But now his chest rose and fell with less effort. Now his face was perfectly serene. Not as one simply asleep, but as one who was fully aware of a peace from another world. As one released into an inexplicable bliss.

For several long seconds I was transfixed by his surrender. I could not comprehend his tranquility, his restfulness as his body hung, pierced by the fangs of deep suffering.

And I knew then that the end would come quickly.

More tears slipped down my cheeks as I stared up at Yeshua, so broken by the cruelty of the world.

I finally placed a kiss on my bloodstained fingers and touched them to the cross. Then I rose to my feet and returned to Saba's side, drained of feeling.

Six hours after the Romans nailed him to that cross, he uttered his last words: "Father, into your hands I commit my spirit." Then he sagged one last time, and I felt utterly abandoned, because I knew then that he really was gone.

Forever gone. Forsaken not only by his Father but by the whole world. *Even as I will not die, so neither will he*, Yeshua had said. But Yeshua had died. And Talya was forsaken.

The ground shook with an earthquake that sent Arim scampering for safety.

The sky was black and I thought, *Now even the dark storm laughs with thunder*. A part of me wished the quaking ground would open up and swallow me.

The earthquake seemed to terrify the soldiers. There

was a flurry of activity around the crosses. They quickly broke the legs of the men hanging next to Yeshua, to hasten their end, and pierced Yeshua's side with a spear to make sure he was dead. Then they fled, leaving only a small group of women and a few men to gaze upon Yeshua's slumping corpse.

That evening, they took down his body and laid it in a tomb belonging to one of his disciples called Joseph, because no one had set aside a place for Yeshua, who would not die.

No one—not his mother, not Mary or Martha, not Lazarus or any of his inner circle, not even Stephen, nor Saba—could speak.

Our hopes had been crushed.

Yeshua was dead.

I would have to save my son, Talya, on my own. And I had to do so quickly, before he too was dead and laid in a tomb.

PETRA

"Father, I have given them the same glory that you gave me.
That they may be one, in the same way we are one;
I in them and You in me."

Yeshua

CHAPTER TWENTY-SEVEN

ONLY SOFT WEEPING could be heard in Bethany that night. Death had overcome not only Yeshua, but all of us who knew him. There were no words to explain what had happened so suddenly and brutally.

What could be said when death overcame the one who had claimed to overcome death?

Mary, who'd anointed him only six days earlier, stayed in Jerusalem with Martha and Miriam to anoint him once again, this time his corpse. They were afraid to leave his body unattended for fear that robbers would steal it. We quietly wept on each other's shoulders, before Saba, Arim, and I returned to Bethany.

Some comfort might have come from the disciple John, who would take responsibility for Miriam now, but not even he could find any words. Nor could Stephen, who'd looked at me as though absent from his body when I told him I was returning to Arabia.

Nor Peter, who, I learned, had repeatedly denied

knowing Yeshua even while he was being sentenced to death by the Roman governor. Nor any of his disciples, because all, including me, felt the weight of our own denial of Yeshua's power. It had been crucified with him.

Who dared to speak of hope?

Saba too was silent and kept wholly to himself except to agree with me that we must return to Arabia. Why he so readily agreed I did not ask. Our journey to Petra would take four days—we would consider our options on the way.

We left Martha's house before the sun rose on their Sabbath. Saba took the lead, followed by me and then Arim, wise enough to remain quiet.

Thoughts slogged through my mind as the camels plodded east, but I did not share them for fear that Saba would only offer more of what I already knew, none of which now made sense or comforted me.

We crossed the Jordan, then turned south, the same way we'd come, and still none of us spoke of Yeshua. When we came to shade beneath towering cliffs, Arim suggested we rest to escape the heat, as was the Bedu way.

"We push on," I said. "There's no need to waste daylight." Neither he nor Saba argued.

When the sun set, Arim again suggested we rest, this time for the night.

"A few more hours, Arim," I said. "While it's cool."

And so we put Palestine farther behind us, Arim now humming quietly to keep himself company.

The stars were bright and the moon high when Saba finally pulled his camel off our route, led us into a small ravine, and came to a stop.

"We must rest now," he said. He dismounted without

seeking my approval. He was right, of course. The night was already half-over.

Arim bounded to life, gathering wood, laying out the makings for tea, building a fire, singing under his breath all the while. Unlike Saba and me, he hadn't been so deeply invested in Yeshua. But I knew that once he began talking, he would speak of what had happened, so I remained silent, as did Saba.

But, having his fill of flatbread and a portion of the small rabbit that Saba had caught, and seated with a steaming cup of tea, Arim could no longer remain quiet. He stared at me across the fire, nursing his drink.

"The Romans are dogs," he muttered, spitting to one side. "One day, they will all be crucified. As Saba says, to live by the sword is to die by that same sword. May a thousand crosses bleed them."

The dying fire popped. Neither Saba nor I spoke.

"Could not one of Yeshua's more accomplished mystics raise him?"

Such a simple question, spoken by such a simple man. I kept my eyes on the fire.

"What I mean," he continued, "is that he said his followers would have the same power as him. Stephen said they have done many works in his name, even casting out devils. Did he not raise Lazarus? This is what I told Stephen—"

"You said this to Stephen?" I blinked at him through the coils of smoke. "Have you no heart, Arim? The man is overcome with grief! None of his followers believe any longer. They are all crushed."

"Yes, of course. And so raising Yeshua would—"

"Don't you understand?" I snapped. "Yeshua wanted to die! We misunderstood his words on death, thinking they were only symbolic, but now they make perfect sense. He went to his death willingly." I turned away. "He orchestrated it. His way is of heaven. One can find heaven only by escaping this world in death. He leaves us to do the same."

"Or perhaps he only meant to test his followers," Arim said. "Daring them to raise him."

My face felt hot.

"Don't be absurd!" I said. "Not even Stephen would attempt such a thing. What did he say when you suggested this?"

Arim shrugged. "Nothing. But Yeshua's power in healing so many... This wasn't true?"

"His power was in life. Not in death."

Saba cleared his throat. "My queen—"

"No, Saba. Do not tell me that I am only blind. Yes, I am. But he is now dead. Which is worse?"

The fire's glow lit his round eyes. Now that I'd voiced a part of my regret, I felt free to speak all of it.

"You cannot deny that he purposefully enraged the religious leaders of Jerusalem by entering on the donkey and then taking a whip into their holy temple. I didn't understand it then, but now I see. He might as well have taken a sword into their inner sanctum and slashed the veil in two. Not even the Romans would dare such an affront to the religion of the Jews!"

Arim stared at me, teacup sagging in his fingers.

I faced Saba. "Nor can you deny that he set up his own betrayal. Nor that he gave himself over to death, offering no defense. You say he rebuked Peter for using the same sword he'd told him to bring to the garden. So he pokes his finger in Peter's eye as well. It is no wonder the man denied him!"

My fingers were trembling. I didn't know where all my words came from but I wasn't able to hold them back.

"This isn't a symbolic death. They butchered him on that tree and he practically begged them to do it. Now he calls us to do the same?"

"Y-you..." Arim fished for words. "You're saying he threw himself on his sword to make a statement, knowing he'd already gone too far by defying the leaders?"

I looked away and lowered my voice. "Of course not. I'm not saying I understand any of it. And I'm not denying the power that he had in life. Yes he raised Lazarus. Yes he calmed the storm. Yes he gave me power in Petra. But all of this in life. Now he's dead, and we are powerless. All of his promises have ended only in death."

"No, Maviah!" Saba's jaw was set. His eyes bore through me. "We are *not* powerless. I felt his power. I breathed it as I stood by his side. His Spirit is alive even now, I can *still* feel it."

"Then you alone, Saba," I said, voice shaking. "Peter denies him. John and Andrew and Philip—all of them are hopeless, after so much time with him. They are crushed! Crushed, Saba!"

"And yet I cannot deny what I have seen and experienced. Our eyes are blinded by grief and so we walk in darkness. We have lost all of our faith and so we flounder in this storm. We suffer only because we haven't followed him in death—"

"Are you going to kill yourself too, then?"

"Not in body—"

"But that's the problem, Saba," I cried, standing

abruptly. "Yeshua is dead in *body*! Do you have any of his power? Any of it at all?"

He stared up at me, speechless.

I snatched up the knife Arim had used to skin the rabbit, strode for Saba's camel couched five paces from the fire, and nicked its hindquarters. The animal roared its protest as a small gash parted its hide.

I spun back to Saba, who had stood, and I shoved the blade back at the camel's small wound. "Show me your power! Heal him!"

Saba's jaw flexed, but he didn't move.

"Heal him!" I cried, then shoved my finger to the south. "Then go and raise my son from his tomb in Dumah! Show me the power of the mighty Saba, who like his master has overcome death!"

The camel, startled by my anger, clambered to its feet and trotted into the night.

Tears blurred my vision. I had said far more than I'd meant to. Even more than was on my mind.

Shame washed over me. I flung the knife to the sand and strode into the darkness, toward a small rise. There, beside a boulder, I sat down, hung my head, and let myself weep.

I wept in shame.

I wept in bitter remorse.

I wept in fear.

But mostly I wept because I knew the light that once had shone into my world of insecurity and shame—that very light that I had shone on Talya and all of the Bedu outcasts—had been snuffed out by my own weakness. Worse, I had railed against the master, who had first given me sight.

Slowly my tears dried. I had few left. Lying down on

my back, I stared at the stars, numb to the world. Judah, who had followed those stars to Yeshua, was dead as well. What hope was left for me?

I closed my eyes. Only Saba. Saba and Talya.

Breathe, Maviah. Gather your strength. Your son depends on you alone now.

My eyes were still closed when Saba came to me, there under the stars. I felt him beside me before I heard him. For a long while, I lay still, accepting his presence. Comforted by it.

And as my heart began to settle, I was able to feel his pain over my own. Being so caught up in my fear for Talya's life, I had once again neglected him.

My shame grew even worse.

I opened my eyes and saw him seated cross-legged next to me, staring out at the horizon. Saba, so strong, so loyal, so unbending.

So wounded and confused.

Without speaking, I pushed myself up and laid my head on his lap, holding his leg in my arms. After a moment, he put his hand on my shoulder and we held each other.

When I finally spoke, my voice was faint, stripped of the emotion that had choked me earlier.

"Forgive me, Saba. I forget myself."

"You forget only who you are." His voice was soft and low, a soothing balm. "There is no shame in you, Maviah. You are my queen and his daughter."

He always thought of me. I wasn't worthy of him. My heart swelled at the thought of being his and he being mine always. What beautiful children we would make, he and I.

The thought caught me by surprise. But rather than pushing it away, I let it warm me.

"I also forget who you are," I said. "The tower who is my refuge and strength." The night was quiet. "I love you, Saba. I love you desperately."

He remained silent.

I pushed myself up and faced him, tempted to smile. "Are you still trying to hate me so that you can love me?"

He brushed my hair off my cheek. "If so, then I have already succeeded."

Because he loved me. This was Saba's way, and I cherished him for it.

I sat beside him, facing the darkness.

"Why is there so much fear in the world, Saba? Even Yeshua, in the garden..." A shiver passed through me at the memory of it, knowing now how terrifying was that cup he'd feared. And yet he'd surrendered his own will and accepted his fate, and was finally embraced by peace.

"He overcame fear," Saba said. "And so he was made perfect, as it is written."

He learned obedience through his suffering, and once perfected became the Way for all who would also obey him. So then maybe Saba was right. Maybe I too could have Yeshua's mind and humble myself by surrendering my own will, as he had. And there find his power...

And yet, his power hadn't saved him in the end.

Such a noble and pure and powerful man, I could scarcely fathom. I couldn't help but to think he'd always known that he would eventually die a horrible death.

"The voice, Saba... *I will glorify my name.* I heard it like thunder. It was so real then, but now I hear nothing."

"Because we do not have ears to hear."

"But what is that glory? The identity of the Father, yes, but what does it look like?"

"We do not know what it looks like when we are blind."

He was unshakable and I loved him for it. But even so, he was both deaf and blind, like me. We were lost together.

I took Saba's hand in mine and kissed his knuckles.

"Then what will we do when we reach Petra?"

"We will show Shaquilath the power we promised to show her," he said, gently caressing the back of my hand with his thumb.

"Do you have this power?"

He hesitated. "No."

"Neither do I."

"No. But he promised his Spirit."

"I feel only the spirit of death."

"I know."

"So then, how will we show Shaquilath his power, if he is dead?"

"I don't know, Maviah. I only know that we too must surrender. We too must let go and forgive the waves that rise against us. How, I no longer know, but we've come too far now." He turned his head and gazed into my eyes. "He said that when you arrive in the desert, you will know. We must only hold on to this promise."

Confusion lapped at my mind again.

"You must find a way to let go," he said. "If not for your own sake, then for Talya's."

I looked down at his hand in mine. "It's like stepping out of a boat and walking on water," I said. "Only now the first water walker is dead." I looked up and searched his eyes. "Will Talya also die?"

He could have said no immediately, but he didn't. He hesitated, and that pause sent a chill through me.

"No," he said.

I laid my head on his chest and swallowed.

"If he dies, I will die with him," I said.

Saba kissed the top of my head. "Then you must let go, my queen," he whispered. "You must forgive. You must surrender."

WE JOURNEYED southeast for three more days, far away from the death in Jerusalem. But with each sunset, my own trouble only grew nearer. Nearly four weeks had passed since Kahil had given me his ultimatum—half of my allotted time.

What if we failed to win Shaquilath? I dared not speak to Saba about such an eventuality, because I knew that I would stop at nothing to save Talya. No amount of bloodshed would keep me from him.

And yet I had no doubt but that without Shaquilath's support, any mission to Dumah would only end in the deaths of myself and my son. So then, if I failed in Petra, I would go to my death in Dumah, because I had no will to live without Talya.

My mind often returned to Stephen and Mary and Martha, still under the shadow of misery there in Jerusalem. To the inner circle once so close to Yeshua. What would become of them now that he was gone?

They were still mourning, certainly, but had they returned to their lives, or did they all remain in Bethany to comfort each other?

Each day the sun rose, each night the moon. The

stars remained fixed in the sky, the wind blew, the sand stretched as far as the eye could see. Nothing had changed in all the world, regardless of what had or had not happened in Jerusalem.

Mary, freed from her shame by Yeshua, surely lived in humiliation once more. Stephen, so hopeful of Yeshua's deliverance, would continue under the fist of Rome. The only begotten Son of God was dead, and so the sons and daughters of God were no more.

We approached the city of rock in the late afternoon on the fourth day, and we stopped when the mountain into which it was carved came into view.

"There!" Arim cried, eager for adventure. "We must go. It grows dark soon."

I was filled with trepidation.

"Arim, what am I to you?"

"My queen, my queen."

I nodded and faced him. "Your queen requires your service now."

"And your servant begs to obey." He dipped his head.

"I give you a very important task that only you can do."

"Anything, my queen. Only say it, and it will be done."

"You must return to the desert. First to Fahak, for news of the tribes, and then immediately to the Garden of Peace, south of Dumah. There you will learn all that you can and wait for word from me."

He stared, dumbstruck.

"You may enter Petra first, of course, to buy what you need and eat what you please. But you must enter alone, after us. We don't know what fate awaits us. I need word of hope to reach the tribes. You will be my right arm in this."

Upon hearing that he could enter the city, he accepted quickly. "I am your arm and your voice and your heart. Say no more, it is done." A pause. "As soon as I've been to the city, only to buy what I need."

"And to eat what you will. You must leave tonight."

"Tonight?"

"You must be gone in the event there is trouble." I sat tall in the saddle, gazing at the distant rock walls.

"Yes, my queen. I will leave in the night and ride like the wind. Five days—it's all I need to reach Dumah."

"Five?" It was a ten-day journey at the least.

"And five nights. Arim needs no sleep in the service of his queen."

I smiled at him. "You are my treasure, Arim. All the desert will know of your courage and strength."

To this Arim slipped to the sand and fell to his knees. "Only because I serve a great queen unlike any the world has yet seen." He glanced up at Saba. "And the mighty warrior who has won her heart."

Saba and I left Arim after endless salutations and entered the city of rock as we always had, under the long shadows of the high red cliffs. The massive monuments to the dead carved into those cliffs had once filled me with wonder. Now they only portended doom.

When we turned onto the main street leading to the king's court, we were approached by four guards.

"They expect us," Saba said.

Yes. Aretas had eyes in every rock. Did they also know about Yeshua's death?

The lead guard dipped his head in respect. "The queen awaits you."

I nodded.

They escorted us, two before and two following, to the same court in which I had first met both Aretas and Shaquilath. Again we left our camels with the servants. Again we climbed the steps leading into the outer court. Again we approached the inner chamber from which Petra's council ruled.

It was all happening too quickly! I had to prepare myself. The last time I'd been tested in Petra, I had arrived with victory flowing through my veins, Herod's gold in my saddlebags, and Yeshua's power in my heart.

But now...

Using my shawl I quickly wiped the sweat from my forehead and tried to ease the pounding in my chest.

Talya. I commanded myself to think only of Talya and his song, his sweet smile, his vision of Eden. *It's still within you, Maviah.*

"Inside," the guard said, showing the way.

We entered. I glanced at Saba, who nodded his encouragement, then I took a deep breath and stepped into the room.

This time I didn't see the opulence of the majestic chamber or think about the power behind such splendor. My eyes were locked on the elevated platform, and my mind was fixed on the hope that the thrones would be empty.

Only the king's seat was vacant. Shaquilath sat in the other, alone.

The tall queen stood as we entered, watching us with piercing eyes that surely undressed my mind. If she didn't know already, one look into my eyes would tell her that I was lost.

Breathe, Maviah. Remember who you are.

I stopped ten paces away, not wanting to be any closer. Bowed.

"My queen."

When I lifted my head, she was still staring at me. A thin smile lifted her high cheeks.

"So, the queen of the dead Messiah returns."

She knew.

She knew, and I knew: unless I threw all caution to the wind, I would drown in this storm. With that realization, my fear subsided and anger replaced it. But I held my anger in check.

"Do you not know, Shaquilath of Petra, that unless a seed falls to the ground and dies, it cannot bring forth fruit?"

Her brow arched. "And she returns full of wit."

The queen gathered her fitted ruby-red dress with one hand, and stepped down to the floor, five paces from me.

"It is true. In the desert death always precedes life," she said. "Are you saying that we must die before we can work the magic of a dead mystic?"

I wanted to tell her it wasn't magic, but raw power from another realm, but that was beside the point.

"Naturally," I said. "Something must die to give space for new life. The question is whether you are willing to count that cost." I was speaking his teachings without fully believing them myself any longer. "But I can assure you, that cost is nothing."

"Nothing?" She placed her hands behind her back, eyes on me. "Do you think I am without my means, Maviah? Since your departure I've learned more of this mystic named Yeshua. He requires the rich to give all they have to the poor. He requires his followers to drink his blood, and now he has no more blood to give them."

My face flushed. "And did your informants forget to tell you that he also raised the dead?"

By her look, I knew she had heard this as well.

"Did you witness his power in your arena two years ago, or have you forgotten this as well?" I asked. I was too bold, perhaps.

"I remember well," she said. "It was you who forgot the power. Remember? And now, hearing the fate of your mystic, I wonder if I'm still interested in it."

What was she saying? That even if I succeeded, she would refuse to keep her agreement?

I scrambled for a strategy.

"What good is it to gain the whole world..."

I looked to my left and saw Saba standing beside a table piled with fruit. He held in his hand an ornament—a golden apple. He finished my sentence.

"And yet have no peace in your soul?" He tossed the apple in the air and caught it in his palm.

"Now your slave speaks for you?" Shaquilath demanded.

"He isn't my slave," I said. "He is my head and my heart, and he speaks for Yeshua."

"If you have a hundred thousand apples made of gold," Saba said, approaching us, "and yet live in misery, longing for another thousand, you live in death. Surely you, Queen of Petra, already know this much. So then, what does it cost you to lose so many golden apples if you find true joy in their stead?"

He tossed the apple to a guard at Shaquilath's side.

"Filled with such joy, would not a queen find her place in history as the greatest among all queens?"

"Joy? What good is joy in the desert?"

"It's the only treasure your heart seeks," Saba said. "But you know this already. For joy, would you not endure some other loss? Or would you remain in your misery, trying to eat apples made of gold?"

Shaquilath returned his challenge with silence, and I knew that Saba's words had shed light in a dark corner of her mind. But that illumination was quickly dimmed.

She looked at me. "Nevertheless, I did not agree to save your son in exchange for comforting words."

"These are not mere words of comfort," Saba said. "They are true words that point to a power far greater than any you can possibly comprehend. My only point, Queen of Petra, is that Yeshua's power comes to so few precisely because it is of immeasurable value. If Maviah chooses to share this power, then you, far more than she, have the greatest reward."

Shaquilath blinked, but she didn't lash out or challenge him again.

"Fair enough." She returned her attention to me. "You have told me what I wanted to hear. I'll put your words to the test, as agreed. Show me your power and I swear to you your son will be freed." She turned to leave. "Follow me."

So she had been leading us into such bold pronouncements. My pulse quickened.

"Would you have me turn the rest of your apples into gold at the snap of my fingers? No, not today. I've traveled far, as you know, and I must bathe—"

"Not apples, Maviah," she said, spinning back. "Phasa." For the first time I noticed deep concern etched about her eyes.

"Phasa?"

"She is not well. Aretas's daughter has been ill for a week now." The fear she had hidden from us until now appeared in her eyes. "Our physicians and priests have been unable to improve her condition."

Shaquilath's fear spread to me. The death of Nashquya, my father's wife and niece of Aretas, had opened the door for the Thamud to overthrow Dumah two years ago. Her illness was my father's test, and he had failed along with all of the Kalb. Saman ruled Dumah because Nashquya had died.

Phasa would be my test.

"She's near death?" I asked.

"No. But she's faint with a fever."

Fever had killed Nashquya.

"I hope that your words are true, Queen of Outcasts," Shaquilath said, voice low and certain. "Because if my daughter worsens and dies, I will personally see to it that your son dies like your mystic. Do you understand what I am telling you?"

My palms were moist and my mind was screaming, but I spoke with as much force as she. "I do... And I am telling you that I must rest."

She stared at me for several breaths, then dipped her head. "In the morning then."

"Yes. In the morning."

She turned her back to me and strode to a side entrance, giving orders to a servant.

"Show them to separate quarters and be sure they are comfortable. Keep them under guard."

And then Shaquilath, queen of Petra, stepped through the door and was gone, leaving me overcome with dread.

CHAPTER TWENTY-EIGHT

ALL OF HEAVEN darkened, leaving me in a despair so deep that I surely would have begged God to take my life, if not for Talya.

They ushered me to a room appointed with red drapes and black pillows on a deep blue bedcover, trappings of comfort and affluence. But those drapes became blood to me. And the black pillows tar pits; the blue my sea in which to drown.

I pounded on the door, crying out to be heard, but when the guard opened it and heard my demand to see Saba, he only grunted, shut the door in my face, and secured the latch once more.

I was terrified for my young son, so innocent. I did not sleep. Jinn tortured my mind. I paced, separated from Saba, who surely would have held me and whispered his words of courage.

I begged God to deliver me. I cried out to his angels to bring me peace and restore my power if only for

Talya's sake. Had angels not found God's Son in the garden of Gethsemane and offered him peace? Then why not Talya and me?

Had they not finally washed Yeshua's mind of torment even as he hung on the cross? When would Talya's suffering and mine finally be over? When would we be able to say, with peace on our faces, *It is finished*?

The queen's servants brought food, but I could eat only a few grapes. Wine sat on a silver tray, untouched. If only I could spend an hour with Saba.

Deep into the night I finally lay on the bed, spent of tears. And there I whispered Yeshua's name. Once again I was there, at the foot of his cross, kneeling in his blood, gripping the post, weeping as his mother.

"Yeshua..." I sobbed. "Yeshua, let this cup pass from me...for you. I beg you, let this cup pass. For your will, for the will of the Father, let me save my son."

And then, over and over to the Father, "Save your son, Talya. Save your son, I beg you. Save your son, save your son, save your son..."

I thought of Yeshua's teaching as told me by Stephen: *If you ask your Father for bread will he give you a stone?* Over and over I begged God to give me the bread of life, and sight to see, and power to overcome, even as Yeshua had overcome death.

But Yeshua had not overcome death. If he had, everything would be different. If he hadn't betrayed me in orchestrating his own death, I would have his life to wield. But how could I now trust the power that had failed him?

If I'd come to Petra a week earlier, while Yeshua still lived, I could have triumphed, surely. Why had he told me to stay in Bethany, knowing my faith would die with him? Why had he not sent me to save my son while he still lived?

My mind was again taken to his suffering. The torture of his body. Then again he became my son, and again I wept for him.

"Yeshua…" He and I and Talya…We were all overcome as one, children of death. "Forgive me, Yeshua," I whispered. "Forgive the one who rages against you even in your death. Forgive me, a wretched woman born to die in shame."

Spent by pain and fear, I finally lay unmoving on the bed, eyes on the window. The dawn came slowly yet far too soon. Now there was only one course for me.

I would rise. I would wash my body and face, I would anoint my skin with perfume and dress and prepare my hair, and I would be the mother who was queen. No one could see me so distraught.

My trust had to be in Yeshua even though I knew it was not. No matter. I would do what needed to be done, praying that the Father would heal Phasa and save my son.

An hour later a knock sounded on the door.

"The queen calls for you."

SHAQUILATH WAITED. I saw her first, standing tall beside the bed, dressed in white, watching me as two servants led me into the large room.

Then I saw Phasa, lying under covers pulled up to her chin, hair tousled on the pillow. Her eyes were closed.

I scanned the room for Saba, but he wasn't present. A tall, bald priest to the Nabataean goddess Al-Uzza stood by the window, watching me with shadowed eyes, nursing a bowl of smoking incense.

"I trust you slept well," Shaquilath said.

I nodded and walked forward, determined to appear confident, but I could hardly feel the floor beneath my feet.

"Where is Saba?"

"This is your test, not his," the queen said. "In any case, I am told he spent the night weeping on his bed."

Weeping... *Saba, dear Saba! What have I done to you?*

She looked me up and down. "You look as weak."

Resolve rose through me, if only because I knew I had little choice now. The time had come. I had to be strong.

"Did I look like a conquering queen when I came blind to your arena two years ago?"

She studied me. "Need I remind you what is at stake now that—"

"No," I said. "You don't." I took a breath. "Please leave Phasa and me alone."

"Alone? No one is allowed to be alone with my daughter."

"You think I would harm her so that you can harm my son? Phasa is a sister to me. If you want Phasa well, leave with your guards and take your priest with you. I must be alone with her."

"I must protest, my queen," the priest said, voice deep. "We don't know what spell comes from this foreign god she invokes."

She looked at the priest. Then me.

"Be quick." She started to leave.

"It will take a day," I said.

"A night and a day? Don't be absurd!"

"Until noon in the least."

"You've had your night to pray. Did you need a day to defeat Maliku in the arena? You have an hour, not a minute longer."

She glared at me, and I finally nodded.

Shaquilath spun on her heels, motioning the scowling priest to follow her, and together they left the room.

I took a deep breath, let it out slowly, and walked to the bed. Sweat beaded Phasa's ruddy face. Strands of damp hair lay on her forehead—how many times had I helped her fix that very hair in Sepphoris?

The white silk cover over her chest slowly rose and fell with her breath, which caught once with a soft rattle of phlegm, then resumed.

For a moment she was only Phasa, my dear friend now desperate for help. Compassion swept me away.

But then I remembered that she was my test. Talya would live or die by what happened here in the next hour.

I didn't know what to do. For several long minutes, I just stared at her, afraid to begin what might not work. I had no incantations or incense or special potions or words of magic. Yeshua had used mud to heal eyes, I'd heard, but mostly he used only words. Sometimes not even those.

I didn't know what to do except to pray. I spoke beneath my breath for fear they were listening at the door.

"Father, hear your daughter, who has no life except through you," I whispered. "Heal this daughter who lies ill. Raise her from her illness and rescue my son through her health."

Her chest continued to rise and fall. Nothing else happened.

So I prayed again. Using new words, claiming what he had promised Saba and me on the path to Jerusalem.

"Spirit of Yeshua, who lives in me and who will do whatever I ask, heal Phasa, whom you love as yourself. Show your power to me and to her and to the world by raising your daughter."

The room was deathly quiet save that faint rattle in Phasa's lungs.

Again I prayed, repeating what I'd said and using new words. Again and again, thinking it would take time for the Spirit so far away to hear. But no, Yeshua had said that Spirit was within me.

Still Phasa slept on, oblivious to the world.

Then I remembered Yeshua's words. *Say to this mountain "be removed," and it will be removed.* So then perhaps I must speak to the illness itself.

I stood by her pillow and extended my hand and I spoke to the illness, commanding it to be gone. I did this several times, but nothing happened.

For many minutes I prayed all manner of prayers as best I knew how. I begged God to save her; I cast out the demons that afflicted her; I invoked the Spirit of Yeshua to fill me and come to her aid.

But nothing happened. Nothing.

I remembered Arim, standing upon the table in Martha's courtyard, proclaiming with such boldness that by following Yeshua we would be like him, full of his power and known for it, the sons and daughters of God walking the earth.

His words, which reflected Yeshua's, now seemed to mock me. But of course they did.

Yeshua was dead.

And I knew then that nothing would happen.

I knew, without any doubt, that the power I'd felt in the arena, spawned by Yeshua in life, would not come to me now. He said that I would live because he lived. But he no longer lived, so his power could no longer live in me.

I felt the last of my sanity fall away. Gripped with panic, I lunged at the bed and I tore the cover off Phasa's dormant body and I yelled at her.

"Get up!"

My body trembled.

"Get up! Be healed! In the name of Yeshua, be healed!"

Phasa lay as though dead but for the rise and fall of her chest.

I beat the bed with both fists, sobbing with desperation. "Be healed! Be healed. Get up!" I grabbed her arm and shook it violently. "Get up! Get up!"

Her body lolled like a cloth doll's, dead to me.

I fell to my knees and threw my arms over her, weeping into the mattress now.

"My son...my son, Phasa! You have to wake, please. Please, Phasa...please..."

I heard a muffled voice through the door. They were coming!

Panicked, I jumped to my feet and pounded on her leg with both fists, full of rage. "Get up! Get up!"

"Back!" Shaquilath's voice shrilled from my left. "In the name of the gods, what are you doing?" she snapped, rushing toward me.

But my eyes were on Phasa, begging movement from her even in this last moment. I grabbed her leg and shook her again.

"Get up!"

Shaquilath gripped my tunic to pull me away. And I, mindless in defeat, flung my arm to deflect her. "No!"

The back of my hand struck her cheek. She staggered back, horrified.

Only then, stunned by what I had done, did I fully realize how firmly I had sealed Talya's fate. Only then did I surrender any notion of being a queen before Shaquilath, the most powerful queen in all of the world.

I fell to my knees and clasped my hands as if in prayer, weeping.

"Forgive me," I breathed. "Forgive me, my queen..."

Her guards were already grabbing my arms to pull me up. Her priest crossed to the far side of the bed and was checking Phasa.

"I beg you..."

They hauled me up, but I kept my eyes on Shaquilath, pleading in the face of her outrage.

"I beg you, have mercy." The words I then spoke came unbidden, spewing from my deepest place, where thought knows nothing. "I deceived you for fear of my son. I thought I could move heaven and earth to raise your daughter, but my heart died when Kahil took Talya. I found the power with Yeshua, but then they took his life, and with it, my own."

The words tumbled out of me.

"Now who is there to save Phasa?" I sobbed. "I can't! I cannot raise your daughter. Neither can your priests. Then who? Who will now save Talya, my son? We are mothers who face only death."

The guards started to drag me away, but Shaquilath held up her hand. Her glare softened.

"But the power is real," I cried. "You saw that power

in the arena with your own eyes. I, who was blind, showed you a power far greater than any you have seen."

"She has cursed her!" the priest cried, straightening from Phasa's form. "Her condition worsens!"

Shaquilath hurried to her stepdaughter, touched her neck, then laid her finger under her nostrils. "She seems the same to me," she said to the priest. "Don't overstep your place here."

"You cannot deny that power, my queen," I said. "It is alive and well, I assure you. But there's only one who now has this power. One untouched by all of this death and these lies."

The queen watched Phasa's chest rise and fall.

"Yesterday you assured me that you would raise her. Why should I now believe a lying serpent like you?"

"Because it may be your daughter's only hope. And if I'm wrong, you lose nothing."

"You think Saba can work the magic that fails you..."

"Not magic. And no, not Saba."

"Then who?"

"The one who is still innocent, like a lamb. My son, Talya."

Her brow arched. "Your son? The boy in Dumah? This is your ploy to save him? Do you think I'm also a child?"

I jerked out of the guards' grasp, fell to my knees before Shaquilath, and grasped the hem of her gown.

"He sees visions of perfection and knows the Way of Yeshua! Send for him. Bring him to Petra. He will show you this power. You have nothing to lose. I beg you."

"Do not listen to her," the priest protested. "She lies like this god of hers. Only Al-Uzza can—"

"Silence, you old goat," the queen snapped. To me: "Get up!"

I rose, trembling.

"Saman will not be pleased to release his leverage on such a preposterous notion. His son gave you two moons, which will soon pass."

I was frantic to make her understand. "Saman came into power only because Nasha fell ill and died under my father's care, infuriating Aretas. Only remind him that if he now stands in the way of your daughter being cured, Aretas will deal with him the same."

She watched me curiously, calculating.

"If Talya fails," I said, "then do what you will. But if you see this power, release us with all of the orphans to live in peace. It is all I wish."

Shaquilath slowly paced, considering this new thought, which had only just come to me.

"Be careful what you wish for," she finally said. "But I will grant you this last request. If he fails, your son will not be the only one to die."

Saba and I as well, I thought.

"My queen," the priest said. "Your daughter will not require their magic."

"Either way, I would see this power that I once saw."

"There is no power greater than—"

"Do not test me," she bit off, glaring at him.

He bowed.

I placed my hands together. "My queen, please send Saba with your men."

"Never. He, like you, will be thrown in the dungeon." Her jaw was set.

"I can't risk you escaping to save your son en route,

now can I? It will take three weeks in the least to get him."

"Then send your men to the oasis south of Dumah first. Find my servant Arim. My son must be with someone he knows, I beg you."

"So be it." She looked me over one last time. "Pray that your god isn't dead, Queen. Or should I call you slave now that you have no power?"

CHAPTER TWENTY-NINE

TALYA DIDN'T know how much time he'd passed alone in the dungeon. He could no longer remember how many times the dream had come and gone, and that's how he'd been keeping track of time. Always the same dream, every night—at least he thought it came at night.

Each time, he dreamed he was back in the garden with the light and the beautiful trees and the flowers. Each time with the lamb. Each time with the song of Eden that flooded him with warmth and joy and peace until he became part of that song.

When he was in the dream with the lamb, all his memories of the snake were gone. Nothing could disturb that peace. Kahil didn't exist. In fact, nothing bad existed, because he had no knowledge of good and evil, only good. So good that he couldn't help but to sing and dance and jump with joy. The dreams seemed to last forever.

But then, every night while he was still lost in the wonder of that realm, suddenly and for no reason he knew, the black serpent with beautiful colors came out of the brush, slithering through the grass.

Every time, as if experiencing it for the first time, he would jump back. And just when he would think, *I can crush its head*, the serpent would dart toward the lamb. Before Talya could move, it spread its jaws wide, sank its long fangs deep into the lamb's flesh, unlatched itself, then sped away, hissing loudly.

Again, the song, so pure and beautiful, became a scream.

Again he dropped to his knees and grabbed his ears.

Again and again he watched in horror as the lamb bleated, faltered, then stumbled to the ground where its eyes closed and it lay still. Dead.

Then Eden would sputter and wink out, leaving him back in the dark cell, panting.

Even so, all through the day when he was awake, he only wanted to dream again so he could be with the lamb, even though he knew it would end badly.

The cell was cold and the food was only bread and a thin broth. He had no idea what had happened to the other children—he'd called out to them several times when his loneliness was at its worst but heard no reply. He was shivering and alone, but the dream kept him alive, reminding him that what he saw with his eyes in that cell wasn't as real as the first part of his dream, even though that didn't really make much sense.

Each time he awoke from the dream, he focused on the light and the lamb. The serpent would come again, yes, but until then his memory of Eden could be his reality as much as possible.

This is what Saba had taught him of Yeshua's Way: he could decide what to put his mind on—the pure and beautiful, or the darkness. The eye is the lamp of the body, Saba said. If his perception was clear, he could see the sovereign realm that was here, in his cell, even now. If not, then he saw darkness and how deep was that darkness.

Faith in Yeshua, who was the light, allowed him to see in the dark. So all he had to do was to learn to see in the dark. That's what faith meant—learning to see in the dark. To trust that Eden was as real as the cell and it was his choice which to see.

That's what would keep him alive until his mother and Saba came for him, and they would come, because they wouldn't leave him here forever any more than the dark ending to the dream could be forever.

These were the thoughts that circled through his mind, over and over.

Father, please give me eyes to see what you see. Help your son see the light instead of this dark cell. Help me remember the forgotten Way of Yeshua.

And each day, he did remember. Just a little bit more would come back to him, until he could fall asleep and dream again and see the light—even if the darkness came again. He knew that darkness would one day be gone. It had to.

No one came to the cell except the guards, and then only to bring him food and take his pots. They were never mean to him. In fact, they seemed to pity him. But they never offered him any kind words either.

Weeks had passed—maybe three or four. Maybe even more.

Then, one day, soon after they'd brought him food

and Talya was still squatting in the corner, wiping the bottom of the broth bowl with his last piece of crusty bread, the gate clanked. He snapped his head up and watched as a guard unlocked the door and stepped back.

"Kahil calls for you."

Kahil? No... No, he couldn't go to the serpent now. He stayed where he was, staring through the open door.

The guard motioned him. "Don't just sit there. He waits for you."

"No, I..." He meant to say *I can't go to Kahil*, but nothing else came out.

The guard looked at him for a long moment, then he came in, stepped around the puddle in the middle of the cell, and reached out his hand.

"They won't hurt you, I promise. One of your own has come for you."

Talya didn't know what to do, because he wasn't sure he could trust the guard. And a part of him didn't want to leave the cell—he would sleep soon and dream of Eden.

The guard squatted on one heel and rested a hand on Talya's shoulder. "I'm sorry for all your suffering, little one. This isn't the Bedu way." He shook his head. "I'm only a warrior, you understand? Under command. But I assure you, you'll be set free today."

Talya's heart was pounding.

"Do you know Arim?" the man asked.

"Arim?"

"He's come with the Nabataeans to take you to Petra. So we can't keep them waiting."

"Where is my mother?"

"In Petra," the kind guard said, standing, hand outstretched.

Talya set the bowl down, took the man's hand, and stood, staring up at him.

"I'll keep you safe, I promise you," the man said. "Come."

Talya hesitated, then nodded. But when they got to the cell door, he stopped and looked back into the darkness. He was learning to see in the dark, he thought. What if he forgot?

"Come." The guard tugged on his hand.

Together they walked down the passage, up the stairs—slowly because his legs were weak—and through a door that led into the palace.

Bright daylight blinded him, and he held his hand up to block it. The stone floor was white. His bare feet were muddy. If he tracked dirt on Kahil's floor...

"Don't be afraid," the guard said when he stopped. "We will go out the back, down to the pool."

The pool. Where he'd last seen his mother and Saba.

"I'm sorry for this, but I've been ordered to cover your head." The man had a black bag in his hand.

Talya nodded and the guard put the bag over his head. The darkness was oddly comforting to him now. Maybe because he was so used to it.

Other guards joined them. They helped him onto a horse behind the friendly guard and led him down the hill. The horses snorted. He could hear children laughing and mothers scolding. How he longed to be with his mother. How good would it be to be with Saba again, walking in his shadow over the sand, learning of great mysteries.

The horse finally stopped.

"Bring him! Take that bag off his head! Is this the way you treat a queen's child?"

Talya immediately recognized the rasping voice of the old sheikh Fahak, and his heart soared. And then Arim's voice, higher and even louder.

"Maviah will surely cut your tongue from your mouth and feed it to the dogs. No one may treat the desert's greatest treasure like this and expect to live!"

"Remember your place, boy." Fahak again, scolding Arim as he always did. Talya had never heard such sweet voices.

The bag was yanked off his head and the kind guard quickly swung him to the ground.

"Be brave," the man whispered, then nudged him forward.

They stood by the platform—Kahil, the serpent, dressed in black with his hands clasped behind his back. Fahak seated high on his camel. Arim on the ground. Eight Nabataean warriors on camels were with them, clearly marked by the green and yellow banners they flew on the end of their spears.

Talya looked back at Kahil, who watched him with dark, empty eyes.

Arim, seeing him standing still, walked quickly toward him.

"He is skin and bones!" Fahak rasped, glaring at Kahil and extending a crooked finger in Talya's direction. "We could have taken him many days ago if not for your defiance of Aretas! You wasted many days in sending your men to Petra to verify his orders—now look at our prince!"

"You are mistaken to think I take orders from any king or queen," Kahil said, eyes still on Talya. "I do only what suits me. You take the boy to his death. This suits me."

Arim dropped to one knee, hands immediately checking Talya's head, his neck, his ears—looking to see that
he wasn't harmed. Fahak went on, demanding to see the
other children, threatening great trouble if even one hair
on their heads was harmed. Kahil said nothing to any of it.

"Do not listen to Kahil," Arim said to Talya. "He is
a vile creature, furious because his hand was forced by
Aretas. We have waited outside the city for three weeks
while his men journeyed to Petra. He risked a great deal
in going to Aretas, only because he knows you are the
greatest treasure in all the sands."

Arim quickly checked his arms, pulling on them to
see if they were broken. "You are well?"

"My mother is in Petra with Saba?"

"Yes. Yes, Talya, I delivered her there myself after
Yeshua was killed. Don't worry, I have protected her.
She waits for you there, over a month now. In only ten
more days you will see her."

Yeshua was dead? Talya blinked, not knowing what
to think of this. But his mother would know. And Saba.

They were taking him to his mother and to Saba.
He was suddenly overwhelmed by this knowledge. Tears
sprang to his eyes, and seeing this, Arim quickly lifted
him from the ground.

"You are safe now, Talya," he whispered. "You are
with Arim, protector of your mother and her son."

And then, spinning with Talya on his hip, jabbing his
finger at Kahil: "You see how you punish a blameless
child? You shame all Thamud. We who love children! I
find myself in the lair of a wolf who feeds on innocent
lambs."

"You speak boldly under the protection of your Nabataean escort," Kahil said. "But even Petra has its

price, my friend. You will all be dead before the moon is full, this I can promise you."

"Do not call me friend!" Arim said, striding for his camel. "There will be no moon to light your darkness."

"Enough, Arim!" Fahak said. "Maviah's god will deal with him."

"Oh?" Kahil said. "Is this god not dead?"

"Are not all gods dead?" Fahak croaked. "Yet Maviah, who flows with his power, will strike you down!"

"Enough of this!" one of the warriors from Petra snapped. "The queen awaits."

Kahil lifted his hand toward the path. "By all means. Go." He looked at Talya. "I'll see you soon, little boy."

Arim hoisted Talya up onto the couched camel, then mounted in front of him. Talya clung to his back as he prodded the beast to its feet. They were still talking, exchanging harsh words, but Arim's comment about Kahil being a wolf who fed on lambs had returned his thoughts to the dream.

It was a serpent in Eden, not a wolf, but was there a difference? What did Kahil mean by saying they would be dead before the next full moon? It was just talk, of course—all men talked in such lofty ways. But in Talya's dream the serpent had deceived the woman. The woman who looked like his mother.

"Pay him no mind," Arim said. "You are safe with Arim, great warrior of the Nafud."

Fahak raised his fist at Kahil. "May the gods curse you and all those who drink the blood of the Bedu! If not for Maviah's mercy, you would be dead already."

And then they were leaving, rocking on the backs of their camels.

Arim twisted in his saddle. "Do not worry, Talya. You will never see this creature again." He lifted a finger. "Never!"

But I will see him, Talya thought. I will see the serpent in my dreams.

And when he fell asleep in their camp that night, he did.

CHAPTER THIRTY

—————⟨⟨⟨ ⟩⟩⟩—————

TWENTY DAYS. This is how long it would take them to bring Talya, I thought. Ten days to Dumah, and ten more to return unless they rode like the wind, collecting extra camels along the way to replace those that died from being pushed so hard.

But no... Twenty days. I wouldn't allow myself to hope it would be less. I'd been in captivity here before, and I'd survived to encounter Yeshua's power.

I hardly knew what awaited me this time. But for twenty days following my failure to raise Phasa, I occupied myself with one thing alone: hope.

Hope that Phasa's illness wouldn't worsen. Hope that Talya would come to find me alive. Hope that Saba had known the truth when he said a child would lead them.

They had placed me in a small room with a single window, one small bed, a stone table, and a narrow hall that led to a rudimentary bathing room. It wasn't part of their dungeon, but here too I was utterly alone.

The servant who brought me food gave me no information about Saba other than to say he was in good health. Clearly, Shaquilath intended to punish me by separating me completely from the one soul who could offer me comfort.

I prayed without end, pacing and begging the silent room to speak to my heart. It never did. But what was twenty days? Only time to pass while I nursed my hope for salvation through my son.

And what if Talya couldn't help Phasa? What other than his innocence and Saba's word made me think he would succeed? But no...I couldn't allow myself to think in those terms.

One day passed. Then five. Then ten. Then fifteen.

Then twenty without word from Shaquilath. Still, it might have taken longer to retrieve Talya. Saman might have objected or stalled. Trouble could have lengthened their journey. Maybe they'd been unable to find Arim. A dozen possibilities could have stretched the time.

I woke with a start on the twenty-third day to the sound of wailing from far beyond my walls. A chill washed down my spine and I hurried to the window that faced only desert, listening for the cause of that mourning.

Had Phasa died?

I could not think of it. This wailing might be for anyone of status. Or for a servant or a priest or even someone from afar. Anyone.

That night, guards came for me and ushered me from the room, offering no explanation. Hope swelled in my breast as we walked down the hall. I imagined Talya was finally here and in the very least I would see him. Once again I would hold my lamb in my arms, and if it was the last time, I would be satisfied to have those few moments with him.

But the guards didn't take me into the inner chambers. Instead, they led me toward the back of the palace. Realizing that something was dreadfully wrong, I screamed out Shaquilath's name and struggled against the strong hands that held my wrists.

A hard slap silenced me. Then they dragged me from the palace to the dungeons, where they dumped me in a small bleak cell with a straw floor.

For three days I paced, demanding to know something each time the guards came with food. They offered no words.

On the fourth day in that cell—twenty-seven days since I'd failed Phasa—the last of my hope drained from my bones and I sank to the floor, numb to the world.

It was the only way for me to cope.

And when that day became another, and another, and another week without a single word from Shaquilath or Saba or any of the guards, I gave up questioning and counting days and all of my imaginations either good or bad.

The brutal slaying of Yeshua haunted me always. Every detail was vividly etched upon my mind. But I could not allow myself to feel any more anger or anguish. Saba's words called to me, but I pushed them away. If I hadn't, my failure to follow the forgotten Way would crush me.

I could only survive. I ate, I washed with a pail of cold water, I slept, I stared at the wall and the ground and the torch flame outside my bars. I was alive and Talya might be as well, and that's all I dared believe.

Every night was the same. I whispered a prayer for

sight because I knew that I was blind, then I slowly fell
into dreams of walking through the dark desert, calling for my son, who'd vanished into an invisible realm
called Eden. Every night I had this same dream, which
always ended the same way it started, without resolution or hope.

"Wake up…"

I opened my eyes one morning to a guard speaking
to me. The latch on the barred door rattled, and I
pushed myself up from the ground, still half-asleep.

Four guards stood outside my cell. One pushed the
door wide and flung a clean tunic at me. "The queen
calls for you."

They were the first words I'd heard since being
thrown in their dungeon. I stared at them, afraid to
think.

The guard shoved his chin at the tunic.

"Dress yourself. They have brought your son."

I DRESSED in the plain white tunic and tied the black
sash hurriedly, uncaring that I was seen by the guards.
I flew from the cell, demanding some water to wash my
face, because I didn't want Talya to see me in such a
wretched condition. We stopped at a small bath on the
way to the main chamber and I quickly splashed water
on my face and tried to straighten my tangled hair. But
I was overwhelmed with my need to see Talya. My appearance would have to do—I was his mother, not his
queen.

The moment they opened the door to the king's
chamber of audience I rushed in, scanning the room for
his small frame.

The queen stood on the platform with arms crossed,

pacing. Aretas was also there, seated on his throne, elbow on the chair's arm, stroking his beard, watching me like a vulture.

And Saba, hurrying forward the moment he saw me. He was thinner perhaps, but clean and tall and dark. My heart leaped at the sight of him, watching me with longing eyes.

I turned, searched for my son, but I couldn't see him. "Where is he?" I croaked. Other than Aretas, Shaquilath, and Saba, only two others were in the room, both guards. The door behind me closed heavily, and I spun to face Shaquilath.

"Where is my son?"

"Stay back from her," Shaquilath snapped, eyes on Saba.

He ignored her and reached me, dropping to one knee and taking my hand. Tears misted his eyes.

"You are safe."

"Away from her!"

I knew by the intense bitterness in her voice that something was wrong. But I could not embrace more pain.

I looked into Saba's eyes, grasping for his strength. "My tower."

"My queen," he said softly.

I nodded. "It will be all right."

Only then did he stand, step to one side, and bow to Shaquilath.

I was accustomed to seeing the queen dressed in striking colors with sparkling jewelry, but today she wore only a gray tunic, and her feet were bare. The king was dressed in a plain white shirt and black trousers, though with boots.

It all came to me at once—the mourning I'd heard the day they'd moved me to the dungeon.

"Phasa..." I said.

"We burned her body on the mountain two weeks ago."

I'd suspected, but my own torment had washed the thought from my mind. Hearing it now, my heart broke. Not only for Phasa and her mother, but for Talya, because I knew already that they would blame me for her death.

"I am so sorry for your loss. Any mother—"

"Silence!" Aretas thundered, rising. He glared at me. "Nasha, who was like a daughter to me, died in your father's care two years ago. And now his daughter, whom I blessed, has killed Phasa, my only daughter..."

I was stunned by the harshness of his accusation.

"I did not make her ill, my king."

"She was ill and now she is dead after your curse. What else am I to conclude? She was only ill! Now I am punished by Al-Uzza!"

I could have told him that his own priest might be the one to blame. I could have explained that all of his beliefs in gods who punished was false. I could have begged for understanding in the face of his absurd allegations. But his mind was too darkened by rage and mine too ravaged by sorrow.

"Talya..." I said.

Shaquilath bore down on me. "He was brought yesterday. The only reason both he and you are alive is because I gave my word to Kahil. I sent for your son over a month ago, as agreed, and Kahil came in person, offering to release him on the condition that he be the one to kill him should your son fail."

Each word was a dagger.

My knees went weak. My mind was screaming with objection. But I could not falter now. The die was cast. Fate had struck its own course, even as it had with Yeshua.

"When?" I asked, voice thin and ragged.

"Kahil arrives in three days. Then, before all, you and I will watch your son die a horrible death."

Saba stepped out, enraged. "She is a queen, he is the prince! The desert will not tolerate this!"

"The desert will embrace this, you fool!" Shaquilath shoved her finger at me. "She was the one to offer her son's life if Phasa died! I only follow her own wish."

Saba turned his head to me. "This is true?"

Not in so many words, but this was the result. It was me. I had sentenced my son to death!

Tears flooded my eyes.

Shaquilath lowered her arm, jaw firm, satisfied.

But now more came to me, like a fire from heaven itself. Yeshua had been betrayed to die in innocence, and now my lamb was to die by my betrayal of him. So then Yeshua's words would come true. He had essentially said that my son's fate would follow his own.

And Yeshua had been crucified. If he lived, it was not here, on this earth...So it would be with my son. My fingers trembled.

"Where is he?"

She turned her back to me and strode for the raised stage as her husband sank into his chair.

"He is bound and secured alone in a hole," she said. "As are the slave and the old sheikh who came with him."

Arim and Fahak? I stepped forward, tentative. "Let me see him. I beg you."

"You will," she snapped, turning back. "In three days' time you may look into his eyes as Kahil takes his life."

Shaquilath took a sharp breath, face twisted with hatred.

"You, on the other hand, are released to find your own misery. You will leave Petra and see the world that your son will never again see. Walk the desert he will never walk. Breathe the clean air knowing with each breath that he will never again breathe. And on the morning of the third day you will return of your own will, because no mother will abandon her son in his darkest hour."

The thought of leaving Petra—this tomb that held my son—terrified me. She wanted me to come to his death of my own will, knowing it would torment me more than being forced to watch.

"And if you try to stop Kahil before he arrives," she said, "I will authorize the immediate death of all the orphans still in Dumah. Then I will send an army to crush the rest of your people. Do you understand this?"

For a long time, I stared at her, unable to think straight.

"Answer me!"

"Yes," I said.

She frowned. "Three days."

Aretas spoke to the guards. "Take them both to the desert with a camel and bread. Spread word throughout the city—the one who killed Phasa, Petra's beloved child, will see her own die before all in the arena in three days' time."

CHAPTER THIRTY-ONE

FOR TWO DAYS Saba and I wasted in the desert east of Petra, where smooth, rolling sands met the base of a large red cliff. From the top of that cliff, we could see endless dunes south, in the direction of the deep deserts of Arabia. The massive rock face protected us from the wind and gave us shade from the high sun in the heat of the day. The cold nights showed us stars that twinkled high above, unmovable in all their distant glory, and then the sun rose to offer us warmth.

It was perfect.

It was death.

For two days, I wept on Saba's shoulder and in his arms, overcome with the finality of our predicament.

He told me how he had been held in a cell also, but that cell meant nothing to him. His mind was only on me and on Talya, fearing for our safety. We were both alive, and for this, he was grateful.

He would not accept Talya's fate, you see? Nor ours.

Not for those first two days. He was too stubborn. He was like the cliff above us, always there for me and for Talya and for himself. His faith could not bend; his heart pumped certainty through his veins.

He spoke little because he knew that words could no longer console me. And he could offer me no power to see because his own sight was gone. He only clung rigidly to his belief that Yeshua could not have lied to us. When the time came, we would know what to do.

Of course, the time had already come and gone.

Yeshua himself had already come and gone.

The warrior I had once known in Saba was gone, replaced by this tower of rock at my side.

We both knew there was no way to save Talya, even with the sword.

I staggered up the dune east of us on the second day, and there I fell to my knees and wailed at the sky, demanding the Father's mercy. When Saba came to comfort me I ignored him, because I already knew all of his answers. There was nothing new to say, nothing new to ask.

Neither the sun above nor the sands beneath were moved by my tears or my words. They, like the Law of Moses, only accused me. The world was set, as was fate.

In the end we would all die. *So then, let me die now.*

I left that dune a shell of the woman I had once been, finally drained of my humanity. But truly, I had been drained at Golgotha, when Yeshua died.

That afternoon I kept to myself, silent and numb as Saba quietly tended to our needs, offering only his presence because I could not hear his words.

But on that last night, as I lay on my side, dumbly gazing into our small fire, I let myself hear him again.

"We have to wake before dawn to be in Petra by morning," I said.

"I will wake us."

I swallowed my bitterness. "We return to the very arena where I had power. Why must we always lose what we find in this life, Saba, round and round, returning to our own vomit, like dogs? Why did even Yeshua fail? Why, if now my son must share his fate?"

Saba was seated by my head, and his answer was what I expected of him, spoken in a low, sure tone.

"He did not fail. We only misunderstood his teaching that he would not die, but this does not mean that the sovereign realm is not real."

"Then his kingdom is like all religions," I said, staring at the flames. "They all offer escape from the suffering in the afterlife by appeasing a deity far away, but give us nothing for this life. This wasn't his teaching."

He wasn't quick to respond.

"His power is still in the air, even now. I've seen too much of it. I've felt it and heard it. In seeing him, we have seen the Father."

"Fine. So then we are saved in the afterlife. But there is no more power to see peace in the midst of the storms or to move the mountain now. Is there, Saba?"

It was an empty statement, not a question. But Saba was a rock.

"There is power, Maviah."

"Then show me. Save Talya."

"We show Yeshua's power by loving the way he loved, without condition. By giving to those in need, because giving is receiving. By judging no man, because in judging we only judge ourselves—this is for God alone. By being light in the darkness lest we become blind. By—"

"No, Saba," I said softly. "Show me this power. Show me how to love in this way. Show me how to ask anything in his name—in his identity. How is that possible if he is dead? Even if he had not died, how is that possible? He is he and we are we."

Another great pause. I knew he didn't have true answers to these accusations. I don't know why I bothered to ask.

"He said he would send us a helper to comfort us. His Spirit."

I stared at the flames, speaking in a whisper. "Then show me his Spirit, Saba. Show me."

"We must surrender all—"

"*No*, Saba. I don't want Talya to surrender his life." The night was perfectly quiet. "I don't want to hold him of no account. I don't want to hate my life or take up my cross. I just want to live in a small tent with you and Talya, away from all of this death. Is that too much to ask of a God who made me to live on this earth? Why must we suffer?"

For a long time I heard nothing but the soft popping of dying coals licked by lazy flames. Finally, Saba had no words. His silence was answer enough. And so I had no further questions.

I heard a soft, muffled sob, and I blinked. Saba's sobs grew more pronounced and when I finally lifted my head I saw him lying on his belly with his hands over his face, weeping into the sand.

I didn't know what to do. I had no more tears to give. I didn't know if he was weeping for Talya or for me or for himself or for Yeshua. It didn't matter anymore, because we had all become the same. I only knew that death could not comfort death, and that we were all dead or dying. Indeed, the moment we had been born, we had begun to die.

But when his weeping grew louder I finally pulled myself up, crawled over to him, and lay down beside him, facing the stars. There, I put my hand on his back and closed my eyes.

Slowly, after many minutes, his sobbing subsided. The night became still once again. Saba lay as though dead, and although I thought I should get up and move closer to the fire, I couldn't find the strength.

In seven or eight hours I would rise to see my son's execution at the hand of Kahil. How that viper would kill him, I didn't know, and I tried desperately not to think about it.

Lying there on my back with my eyes closed, suffering with Saba, I was mercifully pulled into the deep waters of sleep.

Darkness. Sweet darkness, vacant of thought.

THE DREAM CAME to me in that darkness, and in my dream I saw a star streaking across the night sky above our camp, where I stood barefooted. Not any star, but a massive ball of fire that suddenly turned toward me, slicing through the air with lightning speed.

Surprised by its rapid approach, I came alive there in the dream, thinking it might not be a dream at all! I stepped back, heart in my throat. Surely a star could not strike me.

But it kept coming, now with a roar that shattered the still night. I had to run! It was coming too fast and directly for me.

Before I could move more than two paces, the white

ball of fire covered the last of the space between us and slammed into the same dune on which I'd wept that afternoon.

A blinding flash lit the night, perfectly silent now, sending a ring of light out from that point of impact in all directions, like a ripple from a stone landing in a pool of water, only faster, much faster, turning night into day.

I could not breathe.

The moment the wave of light hit me, I felt its power blow through my chest, through my heart, through every fiber of my body, and I staggered back. I expected the roar of a consuming fire, and me in its blast, turned to ash.

Instead it filled me with a single tone. Only one note, beautiful and pure. A note I'd heard before.

Talya's song, I thought. Eden.

I gasped, sucking the light into my lungs, and with that breath my body began to tremble. Not with fear, but with pleasure. Peace and joy as I'd never known them flooded me from the inside out.

I watched, stunned, as grass sprang from the white sand, and vines exploded with grapes, and small saplings grew into large trees heavy with green leaves. Not fifteen paces from me, the ground opened to form a well of clear blue water. On the rolling hills beyond the well were camels and lions and lambs and foxes, and other wonderful creatures that I didn't know. Many birds flew through the sky.

All of it unfurled in the space of only a few breaths.

And with each of those breaths, I inhaled the light so that it became a part of me, and I a part of it.

This was the Eden that Talya had seen in the distance from the high ledge. But now... Now it wasn't distant. Now I was *in* it, knowing it.

I suddenly knew that I had been here for a long time. I knew it as my home. I knew the man, Adam, though he was not present now. I knew the Creator, I knew the fields and the birds and the beasts, and I knew I had dominion. I knew about the tree called life and about tree of knowledge nearby, and I spun around with arms spread wide, lifting my voice to join Eden's pure song.

Here, I experienced each note as if sung for the first time. Each breath as a miracle unto itself. Each sight as a work of wonder.

The water there in the pool drew me, so I hurried to it. The grass caressed my bare soles. I became amazed at such a simple thing as being able to walk, and I was also aware of the infinite complexity behind such a staggering experience.

This was Eden, the realm of God, and I had been fashioned in God's likeness so that I could experience life as he would experience it.

The blue-green water in the pool glowed with light down in its depths. I stopped at the edge and gazed into the glimmering water, and as I did, words from my life outside of my dream filled my mind. *Whoever drinks the water I give will never thirst. From your innermost being will flow rivers of living water to life eternal.* This was Yeshua's teaching, for he was one with the Father in this realm.

I lowered myself to one knee and slowly reached out for the water. Even before my finger touched its surface, I could feel its power, a gentle vibration that warmed my fingertips.

A hiss sounded behind me and I twisted back.

Only then did I see the large black serpent with green and yellow and red stripes sliding through the grass, not ten paces from me. I stared at it, wondering at the beauty of this exotic creature. Had I seen it before?

The serpent slipped through the grass, flicking its tongue, eyeing me with golden eyes. I took a few steps toward it, but then stopped when its hiss extended and grew, louder now than the pure song in the air.

Interest pricked my mind. It was curious, because that sound both repelled me and attracted me at the same time.

It hissed again, and this time a voice filled my mind.

What is it that you shall not do?

Surprised, I blinked. But I knew the answer immediately, and I said it without thought. "I will not eat from the tree of the knowledge of good and evil at the center of the garden, lest I die."

The serpent's tongue flickered.

You surely will not die. If you eat, your eyes will be opened and you will be like God, knowing good and evil.

This was confusing to me. Wasn't I already like God? Had he not glorified his identity by making me in his likeness?

"I am already made in his likeness. How can you say I will become what I already am if I eat the fruit of knowledge? You deceive me in saying I am not in his likeness."

The serpent hissed, agitated, eyes flashing. It coiled as if to strike. For a few moments, it said nothing. Then it repeated itself.

You surely will not die. If you eat, your eyes will be opened and you will be like God, knowing good and evil.

I immediately thought of the tree of life in this garden. It gave me life. Yet the serpent said I would *not die* if I ate of the knowledge of good and evil. That I would be like God, though I already was.

Did he mean I would be a god myself, apart from God?

The serpent slowly opened its jaws wide. I watched, stunned, as a round fruit rolled out of its mouth and onto the grass. It was half-white and half-black—not just white like the sand, but white like that star that had struck the dune. And not just black like shale, but black like a bottomless hole in one's soul.

Fruit from the tree of the knowledge of good and evil.

I was drawn to the fruit in a way that both confused me and intoxicated me at once. What had once been a mere fruit that I'd seen many times before suddenly seemed to contain fathomless power.

I was compelled to pick it up to see more closely. To touch it and feel it.

As the serpent backed away, I stooped and picked up the fruit.

The light from one half glowed around my fingers, while the darkness from the other half seemed to swallow my thumb. What power there must be in this fruit of the knowledge of darkness and light! Could I be a god myself by eating it?

A new thought crossed my mind. The will of the Creator had said not to eat, and I had always shared that will. But now I found another will pulling at me. My own.

Was I made in the likeness of the Creator? I was. So then could I place my will over his? I could. And if I did, my eyes would be opened to know more than I knew.

So I thought, *not your will, but mine*, and I lifted the fruit and bit deeply.

Immediately, a deep and terrifying dread washed up from my bowels and pressed through my chest, then rose up over my face and my eyes like a veil. Darkness as I had never encountered it blinded me.

I could no longer see the garden. My ears filled with a thundering silence, and I was deafened to Eden's song.

I spun, crouching with the fruit still in my hand, terrified. From the corner of my eye, I saw the serpent dart at me from the darkness.

Before I could move, I felt its fangs strike deep into the bones of my heel. Raging pain rushed up my leg and I dropped the fruit, screaming, grasping at my leg.

But that numbing ache didn't stop in my leg. It slammed into my hips and gathered at the base of my spine, then flashed up my back and sank deep into my mind.

Never had I felt such intense pain. I threw my hands to my head and gripped my skull, wailing in agony. But worse than the physical pain was the darkness.

The darkness of unfathomable shame. I knew then how it felt to loathe myself. I had always been transparent and naked to my Maker in this garden, but now nakedness filled me with shame and self-loathing.

And I knew then that the serpent had deceived me when it said I would not die, because I *had* died to the Father's realm by becoming my own god, mastered by my own will.

Retching, I staggered for the trees and threw myself behind the foliage, terrified that I might be seen in such a state of shame. I crouched there in my own horror and self-loathing for a long time, desperate to undo what I had done. But I had no means to do so, for I was my own god of death now.

"Who told you that you were naked?"

Immediately I recognized the gentle voice, and I caught my breath. I had heard his voice always, for as long as I had been in the garden. It was the same voice I'd heard in Jerusalem—then as a thunder in my very bones, now as a gentle rain filled with compassion.

"Who opened your eyes to see that you were naked?"

I knew...I had. I had by eating the fruit. Though I had always been naked, now I was filled with shame. The fruit had changed my perception of myself and the world.

There was no more green grass visible to me. I could no longer see the light. I had been separated from the light and from love, leaving me aware only of a deep shame and self-loathing. I was in a death of my own making. Surely I deserved nothing more. In that moment, I despised the serpent as much as my own self.

"The serpent deceived me." I wept.

"And so you have entered deception and death. In this death you cannot eat the fruit of life."

It was true! How could death create new life? I had become a god of death. I was bound to suffering forever.

My surroundings shifted, and I saw that I was no longer in the garden. Now I was in a vast, dark wasteland of my own making. And there I wept bitterly, swallowed by remorse and loneliness, because by my own will I had separated myself from my Creator.

When I could bear my self-loathing no longer, the voice spoke again, now like a warm breeze that drifted through my mind.

"What is your name, Daughter?"

I blinked in the darkness, straining to see.

Again: "What is your name, Daughter?"

Daughter. How sweet was that word in my ears. How deep my shame for having entered darkness.

"Maviah," I whispered through my tears.

"And what does this name mean?" he asked.

"Ancient life," I said. "Eve."

But of course...I was a part of the story that Judah had once told me. It came back now, fleshed out with new understanding here, in my dream.

In the beginning, the Creator had glorified his name by making man in his own likeness. Adam was the son of God, as it was written. And so I too was Eve.

The children of the Creator, Adam and Eve, had no knowledge of good and evil, only of beauty and love. There, Eve, meaning "life," and Adam, meaning "man," lived in perfect communion with the Father without any thought of judgment or grievance. Love, joy, and peace were their ever-present companions.

But deception had come in the form of a serpent, and they had chosen their own will over their Father's. Eating the fruit of the knowledge of good and evil, they had found the knowledge of light and darkness and were separated from the garden of the Father's eternal life. So blinded, they lived in death.

I too had eaten this fruit. I too was filled with the knowledge of good and evil.

"What is the knowledge of good and evil, Maviah?"

The answer was perfectly plain to me, a woman who now judged herself as loathsome.

"Judgment," I said, trembling.

"More," he urged gently.

"Grievance and offense."

"More."

"Shame."

"More."

What more could there be? But then I knew, because I had once known only good. "Without the knowledge of good and evil, I would know only your glory."

A moment of silence passed.

"And so you will share my glory again," he said. "I will take your shame and your judgment and your offense upon myself and undo what the first Adam has done, and so I will glorify myself in you once more."

By first Adam, he meant me as much me as Adam. Adam and I were the same.

"Have mercy on me, Father!" I sobbed, desperate to be restored. "I have fallen short of your glory and am blind to your eternal life! I am lost."

In the way dreams work, as if my words had made it so, I found myself in the clearing again. I caught my breath. There were no trees, no animals, no life that I could see. But the serpent was still there, writhing slowly on the sand, beady eyes on me, forked tongue licking at the air.

A light came, this time not by a star, but as a white, innocent lamb without blemish that now entered the clearing.

And then I remembered the words spoken by the Baptizer in Galilee: *Behold the lamb of God who comes to take away the sin of the world.*

Then I knew! The innocent lamb is Yeshua! He comes to undo my separation from God's glory. He comes to reunite me with my Father in the eternal realm! If I, the guilty, am the first Adam, then Yeshua, the innocent, is the second Adam, as it was written.

But how? How would the second Adam restore that garden of union in me?

Memory of the garden of Gethsemane flashed through me. Gethsemane, the second garden. The two gardens and the two Adams.

In the first garden, the first Adam, me, had said, *Not your will, but mine*, and eaten of the knowledge of good and evil, which was judgment and grievance.

In the second garden, the second Adam, Yeshua, had said, *Not my will, but yours*, and surrendered his life.

He had undone the choice of the first Adam. He was undoing the knowledge of good and evil that I had found by eating the fruit! This was a great reversal!

All of this I thought in a single moment, and my heart leaped.

The voice spoke again, gently. "Unless a seed falls to the ground and dies, it remains alone. Would you be forever alone, Daughter?"

The seed. The seed of the Father. Which is the Son.

"No," I whispered, weeping again. "Have mercy on me, Father."

Before I could say more, the serpent streaked toward the lamb, spread its jaws wide, and sank its long fangs deep into the lamb's foot.

Immediately, the world filled with a scream and I clenched my eyes and screamed with it, terrified that the lamb would die as Yeshua had, leaving me without hope.

Wind whipped at my face, thunder crashed over my head. I was on Golgotha as the storm gathered to mock the fallen Son of God.

I threw my hands to my mouth and whimpered, eyes shut, afraid to see what I feared.

"Open your eyes, Daughter."

When I did, I saw that the lamb was now Yeshua, in the flesh. He hung from a cross, bleeding. Nails like serpent's fangs piercing his feet. And as I watched, heartbroken, the second Adam—Yeshua—gave up his spirit and died.

The world sputtered once, then winked out, leaving me in utter darkness once again.

Silence.

And then I saw that I too was dead. I knew that I was dead because I was beneath the earth, on my back, in a grave. I, the one who had united myself with the knowledge of good and evil and so became a god of my own making separate from my Creator, had died.

How could this be?

I lay perfectly still, horrified.

I cannot express the dread I felt in that moment. If Yeshua had failed to restore me to the Father's realm, I had no hope. My whole body trembled.

There, above me at my feet, I could still see the serpent slowly writhing, staring at me with yellow, beady eyes, hissing. I could see nothing else, only the serpent, now becoming more frantic, searching the darkness for something.

Suddenly the ground began to tremble, then quake violently. I saw the serpent dart away, but a blazing white fire erupted from the ground where the lamb's cross had been planted, shattering the stillness with a roar.

For a moment, my vision was filled with blinding light.

Then I could see again and I saw a man's foot, still bloodied and pierced, crushing the serpent's head in one blow.

His foot... Yeshua's. Yeshua stood before me now, foot planted on that serpent's head as its body quivered for a moment before going still.

"It is finished," he said, staring at the dead serpent.

Then he slowly lifted his eyes and they met mine. A knowing smile formed on his face as he stared at me through tangled locks.

"The Father put mankind in the garden," he said. "Now... he puts the garden in you. And so he glorifies his identity once more, in you." He stretched his hand out, down into my grave, and seized my hand. "What you were has died with me. Now arise with me and glorify the Father's name once more."

Immediately I felt myself, the ancient one, being pulled up. Light flowed around me, into me, through me. I was there again, in the Garden of Eden with grass under my feet and a warm breeze in my hair, standing before Yeshua, who was smiling.

He had undone what I had done! I was restored into the Father's realm. I was whole once more, swimming in his love there in that garden.

I was weeping with gratitude already, desperate to throw my arms around him and fall at his feet, because that dream felt more real to me than any waking moment.

I dropped to my knees and leaned over to anoint his feet with my tears where he stood, but then he spoke.

"Wake up, Daughter." He slowly turned to my right. "Saba."

And with that command, the world changed again.

Because this time I knew his voice wasn't from my dream.

Startled, I sat upright and gasped. Saba jerked up from the sand beside me, breathing hard, and I knew that he too had heard Yeshua speak his name. And now we saw more.

It was already morning. The fire crackled five paces away.

There, squatting on one heel, tending to that fire, was Yeshua.

In the flesh.

CHAPTER THIRTY-TWO

MY HEART POUNDED.

It was him, I knew that it was, even though he looked somehow different. Not different in his body, but transcendent. Yet there in the flesh, five paces away from me, squatting by the fire with a stick in his hand. He had been stoking the fire.

He saw through me, and his gaze embraced me with the same bright eyes I had longed to look into at every opportunity. His smile was gentle, knowing, worn by one about to reveal great secrets to beloved friends.

Neither Saba nor I could move. For a moment, I dared not believe, afraid I was still dreaming. I had *seen* his tortured flesh on that cross. I had *heard* him give up his breath. I had watched the Roman soldiers shove a spear into his side. I had stood by while his friends sealed his body in a tomb.

And yet I was seeing him now, six or seven weeks after his death, alive as any other man. With new breath.

I must be delirious!

But no. Saba was seeing him as well. I knew this because he was seated beside me, rigid except for a tremble in his always steady hands, breathing hard.

Yeshua dropped the stick by the fire and stood, brushing his hands together to wipe away the ash.

Saba scrambled to rise, and I as well, pushing off the ground with my right hand, trying to get my feet underneath me, and then I was up, clinging to Saba's tunic.

Yeshua walked toward us, chuckling. So now I heard him as well.

"I did not mean to frighten you, my friends. Only to show you."

Saba rushed forward and flung himself to his knees.

"Master!" he cried.

I was too overwhelmed to speak or move, and without Saba to hold on to, I thought my weak legs might give way.

"I now call you friend, Saba. Rise."

But Saba did not rise. He was too overcome, sobbing now.

Yeshua looked up at me and for a long moment, we held each other's gaze. His presence had touched me deeply in Bethany, but now I could barely remain standing in the flood of love and awe washing over me.

He stepped forward, cupped Saba's chin, and kissed the top of his head. "Rise, my son. That day has come."

Saba grasped Yeshua's fingers with both hands and stood with his back to me. He kissed Yeshua's hand. "You have overcome death."

Yeshua offered him a nod. "As have you, my brave warrior."

"We were dead?"

"Are not all? But no longer."

He stepped past Saba and approached me, smiling. "Daughter," he said, extending his hand.

I dared to take it. To feel the warmth of his flesh against my palm. And when I did, I could restrain myself no longer. I stepped into him and wrapped my arms around him, laying my forehead on his chest. And there, I wept with gratitude.

His hands rested gently on my shoulder and the back of my head. He said nothing, but I could feel the rise and fall of his chest, filled with living breath. This, not his words, was what I so desperately needed in that endless moment.

When I finally stepped back, he was still there, in the flesh, fully alive.

Yeshua had been raised from the dead. All of his promises were suddenly and unshakably true to me.

"You..." I said dumbly. "You're..." How could I say what was so obvious?

"Alive?" He took my hand, nodded at Saba, and walked toward the fire, eyes on the flames. "But *I* did not die, Daughter. Only this body, which I surrendered willingly as the atonement for all. I am not of this world; neither are you." He released my hand, crossed to the other side of the fire pit, and squatted again, picking up the stick he'd dropped.

Tears marked Saba's dusty face. He looked like a boy stunned with wide-eyed wonder.

Yeshua poked the fire twice, then gestured to the stick in his hand.

"One day they will learn that this stick is as much the fire as it is the wood." He tossed it into the flames. "Both can be here and gone at once. But love"—he looked up at us—"love never ends, because God is love."

How long had he been alive? I wondered.

"The grave swallowed me for two nights," he said, looking directly at me. "On the third day, I was raised from that death."

So long ago! Did the others know? Surely they must.

"They have all seen me. More than five hundred."

All of my thoughts were bare to him!

"They fear death no more."

"What of Stephen?" Saba said. "He's..."

Yeshua laughed, delighted. "Stephen is like a child overcome with revelation and joy. My precious brother knows no limitations. Nor do the others."

"Mary?" I asked, thinking of the women.

"Like so many of the women, she was among the first to understand and embrace truth. She lives from the heart, as you know."

He looked between us, one to the other.

"But now," he said, standing, "I came to tell you what I told my disciples, and what others will one day write, because it's true. Do you have ears to hear?"

A glint of daring lit his eyes.

"Would you move the mountains, Saba?"

Saba's voice was ragged. "I would."

"Would you walk on the troubled seas of this life, Maviah?"

"Yes."

To both of us: "Would you give sight to the blind, and trample on serpents?" He slowly swept his arms wide. "Would you find joy in all that my Father has created for you here on earth, relishing each breath while you still live?"

I thought of Talya and I blurted my answer even as Saba whispered the same. "I would! Yes, I would."

"Would you walk in eternal life while you still draw breath on this earth?"

I was too overcome to answer aloud. *Yes! Yes, I would!*

Yeshua lowered his arms and winked at me.

"Then know what will be written."

An eagle screamed from the cliff high above us, but he paid it no mind.

"To see me is to see the Father. I and the Father are one. You know about me, but do you *know* the Father? Do you *know* me? This is eternal life."

He was talking of my experience of him.

"At times," I whispered. And I knew that when I did know him, I experienced eternal life, but when I knew only myself, I suffered, and deeply.

"But have joy, Daughter," he said, smiling. "Even when you are blinded and feel forsaken, neither death, nor life, nor angels, nor principalities, nor things present, nor things to come, nor powers, nor height, nor depth, nor any other created thing, will be able to separate you from my love."

Memory of having eaten the fruit filled my mind. But he was saying I would never again be separated...

He dipped his head. "The first Adam, son of God, became a living being. Even so, the last Adam, I, became the life-giving Spirit. And just as through one man sin and death entered the world, in the same way through one man, me, life was restored to all men."

"My dream," I said, astounded by his decree. "You undid the fall of the first Adam, which filled us with the knowledge of good and evil. You did this by dying and rising in Jerusalem..."

He smiled at me. "I was slain before the foundation of the world. And even before the foundation of the world, you were already chosen in me. Because I redeemed you from the curse of the Law by becoming the curse for you, my daughter."

His eyes twinkled.

"But there is more. Your old self was crucified *with* me."

With him. What seemed impossible suddenly made sense, because I had experienced it all in my dream. I— the old me who had eaten the fruit—had died with the innocent lamb, Yeshua.

He grinned at Saba. "And there is even more. You were raised *with* me, and are now seated in the heavenly realm in me."

Saba's attention was fixed on this mystery.

"How is this possible?" he asked.

"It is no longer even you who live, but *I* who live in you. For you to live now *is* me."

"Then..." I was grasping for truth, and it rose from within me. "I am no longer Maviah?"

His brow arched. "Are you?"

"We are in this world but not of it," Saba said with wonder. "Like you."

"Like me," Yeshua said. "Because of me. In me. I am in the Father and the Father is in me. In the same way, you are in me, and I am in you."

His words sank into my mind, but they made no sense.

"How can I be in you and at the same time, you be in me?" I asked. "How can milk be in a bowl and the bowl be in the milk at once?"

"In the same way you are risen and seated in the heavenly realm even now. This truth is revealed to infants but hidden from the wise and the intelligent," he said, tapping his temple. "Instead"—he put his hand on his heart—"may the eyes of your heart be enlightened to know."

He lifted his hand, finger raised.

"Then you will know that I have given you the glory that the Father gave me, so that you may be one *even as* we are one."

Even as... In the same way...

Yeshua used his finger to demonstrate, pointing to himself and to me. "I in you, and you in me. As I said, Maviah, for you to live now *is* me. In this the world will know that the Father sent me and loves them even as he loves me."

His proposition staggered me. He was saying that I had been crucified with him and been raised with him and was even now seated in the heavenly realm, I in him and he in me, in the same way he was in the Father and the Father in him. Like a bowl of milk in which the two were one.

That for me to live now was him so that I could love even as he loved.

As him? Was I then his body?

The voice I'd heard from heaven near Jerusalem echoed again in my mind. *I have glorified my name.* He'd glorified his identity by making man in his likeness. Like him. But then he said more. *I will glorify my name again.* By remaking me in *Yeshua's* identity. The Father restored me to his likeness through Yeshua.

Now restored, I shared in the Father's identity and he shared in mine. This is surely what it meant to believe in his name—to join with his identity.

"When the Spirit of Truth comes you will know that

I am in you and you are in me. Only through the Spirit can this be known," Yeshua said. "Only then can you love as I love. Only then will you know that it is no longer you who live, but I who live in you. That in me you are a new creature, that old things have passed away, that all things have become new." He paused. "Would you hear more?"

"Yes," both Saba and I said as one, drinking in his truth.

"As such you have already been made complete. Is there any more completeness that can be added to what is complete? There is therefore no condemnation for you. You are now clothed in me."

He was feeding us with news too good for the common ear. And yet he was alive, in the flesh, so it was true. All of it.

Yeshua spread his arms wide, lifted his smile, and cried to the sky. "Oh what great love the Father has lavished on you that you should be called the son and daughter of God!"

He pointed to us. "Do you hear me, my friends? He has sent forth my Spirit into your hearts crying, 'Abba. Father!'"

He lowered his arm, eyes fired with zeal and wonder. My pulse was pounding in my ears. I was taken back to the dream of Eden. A smile as wide as his was fixed upon my face.

He paced now, thrilled with his own news.

"The kingdom of God isn't coming with signs to be seen, here or there, because the kingdom of God is already here and within you. And now all of creation groans inwardly for the sons and daughters of God to be revealed."

We stood rooted to that ground, unable to speak in the wake of such earth-shattering good news. This is how and why we would ask anything in his name and see it be done. This is how and why we would move mountains and find perfect peace in the midst of the storm.

This is how we would turn our cheek to the evil man and return love to any enemy.

And yet...And yet we were still here, on the sand, dressed in cloth...

"You see, Maviah," he said, smiling at me. "You see how the accuser already whispers, demanding to know how you can be clothed in me if you stand there clothed in a tunic. Yes?"

I felt exposed, but without shame, because I only wanted to know how to reconcile this truth with my flesh and bone.

"Have hope," he said. "Have faith even when this isn't apparent to you. Now you see through a glass dimly, but then you will see face-to-face. Now you know in part, but then you will know fully, just as you have been fully known."

Saba sank to one knee and looked up at Yeshua. "I saw all of this in my dream, master. I saw how you came as the light into all darkness and undid the fall of the first Adam by taking him to the grave and rising in glory. I saw how I rose with you and am now in you even as you are in me, as one."

He took a breath.

"And yet I find myself in this body walking this earth. Tell us, then...How can we walk this earth free of fear while being the sons and daughters of the Father?"

This was the question that had battered both of us. But now he offered us a soft chuckle.

"Yes... Yes, this is the question, Saba. You would move the mountain without fear and walk on troubled waters and see peace in the storm as the sons and daughters of the Father—on earth as in heaven. You would walk this path that so few find, much less follow, and find joy even in your suffering."

Saba blinked. "Yes."

Yeshua gave him a single nod and spoke with utter resolve.

"Then have this mind in yourselves that was also in me, who, although existing in the form of God, I emptied myself, becoming obedient to the point of death, even death on a cross."

Then must I too take up the cross? Must I too empty myself?

And which self? The one clothed in him or the one clothed in a tunic?

"You know already," he said very quietly, looking directly into my eyes. "Deny yourself."

My old self, I thought.

"How can you see who you truly are when planks of offense blind you? How can you see that you are clothed in me when you clothe yourself in a world that masters you? You cannot serve two masters."

Like a thunderbolt, the truth hit me. A soft hum filled my mind as that truth took voice.

The only way to identify with myself as a new creation was to surrender *all* other identities.

My breathing stalled. But of course! How many different ways and times had he said as much? This was Stephen's obsession as well.

My judgment of myself and others, my offense, my grievances, even against an enemy who persecuted me—

all of these were the knowledge of good and evil consumed by the woman in my dream. All of these were like planks in my eye that blinded me from seeing who I was in Yeshua.

In truth, I was safe already in the Father's arms, complete and without need of anything this world might offer to protect or please me. All these things had nothing to do with who I was—they were only gifts for me. But if I put my faith in them, I would suffer when they failed me, as they must.

I'd known much of this two years ago as one who followed him, but grievance had blinded me to it, so I had forgotten what to surrender.

I had taken on my old way of thinking.

So now I would surrender again. Not to appease a god made in man's image in order to be accepted by him, but so I could *see* who I was. I would surrender all that blocked my awareness of who I truly was. I would surrender my old identity to become aware of my new self.

Even as I thought these things, Saba marveled over them.

"And so we must surrender our identity with the whole world—even as body and self—in order to see who we truly are while yet in this world," he said.

In the Way of Yeshua, I was not a mother. I only played the role of mother in this life.

In his Way, I wasn't even a body. I was only living in a body that would soon return to dust. Yet I had turned my life on earth, even my relationship with my son, into a god that mastered me.

So then, my path in this life was to surrender all that I *thought* I was to find and experience who I truly, already was.

And in Yeshua's Way, surrender and forgiveness and letting go of all worry for tomorrow and giving to others were all forms of the same surrender.

Only by holding my old identity of no account could I love my true life. Only as the daughter of the Father could I find joy in the world he had created for me. As Saba had said, hate in order to love.

"Now you understand? Seek first his kingdom and his righteousness and all these things will be added to you."

"Yes," I stammered.

"The least among you will be the greatest. The last will be first."

"I understand."

Yeshua stepped around the fire and drew close. Saba slowly stood, face fixed with awe.

"You have heard me say, love your neighbor as yourself. Do you know what this means, Saba?"

"To love all as much as you love yourself," he said.

"Did I say as much as yourself?" Yeshua said. "What does this mean?"

Saba hesitated. "As if they were yourself."

"Did I say as if they were yourself?"

Slowly meaning dawned on Saba's face.

"*As* yourself," he said. "*As* myself... As my true self, who is in you, and you, who are in me."

"What you do not do for the least of these, you do not do for me," Yeshua said. "In the same way I love you, love them. Truly, even if you can fathom all mystery and knowledge and have faith to move mountains, but do not have love, it profits you nothing. By this all will know that you are my disciples, that you also love one another."

He spoke with great gentleness now, as if coming to the end. But he could not leave! Not yet. I could not bear the thought of his being gone now. I still wanted to ask him about Talya...What I must do...

Yeshua lifted his hand and rested it on my shoulder, gazing into my eyes. "You will know what to do. Did I not say I would not leave you alone as orphans, Daughter?"

The eagle high above us screamed once again, but to me it sounded gentle, like a dove. Like Talya...I swallowed a lump that had gathered in my throat.

"Do you know what today is in Jerusalem? It is Shavuot. Fifty days since the Passover when I was crucified to rise again, and you with me. They celebrate the coming of the Law to Moses."

He seemed to find amusement in this.

"But you will remember this day differently."

With those words, I knew that something was going to happen. Knew because a great warmth seeped into my bones.

He dipped his head and looked at me, then Saba, like one who has brought an invaluable gift.

"In the beginning, the Father breathed his identity into man and so glorified himself and they were made in his likeness." He lifted his chin a little, eyes bright with wonder, and spoke just above a whisper. "So then, he glorifies his name once more. Receive the Holy Spirit."

Then he pursed his lips and breathed on us. Just a simple breath drawn from his lungs. But the moment it caressed my face, that breath became a roar, like a thundering wind that swallowed me whole and pushed me back at once.

I gasped and instinctively closed my eyes. And with that gasp, I sucked in what felt like raw power that flushed out my entire body of all that was old, replacing all of my blood with a consuming molten fire.

Behind my eyelids, the world burst forth with streaming white light, all of it rushing toward me, then through me, shaking me from head to foot.

A full-throated cry joined the roar—Saba, so stoic, was undone by the light. And now me with him, gasping and weeping at once, trembling as the light continued to flow unrestricted into me, through me, now from me.

Yeshua's Spirit. Nothing less could have possibly filled me with the intense joy and love coursing through my veins, lifting me to the heights of an ecstasy I had never known. It was the Spirit of Yeshua and it was the breath of God himself, smothering me with his love.

Yet I knew that it was only a whisper of his full breath, like the simple caress of only one finger, for I could not possibly contain more and live in this body.

I did not stagger, though the force of the light hit me like a hammer; I did not fall, though I had no strength. I only stood trembling and weeping with joy, held in the embrace of that light.

And then the roar went silent. The shafts of light vanished.

In their place a single, beautiful, pure note filled a world of dazzling light and ribbons of luminescent color arching over the sky. I knew that sound! It was the song that Talya had sung on the cliff. It was the same one I'd heard in my dream.

The song of Eden.

That song swelled, filling my awareness with meaning, as though from a hundred thousand angels bound in those ribbons of light.

High and in perfect harmony, like a chorus of women singing with astonishing mystery and awe in a language I had never spoken but knew to the bone.

The lamb has overcome. Over and over, *The lamb has overcome, the lamb has overcome.* The chorus grew, joined by more, many more, hundreds of thousands, joined by my heart and mind in that same language.

It was all the mothers of the world, I thought. And all the maidens, overwhelmed by love and gratitude. And all the children, with souls as ancient as the mothers'.

They were singing of Yeshua, the second Adam, who had given up his will for the Father's. They were singing of the lamb slain before the foundation of the world. They were singing and I was weeping with joy, trembling in awe.

Because Yeshua had surrendered, the garden was restored. I was in it, and it was in me.

In that state of transcendent bliss, I knew that this song had been and would be sung forever, because the lamb had been slain before the world had ever been formed.

The song suddenly shifted, as if all those who sang had heard my thoughts.

Forever he is glorified.

And then more, joined now by a hundred thousand sons and fathers.

Forever he is lifted high.

The whole world joined with that song, which grew to a thunder as all of creation cried in perfect harmony.

Forever he is risen; He is alive. He is alive!

Over and over now, the words washed through me.

I knew what this meant now. They were singing of Yeshua. And they were singing of me as well because I was alive in him.

Forever he is lifted high…

And I as well, because I had ascended into heavenly places with him!

Forever he is risen… And I as well, because I had risen with him.

Forever he is glorified… And I as well, because Yeshua had given me his glory!

Awareness thundered through my soul.

The song quickly gathered into one note once again, but that note contained all truth. It became high and crystalline, as if sung by Talya himself from that cliff in the desert.

The peace and tranquility that overwhelmed me cannot be described. I can only say that I *knew* it. I experienced Yeshua in me and me in him. I was the daughter of the Father, because he was the Son of God.

Yeshua's words from Bethany whispered through my mind: *Once made perfect, he became the source of eternal salvation for all who obey him.*

To obey him… To enter into alignment with him, surrendering my bond with this world to be one with another, the eternal realm.

I was in the kingdom of heaven, the realm of the Father's sovereign presence, the garden restored on earth within me.

Oh what manner of love the Father had lavished on me that I should be called the daughter of God! And now I could hear that call.

I don't know how long I was in that place, because

time had vanished—perhaps only a few seconds, perhaps an hour.

But when the world changed again, Saba and I were still standing side by side, though farther apart and he on one knee. Both of us were breathing heavily. Both of us gazed about, stunned.

It was as if I, who had been raised and ascended with Yeshua, caught up in such a glorious vision, had been returned to my old body once again, to remain in the world as a new creature. Now I was part of his body. Now I could love as he loved, I in him and he in me.

But the world was just the same old world. The sky seemed bluer. The sun appeared brighter. A breeze swept the sand like the gentle breath of God himself.

I blinked and looked at Saba.

There was no sign of Yeshua.

But no, Yeshua wasn't gone, I thought. He was in Saba and Saba was in him. And in me. We were now like his body on earth, to be Yeshua to the orphans and outcasts and all who were in suffering.

To Talya, who was to face his death today.

His words returned to me. *When the Spirit of Truth comes you will know that I am in you and you are in me. Only through the Spirit can this be known. Only then can you love as I love. Only then will you know that it is no longer you who live, but I who live in you.*

The evidence would be the same love now coursing through my veins.

A great calm settled over Saba. There was nothing to say about what had happened—not then. Words could not convey what we had just known.

It was the third day. Petra lay two hours to the west.

He dipped his head. "Shaquilath awaits us."

CHAPTER THIRTY-THREE

TALYA lay curled up on the straw in the dark cell's corner, desperate to sleep. He knew he had to sleep because he was suffering and only the dream could save him from it.

The journey through the desert had been like heaven to Talya after weeks in Kahil's dungeon. Arim and the cranky old man, Fahak, had made him laugh for joy with all their bold talk.

"There can be no doubt that all trouble is behind you," Arim assured him many times. "Maviah will only have to lift one finger to send all the vipers slithering back into their holes. The desert will soon be singing her praises once again. Even now they sing it!"

Talya laughed, filled with delight, then turned to Fahak, seated on his camel like an old buzzard. "My mother is great, sheikh?"

Fahak glanced at him and looked off at the horizon.

"As great a woman as any who has lived." Then, eyeing him past scraggly gray eyebrows, "Nearly as great as this sheikh, who has faced untold enemies and emerged unscathed."

Talya gave him a nod and said what he imagined Saba would say. "You are indeed great, my sheikh. Loved like no other."

The old man could not hide his toothless grin. "And you are too wise for such a little man."

Then everything had changed. They came into the majestic city called Petra, but instead of taking him to his mother, the Nabataeans separated him from Arim and Fahak and put him in this cell.

The fear that returned when the warriors extinguished the light and walked away had left him trembling. Then weeping. Where was his mother?

The woman had come with two guards a few hours later and peered through into the cell. He hurried to the bars.

"You will take me to my mother, the queen?" he'd asked.

"There's only one true queen in Petra, little boy. It is me, Shaquilath. Do you think she can save you?"

"My mother is Maviah," he'd said.

"Maviah, yes."

"Maviah will save me."

The queen looked at him for a long moment then turned and walked away, leaving him in darkness once again.

For more than four days Talya had waited, full of worry except when he slept and dreamed of Eden before the serpent came and killed the lamb.

He was the lamb, he thought, because his name was

Talya, but he dared not believe that his mother would leave him to die.

He was trying to sleep and dream when he heard feet scraping on the stone and opened his eyes. Yellow light from torches held by two guards filled the cell. At first he thought they'd come with food, because he hadn't eaten in over a day, but they didn't have any bowls.

Talya scrambled to his feet, shaking because he was weak, but eager now. He quickly crossed to the gate and held the bars for support.

"Have you come to take me to my mother?"

The closest guard smiled. "Your mother... Yes, of course. You will see your mother today." He unlocked the gate with a big iron key and pulled it open. "But you can't go to your mother looking like a rat. Put this on."

The warrior handed him a clean, folded tunic, white like Saba's. He quickly pulled off his muddy rags and slipped into the fresh clothing.

"Now this around your neck." The man handed him a necklace with a large wooden pendant on it. Two sticks of wood crossing each other, bound by twine in the middle. The chain was far too big for him, but maybe this is what boys in Petra wore for special times.

"Good. Come with us."

They led him from the dungeon and out into the morning light.

"We're going to the palace?" he asked.

"To the arena. That's where your mother will come for you."

He'd never seen an arena, though he knew the story of how his mother had first become queen.

Talya walked on bare feet, holding the hand of one of the warriors, down a long path into the city. Merchants and Bedu dressed in many different colors turned to watch them. The moment they saw him, they hurried on ahead, as if they all knew what was going to happen. Children ran alongside him, pointing and laughing.

He wasn't sure what this meant, so he smiled with them. "I'm going to see my mother," he said to a small boy.

The boy grinned, toothless, then took his hand, but a woman yelled at him and he ducked away.

Soon many hundreds were running ahead from all directions, and Talya could only assume they were going to the arena, the place where queens were made. Other warriors had joined in, riding horses behind them. It was a big day in Petra. Maviah, the queen from the desert, had come for him.

"Are we close?" he asked one of the guards.

The man pointed to the red cliffs far off. "There."

"There?" Talya stopped. "I don't know if I can go so far." He looked down at his legs. "My feet are bleeding."

The warrior looked him over, then motioned for one of the warriors on a horse. They put him on its back in front of the guard.

When they turned onto a wide path that lead up to the arena, Talya saw that all of Petra must have heard the news, because many hundreds were flowing through the tall gates. All looked at him, many cheering and laughing as they approached the towering walls.

Many also glared at him, and that made him nervous, but he dared not believe any thoughts that darkened his mind. Not now, not after so long.

Not even when, instead of taking him into the arena, they led him underground, beneath the massive walls to a small cell cut into the rock. Not even when they left him alone behind bars once more, without saying a word or answering any of his questions.

Not until he'd been in the cell for a long time, seated on the ground with his new tunic hitched up so he didn't get any dirt on it.

Then he could hold back the dark thoughts no longer. And when they came, they came like a flood in a wadi after a heavy storm.

If his mother was here, she would never allow him to be held in a cell so long. Something was wrong. Something was terribly wrong.

He was the lamb in his dream, and the queen was going to kill him because his mother had failed.

Panicked, Talya hurried to the bars and cried out into the dim light. "Mother!" His voice echoed through the stone passageway. "Mother!"

A beast in his mind growled. Or it could have been a serpent, because his mind was too scrambled to hear anything but fear.

"Mother!" he screamed.

A door opened. "Silence in there!"

The door clunked shut.

Talya backed away from the bars, blinking. He thought he should sleep. If he could dream and remember the place of peace, then he would be safe until his—

The door opened again and two guards marched to the cell, unlocked the gate, and motioned him forward. He walked out, feet numb. They each took one of his hands and led him down the passageway.

"Is my mother here?" he asked.

Without answering, they pushed open heavy wooden doors and led him into the daylight.

Talya stopped, blinking in the bright sun, stunned. Many thousands of people sat or stood in the huge bowl-shaped arena carved from the red mountain. More than all of the people his mother had gathered in the desert.

Some were pointing at him. Then they all turned to watch him and fell quiet.

A high platform sat at the far end where the queen, Shaquilath, and what must be the king sat in tall chairs, both facing him.

The ground was dusty and flat except for a tall post in the middle. A great hush had filled the arena.

"Come," one of the guards grunted, tugging him forward.

They led him out to the wooden post. An iron ring on a thick chain hung from the post, and they clamped this around his wrist, then turned and walked back out through the heavy doors.

The moment it slammed shut, the crowd began to cheer.

Talya stood chained to the post in the center of the huge dirt field, trembling in fear.

I HEARD the roar beyond the high cliff just ahead of us, and I pulled up. The sound was unmistakable—all of Petra had gathered in the arena below us. They had begun. Hearing so many throats joined in unison, my heart went still.

"Hurry!" Saba said, dropping from his camel into a run.

We had ridden the camels hard without uttering a word, cutting time by making a direct route to the arena from the cliffs above. By doing so we could avoid the city streets and any guards who might be posted to intercept us, but we would have to descend into the stadium through the seated crowd.

I slid to the rock surface and ran after Saba, unnerved by what I might see when we broke over the edge to view the arena below. My mind was caught between the staggering reality of peace and love that Yeshua had shown us, and this realm where flesh bled and bone broke.

Two halves. The one half felt a deep and gut-wrenching compassion for my son, for whom I would lay down my life without hesitation. How my mind longed to see him safe; how my arms ached to hold him!

The other half, so brightened with the light of Yeshua's risen reality in me and in Talya, felt no more dread for Talya than Yeshua did.

Had he not wept for Mary rather than Lazarus, his dear friend?

The juxtaposition within me felt like two selves, each battling for supremacy. But in the wake of seeing as I had seen, the dread I'd felt since Yeshua's crucifixion was gone. Only deep compassion remained.

Love, Yeshua had said. This was the manifestation of heaven on earth—for me, as Yeshua, to show compassion to those hurting.

Again the crowd's roar, louder now.

Saba pulled up sharply at the cliff's edge and I knew he'd seen. Then I arrived, grabbing his arm so as not to plunge over the precipice.

There, only a stone's throw below us, Petra's arena was filled to overflowing with countless souls gathered to avenge Phasa's death. There, on the platform, Shaquilath and Aretas soaked in the adulation of their people.

And there, at the center, a post, and chained to that post: Talya, all alone.

Immediately, half my mind screamed its offense. My peace was shattered. To see my son so frail, thinner than he'd been before, trembling under the crushing roar of the crowd—how could this be?

All was well with my soul, I knew this. I knew it but my mind was forgetting, even now, a mere three hours after Yeshua had shown me all was well.

Tears sprang to my eyes unbidden. For a moment I felt like I was back in that grave of my dream, clawing for the surface.

I wanted to throw myself from that cliff and fly to my son's rescue. I wanted to tear apart any enemy that would lay a single hand on him. I wanted to kill them all—every single soul who had gathered for this savage feast.

Love, my daughter. Love them as yourself. Love even your enemy.

I blinked.

I glanced at Saba. Saba, whose eyes were fired with rage. And then he was springing onto a small path that led down the cliff, and I knew that his mind was gone on that rage.

"Saba!" Part of me wanted him to go, because I knew he was going to save my son. But these weren't the words that came to my mouth. "No, you can't take up the sword—"

"To live by the sword is to die by the sword," he snapped, spinning back. "This is only a law and I will accept its consequence!"

"Yes! You will! You'll be killed!"

"But my son," he said, shoving his finger at the arena, "will not!"

And then he was gone, catapulting himself over a boulder and dropping out of sight, leaving me smothered by confusion and fear.

The crowd quieted and I turned to see that Shaquilath had lifted her hand. I could hear her every word rising up from the arena.

"There is only one way for all of man to live on the face of this earth. This is the way of the gods. For every threat against us, we must offer another threat. For every failure, another failure. For every eye taken, we will take an eye. For every hand, we sever a hand. For every life, we take a life."

I could not breathe.

"Today," she cried, "the way of the Bedu and of all living gods in the heavens will be honored."

No... No, I could not allow this. There was another way.

And then I was tearing down the mountain to save my son.

THE QUEEN'S words echoed through Talya's ears as he searched the rows of people for his mother. She had to be here. Maviah, who'd saved him from death in the desert as an orphan, would save him now.

He jerked his head around, frightened, searching. Guards were stationed around the entire top rim; people crowded the long stone benches that circled the arena.

But he couldn't find her.

Still he looked. The queen was still talking, standing on that platform, but he could hardly hear her over the pounding of his heart.

"Mother!" he cried, turning all the way around. His

voice was lost to the sound of a cheer—the queen had said something. "Mother!"

But she wasn't there.

She wasn't anywhere. He looked back at the queen far across the arena.

"It was Maviah, hailed as queen among outcasts, who once showed us her power in this very arena," she cried, pacing. "Maviah, who offered up her own son in exchange for power in Dumah when the power of her god, Yeshua, failed her. Maviah, who tricked me, promising to raise my daughter from her illness, only to curse her with death. Maviah, who runs for her life in the desert, forsaking her only son in his darkest hour."

This couldn't be true.

The queen pointed at Talya from across the arena.

"It is therefore Maviah's son who will die today, according to her own will, at the hand of her vowed enemy."

She pointed to the doors on Talya's right.

"I give you, Kahil bin Saman, prince of the Thamud and ruler of Dumah!"

The heavy wooden doors opened and Kahil rode in, seated tall on a white stallion. He was dressed in black like the last time Talya had seen him. He dipped his head to the queen, then turned his horse toward the post.

No one spoke. They were all looking at him, eager.

Talya began to panic. His mother wasn't coming. Kahil was going to kill him.

He was shaking now, watching the horse plod toward him. All he could see was that horse and the man seated on it, watching him, sneering. The world started to go black.

"Talya!"

He heard his name far away and he thought, *My mother's calling to me.*

"Talya!"

This time he heard his name like a scream from high on his left. This time Kahil also turned his head.

Talya slowly turned to look. She was there, standing at the arena's top rim, reaching out for him, blocked by the people in front of her. Everywhere people were pointing in her direction, calling out. Two guards were rushing toward her, then grabbing her arms.

His heart jumped. She'd come!

"Mother!"

He ran toward her, forgetting that he was chained until he was jerked back and fell to his seat. "Mother, save me!"

"Talya!" She was crying. "My son!"

"Silence!" the queen cried.

But the crowd's commotion only swelled.

Talya scrambled to his feet and was about to call out again when Shaquilath lifted her hand and spoke in a clear voice.

"The woman has come to watch her son die. Allow her the decency we would allow any mother." She lowered her arm. "And then Kahil will take her as spoils before he crushes her bones in the desert."

He heard Maviah cry, "My son, listen to your mother—" One of the guards slapped his mother's face, silencing her.

Kahil chuckled softly.

"Do you think the queen of scavengers can save you, little boy?"

He couldn't think straight. The world seemed to

crush him. His mother was going to be killed because of him.

He jerked his head toward her. "Run away! Run, Mother!"

Laughter batted at his ears. And his mother didn't run. She couldn't. There were three guards around her now, holding her.

She wasn't struggling. She was only looking at him with tears running down her face, trying to help him be brave. And so he had to be brave for her. His bones were shaking and he could hardly breathe, but he had to be brave.

Kahil faced the crowd and spoke so that all could hear him.

"There came into the desert near Dumah a man called Judah, who desired to destroy me. The queen of the scavengers," he cried, pointing up at Maviah, "called him her lion even as she calls this boy, Talya, her lamb. He told me this when I hung him from his neck until he was dead."

Someone laughed and more joined him.

"So then he was no lion, was he?"

"He was not," many cried. "No lion! What lion can defeat the Bedu?"

Kahil silenced them with a raised hand.

"But I have brought him back to life." He reached for a waterskin tied to his saddle and nudged the stallion up to Talya. Now he was close. Talya could smell the horse's sweat, see its frightened eyes.

He didn't move because he had to be brave and was also too frightened.

Kahil pulled the leather string that sealed the bag. "I have brought that lion back to life to feed on the lamb!"

Using both hands, he heaved the contents of the skin at Talya.

He might have ducked, but it came too fast, splashing onto his face and chest, soaking his white tunic.

But it wasn't water, Talya realized. It was blood.

Kahil flipped a key in the air and Talya watched it land in the dust near his feet. Why? He couldn't think...What was happening?

"I give you..." Kahil turned his horse and walked it away, arm extended to a small side door twenty paces away. "Maviah's lion of Judah!"

The hatch slid open and a lion stalked into the arena, growling, eyes shifting between the receding horse and Talya.

And then only Talya.

Gasps filled the arena.

Talya understood what was happening. The lion would smell the blood. This is how Bedu often lured them during a hunt, with a lamb soaked in blood.

The lion was going to kill him.

Talya could not move.

CHAPTER THIRTY-FOUR

⸺⸺

I STOOD as though in death, caught between worlds, because to succumb to either felt like suicide to me. I knew what was happening. I knew it as Yeshua had surely known a kind of death in Gethsemane.

To embrace the rage boiling through my blood would surely leave me in a hell of my own making. Like those who'd driven fangs deep into Yeshua's flesh as the crowd looked on, the vipers in this arena were guilty of terrible savagery. I could not forgive them, for they knew what they did.

To surrender to the whisper deep within me, the one that spoke of peace in the midst of this brutality, felt like its own kind of death. A death of the mind.

So I stood still, trembling from head to foot as Kahil dumped the blood on Talya's body.

Sickened to my bones as he mocked Judah and my innocent lamb.

Horrified as the lion came out, growling. It wasn't

372 • TED DEKKER

enough for Kahil to kill Talya. He would subject innocence to torturous mockery.

Hatred, grievance, fear, terror, judgment, rage. These
were all the fruit of the knowledge of good and evil.

Who are you, Maviah?

I watched, ravaged by anguish, as Talya flung himself
at the key that Kahil had dropped. Wept in silence as he
frantically freed himself from the ring around his thin
wrist while the lion approached, circling, preying, eyes
fixed on my son.

Who is Talya?

I dared tear my eyes away from him for a moment
to search for Saba, desperate to see him there even now,
rushing in to save my son.

A movement near the post recaptured my attention.
Talya was staggering toward the pole, then spinning behind it. The lion started forward in a crouch, and I
knew . . .

The sound of thin, ragged whimpering reached my
ears. It came from Talya, trembling behind that post,
seeing the lion coming faster now, knowing that in only
moments it would rip into him.

Who are you, Maviah?

In that moment, I didn't care who I was. How could
any mother with a sane mind care? I would gladly spend
my life in hell to save him.

Who is Talya?

From the corner of my eye, I saw the large wooden
door across the arena swing wide, and I jerked my head
to see Saba standing in the threshold, chest heaving. He
was stripped of his tunic and his dark muscles glistened
in the hot sun. There was a bloodied sword in his hand.

He'd come! He sprinted for Talya now, leaning into

each stride like a god come to earth, and for a moment my heart dared to soar. Behind him, guards poured through those same doors, fanning out. Scattered cries of alarm from the crowd swelled to a cheer. They thought this was part of the sick play to satisfy their bloodlust.

Who is Saba?

Shaquilath had stood and rushed to the edge of the platform. Aretas pushed himself to his feet. Kahil's stallion sidestepped, disturbed by the intrusion. Kahil, slouched in his saddle, froze at the sight of my warrior.

I knew, far back in my mind, that Saba could kill the lion; that he could kill a dozen warriors and more; that he could reach Kahil and cleanly separate his head from his shoulders. But I also knew that he could not stand against the thousands at Aretas's command, who even now rushed to seal off the arena.

Yet none of this seemed to matter. We would all die. They would kill our bodies.

I blinked, and in that blink, I let go of something deep in me that was desperately clinging to all the old truths that had enslaved me for so long.

Who are you?

This time I heard the voice aloud as if spoken from deep within me and from the sky at once, rumbling like thunder as it had near Jerusalem. And with the voice, the world seemed to stall. Motion slowed. Sound fell away.

A peace beyond my understanding settled over me.

The gathered masses were still cheering. I could see that, but Saba...

Saba had pulled up in the middle of the stadium,

panting hard, sword in his hand by his side, staring at Talya and the lion only twenty paces from him.

He'd heard it too.

"Saba!" The cry sounded distant.

It was Talya, crying out for Saba, trembling behind the post. My son hadn't heard.

"Saba!"

Who are you? Now the voice whispered through my mind like a warm, gentle breeze.

They have all seen me… They fear death no more…

And I knew that those who had seen him and more would willingly give their lives in arenas just like this, because they no longer feared death any more than I did in that moment. Fear was gone.

But my son was in fear… My son, who knew Yeshua and was the son of my Father as much as I was his daughter.

We were safe. Nothing but our own grievance could truly harm us now. Because it was impossible to hold any grievance and know your true self, already at peace.

There in the desert, the Father and Yeshua and his Spirit flooded me with light.

But Talya…

Compassion for him washed over my heart, replacing all the fear I had for his life. I no longer needed him to complete me, because I understood now that I was already complete. I needed nothing from him, not even his love. I only wanted to give all that I had to him, to pour myself out for him, to lay down my own body for him, not because I was desperate for him as my son, but because my surrender would give us both living water.

For the first time since I had called him my son, I loved Talya as Yeshua loved him.

I knew all of this because Yeshua had breathed on me. Saba stood still, arrested by the same breath, I thought. The sword fell from his hand and he dropped to one knee, seemingly oblivious to the guards who rushed toward him, and to Talya, who called out for him.

I saw it all unfold in a great silence save one note that now flowed through my mind, pure and high—the note every fiber of my being knew. The world before me was moving slowly as if in a dream, but the crystalline note filling my awareness was no dream.

Talya knew this love. He who had first heard that song of Eden would hear it again. He would remember who he was and find peace in his storm.

I closed my eyes and I opened my mouth and allowed my throat to give voice to that song. I sent it out into the arena for my son and for Saba and for all who had ears to hear.

THE MOMENT SABA stopped and fell to one knee, the lion growled and slowly swung its head back to Talya. The people were screaming now, crying out for the boy's death, urging the lion to attack.

"Saba!" Talya grabbed the post, keeping it between him and the lion, but he knew the post wouldn't save him. His body began to shake again. "Saba!"

But the crowd was too loud and the lion was moving toward him again and Talya knew no one was going to save him.

It was then that he heard the note. Just one, cutting through the roar of the crowd, piercing his mind. But he knew that note! Only this time, it sounded like his mother. It was her voice!

Talya jerked his head up and saw her again, there at the top. Her eyes were closed and she was reaching one hand toward him, singing. To him.

Immediately everything was quiet except for that one note. The arena was still there all around him, so he knew he wasn't dreaming, but everything was moving slowly and strangely now.

In that one note he could hear her speaking to him gently in his childhood language, which she didn't know. But she knew it now and he could hear every word as if they were the only words in the world.

"Listen to me, Talya. You are safe. You don't need to be afraid any longer. You already believe. You've already seen what so few have seen. You too were chosen before the world began."

It was his mother's voice, but also the voice from the dream! This was Yeshua too? Tears sprang to his eyes as her words touched his mind.

"I want you to let go of everything you see here and find that place deep inside of you that's already at peace, even though you don't feel peaceful right now. But you are already at peace in the Father's realm. Can you do that?"

He held on to each word, believing, but still gripped by fear.

"Let me show you what you saw and believed. Can you do that for me, Talya?"

"Yes," he sobbed.

"I know you're afraid, but I want you to close your eyes and see who you really are. How beautiful you are. How precious you are. I'll be right here, holding your hand."

"Close my eyes?"

"Yes, sweetheart. Just close your eyes and trust my voice. Then you will see."

Now desperate to see, Talya closed his eyes just like his mother told him to. And the moment he did, white light filled the world.

And then he was in the familiar dream once again. He saw all of it all at once as if no time passed.

He saw the garden and felt the same love he'd felt before.

He saw the woman and the serpent and felt the fear. But this time he saw more.

He saw Yeshua crushing the serpent's head under his heel.

Then Yeshua breathed into him like the Father had breathed into the first man and his mind lit up with a thousand stars.

He gasped. He gasped because he saw who he really was. How greatly his Father loved him. He was the Father's son, loved as no other son and all sons at once!

Streams of living light flowed into his body, shaking him from head to foot, not only here in the world of light, but here in the arena too.

Yeshua was laughing in that light, and Talya wanted to laugh with him. He wanted to run and leap and roll in the grass and jump up to touch the nearest star because he knew he could. He wanted to throw his arms around Yeshua and hug the lamb and dance with the woman who looked like his mother.

He wanted to do all of this because he'd never, not even in his dreams, felt such joy.

I DIDN'T know what Talya heard other than the note I sang—the same one he himself had once sung from the cliff. I was only loving him the same way that Yeshua had told us to—as myself.

But when I opened my eyes I saw that his body was trembling. A look of wonder had filled his face and I knew that he was enveloped in a realm as real as this one here.

Only a few moments had passed. The warriors had spread out and were just approaching Saba from behind. Saba, who knelt on one knee with his eyes closed and arms spread wide, at peace. The guards who'd held me released my arms and I extended one hand toward Talya.

Still I sang.

The lion was still approaching Talya, crouched low, preparing to launch itself onto its bloodied prey.

Sing, Talya, sing! I thought. *Join me in the sovereign realm and sing to your Father!*

He immediately opened his mouth and began to sing the same note with me. I could feel it more than hear it. But even more, I could see it. Because the moment Talya began to sing, everything in the arena changed.

Motion, once slowed, now returned to normal. Sound, once muted, swelled to a roar in my ears—the crowd, the lion, the screaming of Kahil, who was driving his horse toward Saba.

But when Talya issued that long, pure note from pursed lips, they all stopped.

The lion was first. Immediately he withdrew and lay down like a scolded cat. Then the crowd fell to a hush, then Kahil's horse froze with ears perked. They were all gripped by this one single note filled with raw power.

My heart leaped in my breast and I smiled, delirious

with joy. I wanted to hear Talya's note more clearly, so I let my voice trail off and lowered my hand.

Now only this, a young boy's song, held all of Petra in its love and peace. As one, thirty thousand Nabataeans and Bedu stood aghast. They couldn't know what they heard, only that it called to a place deep within them that refused to be denied.

It was wonder to behold, and I thought, *What wonders will they see in Jerusalem if Talya's voice can still Petra? Could even Stephen's shadow now heal what it touched? Surely!*

Still Talya sang, only that one note, extending far longer than it should have.

AS TALYA sang he knew more...Much more. Far, far more than he had words to express or even a mind to understand. Truth came to him in pictures that he could not describe, and in words that had no meaning in his own language. It came to him as if he was experiencing it, not thinking about it.

Yeshua was the Way. He was the Truth. He was the Life. He was the innocent lamb who had overcome death, and the knowledge of good and evil and all that came with it.

All of this came to him and far more, in that language from something closer than his own breath and yet greater than all things combined. And he heard himself speak in his mind, but in a language known only to his mind.

"You are my Father?"

I am.

His bones trembled.

"I am your son?"

You are.

He could hardly breathe there in the stadium, but here he was breathing only power. Because a Father would show his son everything, so that he could do what the Father did!

Surrender who you think you are...

"To see who I really am," he whispered.

Surrender what you think you need...

"To see what I already have."

Surrender all that you think you know about...

"To know you."

He could feel his Father's pleasure like a kiss on his forehead.

Then Talya knew that he was glorious. Shining like a thousand suns because he—not his body, which was also beautiful—was now joined with Yeshua like one whole fruit, not two halves like the black-and-white one the woman had eaten in the garden. So he was the son of the Father, here and now and unafraid and more powerful than all of the lions in the world. Anything else was only a lie.

This was the knowing that thundered through him like a storm made from that one simple yet forever note. Like when Saba said *eternal.*

And suddenly he thought: *Sing to your mother.* Share this with her because you are one with her! Sing to your mother the wonder of the Father! And sing to Saba too... Sing to them both. Sing to the whole world.

So he did. And the truth in that song was far more than his mind could hold.

I WAS STUNNED by the beauty arising in my heart and mind and soul, quickened by Talya's song—I could barely contain it all.

And even then, as I was thinking the beauty was too great for such frail vessels as mine and little Talya's, he sang more, and now to me. And to Saba. And to all who had ears to hear.

My son was singing to us of our Father! Of Yeshua...Of himself, the truest part of him, and of me, the me that was now risen and complete, joined in Yeshua's identity, like water in a bowl and the bowl in the water at once. He was the Way. The Truth. Life. No one could know the Father without this joining.

And the song said more, all at once, like the opening of eyes to see an entire landscape once darkened by blindness. The mystery Talya sang to me in that single note could fill a hundred scrolls.

I stood high in that arena and I trembled with wonder.

TALYA'S EYES were closed, but he was seeing and he was singing. And Talya was so filled with joy that he suddenly had to laugh. He had to use his mouth to laugh and so he had to stop singing. So he did.

He started to chuckle with delight even before his voice trailed off. The laughter bubbled up and spilled out of his mouth, and even in the middle of all the light he thought that laughter was wonderful too. *What an incredible body I have that can laugh like this!*

So he threw his arms in the air, eyes still closed and full of light, and started to jump up and down, giggling. What a wonderful, wonderful body he had!

And then he remembered that he was still in the arena, and he stopped in the middle of his laughter and opened his eyes.

The brilliant, colorful light was replaced by the sight

of many thousands in that bowl-shaped arena, all staring at him. But half his mind was still aware of that light, so everything seemed to glow a little.

He was standing alone, three paces from the post, and there ahead of him was the lion, lying on its belly with its tongue hanging out of one side of its panting jaw. The beast watched Talya like a cat resting after chasing a mouse.

Talya was so taken by the magnificent creature that for a moment he forgot where he was. But then he remembered, and he looked up to see Saba on both knees, his arms spread wide and his face lifted to the sky, weeping softly. How wonderful was Saba!

And beyond Saba, Kahil, seated tall on his stallion, staring at him with black eyes, frozen in shock. Lost. How beautiful was this poor man, so wounded to hurt so many!

Still not a soul moved.

Talya looked past Kahil to the warriors, who seemed not to know what to do, and beyond them to the platform where the queen and the king stood, staring dumbly. *Shaquilath has lost her daughter*, Talya thought, and his heart broke with hers. *The king has great kindness that's been covered up by fear and greed.*

How or why these things came to Talya, he didn't know, because he wasn't as much knowing them as experiencing them.

And more, he was experiencing the truth, which was this: here he was in a small body that could easily be torn in two by the lion's jaws or cut down the middle by Kahil's sword, but this would lessen him no more than losing a finger, because he wasn't his finger any more than he was his body.

Here he was, that small boy, but here he was also: the son of the Father, who was more powerful than a hundred thousand bodies.

A voice whispered to him from his memory of the light. *In this world you will have trouble*, it said, *but take heart... I have overcome the world.*

Talya looked at the lion again, then walked toward it. He could feel the dust under his bare feet, soft like clouds. The lion, seeing him come, flicked its ears, then continued its panting, looking about lazily.

Talya stopped in front of the beast, mesmerized by its golden fur.

Still no one spoke. The lion looked up at him, stretched its neck, and yawned before returning to its lazy distraction.

Talya, the lamb, was loved even by the lion. And then Saba's words from Dumah came to him.

A child will lead them. Today, he was that child.

"What is this?" Kahil snarled.

But nobody was paying him any mind.

Talya walked up to Saba, who was watching him in wonder. They smiled at each other and Saba beamed with pride.

"What is this?" Kahil repeated, twisting back to glare at the platform. "I demand what I was promised!"

New voices rippled through the crowd, as if Kahil's objection had broken their spell. But they were exclamations of wonder for Talya.

The king, Aretas, lifted his hand and they quieted. He stared at Talya curiously for a moment.

"My word is my word. You will have what was promised." He paused. "But let the boy speak."

Saba rose to his feet.

Talya stared at the king. They were going to kill him then? For a brief moment fear shot through his heart, but then he saw a young boy like himself, maybe only eight years old, smiling at him from the one of the nearest seats. The boy was dressed in rags and his face was dirty and Talya suddenly remembered the orphans still in Dumah and everywhere in the desert.

I will not leave you as orphans...

He looked along the crowd and saw many children. Whether orphans or not, he didn't know, but weren't they all lost, alone?

A child will lead them.

Suddenly this was all he could think about. His mother had gone to save them two years ago and assumed she'd failed, but she was wrong. This was a part of how she would save them, by saving him. All of what had happened was part of what had to happen for the sake of so many.

He turned to where his mother stood high in the arena. Tears wet her face but she stood tall, the greatest of all mothers in his eyes, so proud of him.

The king had told him to speak. So then he must speak.

"Mother..." For a moment he couldn't say more because he was overwhelmed by love for her and his throat was knotted.

Her soft voice reached down to him, gripped by emotion.

"Speak to me, my son."

He looked at the king, who seemed curious; at Kahil, scowling; at Saba, who had fresh tears on his cheeks. Then back at his mother.

"We have to take comfort to the others in Dumah.

All of the orphans, everywhere...they wait for us. I see now. We must return to the desert and show all the motherless their Father."

She looked at him for a long moment, then started to descend. The people parted before her.

"You are right, Talya," she said, stepping slowly down the stone benches, eyes fixed upon him. "Do not be afraid."

Talya looked at Kahil, only eight horse lengths away. The prince sat on his stallion, trembling with rage, eyes black and fierce, and Talya thought, *The jinn are shaking his body. He's afraid.*

But Talya wasn't afraid.

He turned to Aretas. "You must allow us to return to Dumah and to the desert." His voice rang out for all to hear. "We have to tell the outcasts that they are loved! Maviah is the queen of those who need to hear, the mother of all the orphans who cry. She, not Kahil, is the one who will bring the kingdom of power to the desert."

He knew, even as his voice carried to every ear in the great stadium, that he was speaking words their old minds could not understand, but he must speak them anyway.

He pointed at the viper, keeping his eyes on the king. "Kahil is blind and afraid, because his eyes have been scraped out by the hatred of his fathers and jinn, but he could learn to see. Then he too will love the outcasts as he loves—"

A terrible scream of rage cut him off. Motion blurred in the corner of his eye.

Turning slowly, he saw it all unfold, and he knew he must allow it to happen.

He saw Kahil screaming, standing in his saddle, leaning forward with his long, curved blade in his hand, pounding the white stallion's flanks with his heels.

He's coming for me. He's going to cut my head off with his sword.

And he did come, flying past Saba, who was shoved back by the sudden onrush. Closing in on Talya, now only ten paces away.

Alarm flashed through his body, and with it realization. He was going to die. Still, it was only his body here that would die, now instead of later. Yet there was no now or later in the eternal realm.

Kahil drew his blade back, mouth wide like a viper that had learned how to roar.

He's going to kill me!

But there was another roar. One to Talya's left—low and rumbling at first, then rising to a snarl, then a sound of fury that shook the ground.

A rush of golden fur and sinew and rippling muscle streaked low to the ground to intercept Kahil.

Talya watched, stunned, as the lion launched itself to the air, claws extended, fangs wide. Kahil jerked his head toward the threat, but his awareness had come too late.

The lion took the dark prince from his saddle in full flight. His jaw crushed Kahil's head while they were still in the air, before the man's scream of rage could turn to fear.

They landed, lion on top, ten paces from the frightened stallion, who veered to miss Talya's body.

Then there was only the lion hunched over his kill.

It had happened so fast and with such brutality that none could react.

The lion released his prey, gazed down at the fallen warrior for a moment, and looked around, growling softly. Satisfied, he turned and trotted toward Talya, tongue lolling out of its mouth, gently panting.

The lion stopped two paces from him and sat down on his haunches, looking about as if nothing had happened.

Talya blinked, realizing that he had forgotten to breathe. So he breathed now, drawing his fingers into loose fists because they were trembling.

Kahil was dead, and for this he felt only empathy.

The lion was his friend. Imagine that!

The lion and the lamb.

His mother was in the arena now, walking toward him, calm and queenly. She reached him and took his hand. Then gave it a gentle squeeze.

"What a beautiful boy you are," she breathed.

Then she reached out for Saba, who'd approached from the side, and all three stood and faced the king and queen of Petra.

"You have seen and heard the power of Yeshua as promised," his mother said, as a queen in this realm might say it. "Now we are needed in the desert."

CHAPTER THIRTY-FIVE

I HAD HEARD of kingdoms far beyond the oasis of Dumah that give birth to life where none should be, kingdoms beyond the vast, barren sands of the Arabian deserts.

Yet none of these kingdoms were real to me because I, Maviah, was born into shame without the hope of honor.

But there came into that world a man who spoke of a different kingdom in words that defied all other kingdoms.

His name was Yeshua.

One look into his eyes would surely bend the knee of the strongest warrior or exalt the heart of the lowest outcast. One whisper from his lips might hush the cries of a thousand men or dry the tears of a thousand women.

Some said that he was a prophet. Some said that he was a mystic. Some said that he was a fanatical Zealot, a heretic, a man who'd seen too many deaths and too much suffering to remain sane and so had given himself to be crucified.

But I came to know him as the anointed Son of the Father, from whom all life flows; a teacher of the Way into a realm that flows with far more power than all the armies of all the kingdoms upon the earth joined as one; the Son of Man, who undid what the first Adam had done.

Yeshua, the only Way to know the Father. The only Truth, the only Life.

It was Yeshua who told me that I'd been created with the breath of God in his image and then glorified his identity in me. Yeshua who'd shown me how the knowledge of good and evil had darkened my world, causing me to live in grievance and shame so that I could only stumble in darkness and death, lost to that glory.

It was Yeshua who showed me how the Father had raised me from my death with him, and breathed his life into me through him, and so glorified his identity in me once again. Yeshua who showed me how beautiful and powerful he is in that realm, and how beautiful and powerful I was as well—he in me and I in him. All else was only the lie of that serpent, who accused me.

It was Yeshua who showed me that my purpose was to be like him on earth, sharing my love with a world still enslaved by darkness.

To love them as myself.

In the wake of such a stunning display of power, Shaquilath released Arim and Fahak but remained distant upon reuniting us. Twice now, she'd seen Yeshua's power, but her grievance over the loss of Phasa, her daughter and her idol, darkened her heart. She was fearful of what she could not comprehend.

Aretas again restored my right to find my way in the desert as queen without either his support or rejection. So long as he received his taxes, he would let me contend with the Thamud and Dumah, he said. Then he ordered that we be supplied with all we needed for our journey and sent us away.

We left within the hour.

Now we sat upon our camels three hours east of the city. Here, where Yeshua had appeared to Saba and me in the flesh and opened our eyes to the truth of who he was and who we now were.

Saba, Fahak, Arim, and Talya faced south on the dune with the towering red cliff to our rear. Spent coals from our fire still darkened the white sand in the wadi beside us.

"You say he made this fire?" Arim asked, staring down the slope. "This very fire just here, with his own hands?" His camel shifted under him and he twisted to us, beaming. "Then was I not right? He raises the dead even as he raised Lazarus and now himself!"

"Not only Lazarus," Saba said, eyes fixed ahead. "Us as well."

The old sheikh Fahak stared at Saba, still at a loss, as he had been since leaving Petra. "Raised? Then my sagging flesh could be young to love many wives once again," he muttered. "To this god I would enslave myself."

I could not help but grin. "Be careful not to enslave yourself to your body, mighty sheikh. It will soon return to dust."

He grunted but remained silent.

He would know soon, I thought. Both he and Arim, in ways not even Arim could yet comprehend.

Saba sat to my left, Talya to my right atop his camel, bared of shirt now, to be like Saba. The calm that now lived in his eyes filled me with wonder. He was still a child, only eight, but I was humbled to be in his presence.

He turned and gazed at the dune a hundred paces to our right. There, the lion lazed on its haunches, watching us. Talya had asked if he might take it, and Shaquilath had agreed. But Talya didn't need to take the lion. It followed without encouragement.

That a lion should be drawn to a boy was a marvel to all of us, particularly Arim, who kept as much distance between his camel and the lion as possible without appearing to have lost his bravery.

I glanced at Saba and he gave me a gentle, knowing nod.

Saba, whom I hated so that I could love and whom I would wed. And how deep was that love, which I had never thought possible. I would expect nothing of him; I would give my life for him.

"We should go, my queen," he said, gazing south again. "They await us."

I nodded. It would take us ten days to reach the orphans in Dumah.

My thoughts returned to the question that had bothered Saba for so long before returning to Judea. If clear vision was required to see the path of faith into the kingdom, by what means could one's sight be restored?

"Tell me, Saba," I said, following his eyes. "How can one see the eternal realm of the Father here on earth?"

He nodded. "By placing your identity in Yeshua's identity. Only then can you see the Way."

"And what is that Way that is so easily forgotten?"

Saba thought only a brief moment.

"In any given moment, you, as the son, the daughter, of the Father, believe in and so are mastered by one of two perceptions of reality. One is seen in flesh—the passing system of the world, darkened by the knowledge of good and evil, deceiving and so enslaving all those sons and daughters who put their faith in it. The other realm is seen in the light, the eternal dimension of the Father flowing with love and power without grievance."

He paused.

"Yes?"

"Yeshua, the second Adam, came as light into all darkness and undid what the first Adam did, restoring communion with the Father once more and making it possible for all who so choose to see in the light, and to know, as a child, their Father and his sovereign dimension of peace, power, and love, even now. This is eternal life—to know and so experience the Father and his eternal realm, now and beyond all time."

My heart beat faster…I was eager to hear the rest. Saba continued.

"Our journey is to now believe who we truly are, having been raised from the dark grave into that realm of light with and in Yeshua."

He faced me.

"Belief in Yeshua is this: identifying with him in his death, resurrection, and glory even now, he in you and you in him. Your true identity is this: you are the daughter of your Father, already made complete and whole, already at peace and full of power, though you often forget, each day, whenever you are blinded to your true identity and so search for and cling to whatever else might save you in this life."

I smiled. Identity. It was all about our identity.

But Saba wasn't done. He faced the desert again.

"The only way to identify with your true identity is to let go of all other identities, and all offense that blocks your vision, and all vain imaginations of what else might fulfill you or save you from trouble in this life and that to come."

"*This* is true surrender," I said.

"Walking in the realm of the Father's sovereign presence here on earth, we will find peace in the storms; we will walk on the troubled seas of our lives; we will not be poisoned by the lies of snakes; we will move mountains that appear insurmountable; we will heal all manner of sickness that has twisted minds and bodies."

I finished it off for him, because I knew as well as he.

"The fruits of the Sprit—love, joy, and peace—will flow from us as living waters, because the manifestation of the kingdom of heaven on earth is love. This is the evidence of the Spirit. In this evidence, all will see: there goes one who knows God and walks in the eternal realm."

For a long while, we sat in silence, lost in awe at such good news. Imagine, if all people could love both themselves and their neighbor this way. This was our purpose now: to share this good news and to love as Yeshua loved us.

His teaching there by the vines near Bethany came to me. *Many will say to me, Lord, Lord... did we not do many mighty works in your name? And I will tell them* plainly, "*I never knew you.*" And... *Many will come in my name, saying "I am Christ," and will deceive many.*

I wondered how many... Perhaps many thousands or perhaps whole nations, for surely news of his power could not be contained, yet many who called him Lord and served him would still be blinded by their offenses and still lost in their storms of fear, misery, grievance, and judgment. My heart broke for them.

You will know them by their fruit, he'd said.

Good fruit was unconditional love, without which all dogma and claims of authority were only noise.

What you do to the least of these you do to me, he'd said.

Oh that everyone would know the Father! Oh that all would see what I saw and know as I knew such boundless rivers of love for all who were weary and downtrodden in this life! That they would taste the fruit of Yeshua and *see* that he is good. That this taste would forever wash away the bitter taste of the fruit that had opened their eyes to darkness and grievance.

Truly, the Way of Yeshua was profoundly simple. His meaning was simple, his burden was light... but the serpent's lies made for the weight of the world.

What great hope we had for all that was to come! And how powerful we were in his Spirit while yet in this realm!

We were the sons and daughters of God on earth. *Your kingdom come, your will be done, on earth as it is in heaven.* Now and always.

I turned to my son who was not my son and whom I loved as myself. What a beautiful, beautiful boy he was. I had no doubt that he would one day flood the dry desert with the living water of a single word. He, who now sat shirtless on his camel like Saba, though thin and pale. Talya, a tenth of Saba's size. Talya, who was loved by the lion.

He looked up at me with bright, innocent eyes and my heart soared.

"The orphans are waiting for us," he said.

I smiled.

"The whole desert awaits you, my son," I said softly.

Then I nudged my camel and took us into the sands.

AUTHOR'S NOTE

EVEN AS Yeshua's Way to peace and power was so easily forgotten by Maviah, it is as easily forgotten by most today. For more information on *A.D. 33* and *A.D. 30* or to explore The Forgotten Way for yourself, two thousand years later, visit the website below. This is only the beginning...

theforgottenway.com

Every teaching spoken by Yeshua in *A.D. 33* is taken directly from the record of his teachings, referenced in the appendix below. How his teachings were understood by various characters in the story is a matter of their interpretation.

In addition, though I have fictionalized Maviah's journey, none of what otherwise occurs in *A.D. 33* contradicts well-supported historical records of what happened within the scope of this novel. Scholars agree that Yeshua would have repeated his teachings many times throughout his ministry from beginning to end, yet I have focused primarily on those teachings recorded in the last weeks of his life on earth. His earlier teachings are explored in far greater detail in *A.D. 30*.

Please note that there is little agreement in the scholarly community regarding specific dates for certain events—whole books have been written to argue various points of view. But in the end, the lack of consensus about the specific timing of some events has little bearing on the significance of those events. I contend that when an event occurred is not nearly as important as the fact that it did. I have thus chosen a scholarly calendar that best facilitates Maviah's story.

APPENDIX

References for the teachings of Jesus. Unless otherwise noted, all references are from the NASB.

Chapter Six

Matthew 26:52 "Then Jesus said to him, 'Put your sword back into its place; for all those who take up the sword shall perish by the sword.'"

Matthew 10:34 "Do not think that I came to bring peace on the earth; I did not come to bring peace, but a sword."

Matthew 5:44 "But I say to you, love your enemies and pray for those who persecute you."

Matthew 5:39 "But I say to you, do not resist an evil person; but whoever slaps you on your right cheek, turn the other to him also."

Luke 4:18 (ESV) "The Spirit of the Lord is upon me, because he has anointed me to proclaim good news to the poor. He has sent me to proclaim liberty to the captives and recovering of sight to the blind, to set at liberty those who are oppressed."

Matthew 5:5 (ESV) "Blessed are the meek, for they shall inherit the earth."

Matthew 6:24 "No one can serve two masters; for either he will hate the one and love the other, or he will be devoted to one and despise the other. You cannot serve God and wealth."

Chapter Sixteen

Matthew 11:25 "At that time Jesus said, 'I praise You, Father, Lord of heaven and earth, that You have hidden these things from the wise and intelligent and have revealed them to infants.'"

Matthew 19:14 (ESV) "But Jesus said, 'Let the little children come to me and do not hinder them, for to such belongs the kingdom of heaven.'"

Mark 10:15 (ESV) "Truly, I say to you, whoever does

not receive the kingdom of God like a child shall not enter it."

Luke 15:4–6 "What man among you, if he has a hundred sheep and has lost one of them, does not leave the ninety-nine in the open pasture and go after the one which is lost until he finds it? When he has found it, he lays it on his shoulders, rejoicing. And when he comes home, he calls together his friends and neighbors, saying to them. 'Rejoice with me, for I have found my sheep which was lost!'"

Mark 14:6–7 (NIV) "'Leave her alone,' said Jesus. 'Why are you bothering her? She has done a beautiful thing to me. The poor you will always have with you...But you will not always have me.'"

Matthew 6:24 "No one can serve two masters; for either he will hate the one and love the other, or he will be devoted to one and despise the other. You cannot serve God and wealth."

Luke 18:29–30 "And He said to them, 'Truly I say to you, there is no one who has left house or wife or brothers or parents or children, for the sake of the kingdom of God, who will not receive many times as much at this time and in the age to come, eternal life.'"

Matthew 16:24 "Then Jesus said to His disciples, 'If anyone wishes to come after Me, he must deny himself, and take up his cross and follow Me.'"

Luke 14:27 "Whoever does not carry his own cross and come after Me cannot be My disciple."

Matthew 16:26 "For what will it profit a man if he gains the whole world and forfeits his soul? Or what will a man give in exchange for his soul?"

Luke 14:26 "If anyone comes to Me, and does not hate his own father and mother and wife and children and brothers and sisters, yes, and even his own life, he cannot be My disciple."

Luke 14:28, 31–32 (NIV) "Suppose one of you wants to build a tower. Won't you first sit down and estimate the cost to see if you have enough money to complete it? Or suppose a king is about to go to war against another king. Won't he first sit down and consider whether he is able with ten thousand men to oppose the one coming against him with twenty thousand? If he is not able, he will send a delegation while the other is still a long way off and will ask for terms of peace."

Luke 14:33 (NIV) "In the same way, those of you who do not give up everything you have cannot be my disciples."

Luke 14:28 (ESV) "For which of you, desiring to build a tower, does not first sit down and count the cost, whether he has enough to complete it?"

1 Corinthians 15:57 (NLT) "But thank God! He gives

us victory over sin and death through our Lord Jesus Christ."

John 11:26 "And everyone who lives and believes in Me will never die. Do you believe this?"

Chapter Seventeen

Hebrews 5:7–8 (NIV) "During the days of Jesus' life on earth, he offered up prayers and petitions with fervent cries and tears to the one who could save him from death and he was heard because of his reverent submission. Son though he was, he learned obedience from what he suffered."

John 15:1–2 "I am the true vine, and My Father is the vinedresser. Every branch in Me that does not bear fruit, He takes away; and every branch that bears fruit, He prunes it so that it may bear more fruit."

John 15:4 "Abide in Me, and I in you. As the branch cannot bear fruit of itself unless it abides in the vine, so neither can you unless you abide in Me."

John 15:5 "I am the vine, you are the branches; he who abides in Me and I in him, he bears much fruit, for apart from Me you can do nothing."

John 15:7 "If you abide in Me, and My words abide in you, ask whatever you wish, and it will be done for you."

John 5:39 (NIV) "You study the Scriptures diligently because you think that in them you have eternal life. These are the very Scriptures that testify about me."

John 17:3 (ESV) "And this is eternal life, that they know you the only true God, and Jesus Christ whom you have sent."

Luke 17:21 (KJV) "Neither shall they say, Lo here! or, lo there! for, behold, the kingdom of God is within you."

Matthew 24:5 "For many will come in My name, saying, 'I am the Christ,' and will mislead many."

Matthew 7:15–16 "Beware of the false prophets, who come to you in sheep's clothing, but inwardly are ravenous wolves. You will know them by their fruits."

Matthew 7:22–23 (ESV) "On that day many will say to me, 'Lord, Lord, did we not prophesy in your name, and cast out demons in your name, and do many mighty works in your name?' And then will I declare to them, 'I never knew you; depart from me, you workers of lawlessness.'"

John 5:22 (ESV) "The Father judges no one, but has given all judgment to the Son."

John 5:45 "Do not think that I will accuse you before the Father; the one who accuses you is Moses, in whom you have set your hope."

John 16:33 "These things I have spoken to you, so that in Me you may have peace. In the world you have tribulation, but take courage; I have overcome the world."

Hebrews 5:8–9 (NIV) "Son though he was, he learned obedience from what he suffered and, once made perfect, he became the source of eternal salvation for all who obey him."

John 14:18–19 "I will not leave you as orphans; I will come to you. After a little while the world will no longer see Me, but you will see Me; because I live, you will live also."

John 14:16–17 "I will ask the Father, and He will give you another Helper, that He may be with you forever; that is the Spirit of truth, whom the world cannot receive, because it does not see Him or know Him, but you know Him because He abides with you and will be in you."

Chapter Nineteen

Luke 19:43–44 "For the days will come upon you when your enemies will throw up a barricade against you, and surround you and hem you in on every side, and they will level you to the ground and your children within you, and they will not leave in you one stone upon another, because you did not recognize the time of your visitation."

Mark 11:11 "Jesus entered Jerusalem and came into the temple; and after looking around at everything, He left for Bethany with the twelve, since it was already late."

John 12:25 "He who loves his life loses it, and he who hates his life in this world will keep it to life eternal."

John 12:27 "Now My soul has become troubled; and what shall I say, 'Father, save Me from this hour'? But for this purpose I came to this hour."

John 12:28 "'Father, glorify Your name.' Then a voice came out of heaven: 'I have both glorified it, and will glorify it again.'"

Chapter Twenty

Matthew 21:19 "Seeing a lone fig tree by the road, He came to it and found nothing on it except leaves only; and He said to it, 'No longer shall there ever be any fruit from you.' And at once the fig tree withered."

Mark 11:23–24 (NIV) "Truly I tell you, if anyone says to this mountain, 'Go, throw yourself into the sea,' and does not doubt in their heart but believes that what they say will happen, it will be done for them. Therefore I tell you, whatever you ask for in prayer, believe that you have received it, and it will be yours."

Mark 11:17 (NIV) "And as he taught them, he said, 'Is it not written: "My house will be called a house of prayer for all nations"? But you have made it "a den of robbers."'"

Mark 12:17 "Jesus said to them, 'Render to Caesar the things that are Caesar's, and to God the things that are God's.' And they marveled at him."

Chapter Twenty-Three

Luke 10:18–19 "And He said to them, 'I was watching Satan fall from heaven like lightning. Behold, I have given you authority to tread on serpents and scorpions, and over all the power of the enemy, and nothing will injure you.'"

Luke 10:20 "Nevertheless do not rejoice in this, that the spirits are subject to you, but rejoice that your names are recorded in heaven."

Matthew 19:26 "With God all things are possible."

Luke 22:42 "Father, if You are willing, remove this cup from Me; yet not My will, but Yours be done."

Hebrews 5:7–10 (NIV) "During the days of Jesus' life

APPENDIX • 407

on earth…Son though he was, he learned obedience from what he suffered and, once made perfect,
he became the source of eternal salvation for all
who obey him."
Luke 22:42 (NIV) "Father, if you are willing, take this
cup from me; yet not my will, but yours be done."
Matthew 26:41 (ESV) "Watch and pray that you may
not enter into temptation. The spirit indeed is willing, but the flesh is weak."

Chapter Twenty-Six

Luke 23:34 "Jesus was saying, 'Father, forgive them; for
they do not know what they are doing.'"
Matthew 27:46 (ESV) "And about the ninth hour Jesus
cried out with a loud voice, saying, 'Eli, Eli, lema
sabachthani?' that is, 'My God, my God, why have
you forsaken me?'"

Chapter Thirty-One

Genesis 3:4–5 "The serpent said to the woman, 'You
surely will not die! For God knows that in the day
you eat from it your eyes will be opened, and you
will be like God, knowing good and evil.'"
Luke 3:38 "Adam, the son of God."

John 1:29 "The next day he saw Jesus coming to him and said, 'Behold, the Lamb of God who takes away the sin of the world!'"

1 Corinthians 15:45 (ESV) "Thus it is written, 'The first man Adam became a living being'; the last Adam became a life-giving spirit."

John 12:24 "Truly, truly, I say to you, unless a grain of wheat falls into the earth and dies, it remains alone; but if it dies, it bears much fruit."

Chapter Thirty-Two

John 15:15 "No longer do I call you slaves, for the slave does not know what his master is doing; but I have called you friends, for all things that I have heard from My Father I have made known to you."

John 10:17–18 (ESV) "For this reason the Father loves me, because I lay down my life that I may take it up again. No one takes it from me, but I lay it down of my own accord. I have authority to lay it down, and I have authority to take it up again."

John 17:16 "They are not of the world, even as I am not of the world."

1 Corinthians 15:6 "After that He appeared to more than five hundred brethren at one time, most of whom remain until now, but some have fallen asleep."

John 14:9 "Jesus said to him, 'Have I been so long with you, and yet you have not come to know Me, Philip? He who has seen Me has seen the Father; how can you say, "Show us the Father"?'"

Romans 8:38–39 "For I am convinced that neither death, nor life, nor angels, nor principalities, nor things present, nor things to come, nor powers, nor height, nor depth, nor any other created thing, will be able to separate us from the love of God, which is in Christ Jesus our Lord."

1 Corinthians 15:45 (ESV) "Thus it is written, 'The first man Adam became a living being'; the last Adam became a life-giving spirit."

Romans 5:18 "So then as through one transgression there resulted condemnation to all men, even so through one act of righteousness there resulted justification of life to all men."

Revelation 13:8 (KJV) "And all that dwell upon the earth shall worship him, whose names are not written in the book of life of the Lamb slain from the foundation of the world."

Ephesians 1:3–4 "Blessed be the God and Father of our Lord Jesus Christ, who has blessed us with every spiritual blessing in the heavenly places in Christ, just as He chose us in Him before the foundation of the world, that we would be holy and blameless before Him."

Galatians 3:13 (NIV) "Christ redeemed us from the curse of the law by becoming a curse for us."

Galatians 2:20 (ESV) "I have been crucified with Christ. It is no longer I who live, but Christ who lives in me. And the life I now live in the flesh I live by faith in the Son of God, who loved me and gave himself for me."

Ephesians 2:6 "And raised us up with Him, and seated us with Him in the heavenly places in Christ Jesus."

Philippians 1:21 "For to me, to live is Christ and to die is gain."

John 14:16–17, 20 (ESV) "I will ask the Father, and he will give you another Helper, to be with you forever, even the Spirit of truth...In that day you will know that I am in my Father, and you in me, and I in you."

John 17:22–23 "The glory which You have given Me I have given to them, that they may be one just as We are one, I in them and You in Me, that they may be perfected in unity, so that the world may know that You sent Me and loved them even as You have loved Me."

Matthew 11:25 "At that time Jesus said, 'I praise You, Father, Lord of heaven and earth, that You have hidden these things from the wise and intelligent and have revealed them to infants.'"

Ephesians 1:18 "I pray that the eyes of your heart may be enlightened, so that you will know what is the hope of His calling, what are the riches of the glory of His inheritance in the saints."

2 Corinthians 5:17 (WEB) "Therefore if anyone is in Christ, he is a new creation; the old things passed away; behold, all things have become new."

Colossians 2:9–10 "For in Him all the fullness of Deity dwells in bodily form, and in Him you have been made complete."

Romans 8:1 "Therefore there is now no condemnation for those who are in Christ Jesus."

Galatians 3:27 "For all of you who were baptized into Christ have clothed yourselves with Christ."

1 John 3:1 (NIV) "See what great love the Father has lavished on us, that we should be called children of God!"

Galatians 4:6 "Because you are sons, God has sent forth the Spirit of His Son into our hearts, crying, 'Abba! Father!' "

Luke 17:20–21 "Now having been questioned by the Pharisees as to when the kingdom of God was coming, He answered them and said, 'The kingdom of God is not coming with signs to be observed; nor will they say, "Look, here it is!" or, "There it is!" For behold, the kingdom of God is in your midst.' "

Romans 8:19 (NIV) "For the creation waits in eager expectation for the children of God to be revealed."

1 Corinthians 13:12 (ESV) "For now we see in a mirror dimly, but then face to face. Now I know in part; then I shall know fully, even as I have been fully known."

Philippians 2:5–8 (ASV) "Have this mind in you, which was also in Christ Jesus: who, existing in the form of God...emptied himself, taking the form of a servant, being made in the likeness of men; and being found in the fashion as a man, he humbled himself, becoming obedient even unto death, yea, the death of the cross."

Matthew 6:33 (ESV) "But seek first the kingdom of God and his righteousness, and all these things will be added to you."

Luke 9:48 (NIV) "For it is the one who is the least among you all who is the greatest."

Matthew 20:16 "So the last shall be first, and the first last."

Mark 12:31 "The second is this: 'You shall love your neighbor as yourself.' There is no other commandment greater than these."

Matthew 25:45 (ESV) "Then he will answer them, saying, 'Truly, I say to you, as you did not do it to one of the least of these, you did not do it to me.'"

John 13:34 (ESV) "A new commandment I give to you, that you love one another: just as I have loved you, you also are to love one another."

1 Corinthians 13:2–3 "If I have the gift of prophecy, and know all mysteries and all knowledge ... but do not have love, I am nothing. And if I give all my possessions to feed the poor, and if I surrender my body to be burned, but do not have love, it profits me nothing."

John 13:35 "By this all men will know that you are My disciples, if you have love for one another."

Chapter Thirty-Five

Matthew 7:22–23 (ESV) "On that day many will say to me, 'Lord, Lord, did we not prophesy in your name, and cast out demons in your name, and do many mighty works in your name?' And then will I declare to them, 'I never knew you; depart from me, you workers of lawlessness.'"

Matthew 24:5 (KJV) "For many shall come in my name, saying, I am Christ; and shall deceive many."

**Look for book one of the epic
A.D. series by
New York Times bestselling author
Ted Dekker**

The outcast daughter of one of the most powerful
Bedouin sheikhs in Arabia, Maviah, is called on
to protect the very people who rejected her. When
their enemies launch a sudden attack with devas-
tating consequences, Maviah escapes with the help
of two of her father's warriors: Saba, who speaks
more with his sword than his voice, and Judah, a
Jew who comes from a tribe that can read the stars.
Their journey will be fraught with terrible danger.
If they can survive the vast forbidding sands of a
desert that is deadly to most, they will reach a brutal world subjugated by kings and emperors. There
Maviah must secure an unlikely alliance with King
Herod of the Jews.

But Maviah's path leads her unexpectedly to

another man. An enigmatic teacher who speaks of a way in this life that offers greater power than any kingdom. His name is Yeshua, and his words turn everything known on its head. Though following him may present even greater danger, his may be the only way for Maviah to save her people—and herself.

Available in print, ebook, and audio formats wherever books are sold.

**CENTER
STREET**